"Hey, McCoy, here's your new partner."

David took one look toward the door and felt an inexplicable urge to run. Walking toward him was Kelli Hatfield. The same sexy, innocently insatiable, utterly feminine Kelli Hatfield he'd shared a bed with last night. Her face mirrored the shock he felt. He could not believe that *she* was his new partner. The reality that this gorgeous woman was actually a cop was enough to send him reeling. Kelli appeared to regain her bearings before he did.

"Officer McCoy," she said, clearing her throat, apparently remembering where they were, and thrusting her delicate hand toward him.

David took it, tempted to pull her into the nearest room where they could have a little talk...and then some. He looked up to find Officer Kowalsky studying them guardedly.

"You know each other?" he asked.

David looked into Kelli's eyes. "Yeah," he said, tempted to add, *In the biblical sense.*

MINISERIES

SEDUCING McCOY

Tori Carrington

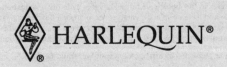

HARLEQUIN®

TORONTO • NEW YORK • LONDON
AMSTERDAM • PARIS • SYDNEY • HAMBURG
STOCKHOLM • ATHENS • TOKYO • MILAN • MADRID
PRAGUE • WARSAW • BUDAPEST • AUCKLAND

ISBN 0-373-83711-9

SEDUCING McCOY

Copyright © 2006 by Harlequin Enterprises S.A.

The publisher acknowledges the copyright holder
of the individual works as follows:

YOU ONLY LOVE ONCE
Copyright © 2001 by Lori and Tony Karayianni

NEVER SAY NEVER AGAIN
Copyright © 2001 by Lori and Tony Karayianni

CONTENTS

YOU ONLY LOVE ONCE

We heartily dedicated this book to romance-friendly
booksellers and librarians everywhere, especially
Mark Budrock, Dawn Rath, Kathy Andrico, Jim Beard,
Chris Champion, Barb Kershner, Sharon Harbaugh,
Kathie Freedly, Joan Adis and her lovable staff, Lisa Hamilton,
Kristin Fennell, Kery Han, Betty and Fred Shultz and their
partners in crime, Joan Selzer, Cathy Bartel, John Cleveland,
Colleen Lehmann, Kathy Hendrickson, Heather Osborn,
Lori Grassman, Judy and Bob Dewitt, Cy Korte,
Michele Patrykus, Gayle Davis, Tracy Marr, Molly Carver,
Rosechel Sinio, Bessie Makris, Eileen Masterson,
Linda Membel, Donna Leaver, Delores Silva and
last but not least, Donita Lawrence.

Although we write the stories and Harlequin publishes them,
it's each and every one of you who makes sure our books
find their way into the readers' hands.
Thank you doesn't begin to cover it.

CHAPTER ONE

"YOU'RE LATE."

David McCoy slid onto a stool next to his brother Connor and shrugged out of his sheepskin coat. He glanced at his bulky black sports watch as he rubbed his hands together to warm them. It was cold even for December in D.C., the kind of cold that inspired the saying, "it's too cold to snow." But the bar was pleasantly warm and decked out festively for the holiday season. Green garland laced with red lights hung behind the counter, and hurricane candle centerpieces were placed on tables around the room. He motioned for Joe, the bartender at The Pour House, to bring him a brew when he finished serving a guy down the long length of the oak bar. "Yeah. Lieutenant Kowalsky wanted to have a few words after I knocked off tonight." He greeted a couple of fellow officers taking their seats a few stools down. "Looks like I get a new partner tomorrow."

Connor knocked back what remained in his own glass. "Should be interesting."

"Yeah." David paid Joe and made a comment on the busyness of the place this early on a Thursday night. Joe shrugged and told him whatever paid the bills.

"What will this be? The third?" Connor asked as Joe took an order down the bar.

David grimaced at his older brother. Connor knew how

many partners he'd gone through. He could probably recite their names, and exactly how long it had taken David to scare them off. Connor was good that way. Always the one to remember when one of them had gotten the measles, when their homework had been due and which forms he had to forge so they could participate in school-sponsored road trips. Mostly, his diligence was welcome. There were times, however, when he wished Connor would get a life—preferably, his own.

He had the sinking sensation this was going to be one of those times.

He drank more of his beer than he intended and gritted his teeth at the onset of a cold headache. Of course, in the case of his last partner, Lupe Ramirez, he hadn't exactly scared her off. In fact, she'd very nearly been killed off. A perp at a twenty-four hour convenience store had taken a potshot at her while he'd been making his way around the back. Lupe was still in rehab, learning how to walk on her reconstructed knee.

"At least the odds are against me getting another female," he said.

Connor grinned. "You sure about that? If Ramirez filled some sort of gender quota, odds are probably in favor of you getting just that."

David shook his head adamantly. "No…Kowalsky might not like me very much, but he wouldn't do that to me again. Uh-uh."

His brother shrugged. "No skin off my nose who you work with or don't. I'm just pointing out the possibilities."

"And I'm telling you the possibility isn't even remote, not even slim. In fact, the possibility is so remote, it's an impossibility."

Connor's grin grew wider.

"What?"

His brother shook his head. "Did I say anything?"

"No. You didn't have to. That stupid grin of yours says it all." David sat up and straightened his denim shirt. "Anyway, at least I do know my partner isn't fresh from the academy. He's a transfer from outside. And no matter what you say, he will be a *he*. I've done my duty as far as equality between the sexes goes. Is it too much to ask to be assigned a guy this time around?"

Connor seemed exceedingly interested in the bottles lining the wall behind the bar and took a slow sip of his beer, his grin apparently making it difficult.

David couldn't resist. He slapped his hand against his older brother's back, nearly causing him to spew the contents of his mouth all over Joe, who now stood before them putting together a purple concoction on the other side of the counter.

"So tell me, Con, what's the deal with you? Why did you want to meet here?" He held his hand up. "Wait, don't tell me, you're getting married, too, aren't you?"

Connor's expression grew darker with each question until he looked a word away from knocking David from his stool.

David held up his hands. "Hey, don't look at me that way. You're the one who called me, remember?"

"Yeah, I remember, all right. Though I'm having a hard time recalling why." He visibly winced. "Married? What on God's green earth would make you ask that?"

For some reason David had never tried to decipher, he'd always loved getting under Connor's skin. Maybe because it was so easy. Or perhaps because it was so much fun to watch Connor go from self-righteous know-it-all to a put-up-your-dukes teen in a blink of an eye. Pops had warned him that one day he'd take his banter a little too far and find himself knocked into the middle of next week. But somehow David had always known Connor would never lay a fist on him.

And, for other reasons he preferred not to pursue, he suspected it was why he'd always felt slightly separate and apart from his brothers. Too young to participate in all the older McCoy guys' reindeer games. The one to be sent to his room when discussions grew serious. Hell, he didn't even look like them, what with having blond hair and being a tad bit shorter than them all at five foot ten. And he didn't even have the benefit of a red, glowing nose so he could prove to them that he was up to the task of leading them through a foggy night— or any task, for that matter.

He shrugged. "Why not marriage? Seems like everyone else is getting hitched these days. Why should you be any different?" He knew the quickest route to pissing Connor off was mentioning him and marriage in the same breath, and he'd done it not once, but twice. His brother had been miserable during Thanksgiving dinner at the McCoy house three weeks ago. Grumbled comments ranging from "all these damn women running around the place" to "you've all turned into a bunch of wusses" encompassed the whole of Connor's contributions to any ongoing conversation.

David braced himself for another Connorism as his brother scowled. "What was it you said to Mel when she asked when *you* were going to settle down? When Satan takes up snow skiing?"

Connor's grin made a comeback. "Yeah. Well, that's about the time I get anywhere near an altar, too."

David leisurely watched a woman in tight jeans walk by, then turned back toward his beer and his brother. "So why did you call then?"

"Does there have to be a reason?"

He watched the way Connor shifted on his stool. Yeah, he'd say his brother had something on his mind, something heavy. "With you, uh-huh. There definitely has to be a reason." He took a long pull from his own bottle. "Come on, Con, just spill it, will you? You've never been the kind of guy for a boys' night out drinking. Actually, you were always telling the rest of us when it was time to lay off the stuff. So what gives?"

Connor grimaced. "I don't know. It's just this thing with Pops...."

David waited for him to continue...and waited...and waited.

"Man, you're about as talkative as Jake tonight. You know, if you really want this to begin resembling a conversation, you're going to have to start with finishing your sentences. I'm no mind reader."

Connor leaned back and released a long-suffering sigh. "Look, this isn't easy for me, you know? You guys are usually the ones coming to me for advice."

"Yeah, it must really eat you that you're stuck with me."

Connor looked at him, a question in his blue-green eyes. "Is that what you think?"

David was the one who shifted in his seat this time. "Come on, Con, quit pussyfooting around and get to the point already, will you?"

"It's just...aw, hell, David, do you think I did the right thing with Pops? You know, telling him I didn't approve of his going out with Melanie's mother?"

David remembered the incident at the cemetery. His brows shot up. "Didn't approve? You practically told the old man you'd disown him if he didn't stop seeing Wilhemenia." He motioned for Joe to bring Connor a fresh bottle. "Have you two even spoken a civil word to each other since then?"

His brother looked away.

"You haven't, have you?" He rubbed his chin, thinking of the times the family had gathered together over the past couple months. He couldn't come up with a single time when he'd seen Connor and Pops talk to each other. Oh, yeah, Connor may have mumbled a jab or two under his breath, but he'd never directly spoken to their father. "Out of all of us, you were always the closest to Pops. I don't know if it's an age thing…" Connor gave him a glowering look. "Sorry. What I'm trying to say is that if two men ever understood each other, it was you and Pops."

"Yeah, well, I guess this Wilhemenia stuff really got to me, you know? Thanks." He grabbed the bottle Joe put in front of him. "Of all the women Pops could have chosen, why did it have to be that sourpuss excuse for a human being?"

David's burst of laughter died down. He thoughtfully rolled his beer bottle between his palms. "I don't know what you're looking for here, Connor, but if it's reinforcements, you're looking in the wrong place. I, for one, don't happen to see anything wrong with Pops getting a little—"

Connor whipped up his hand to stop him. "Don't. What I'm interested in finding out is how you would feel about him…well, actually bringing her into the family."

David thought that if his eyes had widened any farther, his eyeballs would have splashed into the bottle he was just about to press to his lips. "You mean, like *marry* her?"

A shadow of a smile played around Connor's mouth. "See, it bothers you, too."

David put his bottle down on the bar. "I wouldn't say that, exactly."

"So what would you say…exactly?"

"I…I don't know." He looked at his brother. "Do you think it's that serious?"

Connor sighed. "I don't know. Right now, no. I think after…our little talk, Pops did stop seeing her. But it's only natural to think that he was serious about her. I mean, it's not like Pops has ever dated before."

David frowned. "Wait a minute here. If he's not seeing her anymore, then what in the hell are you worried about?"

Connor fell silent, staring at his bottle as if a genie would appear any moment and supply him with the answer. "It's just that…I don't know. Pops looks so…"

"Miserable?" David grinned at Connor's quick glare. "Hey, I'm capable of noticing some things, too. And Pops is definitely miserable."

"Yeah, well, he'll get over it."

"If that's how you really feel, then why are we talking about it?"

Connor looked at him as if he was surprised by the realization. "I don't know."

A wink of neon pink distracted David. He turned to watch the tantalizing back of a woman walking toward the pool tables. The pink of her top clung to slender shoulders and a narrow waist before giving way to form-fitting black slacks designed to drive a man wild. She met another woman, then picked up a pool stick, flicking her silky blond, shoulder-length hair over a sculpted shoulder. David got a good look at her face. Heart-shaped. Large green eyes. A bow-shaped pink, pink mouth. Everything about her seemed delicate in some way. Utterly, totally feminine. Innocent. So unlike most of the women he typically dated.

His gaze drifted lower. Whoa. There was nothing innocent about the way that top fit. The curve-hugging material outlined her breasts perfectly, and hid very little—like the fact that she was either cold or tuned in and turned on by his slow visual examination.

He groaned deep in his throat. He managed to croak out a response to Connor. "Yeah, well, you might want to try figuring out the answer to that question before you go on to the next." His gaze again strayed to the pool table.

Damn, but she's more woman than any two men could handle, David thought as she returned his measuring gaze. A smile turned up the sides of her mouth and he came close to letting loose a long, appreciative whistle. Despite the fact that they were in a cop bar, there was no way this woman was one. Nor was she a cop groupie like the table of women nearby who consistently went to cop bars pretending to be out for nothing more than a good time, but were really angling for a wedding ring.

No. This woman was neither. She probably did something…womanly. Sold wedding dresses, worked in an antique shop, sold perfume at an upscale department store. She probably wouldn't know how to hold a gun, much less fire one. The thought was altogether appealing. Especially since he didn't plan to repeat the mistake of sleeping with someone on the force again.

He cleared his throat, then slanted a loaded gaze his brother's way. "Speaking of the weather, I think I just heard that Hell's forecast calls for a blizzard." He pushed from his stool as if compelled by a force greater than himself. "I just spotted me the woman I'm gonna marry."

"Who was talking about the…" Connor's spine snapped military straight as he apparently realized what was going on. "Aw, hell, David, I didn't come over here to watch you play Casanova."

"You can have the friend," he said, straightening his shoulders.

"Gee thanks, but no thanks."

"We're done, here, right? All we're doing is talking in circles anyway. Come on. Let's see if we can go get in on some of this action."

Connor hiked a skeptical brow.

"I'm talking about pool, doofus. What did you think I meant?"

"I don't play pool."

David barely heard him, his gaze fastened on the woman even now bending over to set up her next shot. Her toffee-colored hair swept down over her face and, with cleanly manicured nails, she pushed it so the strands mingled with the hair on the other side of her perfect head. Her gaze shifting back to him, she pulled the pool stick back then scratched, completely missing the ball. She might not know much about the game of pool, but she'd look damn hot stretched across the green felt…naked as the day she was born.

"Look out, here he goes again," he overheard a fellow officer say to another as he walked by them, the comment punctuated by laughter.

David's grin merely widened.

"IF THE DEVIL wore jeans, this is what he'd look like."

Kelli Hatfield laughed at her friend's whispered comment, then self-consciously tugged the snug, unfamiliar pink material of her new top away from her skin. She didn't have to ask who Bronte was talking about. The blond guy from the end of the bar, who could easily have posed for Michelangelo's *David,* was sauntering their way. And saunter was about the word for it. With his sexy gaze openly fastened on her, he gave the impression that she might be his destination. She swallowed hard, straightened, then resisted the urge to pluck at her top again. She caught her friend's cautionary gaze but purposefully ignored it. The same way she had ignored Bronte's groan earlier when she saw what she was wearing. And her arguments when Kelli had suggested they go to the renowned D.C. cop bar for "just one drink and a game of pool." And her warnings that she was just looking for trouble by shimmying like that when she bent over to take a shot. Until that moment, Kelli hadn't known she *could* shimmy.

A delicious, reckless shiver glided down her spine.

Bronte leaned closer. "Don't even think about it, Kell. The guy's Grade-A trouble. In capital letters. Bolded. Underlined. A lady-killer and a half."

Kelli's smile widened as she brushed off her friend's warning. When was the last time she had felt this way? Keyed up? Sexy? Ready to take on the world? Well, okay, maybe not the world, but certainly the prime male specimen heading her way. She frowned slightly, not knowing what was worse—the fact that she couldn't remember the last time she'd felt this way, or the suspicion that she never had. The unclear answer made her all the more determined to pay attention to the fiery emotions.

Sure, she admitted it probably wasn't very wise to openly encourage a guy in a cop bar, considering her circumstances. But it was her first night living in D.C. after three long years. And, by God, it felt good to be home, in the city where she'd been raised and where she planned to live out the rest of her life. It felt good thinking about her new job and knowing she had a choice apartment in Columbia Heights, the equivalent of which she would never have been able to afford in New York City. Overall, she felt good. And the instant she'd exchanged glances with the man now close enough for her to see the color of his eyes—a warm, vivid blue that sent another shiver sliding behind the other—she'd felt the overwhelming need to cut loose in a way she never had.

"Tonight, maybe Grade-A trouble is what I'm in the market for," Kelli said, enjoying her friend's shocked expression.

There wasn't much capable of shocking Bronte O'Brien. If she were to be honest, Bronte had always been the shocker out of the two of them. Ever since forming an odd union of sorts while taking pre-law at George Washington University, Bronte had been the racy one, reckless, the girl on scholarship who hid her brains behind her good looks. Kelli had lived vicariously through her best friend for years, though she had to admit Bronte's life had become boring as of late. Still, it was long past time Kelli started doing her own living.

Bronte rubbed the smooth skin between her brows and

sighed. "You know, Kelli, I take back everything I've ever encouraged you to do. For years, I've been telling you that you need to loosen up. Get out and experience life. *Get* a life." She slowly shook her head, the dim light burnishing her short red hair. "But this is definitely *not* what I had in mind. If you won't take the advice from me, personally, take it from your trusted attorney—you don't want to do this. I know the guy he's with—I've run across him on the job. He's a marshal. Anyway, a guy like this one making a beeline for you…well, he has catastrophe written all over him. He should come with a warning label—Commitment Phobic—Use For One-Night Stand Only."

"You're not my attorney, Bronte. You're a U.S. attorney. And I'm not interested in his friend. I'm interested in him." Kelli looked her full in the face. "Besides, maybe a one-night stand is all *I'm* looking for."

"That's what you say now. Let's see how fast that story changes afterward."

Kelli leaned against her stick. "Come on, Bron, lighten up. You're acting like my sleeping with this guy is a forgone conclusion." She held up a rigid finger. "One. That's the whole of my experience with the opposite sex." An experience she didn't want to repeat much less remember. "Only then I was so green you could have planted me."

"So you say. Mark my words, Jed was an amateur. This one's a pro." Bronte hooked a thumb to where the guy in question stopped to talk to a couple of men at the bar, though his gaze never strayed from their direction. "A regular heartache waiting to happen."

Kelli rolled her eyes to stare at the ceiling, then laughed. "Why don't you let me be the judge of that?" She drew her thumb along the smooth wood of the pool stick then bit softly on her bottom lip. "Come on, Bronte, I'm tired of being a good girl. Fed up with always doing the right thing, both in my job and my personal life. The perfect worker who passes up a vacation day because a coworker needs to go to his kid's school play. The friend who's always home because she never goes anywhere, never does anything. The boring neighbor who doesn't mind feeding your pets while you're away sipping Bahama Mamas on some tropical island. I want to step outside my safe little box, live a little, even if just for this one night."

Kelli swallowed, not understanding the scope of her restlessness until that very moment. There had been hints over the past few months. The Egyptian silk sheets she'd dropped a fortune on because she thought they were sexy. Her new interest in cooking exotic foods; she'd even bought a wok, for God's sake. Her sudden, insatiable hunger for romance novels, addictive books she had only picked up on occasion before, but now her collection had grown so large it had taken five huge boxes to cart it from New York. The simple truth was that she no longer wanted to rub her legs against the sheets…alone. She didn't want to spend hours concocting the perfect meal only to be disappointed when she discovered she and her dog Kojak were the only ones around to eat it. She wanted to *live* the lives of those romance heroines rather than just read about them.

"And as for your worrying about me getting my heart broken," she continued, "give me a little credit, will you? I think I deserve at least that after all the heartaches I watched you experience. I never said one word to you all those times you got yourself in trouble over some walking stud muffin."

"What, are you actually inventorying each of my doomed romances so you can be sure to get in all your I told you so's?" Bronte grimaced and held up her hand. "And don't try to give me that innocent look either." Her blue eyes twinkled as she sipped her purple drink. "Just how do you think I learned how to give you a hard time now?"

Kelli squinted at her.

"Every little jab I've just hit you with, you've poked at me over the years."

Touché. She leaned over the table and lined up her next shot. Right before she would take it, she glanced past the cue ball and directly into the suggestive eyes of the man in question. She scratched so badly she nearly tore a hole in the green felt.

The guy grinned and began swaggering their way again.

Bronte dropped her voice. "Just don't say I didn't tell you so, you hear?"

Kelli didn't absorb her friend's words, concentrating instead on the heat spilling through her bloodstream, the tingly tightening of her breasts. Tonight she wanted to be the ravisher *and* the ravishee. She wanted to throw her hands up in the air and say "I am woman, hear me roar." And she wanted to swallow the gorgeous guy moving toward them whole.

Shamelessly she openly eyed the man's physique. Oh, he was a cop all right. There was no denying that. Everything about him spoke of cockiness and authority, a rough-around-the-edges attitude that stemmed as much from knowing himself capable of saving someone's life as from the certainty that he could take a suspect's. And he was still young enough to think himself immortal.

She briefly caught her bottom lip between her teeth again. Maybe he was just the thing this good girl needed to turn very, very bad.

He reached the pool table just as someone finished feeding the jukebox a slew of coins. Bronte rolled her eyes as Bob Seger's "Night Moves" attempted to drown out the hum of conversation and clink of glasses from behind the bar.

The devil in blue jeans slapped a fiver on the edge of the pool table near the coin slot. "I play the loser." His grin made her heart race. "David McCoy."

Kelli repositioned her pool stick and slowly shook his hand, the heat the simple touch generated exhilaratingly cathartic. "Kelli Hatfield." She released his hand then tapped the stick lightly against her side. This was one game she was going to enjoy losing. "You're on."

TWO HOURS LATER, David launched a renewed assault on Kelli Hatfield's luscious mouth and backed her toward her stripped bed in the corner. Her hungry but obviously inexperienced response made him harder than steel. As drop-dead sexy as the woman was, an innocence clung to her silky skin like an irresistible perfume, making him want to breathe her in, eat her alive, thrust into her like nobody's business.

And that's exactly what he intended to do. That is, if he could pull his thoughts together long enough to take things further than kissing.

The strength of his reaction was like a sucker punch to the gut. Even he had to admit surprise at how quickly they'd ended up back at her place, clawing at each other's clothes, devouring each other's mouths. He'd lay ten-to-one odds that the woman even now clumsily unzipping his fly had never uttered the words "one-night stand" before, much less indulged in one. Still, he hadn't had to resort to any of his old come-on lines at the bar. It had always been a bit tricky trying to get a woman between the sheets while keeping her well away from serious commitment territory. After their sexually charged game of pool, he'd simply suggested they get out of there, and she'd agreed. Even Connor and her friend, Bronte, had held up their hands as if their leaving were inevitable and said little more than "Bye" when they grabbed their coats and practically ran from the bar.

Just thinking about the remarkable, lightning-fast string of events sent David's pulse rate skyrocketing off the charts. Hell, he felt he might lose it if he couldn't bury himself in her hot flesh right then and there.

He supposed she might be drunk, but he knew what signs to look for and she displayed none of them. In fact, he didn't detect a hint of liquor. Rather, he tasted something hot and undeniably sweet on her tongue. Then there was her skin….

Peaches. She tasted like peaches, for crying out loud.

Off went that stretchy pink top and her lacy bra. He palmed her breasts and groaned at their nicely rounded weight. Not too big. Not too small. Pure heaven.

"Wait…I…" she whispered huskily.

He pulled an engorged, pale nipple into the depths of his mouth. She gasped and ceased trying to speak.

With more strength than he would have thought possible, she reversed their positions then pushed him toward the mattress. Off went her slacks, his jeans. Before he knew it, his fingers were entangled in her hair, his mouth greedily pulling at hers, and she was poised, ready, above him.

He tugged his mouth from hers and met her eyes. In the fleeting beams of passing headlights, he saw on her face a gravity, a need, a beauty that made him groan. He'd experienced one or two one-night stands in the past, but this was different somehow. Rather, Kelli Hatfield was different. He'd never felt so in tune with a woman, so completely wrapped up in her. And though they didn't know each other well, he felt that he *knew* her on a level that transcended the trivial details normally exchanged during the traditional first few dates. He didn't know what college she had attended in New York, where she'd said she just moved from, but he knew that she wanted him as much as he wanted her. And that was saying a whole lot.

Her gaze remaining locked with his, Kelli lowered herself. His hips bucked and suddenly her tight, slick flesh surrounded him.

He recaptured her mouth and closed his eyes, feeling an odd sensation of inner calm even as their movements grew restless, their breathing ragged. When they climaxed together minutes later, he felt an odd sense of completion that stemmed from more than just the physical. The sensation was foreign, frightening, electrifying, and completely blew his mind.

"Wow," Kelli whispered, her damp flesh resting against his.

"Yeah…wow," he repeated.

Slowly, his breathing evened, his heartbeat went back to normal, and the world came back into focus. He glanced around the room. Boxes everywhere. There weren't even sheets on the bed, though the old radiator in the corner emanated so much heat, it didn't matter. He vaguely wondered if she'd just moved in, but didn't have the energy to ask. For the first time since he could remember, David McCoy was completely devoid of words.

She rolled off of him and reached for a robe pooled on the bare wood floor. He fought the urge to pull her back.

"I could do with a glass of something cold. How about you?" she asked, tucking her tousled hair behind her ear.

David noticed the way she didn't look directly at him, rather concentrated on a spot just over his right shoulder. His brows shot up. He recognized her actions all too well, because, simply, he was usually the one who made them after sex. He pushed himself up onto his elbows. God, this was a first. "I…yeah, sure. I could go for some water or something."

A whole holding tank full of ice-cold water, he thought.

Tying the robe around her trim waist, she scooped up the empty condom packet from the nightstand, then padded barefoot from the room.

David lay still for a long moment staring after her. So that was it, huh? The most explosive sex he'd had…well, that he'd ever had, and it was over. It was time for him to leave.

He closed his eyes and groaned. Mitch had always warned him that one day he'd pay for his errant ways. He absently scratched his head, the thought of one brother leading to thoughts of another. Was Connor somewhere getting better acquainted with Kelli's friend, Bronte, right now? Or had he taken off right after he and Kelli had?

For the life of him, he didn't want to move. He wasn't sure what exactly had happened just now. The sex between him and Kelli was…well, whatever it was, he had to get himself some more of that.

Something cold and wet nudged against his foot. David went from complete relaxation to nearly catapulting from the bed at Olympic record-setting speed. He thoroughly searched the area but found nothing on the quilted blue-flowered mattress. If that was a bug, it had to be one of the slimiest…

There was a click-click against the wood floor. David looked anxiously around the room for something to defend himself with. He settled on one of his hiking boots. He slowly moved toward the end of the bed aided only by the boot and the dim light filtering in through the window. Not only did it have to be the slimiest, it must be the biggest damn bug—

A hulking, jowl-drooping blond boxer stuck his head out from around the corner of the bed and eyed him, his tongue seeming to curve upward toward his nose. David sagged with relief. A dog. It was a dog. Sensing that the crisis had passed, the ugly pooch came loping around the corner, his wagging short tail making his entire overly plump body shimmy.

David reached down to let the canine sniff the back of his free hand. "Hey—" he craned to see "—boy. How are you doing, huh?" He heartily rubbed him behind the ears.

A switch clicked, then an overhead light filled the room with its harsh glare. David blinked rapidly to adjust his eyesight, then looked at where Kelli stood in the doorway, a brow raised in question. David grimaced at his undressed state and the hiking boot he still held. *Way to go, McCoy.* It began to sink in that he wasn't going to be getting anymore of anything anytime soon.

Wow.

The word ran through Kelli's mind like a hit compact disc on permanent replay, despite the strange scene she encountered when she returned to her bedroom.

Her brain had effectively stopped working, oh, about an hour and a half ago at the bar, when she'd basically decided she was going to take one delectable David McCoy home with her. And it hadn't switched on again until she found herself lying on top of David, gloriously sweaty, wondering what in the world had just happened.

Despite her arguments to Bronte to the contrary, the limited scope of her experience had left her criminally unprepared for this man and her phenomenal reaction to him. She pulled her white, threadbare robe more tightly around herself with one hand. If this was what made Bronte jump into every bed she came across, then she herself had definitely been missing out on a whole lot of something for much too long.

The only problem was that remembering how very bad she'd just been made the good girl come out to do some mental finger-shaking.

The boot David held clunked to the floor and he grinned boyishly. "Uh…your dog and I were just getting acquainted."

Dog… Oh, God, her dog! "Kojak! Come here, boy." She'd purposely closed the bedroom door when they'd come in, but the pooch must have snuck in while she was in the other room. "There you are."

"I thought he was a bug."

"What?"

David was tugging up his jeans, his back to her, his firm, rounded behind tempting her touch. She averted her gaze and felt her cheeks color—which was ridiculous, because mere moments before she'd shamelessly run her fingers all over the flesh in question. "Never mind."

"I have your water," she blurted needlessly, the plastic glass in her hand.

Clad only in jeans, he sauntered over to her and accepted the cold drink. While he drank, Kelli covertly skimmed the well-toned body she had hungrily molested in the dark and was shocked by the rush of desire to consume him all over again. She mimicked his movements by swallowing hard. The guy was perfect in every sense of the word. His abs stood out in wondrous relief, making her itch to run her fingers over the sculpted muscles, down to where a thin line of blond hair disappeared into the waistband of his jeans.

"So that's it then, huh?" he asked, holding out the glass to her.

Kelli took it. "Did you want more?"

The odd way he looked at her made her rethink her question. "Depends on what you're referring to."

Kelli's cheeks burned hotly all over again. He wasn't talking about water. He was likely referring to the fact that she hadn't given them the chance for more. After they'd…had sex, she couldn't have run from the room quicker had it been on fire.

The dog butted his head against her shin, then ran around her legs in an attempt to gain her attention. "Not now…Jack."

David's grin nearly knocked her over. "Good thing you clarified who you were talking to, 'cause I was just about to grab my shirt."

Bronte would be happy to know that every last thing she'd uttered about David McCoy was absolutely, positively, one hundred percent true. He was a pro. And now that Kelli's head was working again, she was beginning to fear she was greener now than she'd ever been. Beginning to fear that it was impossible for her to have casual sex, because tomorrow kept intruding, making her wonder about stupid things like whether or not he would call her, or if he liked Chinese food.

Her gaze drifted down the sculpted planes of his chest and her own breathing grew curiously ragged. Green or not, she still wanted this man with every fiber of her being. She looked at his flat, beaded nipples and her own tightened and ached to be touched. She saw the thick ridge pressing against the zipper of his jeans, and felt a rush of hot desire between her bare legs.

She flicked her eyes up to stare into his, recognizing and instantly responding to the need reflected in the midnight blue depths. The hungry, sex-deprived wanton may have abandoned her, but she was finding that the good girl wanted everything she had…and more.

A tiny whimper gathered in her throat. Oh, to hell with tomorrow and consequences and hearing Bronte say "I told you so." The simple truth was that it was still night, and she wanted to spend every single last moment of it with David McCoy cradled between her thighs.

Forgetting the dog, she practically leapt on David, circling her arms around his neck, pasting her mouth against his and hungrily letting him know exactly what she was feeling. He slid his hands inside her robe and the ineffective belt slid to the floor…right along with the empty plastic glass. David grinned then scooped her up and practically tossed her back on top of the bed.

CHAPTER TWO

"YOU'RE LATE, Officer McCoy. Again."

David waved away O'Leary, the desk sergeant, and his penchant for protocol as he rushed by on his way to the briefing room. He'd run into bumper-to-bumper traffic near Dupont Circle, so had parked his car in the station commander's spot in front of the street level building to save time. His uniform shirt was wrinkled because when he'd looked for it on the passenger's seat—where he thought he'd put it when he leapt into the car half-dressed—he found instead that he'd been sitting on it. And he hadn't had a chance to clean and check his firearm, as he did every morning.

Despite all that, he caught himself whistling.

Okay, so it was tuneless, and he was also pretty sure he looked like Gomer Pyle on drugs, but he couldn't help himself.

Slowing his step, he made sure the back of his shirt was tucked in, folded his police issue winter jacket over his arm, and started to turn the corner. Lieutenant Kowalsky would have his ass for being late again. Still, suffering through old Kow's impending wrath didn't bother him half as much as it normally would. His good humor might have something to do with last night, and the incredible mind-blowing sex he'd had with Kelli Hatfield.

Kelli Hatfield.

If it was true what they said about the whole Hatfield and

McCoy feud…well, then, he and Kelli had made it their duty to put a huge dent into righting old wrongs.

"Nobody's in there."

O'Leary's words reached him the instant David opened the door to find the briefing room empty. He relaxed his shoulders from their stiff at-attention angle then glanced at his watch. Certainly, he hadn't missed roll call.

"Okay, O'L, what gives?" David stalked back to the front desk.

"Didn't have your radio on during the drive in, did you, kid? Everyone's downtown. Some guy's holding his little girl hostage until he can talk to his estranged wife. The whole city and county forces are down there now, not to mention every branch of the news media."

David felt the familiar, all-powerful burst of adrenaline kicking in. A hostage situation. Now that was a meaty way to start a day. He sprinted for the door, shrugging into his coat as he went.

"McCoy!"

David winced at Kowalsky's shout. He'd recognize that low, eardrum-popping sound anywhere. The guys around the station joked that you could hear his voice in the next county if you listened hard enough.

"Yes, Lieutenant?" he said, turning to face him, though he maintained his momentum.

"Going somewhere?" Kow asked, eyeing his shirt and raising a brow.

David either had to go through the door or stop. Given the warning written all over his superior's face, he opted for stop. "Yes, sir, I thought I'd head downtown to see if I could be of assistance."

"Aren't you forgetting something?"

"Sir?" Methodically, he patted his badge, his firearm, his cuffs. All there.

"Your new partner, McCoy. I'm talking about your new partner."

David winced for the second time. That's all he needed. A new guy to play getting-to-know-you with during the ride downtown. He quickly rebounded. "Sorry, sir. I'd assumed that since I was late, he would already be on the scene."

Contrary to his name, Kowalsky was a six-foot-five African-American with the manner of a drill sergeant and a monstrous grin he used only to his advantage. That he grinned now made David mutter a mild oath.

"What was that, McCoy?"

"Nothing, sir. My new partner… Where can I find him?"

Kow's grin widened. "Right here, McCoy."

He turned to find the hall empty. The grin left his face. "Hatfield!"

The bottom of David's stomach dropped out. *Hatfield.* His mind quickly calculated the odds that he would meet two Hatfields in less than twenty-four hours. They were very small. So small as to be minuscule. So tiny as to be impossible…

Naw. He had Hatfield on the brain, that's all.

He made the mistake of looking at Kow's suspicious grin, noting the telling absence of his new partner—as if he or *she* didn't want to be seen—and felt the sudden, irresistible urge to run. Especially when the sweetly sexy, innocently insatiable, utterly feminine Kelli Hatfield popped out from around the corner, her face mirroring the shock he felt.

Forget his stomach. The floor had just dropped out from beneath his feet.

It couldn't…wouldn't…there was no way in hell that this…that *she*…was his new partner. Hell, last night he judged her competence to be somewhere between squirting perfume on little blue-haired ladies with platinum credit cards and helping panicky brides try on their wedding dresses. The reality that she was actually a cop was enough to send any man reeling.

Kelli appeared to regain her bearings before he did. "Officer McCoy," she said, clearing her throat. Apparently remembering their company, she moved her coat from her right to her left arm, then thrust her hand—her soft, slender, *delicate* hand—toward him.

David took it, tempted to use it to pull her into the nearest room so they could have a little talk. *Now.* Kow be damned.

Speaking of Kow, he glanced to find him staring at them guardedly. "You two know each other?"

David nearly choked on the words, "yep, in the most sinful sense."

"Yes, sir," Kelli answered instead. "We met last night at The Pour House. First night back in town, as luck would have it."

"Good." Kow nodded. "Now isn't there some place you guys need to be?"

He had to be dreaming. That was it. This was all some sort of sick, twisted nightmare brought on by what happened to his ex-partner and his anxiety of who his new partner would be. At any moment he would—

"McCoy!" Kow barked. "Get with the program, man."

David winced. If this was a dream, what the hell was Kowalsky doing here?

Kelli gave him a pointed look. "We're on our way, sir," she said.

Completely dumbfounded, David watched her walk by him. Catching a whiff of her subtle scent didn't help matters any. His gaze zipped around the station lobby, but he didn't find any chuckling officers hiding behind any doors or around the corner. O'Leary wasn't even watching them. And Kow's expression darkened further with each second that passed.

This is for real. It wasn't some really bad practical joke being played on him by fellow, prankster officers. Kelli Hatfield truly was his new partner.

Yeah, and he was the king of Siam.

Picking up his jaw off the gritty tile, David hurried after Kelli's trim little bottom. The door closed after them and he stopped again. After a few steps, she turned toward him, shrugging into her coat. "Are you coming, McCoy?"

"There's no way…I mean, I don't believe… Come on, Kelli, you *can't* be a police officer," he blurted.

She planted her fists on her hips, her expression altogether thunderous. "Which one's ours?"

"Huh?"

"The car, Officer. Which is our vehicle?"

David pointed left to the cruiser in the lot and watched her head for it. She reached the driver's side. The impact of what her actions meant provided the impetus he needed to finally move. He was next to her in no time flat. "I'll drive."

Rolling her eyes toward the sky, she took her hand off the handle, then rounded the car and got in the passenger's side.

David stood still for a long moment, concentrating on little more than his breathing. This couldn't be happening. Any second now he expected to wake up from this dream—*nightmare*—and find his mind was playing some sort of sick joke on him after last night's recklessness. He bent over and looked through the window. Kelli was fastening her seat belt. He snapped upright again. Nope. She was still there.

Damn.

KELLI SAT flagpole straight, staring at the dash like a dazed crash victim waiting for the airbag to deflate. Her friend Bronte's words of warning from the night before echoed in her mind. "Just don't say I didn't tell you so…."

Somehow she didn't think this was what Bronte had in mind. Though her friend would probably argue it was exactly what she deserved—right after she laughed herself into hysteria.

Kelli closed her eyes tightly. Only to her. This could happen only to her. Her first night back home in D.C., the one and only night out of her entire life that she had thrown caution to the wind, and she wound up spending it with her new partner, screwing up both her personal and her professional life.

She scrubbed her damp palms against the scratchy material of her police issue slacks and whispered a long line of curses that would have done her police chief father proud. Well, it would have done him proud if, indeed, she'd ended up being the son he'd wanted instead of his only daughter. But she hadn't, and it was a fact he never let her forget. Not when she'd played little league baseball. Not when she'd enrolled in the academy at twenty. Not when she'd graduated and was denied a spot with the D.C. Metropolitan Police. It hadn't helped any when she learned that her father made sure her status was knocked down to third tier standby, essentially barring her from a job on the force. Apparently he had thought she would lose interest in her pursuit while in the academy. He'd always been so overprotective. As he'd told her, no little girl of his was going to get her butt shot off so long as he had any power within the department. And as Regional Assistant Chief for the East, he had more than enough to waylay her…at least in D.C. In New York, however, his power was nil.

The driver's door finally opened and Kelli nearly launched from her seat. David slid behind the wheel. She pointedly avoided his gaze and suspected he did the same beside her.

He's just as much a victim in this as I am, she reminded herself. But for some reason his undisguised disbelief when they were introduced irritated her. Shock, she expected. Disbelief? Suddenly agitated, she shifted. She told herself to give him the benefit of the doubt. That there was a good chance he wasn't like eighty percent of the other males she'd worked with who thought her completely incapable of her job as a police officer. Okay, maybe not a good chance. But there was a chance. And after last night, she, um, owed him at least that much consideration.

He moved. She forced herself to look at him. His mouth was moving, but no words made it past his impossibly wicked lips. She swallowed, reminding herself that she wasn't supposed to notice what a great mouth he had…or remember all the naughty places that mouth had been mere hours earlier.

His attempts at speech continued, nudging up her impatience level. Finally, she said, "Look, I didn't expect this anymore than you did, David…um, McCoy." *Stick to last names.* Maybe that would afford her the distance she so desperately needed right now.

His crack at imitating a wide-mouth bass out of water stopped and he seemed to relax. "Actually, Hatfield," he said, stressing her last name. "That's not entirely true. Last night *you* knew you were going to be reporting to work at *this* station and that you would be assigned a *new* partner. That's a helluva lot more than I was privy to."

She sighed and stared at the ceiling of the car. Okay, she'd give him that. Still… "Come on, David, we met at a cop bar. Surely you had to know there was some connection."

"All right. Sure. Maybe. But as someone's daughter. Or sister. Or…"

She raised a brow, daring him to say "cop groupie."

He cursed under his breath. "I didn't expect you to be a blasted police officer."

She stared out the windshield as a couple of uniforms walked by, openly curious about the couple in the squad car a few feet away. "Don't you think we should get going?"

"Huh?" He followed her line of vision. His long-suffering sigh told her he'd somewhat snapped out of his momentary trance.

"Look, David, when I came in this morning, this was the last thing I expected." She hated that she noticed his eyes were an even more vibrant blue in the light of day. "I say we do this. Go on about our business for now and pretend last night never happened."

He blinked as if the effort took every ounce of his concentration. "Are you crazy?" he said, startling her with his intensity. "I have the best friggin' sex of my life and you tell me to forget about it? Act like it never happened?"

Heat spread quickly through Kelli's veins, making her remember just how incredible last night had been for her, too. But last night was last night. And, oh boy, did the guy who sang "What a Difference a Day Makes" ever know what he was talking about.

David started the cruiser and began to back out. "Ain't a chance in hell I'm going to forget about last night, Kelli." He looked at her. "And I'll be damned if I'm going to let you forget either."

THEY ARRIVED on the scene to find the street glutted with blue-and-whites. David spotted the scene commander and within moments he and Kelli were next to him. A brisk December breeze brought her scent to him. Damn, but she smelled good. Like ripe peaches picked fresh from the tree.

He grimaced. Yeah, she was a peach all right. A peach with a gun.

"Glad you could join us, McCoy," Sutherland said dryly.

An officer David recognized as being at the bar the night before chuckled as he elbowed his partner.

"Look, loverboy has himself a new partner."

"Can it, Jennings," David told him. His gaze rested on Kelli's face to find bright spots of red high on her cheeks. But whether her flush was a result of the cold, or the obvious gossiping going on, he couldn't tell. Her shoulder-length toffee-colored hair was caught back in a neat French braid, her skin nearly flawless where the gray morning light caught it.

She looked at him. He immediately looked back at the commander. "Why don't you bring me...us up to speed on what's going on?"

Sutherland did, covering much the same ground O'Leary had at the station. Except his details were more specific. The perp was on the third floor. Door was open, but there wasn't a clean shot. He pointed to where the perpetrator's estranged wife stood shivering next to a nearby patrol car, then to a fire escape on the side of the building. Across the way on the roof of a neighboring building a couple of sharpshooters were setting up shop.

"The perp demands to talk to his wife before he'll give up the three-year-old girl."

"The perp is the child's father?"

"He ceased being a father the minute he took his own child hostage, McCoy."

David stepped backward until the fire escape was in sight, ignoring the red-and-white flashes of light against the brick building.

"What is it?" Kelli asked, coming to stand next to him.

He looked at her again. Damn, but just looking at her did all sorts of funny things to his stomach. "Just that the guy couldn't have picked a worse time to do this, that's all. You've got the tired third shifters exhausted and pumped up on caffeine, their trigger fingers itchy as hell. Then there are the first shift guys barely awake and pissed as hell that their coffee-and-donut run was interrupted." He grimaced. "Really bad timing."

Her gaze swept him from forehead to mouth. Was she remembering last night as vividly as he was? Was she thinking about how great it had felt to be joined together, far, far away from this mess? She looked quickly away and this time he was sure the color of her cheeks wasn't due to the cold. "Any ideas on how to end it?" she asked.

He mulled over her words. "Yeah. I think what I just said makes a lot of sense."

"What, let SWAT take him out?"

"No. The donuts part. If the father's just coming off third shift he probably hasn't had breakfast yet. A guy can get awful hungry after putting in a full one."

"Are you saying we should feed the perp?" she asked, a suspicious shadow darkening her green eyes.

"The father, Hatfield. The guy is the kid's father." He grinned. "And yeah, I think we should try feeding him." He shrugged. "Couldn't hurt."

He scanned the street. At the corner was a small donut shop. He thrust five dollars at her. "Here. Get a half dozen and a couple of coffees."

Kelli frowned. "But—"

"Do it, Hatfield."

Her eyes flashed, but she started toward the shop—though not without looking back a couple of times first.

The instant she was out of sight, David grabbed a bulletproof vest from the back of a riot wagon, then strode toward the fire escape. He pulled down the ladder even as he shrugged into the vest. He pulled his weight up on the first rung, then methodically climbed until he reached the third floor landing. Ducking off to the side, he peeked in through the window. The father was sitting on a couch out of view of the front door and of the sharpshooters across the street, grasping his little girl in one hand, a twelve-gauge shotgun in his other. The little girl looked unharmed. More than that, the toddler didn't seem to have the slightest idea that things were out of control as she giggled and toyed with the buttons down the front of her father's work shirt.

David ducked back out of sight and took a deep breath. He figured out the scenario in his mind. The father had just knocked off work at a nearby factory, had stopped by to see his daughter, his soon-to-be ex refused to allow him to, and he'd taken matters into his own hands.

Any way you cut it, what had begun as a harmless domestic squabble had spiraled out of control until you had the situation he now faced.

"I've got a clean shot," a sharpshooter's voice crackled over the radio fastened to David's gun belt.

"Be at the ready," scene commander Sutherland's voice responded.

Shaking his head, David reached over and tested the old wood-frame window. Unlocked. Hoping the bit of luck would stay with him, he pushed the window up before the guy inside, and the commander outside, had time to react.

"Whoa, there, cowboy," David said, swinging his feet over the sill and sitting with his hands up. "My name's McCoy and I'm here to make sure no one gets hurt." He grinned. "Especially me."

OFFICERS, uniformed and otherwise swarmed the small, neat apartment, talking into radios, issuing orders and generally making a mess out of things. In the middle of the chaos, Kelli finished reading the perp his Miranda rights, then cuffed him. Distractedly, her gaze trailed over to where David stood near the door holding the little girl. She clung to him like a young chimp. He leaned in and whispered something into her ear, then chucked her under her dimpled chin. She twirled her blond, sleep-tousled hair around her chubby index finger, then giggled shyly. Somehow, David had not only skillfully managed to keep the girl from seeing her father being arrested, he had made her laugh. Kelli couldn't help noticing how… right he looked holding the little cherub.

Testing the cuffs, she forced the unwanted thought aside and concentrated instead on her total lack of amusement only moments before. David's sending her off on some two-bit, phony errand so that he could play maverick hero set her blood to simmering.

"This way," she said, grasping the perp's elbow, then angling him toward the door.

He hesitated. "I didn't mean for any of this to happen. I just wanted my face to be one of the first she saw this morning, that's all," he told her. "It's her birthday, you know. All I wanted was five minutes to give her a hug and her present. I would never have hurt my little girl."

Kelli took in his aggrieved expression. "I hope not. But that's for a judge to decide, isn't it?"

David handed the child off to another female officer who would likely take the toddler to her mother and Kelli passed the handcuffed perp off to the first officer on the scene.

"That was a stupid stunt you pulled, David," Kelli muttered as they walked out of the apartment together.

"Just so long as it's over and no one got hurt." He acknowledged a hearty slap on the back from one of their colleagues with a nod. He flashed a loaded grin at her. "I didn't know you were so concerned about my backside."

"I'm your partner," she said, her breath catching at the teasing expression on his face. "I'm supposed to be concerned about your backside. But that's not what I was talking about. I didn't much care for your little diversionary tactic, David. Do you even know the definition of the word partn—"

"McCoy! Get your ass over here now, boy," Sutherland's voice boomed up the stairwell.

"Speaking of backsides…" David groaned. "I'd better go see what he wants."

Kelli opened her mouth, then snapped it closed again. She got the impression that whatever she had to say wouldn't make one iota of difference anyway.

She stopped and let him pass in front of her. "Go ahead. I just might enjoy watching the scene commander take a piece out of you."

David's grimace was altogether too cute. "Be careful what you wish for, Hatfield. At this rate, I won't have any behind left to risk." He waggled his brows.

Sutherland was at the bottom of the steps and was apparently ready to do just as David forecasted. Even so, Kelli couldn't help eyeing the backside in question. The clinging, unattractive material and bulky weapons belt was unable to hide the fact that David McCoy's behind was the stuff of which fantasies were made. She started to push wisps of hair from her forehead only to find her hand shaking. She greeted an officer, then outside on the street away from the crowd she took a deep, calming breath.

Why did she get the feeling that everything in her life had just been turned upside down? And why was it that she suspected that a certain precinct Casanova named David McCoy was solely to blame?

CHAPTER THREE

THE FOLLOWING MORNING, Kelli caught herself daydreaming as she stood in front of the toaster. She'd been thinking about David in a way that had nothing to do with the way he'd treated her yesterday, nothing to do with her plans to nab a detective's shield, and everything to do with hot flesh and cool sheets.

Sighing in a mixture of wistfulness and frustration, she pushed her run-dampened hair from her cheek, then stuck half an onion bagel smothered with grape jelly between her teeth. Ignoring the dirty dishes stacked in the sink, and the empty carton of orange juice on the counter, she clutched her full coffee cup, then elbowed open the kitchen door. She had forty-five minutes before roll call. Plenty of time to peel off her sweats, catch a shower and get down to the district three station to have that little talk she and David had never really gotten around to yesterday.

The tension she had just spent a half an hour and three miles running off settled solidly back between her shoulder blades.

After the hostage case and Sutherland, there had been the press to deal with. She remembered how David's easy grin and easygoing personality had transferred well over all forms of media and felt her stomach tighten along with her shoulders. Reporters, especially female—although she'd noticed a couple of males responding to David's charming, daredevil ways—were all over him. When they'd *finally* gotten back to their squad car, it seemed a quarter of D.C.'s population had a crisis of some sort that needed attention. She and David had spent the day on back-to-back runs ranging from the simple—helping find an elderly woman's "stolen" social security check in a neighbor's mailbox—to the complicated—an obvious gang member who would probably lose an eye but would never give up the names of his homies or the opposing gang.

Still, no matter how many calls came in, how much paperwork they had to fill out, a thread of awareness had bound her and David together. It was a connection not even her sharpest retort could hope to cut.

Yeah, well, today she planned to take a machete to work. She'd get a handle on her runaway hormones if it was the last thing she ever did.

Kelli wove her way through the maze that was currently her apartment into the dining area of her living room. She dodged precariously stacked, half-unpacked boxes, a hundred pound bag of diet dog food and her treadmill. Finally she nudged a manila folder aside with her mug, then put her coffee on the cluttered dining room table. Her attention catching on a pink message slip, she freed the bagel from between her teeth and took an absent bite. The message must have slipped from one of the files, the blue ink nearly faded. She leaned closer to see the date. March 25, 1982. The day her mother was murdered. The day she'd decided she wanted to be a homicide detective.

A sharp bark made her jump.

"Yikes, Kojak, you just about gave me a coronary." Frowning down at the drooling blond boxer she'd rescued from a New York animal shelter, she considered the disgusting concoction that served as her breakfast then held it out to him. He sniffed, licked, then whined and walked away.

Kelli stared at the now inedible bagel half. "Thanks a

lot." She tossed it into a nearby bag she hoped was empty, then switched on the television across the room with the remote. The local news broadcaster's voice filled the apartment reminding her again how David had charmed the reporters. His too handsome mug had been plastered all over the news last night, every hour on the hour, if not on the news itself, then in the news previews. "You don't want to miss our story of the day as local man in blue David McCoy saves the day…."

It was enough to make a person ill.

Kelli plucked up the remote again, moving to switch off the television before the news could launch into another "local hero" bit featuring her partner the sexist cad, when a completely different scene stopped her. *We're on the outskirts of Georgetown where a woman was found dead in her apartment, earlier this morning. Eyewitnesses tell us the murder of this quiet, private school teacher bears all the markings of the work of the man dubbed the D.C. Degenerate.*" The female spot reporter looked over her shoulder.

Kelli wryly nodded. "Zoom in on the standard body shot," she said under her breath.

The reporter looked back at the camera. *"If so, then I, for one, think we need to upgrade his name to D.C. Executioner. Because it appears he's just lost interest in playing out sick sexual fantasies and has just graduated to full-fledged killer."*

Kelli pressed the mute button, the case too similar to another for her comfort. She picked up the message slip lying on the table in front of her, wondering how much detectives knew about this latest guy. And if they would do any better catching him than they had her mother's killer.

It had been awhile since she'd reviewed the contents of the folders strewn out before her. Three years, in fact. Ever since transferring to New York where doing any footwork on the case would have been impossible. She sat down and curled her right leg under her. Now that she was back home, though...

The telephone chirped. Propping a file open with one hand, she reached for the cordless with her other.

"Yeah?"

"Jaysus, Kelli, is that the way you answer the phone?" her father asked with obvious exasperation.

Kelli closed the file and reached for another. "I don't know, Dad, you'd be the better one to answer that question since you are the one who's calling me every five minutes since I got back in town."

She winced the moment the words were out of her mouth. Not because she shouldn't have said such a thing to her own father, but because of what it would ultimately lead to.

She closed her eyes and waited for the inevitable speech.

"Yes, well, I wouldn't have to call you if you were staying here, now would I?"

"No, Dad, you wouldn't," she said almost by rote.

"You know I have more than enough room for you. There's no sense in your going off and getting an apartment."

"Yes, Dad, I know."

The sound of crumpling paper caught her attention. She turned to find Kojak nosing around in the bag for the uneaten bagel.

"Have you watched the news lately? It isn't safe for a woman to be living on her own in this city."

Kelli nodded. "Not safe."

"And that damn mutt of yours is no kind of security either, if that's what you're thinking. He's nothing but an overgrown cat."

"Cat..."

"Kelli Marie, are you even paying attention to what I'm saying, girl?"

"Sure, Dad. Though I really don't have to because you've

said it so often it's etched in my brain." She pulled another file in front of her and flipped it open. "Was there a specific reason you called, Dad? Or is this just another of your check-ins?"

Silence, then, "Can't a dad simply want to talk to his daughter?"

Kelli slowly spread her hand out palm down on the table. She should have seen that one coming as well but stepped right through the open barn door all the same. Her voice was decidedly more subdued when she said, "Of course you can, Dad." She leaned back in her chair. Sometimes it seemed it had always been just her and her father. "You and me against the world," he'd said when he'd found her crying in her mother's closet after the funeral. Words he'd repeated time and again after she'd gotten knocked down over and over while proving to everyone and to herself that she was just as good as the guys. "It's just you and me against the world, kid."

She curled the fingers of her free hand into a loose fist. "Dad…I know it makes you uncomfortable to talk about it…and Lord knows I've avoided bringing the topic up enough times…but I have to know." She took a deep breath that did nothing to calm her. "Does it ever bother you that Mom's killer was never caught?"

She regretted the question the instant it was out. The silence that wafted over the line was as palpable as her own unsteady heartbeat. "You know I don't like talking about the past, Kelli."

"I know, but—"

"What's done is done. Nothing can change it."

I can change it. "But don't you think sometimes that it can be changed? That by—"

"No."

She bit her tongue to stop herself from asking anymore questions, no matter how much she wanted to. She knew from experience that she would only upset her father more. And the more upset he got, the more he clammed up, locking himself away even from her. She didn't want to make that happen. Not in her first few days back home, no matter how desperately she needed answers.

"Okay, Dad. We don't have to talk about it if you don't want to."

She switched the phone to her other ear, focusing her entire attention on lightening the conversation, coaxing it back to safer ground. "So tell me, big bad police chief…did you go for the Café Vienna or the French Vanilla this morning?"

For the next ten minutes she and her father talked about everything and nothing, with Kelli carefully redirecting the conversation whenever it moved too near career territory…too close to family issues that might include mention of her mother. It was altogether easier for both of them to forget that she was a police officer. Um, edit that. It was infinitely easier to make her father forget she was a police officer, much less why she had chosen the career to begin with. She wasn't sure what he told everyone about her time in New York, but if she knew Garth Hatfield, and she did, it probably had something to do with art school.

Of course that explanation would not only raise some brows now that she was back in town, it would call into question his mental capacity.

Kelli glanced at her watch. "I gotta run, Dad."

"Oh. Sure. Okay."

She methodically closed each of the files in front of her and piled them back up, chucking any idea she had of going through them this morning. "I'll talk to you later, then?"

"Later."

"Goodbye." She started to get up and nearly tripped over where Kojak was licking a jelly stain from the wood floor.

"Hold up a second, Kell." Her father's voice stopped her

from hitting the disconnect button. "There's something I wanted to ask you."

She absently watched the muted images slide across the television screen. Stories of murder and corruption, all against the background of the most powerful capital of the world. Never a dull moment. "What is it?"

"How did it go yesterday?"

Kelli paused, wondering at the neutral sound of her father's voice. She decided to play it as vaguely as he was. "It went well. Really well." *Liar.* Although she was sure her dad would approve of her trouble with David even less than the idea of her putting on a uniform every morning.

"You meet your new partner yet?" he asked.

She slowly reached out and switched the television off. "Yes."

"Are you getting on well?"

Kelli crossed her free arm over her chest. "Yes."

Her father's sigh burst over the line. "Come on, girl, this isn't an official interrogation. You can give more than a yes or no answer. Do you like the guy or don't you? Do you want me to have you assigned somewhere else? Another district station, maybe?"

"Like out in Arlington where the most serious crime is loitering? No, Dad, but thanks just the same." She rubbed her forehead. So much for avoidance measures. "And my partner's name's McCoy. He's a pigheaded, male chauvinist who needs an ego adjustment, but I can handle him." At least she hoped she could.

There was a heartbeat of a pause. Kelli fought the desire to ask him if he was still there.

"McCoy?" he finally said gruffly.

"Yeah. David. Do you know him?"

"Of him. I know his father."

"That's nice, Dad. Maybe you and he can get together and

plot how to scare your kids off the force over a beer sometime. Look, I've—"

"If Sean McCoy and I ever end up in the same room together where there's beer, I'd just as soon crack a bottle over his head," her father said vehemently.

Kelli's mouth dropped open. She'd never heard him say such a thing about another person. Yes, he was quite adamant on where he stood on her decisions, but that was different. In almost every other aspect of his life he was as open-minded as they came. "Dad...I don't quite know what to say. I'm...shocked."

"Yeah, well, you wouldn't be if you knew the guy. They don't make them any cockier than Sean McCoy."

He hadn't met David yet. "When's the last time you spoke to this...Sean?"

He mumbled something she couldn't quite make out.

"What was that?"

"Twenty years."

Kelli smacked her hand against her forehead. "Gee, and here I thought it was something a little more recent. Like yesterday."

"It was. I might not speak to the old geezer, but I see him just about every day on the job."

"Wait, don't tell me. He's on the force, too. What is he? Regional Assistant Chief for the West or something?"

"Chief?" Garth nearly shouted. "Hell, Kelli, aren't you getting the drift of anything I'm saying? The guy's a damn beat cop. Always has been, always will be."

"So?" she said carefully. "Look, Dad, call me slow, but I'm not getting this. What is this, a modern day replaying of the old Hatfields and McCoys thing?" She glanced at her watch and nearly gasped. "I gotta run, Dad. We can talk about this later, okay?"

She pressed the disconnect button while he was still blathering on. She cringed. No doubt she would hear about *that* later, as well.

DAVID STARED at his watch for the third time, although no more than a minute had passed since the last time he'd looked. The briefing room was already filled to capacity. Which wasn't abnormal in and of itself, except the collection of plainclothes at the front of the room had ignited gossip among the officers surrounding him.

Where is she?

"What do you think's up?" Jones, next to him, asked.

David shrugged. "Beats me."

"Harris thinks it's the Degenerate case."

He grimaced. "All this attention for a sexual deviant? Seems a little excessive."

"Where you been, man? The guy's been promoted. He's chalked up his first killing. Body was found this morning, though they think she's been dead a couple of days."

David recalled the case. "Damn."

Jones chuckled. "You got that right."

"Did I miss anything?"

David looked to his left where Kelli had claimed the seat he'd been saving for her. She looked far too fresh, too alert, for first thing in the morning. And far too enticing. It was all he could do not to pant all over her like a Chihuahua, bug eyes and all.

"You're late," he said, unhappy with the simile. A Chihuahua? He should be something more manly, like a German shepherd at least.

And Kelli was one hundred percent groomed white poodle, pink bow and all.

She smiled. "Yes, I am, aren't I?"

It took David a full second to realize she was referring to her lateness, not to his mental comparison.

She shifted her weight so that she could slip his notepad out from under her curved bottom. "This yours?"

David snatched it away, telling himself the paper couldn't possibly be warm after so brief a contact.

"Did I miss anything?" she asked again.

David crossed his arms, tempted to ignore her. After her dumping maneuvers yesterday after they kicked off work, he'd spent the entire night at his father's place glowering…and watching Pop glower, too. Not a fun way to pass the time. "It's about the Degenerate case."

Her eyes lit up. "You mean the D.C. Executioner case now, don't you?"

"You know?"

"Of course I know. Don't you watch the news, McCoy?"

He wanted to tell her that no, he got enough of real life on the job, but he didn't think it would reflect well on him. So instead he said nothing, because to imply that he usually did watch the news, but had missed it now, might hint at a break in his routine. Which might then lead to her assumption that she was the cause for this disruption. He wouldn't in a million years let her think that. No matter how on the mark the assumption would be.

Instead, he grinned. "I, um, had other things to do last night."

The light extinguished. "The news came through this morning."

David shrugged. "Same difference."

Kelli sat back in her seat and sighed. "Please, do spare me the details."

He leaned in a little closer, eyeing the clean stretch of flesh just below her ear. "Oh, I don't know. I was hoping you and I could, um, go over them blow-by-blow. Say tonight? Over dinner?"

He never saw her fist coming, but he had no doubt that's what hit him in the arm. "Ow," he said, rubbing the sore spot.

"Come on to me again on the job and you'll be hurting a lot worse than that, McCoy. Now stop your whining. They're about to start."

And start they did. But David only listened with half an ear about the formation of a special task force headed up by homicide in cooperation with the Sex Crimes unit. They were looking for a few good men and women to go undercover. SC already had three detectives working undercover at three different sex shops across the city that the earlier victims may have frequented. They needed another.

David couldn't care less. His academy test scores had all basically come up with "does not play well with others." It was exactly the reason he'd been through three partners in less than seven years. Even if he had a mind to apply for a position on the task force—and he didn't—they'd probably laugh him out of the interview.

Still, it wasn't his lack of interest in the goings-on that worried him. Rather, his intense interest in the woman next to him.

Why had she dodged his attempts to get her alone last night? One minute he'd been shooting the breeze with a couple of other officers back here at the station, the next he'd turned around to find her gone.

He'd thought about showing up at her place unannounced with a six-pack. And probably would have had she been anyone else. But for some reason the thought of her shutting the door in his face had chased him out to Pops's instead.

Was it his imagination, or had the sex between them the other night been as good as he remembered? And if that was the case, why was it that Kelli looked like she'd rather be anyplace else on earth than sitting next to him?

Unless…

Oh, God, he couldn't even bear to think that he'd somehow fallen short of the mark performance-wise. Missed the three-pointer. Left her swinging in the proverbial wind.

He shifted and covertly eyed her. Naw. It wasn't even remotely possible that lady-killer David McCoy had left a woman sexually unsatisfied. Hell, he had a black book full of names to prove differently. An endless list of women just begging for a phone call from him.

He crossed his arms. It wasn't possible.

He slanted her another glance. Was it?

"That's it. If anyone has any questions, feel free to ask the detectives here. We should be getting a suspect sketch out to all units before the end of first shift." A pause. "And officers, I won't kid you. We don't know what we're dealing with here, what the suspect's capable of and how far he intends to go. The female officer who signs on will be faced with a very dangerous situation. We want you to take that into consideration before tendering your name."

David practically sprang from his chair. "Thank God, that's over. You ready?"

Kelli grimaced. "I've got…something to do first. Meet me out at the car?"

He shrugged. "No prob."

Women. Probably had to go powder her nose or something. Lord forbid she should look less than her best to apprehend a shoplifter.

KELLI DISCREETLY wiped her sweaty palms down the length of her slacks when she finally left the briefing room. Her chances of winning the grand prize in the Publisher's Clearinghouse sweepstakes were probably better than getting on that task force. She'd only been on the job in D.C. for two days. What did it matter that she had three years of solid experience in New York? Or that she'd gone undercover twice there as a prostitute to arrest potential johns?

Still, she'd had to submit her name for consideration, no matter what the outcome. Chasing down men who preyed on women was exactly what she'd always been driven to do. If she couldn't find closure in her mother's case, she could make damn sure no other young girl had to face what she had. She would offer them closure. A chance to see the offender punished for what he'd done to a loved one. An opportunity to go on with life knowing that there was some justice in the world.

She had to do it. No matter how dangerous the road she had to take to get there.

She shrugged into her coat and opened the outer door, admitting that maybe her chances at the assignment were better than she thought. Even she was surprised to find the task force already had her personnel file. Written there in black and white for the entire world to see was her career goal: become a full-fledged homicide detective before she reached thirty. She cringed. Sure, that was her goal. But what had she been thinking when she wrote that little tidbit down for her supervisors to see? She might as well have written that when she was ten she'd wanted to be president of the United States.

"Smooth move, Hatfield," she muttered to herself as she put on her hat.

She wasn't surprised to find David glowering in the squad car, tapping the face of his watch like a taskmaster. Kelli climbed into the passenger's side, inclined to tell him that she had enough on her hands with one father, she didn't need another. But that might lead to her revealing who her father was, and she wasn't quite up to dealing with that can of worms right now.

"Took you long enough," he said, backing out. "What did you do, eat some bad Chinese or something last night?"

Kelli stared at him, her mouth agape. Of course he would

think she'd needed to make a pit stop at the bathroom. She wouldn't be surprised if he thought she'd needed to powder her nose, or whatever men thought women did nowadays. Lord forbid she'd have any interest in joining the task force. And far be it from her to fill him in. It would only make it worse when she found out she hadn't made it.

She snapped her mouth shut. "Yeah, something like that." She switched on the radio and picked up the handset. "Dispatch, this is Five-Two, heading out." She settled back into her seat. "Look, David, you and I *really* need to have that talk I mentioned yesterday."

"About what?"

His blank expression told her he truly didn't have a clue. "About the little stunt you pulled yesterday morning."

He didn't look enlightened.

"When you sent me out for donuts while you, by your lonesome, went out and saved the world."

"Oh, that," he said, grinning. "I didn't save the world, Kelli. Just kept a guy who needed some sleep from mucking up his life any more than he already had."

"Did it ever cross your mind to consult with me first? To work out a plan together, then have Sutherland approve it?"

He appeared to think her question through, then shook his head. "Nope."

She pointed her finger in his direction. "That's exactly the reason we need to talk. Just what did you think you were doing climbing that fire escape without backup? Without anyone knowing just what you were doing? Then barging through that open window like…like some uniformed supercop there to save the day?"

He arched a brow. "Uniformed supercop?"

Kelli bit her tongue. She'd picked up the description from one of the many news reports the night before.

"Look, Hatfield, you and I could argue about this all day…and all night—" a decidedly suggestive twinkle entered his eyes "—but when all is said and done, there was no time to plan. SWAT had a shot and Sutherland was about to give the order for them to take it. I had to act, and I had to act fast." He stopped at a red light. "Okay, I admit, sending you to get donuts was a pretty rotten thing to do—"

"Downright crappy."

He grinned. "Yeah. But, hell, I was still shocked to find you were on the force, much less my partner, and I needed some time to adjust before going out and playing Butch Cassidy and the Sundance Kid, you know?"

His explanation made Kelli more agitated. Only because it made a twisted sort of sense. What was the world coming to when she understood the inner workings of a mind like David's?

Worse yet, what was with her desire to keep looking at the way the material of his slacks clung to his hunky, well-defined thighs?

"Just don't do it again, McCoy, or else you won't have to worry about Sutherland taking a piece out of your behind. I'll be the one with that honor."

He flashed that devil-may-care grin at her again, making her want to smack her forehead against the dash in exasperation. "Sounds fun."

She mumbled a series of unflattering remarks under her breath.

David's grin vanished. "That was just a joke. Hey, if it makes you feel any better, I'll let you take the lead on the next call that comes in, okay? Whatever it is—bank robbery, car chase, shoplifter. You name it, I'll stand back and let you handle it any way you want to. You'll be completely, totally, in charge."

Naughty images that had nothing to do with police work

slid through her mind. Finally, she managed to say, "I don't want to be the leader, McCoy. I just want to be your partner." She uncrossed her arms and smiled. "But you've got a deal."

Just then, the radio crackled. The dispatcher named a code and a location. "All officers in the vicinity, please respond."

Kelli rolled her eyes. A domestic dispute. It figured. The one call she was going to get to control and it would probably be settling an argument over who left the cap off the toothpaste.

"Aren't you going to call it in, Hatfield? We're only two blocks away," David said, then laughed so hard he had to slow down the car.

Kelli glared at him. "I was thinking about letting another patrol get it." Then she sighed and picked up the handset. "Dispatch, this is Five-Two. We've got it. ETA five minutes."

CHAPTER FOUR

BOY, SHE'S EVEN more beautiful all worked up. David slipped his nightstick into his weapons belt, then closed his car door. On the other side, Kelli did the same, the high color on her cheeks reflecting how she felt. And he knew it was in response to him. He inwardly grinned. She might act like being around him didn't affect her one way or another, but her sparkling green eyes told him differently. He'd be the first to admit that having her pissed at him wouldn't be his first choice in responses, but hey, he'd take it over her pretended indifference any day.

They stood on the curb looking at the four-story, low-rent walk-up. Nothing out of the ordinary jumped out at him. Windows were closed against the December cold. A man in his thirties was leading a bicycle from the door and carrying it down the ten or so cement steps.

"So…" David began. "Lead on."

And Kelli did. Catching the door before it had time to close after the cyclist, she switched on her shoulder radio to let dispatch know where they were. No elevator. Nimbly, she climbed the interior steps to the third floor, then crossed to the door farthest to the left. Slipping her nightstick out, she rapped on the door.

Footsteps, then a voice called out, "Who's there?"

"Police. We got a call reporting a disturbance."

David noticed that she didn't say "sir" or "ma'am" likely because he couldn't identify the sex of the person inside either.

"Who?"

Kelli looked at him. "Metropolitan P.D.," she said louder.

"I didn't call any poh-leece."

David stepped down the hall and switched on his radio. "Dispatch, the resident said there was no call made."

"My records show there was. Right from the apartment in question. Do you want back up?"

Very curious. David told the dispatcher to stand by, then rejoined Kelli at the door. She nodded, indicating she'd heard.

Kelli rapped lightly on the door again. "Someone did call, *ma'am*," she said with raised brows. David shrugged. She had a fifty percent chance of getting the sex right. "Could you please open the door?"

"But I'm not dressed."

"We'll give you a few moments to put something on, ma'am. But we're going to have to insist that you open the door."

There was no mistaking the long-suffering sigh on the other side of the wood. "Okay. Just a minute."

The sound of another voice filtered through the door, then there was an ominous thump. David slipped his stick out as well. What was going on here?

Abruptly, the door opened. Kelli held her ground, but David took a protective step back. His position allowed him a better view of just how enormous the woman in the apartment was. And he guessed that she was a woman, given the brightly colored flower-print…dress she had on.

The resident filled the entire length and width of the door. In fact, she would probably have to turn sideways in order to get out of it. Kelli tossed him a nervous glance over her shoulder. Talk about David and Goliath….

"Ain't nobody make no call from here," the woman said. "I've opened the door. So you gonna leave now?"

David heard Kelli swallow. "Step away from the door, ma'am."

"Why? Ain't nothing here to see but me."

"I'm afraid I'm going to have to insist," Kelli said.

The resident held her ground. "You got a search warrant?"

"The phone call was all the warrant we need, ma'am."

"I done already tol' you—"

"Help."

David stepped up at the muffled sound of the voice emanating from somewhere behind the woman.

"I told you to shut up," the woman said, turning just enough so that they could see the person who had made the weak plea.

David heard Kelli's gasp and nearly had to put his hand to his mouth to stop his own burst of shocked laughter.

Kneeling in the middle of the living room floor was a man about a quarter the size of the woman in front of them, his skinny ribs clearly visible through the flaps of a fluorescent pink robe edged in red feathers.

"Please help me," he repeated.

"If there's no one else here, who's this, ma'am?" Kelli asked, elbowing David when his laughter threatened to spill over.

The woman hooked a beefy thumb toward the man. "That's my boyfriend, Ethan."

It took all kinds, David thought as he slid his stick back into his belt.

"You mind explaining what's going on here?" Kelli asked, obviously preferring to hold on to her stick.

"She took my clothes," the man whined.

"Took...your...clothes," Kelli repeated carefully.

The guy crawled a couple of steps closer on his knees,

allowing them a peek at the pink mules he wore on his bony feet. David couldn't help himself. He made it halfway down the hall before he burst out laughing. Kelli shot him a repri-manding look, though her eyes gave away just how close she was to losing it.

She turned back to the woman. "Ma'am, would you care to explain why you took his clothes?"

"I sure would. The no-good, dirty rotten bastard stole twenty dollars out of my wallet, that's why. I told him the last time he took something from me that if he did it again, I'd make him pay." She crossed her arms over her chest. "Well, all he had to pay with was his clothes."

Kelli motioned to the pitiful looking man. "And what he has on…now?"

"Them's my things."

"Uh-huh." Kelli tucked her stick under her arm and flipped open her notepad. She took both their names. "Do you two reside here together, Mrs. Smith?"

"You can bet your narrow little behind that he don't live with me. He's lucky I even let him visit."

"Okay. What did you do with Mr. Watson's clothes?"

"I burned 'em."

Kelli's eyes widened. "You burned them?"

"I surely did. Put them in the bathtub and squirted lighter fluid all over 'em, I did. Then I flicked a match." She snapped her fingers, then hooked a thumb over her shoulder again. "That's when Mr. Shady decided to borrow some of my things."

"I see," Kelli said slowly. She eyed the situation in front of her again, then looked back at David. He shrugged. "Do you want to press charges, Mr. Watson?"

"Press charges? Against me? What about my twenty?" Betty Smith whipped it out and waved it back and forth.

"Well, ma'am, since it looks like you've recovered your property, what remains in question is Mr. Watson's property, which, of course, can no longer be recovered."

"Not to mention whatever dignity the guy had left," David murmured into Kelli's ear.

She cracked a smile, then cleared her throat. "Mr. Watson?"

Apparently sensing that things were moving in his favor, the man finally got up. David wished he hadn't. He watched Kelli cringe, then look the other way as the robe gaped open and revealed that Mrs. Smith had indeed stripped him to the skin.

"Please cover yourself, Mr. Watson."

"Oh." He quickly did as asked. "I suppose I don't want to press charges, officers. Am I free to go?"

Kelli nodded. "Yes, sir, I'd say you are."

He rushed for the door, stumbling in the mules he wore.

"You ain't goin' anywhere wearin' my stuff!"

Kelli extended her stick, preventing Mrs. Smith from grabbing Mr. Watson. "He can't leave here wearing nothing, ma'am. He'd be breaking the indecent exposure laws."

She snorted. "You can say that again. Ain't a damn thing decent about his sorry ass."

David burst out laughing again. Kelli looked about ready to beam him over the head with her stick.

Kelli turned back to Mr. Watson. "Promise you'll bring… No, scratch that. Promise you'll mail Mrs. Smith's things back to her."

"I promise."

Then he darted between them and stumbled down the hall.

"And make sure you keep that robe closed," Kelli called after him.

"I ABOUT DIED LAUGHING when he got up with all of his…um, privates just a flapping in the wind," David said, grinning.

Kelli winced. "Did you have to remind me? I could have done without that little peep show, thank you very much."

"*Little* being the operative word."

Despite her best intentions, Kelli sat back in the diner booth and gave into the laugh tickling the back of her throat. Her eyes began watering. Not from the piles of onions on her hot dog, but rather from the effort it took not to completely give herself over to the hysterics that threatened. It was a relief to release the tension accumulated during the long, busy morning. It was a blessing to release the tension of a whole other nature that had been building between her and her, um, partner. Sitting across from him and dishing like partners after an emotionally trying morning helped to dispell the awkwardness. Over the years she'd come to see that these little chats with fellow officers were just as important to her sanity as knowing her partner was a capable backup. Given her history—however brief—with David, she was afraid that they'd lost all ability to objectively converse as two coworkers.

He grinned and took a hefty bite of his own chili dog.

Kelli took a long, thoughtful swallow of soda. She looked around the interior of the diner, just now noticing there wasn't another officer in sight. Considering she'd left today's choice of lunch spots up to David—her own choice of Thai food the previous day a major mistake—she was surprised he even knew of any places outside the perimeter of the station, much less one that didn't include at least a dozen macho pals. The diner wasn't only private, it was…nice.

She put the drink straw in her mouth again, watching him closely. "You know that call could have turned out very differently."

His gaze skated away from where it was locked onto her mouth and on up to her eyes. "Don't I know it." He grinned.

"Mrs. Smith could have given us a peep show too, which neither one of us would have soon forgotten."

She smiled and picked up her hot dog. "I'm serious." She took a bite, then swallowed. "I learned really quick that the fastest route to a disability pension was accepting situations at face value."

"In New York?"

She nodded. "Yeah. First day on the job. Or night, rather, since I started on third shift. Anyway, my partner and I were sent out on a domestic disturbance call. By the time we showed up at the place, all was quiet. The wife answered the door and assured us that everything was fine. Her husband had come home drunk and they'd had a little argument, but that he had since fallen asleep."

Apparently picking up on the seriousness of her tone, David's chewing slowed.

Kelli shrugged. "We had no reason to dispute her story. There were beer bottles littering the floor, the television was running full blast, and there was a kid in a diaper sitting on the floor by his father's feet, you know, where he was passed out on a recliner." She gave a tiny shudder, remembering the scene. "Both of us put our sticks away and were about to sign off on the case when something caught my attention."

"Ah, the rookie sees all."

She gave him a wry smile. "Something like that. Anyway, I decided that I wanted a closer look. I went into the living room and tried to prod the husband awake. Nothing. I gave him a more insistent poke and he slumped over…to reveal that he'd been shot in the back of the head. He hadn't been sleeping. He was dead. And the gun? The wife had put the toddler on top of it, still loaded, the safety off."

"Ouch."

Kelli sighed. "Yeah. Not exactly a banner first day. I had nightmares for weeks afterward."

"The first corpse is never easy," he said.

She studied his striking face then gave a small smile. "Somehow I can't imagine you having a hard time with anything."

"Are you kidding?" he said seriously, putting his hot dog down. "I'm going to be having nightmares about Mr. Watson for the next month, at least."

She picked up a fry and tossed it at him. "Very funny."

He plucked it from his shirtfront and popped it into his grinning mouth.

Kelli forced her gaze away from him, finding him far too attractive for her own well-being. "I'm serious. Aren't there times when this job, you know, really gets to you? Makes you wonder why you ever signed up?"

David took another huge bite of his dog, then sat back, appearing to think it over. Finally, he shook his head. "Nope."

"You would say that."

"So tell me," he said, putting fries into his mouth two at a time and talking with his mouth full, "what does your family think of you being a cop?"

"I prefer police officer." She took a bite of her own dog.

"You would."

She wiped her mouth with a napkin. "There's just my father and me. And, well, to say he doesn't think much of my being a police officer would be a major understatement." She found herself unable to meet David's gaze for fear of what she would give away.

"He still in New York?"

She shook her head. "No. I'm originally from here. How about you? How does your family feel?" she asked, hoping to switch the conversational spotlight over to him for fear that she would end up just throwing her hands up and say, "Okay, my father's a police chief and why does he hate your father anyway?" She'd never been much good at deception. Except when it came to the little white lies she told herself.

Ignoring his napkin, he brushed his hands together. "Well, let's see. There are my four brothers. They couldn't care one way or another if I was a cop or not. You see, each of them is or was in law enforcement in one form or another. Then there's Pops." He flipped over his coffee cup on the saucer to indicate to the waitress that he wanted coffee. "I don't think I've ever seen him so proud as he was the day I graduated from the academy. Out of all of us, I was the only one who followed him onto the force."

She battled against a frown. Her father had stood at the back when she graduated, then hightailed it out of there without even a congratulatory hug. She suspected he'd come only to see if she'd go through with it. "He's with M.P.D.?"

"How'd you know?"

Kelli shrugged, and crossed her fingers under the table. "Lucky guess?"

"Then you're a good guesser. Yeah, he's with the M.P.D. A thirty-five year veteran."

Thirty-five years. The same amount of time as her father. Hmm… It made her wonder if they'd met way back then.

She noticed that David hadn't said anything about his mother. Given her own experience, she was careful about asking others about family members they didn't mention on their own. She hated the awkwardness when someone asked her. Lately she'd begun saying that her mother died when she was young. It sounded better than revealing that her mother was murdered when she was seven and the killer was never caught.

Talk about a conversation stopper.

"How long you been on the force?" she asked him instead.

"Seven years. How about you?"

"Three with N.Y.P.D." She polished off the last of her dog and started on her fries.

"Do you always eat like that," he asked, motioning toward her plate.

"Like what?"

"One food group at a time? First you ate your hot dog. Then you started on your fries."

She looked down to where she held a French fry. "Yeah, I guess I do. Do you have a problem with it?"

"No. But don't you think it's a little strange?"

She pointed at his plate, which was coated with a little bit of everything he'd eaten. "Oh, and I suppose you think stuffing everything into your mouth at the same time is better."

"At least it's normal."

"Are you saying I'm not?"

He stretched his arms along the length of the booth, allowing his gaze to skim over her from head to…chest. "Oh, I'd say you're not in the least bit normal."

Kelli rolled her eyes. "Just when I begin to think you're almost human."

He sat forward and rested his forearms on the table. "You know, Kell, we still haven't talked about…well, you know, what happened the other night."

She nearly choked on her food. Deliberately taking her time, she reached for her soda, swallowed, then took a long, delaying sip. "Yes, we have. When we were partnered together."

"Oh. You're talking about when you said that we should act like it never happened."

"That's exactly what I'm talking about."

He opened his mouth to respond, but the waitress swept by and filled David's coffee cup. "Would you like any dessert today, officer?" she asked him, seeming to overlook that there were two officers at the table.

Kelli raised her brows. There was no mistaking that the waitress was offering herself up as an additional menu option.

She was surprised when David didn't even take notice of the attractive blonde. Rather, he waved her away.

"Come on, Kelli, you can't be serious."

"Who says I can't?"

"I say." He sat back, causing the plastic on the booth to creak. "There isn't any departmental policy saying two officers can't…date."

She lifted a finger. "Unless those two officers are partners. Then it's their duty to report the situation to their commanding officer and asked to be reassigned." She polished off the last of her fries and visually challenged him. "Anyway, who says I want to date?"

His eyes widened to nearly pop out of his head. "What do you mean you're not interested in dating?"

She sighed deeply, finding it difficult not to be amused by his reaction. "You know if you keep answering my question with a question, we're never going to get anywhere in this conversation."

"Well, if you start making some sense, maybe I'd stop asking so many questions."

She held up her hand. "Now I think you've just insulted me."

"This isn't about insulting anyone, Kelli."

"Don't take this personally, David, but I'm…well, I'm really not interested in dating anyone right now. So don't think it's just you. It's not. I have…" How did she put this without setting herself up for target practice? "I just got back into town. I haven't even completely unpacked yet. Now is definitely not the time to get…involved with anyone. The other night… Well, the other night was the other night. And I really do think it's a good idea if we just pretend it never happened."

She sipped on her soda, noticing the way he watched her mouth as she did so. She fought a smile, realizing she was enjoying his discomfort a tad too much.

"Come on, Kelli. Both you and I know you're not that kind of girl."

She slowly took the straw out of her mouth, satisfied by his visible swallow. "What kind of girl?"

He waved his hand. "You know what kind."

She carefully put down her cup. "You mean the kind of girl that sleeps with a guy on the first date?" She tilted her head. "Although I don't think our meeting at the bar really counts as a first date, do you? It's more like a first meeting. So what kind of girl does *that* make me?"

His grimace was so endearing she had to smile. "This isn't funny, Hatfield."

"Oh, I think it's very funny." She leaned forward this time, resting her forearms on the table between them. "Be truthful, McCoy. Would we even be having this discussion if I were a guy?"

His brows shot up high on his forehead.

She laughed. "That's not what I meant. What I'm trying to say is that you think it's perfectly all right for a guy to indulge in one-nighters, but for a woman—" she shrugged "—well, it's a whole different ball game then, isn't it?"

His face relaxed, making Kelli wonder if she'd overplayed her hand. "Oh, I get it. You're trying to set me up as sexist, aren't you? You know, a primitive jerk who thinks there is one set of rules for men, quite another for women." He slowly shook his head. "Oh, no, Kell, you're not going to paint me into that losing corner." He leaned closer as well, putting them mere inches apart across the table. "Uh-uh. I'm not saying that women as a group aren't emotionally equipped for one-night stands." His gaze trailed to where she was sure her pulse was throbbing a mile a minute at her throat. "I'm saying *you* aren't."

"That's a load of crap and you know it," she said, disappointed to find her voice huskily breathless. "What you just said leads me to believe that you're a selective chauvinist. A new generation sexist. Which, in my opinion, is the worst kind." She fought the desire to tuck a wisp of hair behind her ear for fear of what the nervous gesture would reveal. "Oh, yeah, you pretend you're a new millennium man. Equal rights for women and all that. You've done your homework. Know exactly what to say and when to say it to represent yourself in this light and chuck the chauvinist argument out the window." She poked a finger against his chest. "But when all is said and done, you're as sexist as they come. A place for every woman and every woman in her place." She leaned back. As much to emphasize her point as to put some much needed distance between them. "Admit it, McCoy. You probably think a woman has no place on the force."

As in control as he appeared to be, the brief flicking away of his gaze told her she'd hit the nail right on the head. But while the lean, corded muscles in his forearms tensed, her jab barely knocked him off balance. "I'll have you know that my previous partner was a woman, Hatfield. And a damn good cop at that."

She crossed her arms over her chest, then immediately wished she hadn't as it drew his gaze there. "Uh-huh. And I'll lay ten-to-one odds that when you were due for a new partner, you thought you possibly couldn't be stuck with another woman, didn't you? That you had already done your part for equality between the sexes and that you couldn't possibly be put through that hell again."

Bull's eye. While the politically savvy David McCoy was nowhere near down for the count, she'd definitely landed a solid punch. He blinked and slowly began to sit back.

Smelling a victory, Kelli pushed her plate aside and leaned forward again. "And tell me this, David. Would we even be having this discussion if I were the one interested in repeating the other night?"

"Come again?"

She purposely ignored the double entendre of his words and cleared her throat. "I'm talking about the whole hard-to-get thing. Admit it. If I had asked for your phone number, invited you to come over last night, begged you to stay, right now you'd be running so fast in the other direction I'd have to be a marathon runner just to keep your fine butt in sight."

Uh-oh. Wrong choice of words. She knew that even before he had the chance to grin. "You think I have a fine butt?"

She scrambled to recover lost ground. "Well, that just makes two of us, doesn't it?"

"Ooooh, that was low."

She couldn't help smiling.

He slowly recrossed his arms. "So what you're telling me, Kelli Hatfield, is that the other night was no more than a one-night stand as far as you're concerned."

"Uh-huh."

"And that since we're now partners, we should just forget it ever happened."

"Yes."

"And that you're not only okay with that, you have no problem being around me without wanting to…jump my bones."

She briefly glanced away, then cringed at the dead giveaway reaction. Still, she somehow managed to hold her chin straight as she met his knowing gaze and said, "Right."

He grinned. "Wrong."

Something touched her foot under the table and she nearly jumped out of her skin, especially when she realized it was his foot.

"Oh, you're good," he said, tapping the front of her shoe with his. "But not good enough."

To her chagrin, she felt her cheeks heat. "You don't know what you're talking about."

"But you haven't even given me a chance to speak yet."

She made a production out of looking at her watch. "I think—"

"I already know what you think. Or at least what you want me to think. Now I deserve equal time, don't I?" he asked, putting the emphasis on equal.

She tried to hide her deep swallow and mentally armed herself against whatever he was about to throw at her. "Shoot."

He chuckled, the rich, wicked sound sliding down her spine like a hot, feathery touch. Bronte was completely right when she'd said David McCoy was a pro. And she was afraid she was going to find out just how substantial his skills were.

He reached across the table and tapped the very tip of his index fingers against the sensitive skin of her hand. "I want to ask you a few questions and I ask that you be honest in your answers. No lying allowed."

She smiled enigmatically.

He groaned. "You are good at this, aren't you?"

"You sound like you think this is some sort of game."

"Well it is, isn't it? The courtship battle?"

Courtship? Kelli couldn't move her hand far away fast enough from his.

"First things first. I'd like you to tell me that what happened the other night is an ordinary, everyday occurrence for you. That your past is littered with poor guys you used as one-night stands."

Her throat tightened.

"You can't, can you? Because that night was your first night. First one-night stand, that is."

Okay, she supposed she could give him that much. "I'll admit it. It was my first one-night stand."

"Not *it*. *I* was your first one-night stand."

She tried to figure out where he was going with this.

He caught her pensive gaze. "Oh, no. No overanalyzing allowed. If we're going to do this, it's got to be here and now, head-to-head. No strategizing permissible."

"You can't regulate something like that."

He shrugged lightly. "You think so, huh?" At her nod, he grinned. "Okay then. You're only going to make it tougher on yourself."

She opened her mouth to ask what he meant but found out before she could get the first word out. Leaning forward with the most innocent of grace, he stretched his hands out under the table and trapped her knees in his long-fingered grasp. She gasped and tried to jerk back out of the way, but there was nowhere to go.

"Uncle," she croaked. "No strategizing."

He slowly removed his fingers.

Kelli quickly moistened her lips with a flick of her tongue. "You play dirty, McCoy."

"Whatever it takes." He shrugged. "Now, back to what I was saying. Seeing that I was your first one-night stand, then the whole modern woman argument goes right out the window. Call it a spiraling out of control, or spontaneous combustion—"

"Or a mistake in judgment," she added.

He grimaced. "Call it what you will, but don't try to play it off as if the situation was just par for the course, because I know better."

"And just how, exactly, do you know that?"

His grin widened. "I know."

Ask a dumb question, get a dumber answer.

"Anyway, I'm the one doing the asking now, remember?"

How could she forget? She looked at her watch again and he raised a brow. She sighed and sat back.

"Now that we've established that your argument is basically moot, that brings us back to the reason why you don't want to go out with me again."

"Don't you usually have to visit a subject before you can return to it?"

He leaned forward again, his hands conspicuously hidden from view.

She sat back as far as she could and murmured, "Okay, okay. No more smart comments."

"Fast learner. I like that in a woman."

She sniffed. "I'd guess there isn't a whole lot that you don't like about women."

His skillful fingers found her legs under the table, this time sliding a little higher up. She drew in a quick breath and plunged her own hands down to pluck his away. He merely trapped her hands beneath his, forcing her to lean in closer to him across the table.

His gaze flicked to where her mouth was mere inches away from his. "What was I saying? Oh, yeah. You think we shouldn't… date, for lack of a better word, because we're partners."

"Uh-huh. And don't forget that I think your continued interest in me is due solely to the fact that I'm playing hard to get."

"So you say." He hiked a brow. "*Are* you playing hard to get?"

She tried to yank her hands away from the persuasive warmth of his. "Don't be ridiculous. I'm just saying—"

"We already know what you've said." He began moving his thumb in slow circles on her lower thigh. The touch itself was maddening, but when combined with the tugging on the fabric of her slacks against certain, nearby areas…well, she was finding it increasingly difficult to concentrate. Talk about conduct unbecoming an officer. Her gaze darted around the diner, but the few people who were there weren't paying them any mind. Yet.

She needed to end this conversation and fast. "So tell me, then, David, why *do* you want to go out with me again?"

"Aside from the fact that it was the best sex I've ever had and I'd like to repeat the experience?"

"Uh-huh."

"Simply…because I like you."

He liked her. The simple words caused her heart to dip low in her belly, and intensified the growing tension between her legs. Oh, boy. She hadn't expected him to be so honest. And she had no doubt that he was. She'd expected him to pull out every weapon in his armory, but this was one she didn't know how to protect herself against.

Still, she had a few more weapons in her own arsenal. "Are you saying you want to go talk to Lieutenant Kowalsky about this?"

She felt herself regain some all-important ground with his immediate grimace. "No…I'm saying that I think we should give this thing between us a chance to see what develops."

"A couple of one-night stands," she said, growing stronger.

"Uh-huh."

She moved in for the kill. Tilting her head to the side, she purposely drew the tip of her tongue along her upper lip. "What's really eating you, David? That I slept with you on the first night? Or that I slept with you and I'm not interested in seconds?"

His hands moved away from her knees so quickly, she had to laugh.

The radio on her weapons belt beeped at the same time his did, effectively slicing through the sensual web that had formed between them.

She was the first to answer. Dispatch asked if they were through with lunch and were able to take a nearby breaking and entering call.

"Got it, dispatch," she told the man.

The way David avoided her gaze, she was beginning to suspect that she'd really hurt him. Then she decided that at best she'd probably put a little ding in that monstrous ego of his, and she slid from the booth.

"We're nowhere near finished with this discussion, Hatfield," he said in a low, gravelly voice.

She blinked before looking at him, noticing the dark determination on his handsome face. Why did she have the sinking sensation that she was in way over her head with Officer David McCoy?

AT THE STATION at the end of the day, David reasoned that what happened the day before was not going to happen again. Kelli was not going to duck out on him. Not when they had their…discussion to finish.

Even though four and a half hours and five official calls separated now from their time at the diner, he still felt vaguely like he should be doubled over from the beating he'd taken during that conversation.

Pretending an interest in talking to a fellow male officer, he covertly watched Kelli hang her weapons belt in her locker in the next row. She was closer to the door, but he was coming to accept that he was at a permanent disadvantage where Kelli Hatfield was concerned. He'd just have to compensate for it.

She looked in his direction and he offered up a quick grin. Her slightly smug return smile put him on alert. She'd been giving him that smile all afternoon. At one point he'd been sorely tempted to pull the patrol car to the side of the road and kiss the damnable expression from her delectable little face.

Oh no, Kelli definitely didn't fit into the "sugar and spice and everything nice" category, as he had made the mistake of believing the other night. No, vinegar, jalapenos and red pepper were part of what went into making her. And, damn it all, the recipe made him even hungrier for her.

She closed her locker and made a beeline for the door. David slammed his own locker door shut and hurried after her.

"Hatfield, hold up!" he called out.

She quickened her step.

But no matter what mental ground he may have lost, physically he was still way ahead of the game. She didn't dare break into a run within the station house without raising suspicion, and his long strides quickly brought him next to her.

"Where are you going?"

Her grimace was altogether appealing. "Home. Alone."

That's what *she* thought. If he had it his way, he'd be tagging there right along with her. But he was going to have to do some quick stepping before that had a remote possibility of happening.

He plowed right into a fellow officer. Speaking of stepping, he'd better concentrate on where he was going right now.

Mumbling an apology, he began to skirt around the obstruction when he realized that the wall blocking his way was none other than Lieutenant Kowalsky.

"Officers Hatfield and McCoy. Just the two people I was looking for." He looked up to find Kow grinning. "You mind removing yourself from my uniform, boy?"

Damn. David's gaze slid from the towering man to his new partner. Remembering their words at the diner, he wondered if she'd gone ahead and said something to their superior officer anyway. Not because she was interested in pursuing a further relationship with him, but because she was the type who would be on the up-and-up in any situation. And she probably viewed the circumstances surrounding their odd relationship as compromising.

Double damn.

His suspicions only deepened when Kow focused his gaze on Kelli. "First of all, I want to congratulate you, Officer Hatfield. Second official day on the job and you've already been promoted—temporarily, of course."

"Sir?" both David and Kelli said simultaneously.

"The special task force, Hatfield. You nabbed yourself a spot. You're to report in for briefing bright and early, as they say."

"You put in for the task force?" David asked, incredulous.

Kelli beamed at him, her smile a little too wide, her eyes a little too full of mischief. "What did you think I was doing when I kept you waiting this morning? Powdering my nose?"

Geez...

"You can't," he said vehemently, surprising even himself.

Her eyes instantly narrowed and the hall went, suddenly, deafeningly silent. "Define 'can't,' Officer McCoy," she said finally.

He shrugged ineffectually, searching for a reason that would make some sort of sense. Only problem was, he couldn't put it into words. He only knew what he felt, and that was until he knew her a little better, trusted what she was capable of, he didn't want to see her put in any unnecessary danger. And that damn task force assignment had danger written all over it. "I don't know. You just can't accept that spot on the task force. I won't allow it."

"Pardon me, but just when, exactly, were you put in charge of my decisions?"

"Since I became your partner."

She appeared on the verge of laughter. "That's rich, coming from a guy who doesn't even know what the meaning of the word is."

"She's got you there, officer." Kow seemed to find their exchange as amusing as Kelli now apparently did. "I didn't see your name on the list of potential candidates, McCoy. Why is that?"

"Because I like my uniform just fine, thank you." And he thought Kelli did, too. What was all her talk about equality between the sexes if the first thing she did was run off and join up with the task force?

Kowalsky's chuckle got under his skin. "And your uniform likes you, too, McCoy—most of the time." He pulled a pack of gum out of his front shirt pocket, then offered them a piece. They both shook their heads. "Since Officer Hatfield here will no longer be available to be your partner, I've taken the liberty of matching you up with someone else. Phillips has opted for a desk job until after she comes back from maternity leave, so that leaves Johnson minus one partner. I think you two are a match made in heaven. If everything goes the way I expect, and there's no reason for me to believe otherwise, then you'll both get your partners back at the same time."

"Johnson?" David repeated.

"Yep. First thing in the morning." He popped a piece of gum into his mouth and chewed with immense satisfaction. "Got a problem with that, officer?"

David scratched his head. "No. No, sir, I guess I don't."

"Good."

Kelli thrust her hand forward and enthusiastically pumped Kow's. "Thank you, sir, for allowing me to accept the position with the task force. You won't be sorry."

"I know I won't, Hatfield. I just hope the same applies to you."

The big man neatly continued on his way down the hall.

David could do little more than stand cemented to the spot as Kelli waggled her fingers at him and went the other way.

CHAPTER FIVE

ANOTHER NOTE. Kelli plucked it from where it was stuck in the jamb of her door and slid it inside one of her shopping bags. A full day had passed since she'd left David standing in the station hall looking like a bomb victim. She didn't have to read the note to know what it said. "We need to talk," signed D., were the words on the last two notes, one left last night, another this morning. It was likely what this one said, too.

"What was that?" Bronte asked, trying to sneak a peek over Kelli's shoulder.

Kelli jiggled the bag so the note fell down to the bottom. Just because the guy monopolized her thoughts every minute of every day didn't mean she was up to sharing that piece of information with her best friend. "Nothing. Only the landlord telling me when the rent's due."

She led the way through the open door, leaving Bronte to close it behind her. "Uh-huh. You just moved in and the landlord's worried about the rent. Sure, I'll buy that one." She gestured to the bags. "I figure I should buy something, considering all the money you just spent."

"I didn't know how much fun it would be to spend the department's money." Kelli dropped her shopping bags on the couch, then collapsed alongside them. "Have I ever told you that you have a suspicious mind?" she said, slipping off her coat.

Bronte hung it along with her own sleek pale leather

jacket on the tree next to the door, then she dropped into the chair across from Kelli. "Comes with the territory." She cast a glance around the apartment. "Are you ever planning to unpack?"

Grimacing, Kelli took in the boxes stacked in every available spot in the place. There were three clear paths. One that ran from the doorway to the couch and on into the kitchen. Another to the bathroom. The third to her bedroom. "Are you volunteering to help?"

Bronte laughed. "Not in this lifetime. I have enough trouble keeping up with my own place." She rolled her head to look at her, her short red hair immediately falling back into place.

Kojak came panting down the path from the kitchen and plopped his plump butt at Kelli's feet. She heartily rubbed the dog's jowls and made kiss-kiss noises at him.

Bronte made a face. "Have I ever told you how disgusting that is? I don't get that close to the men I date." She leaned forward and emptied out the contents of one of the bags onto the floor. "So I take it you're not going to tell me who the note was really from then."

Kelli smiled. "Nope."

She wrinkled her nose. "Heartless witch." She picked up a miniskirt and turned it first one way, then another. "Just remember that when you're curious about what's going on with my life and I tell you to buzz off. Are you really going to wear this?"

Kelli snatched the skirt from her fingers. "I don't have to remember it because I already know there's absolutely nothing going on in your life. Hasn't been for at least six months. And yes, I'm going to wear that. It's part of my job." She grimaced at the scrap of red suede. Knowing it was right for her temporary reassignment was one thing, actually shimmying into the thing was quite another. She tossed it onto the couch. Too late for second thoughts. "By the way, why isn't anything going on with your life?"

"Ha!" Bronte flipped the strap of a jewel blue Wonderbra around and around her index finger. "The author of the note first."

"God, did I really buy that?"

Bronte positioned it like a sling shot and launched it at her. It landed on Kojak's head. "Yep. I was there so there's no denying it."

Kelli collected the bra before the dog could catch the silky fabric in his slobbery jaws. He got up, ran this way, then that, down the only path available to him, then barked. "No, you can't have it. Sheesh, buy the pooch a million play toys and he salivates after my bra."

Bronte hiked a feathery red brow. "That's a male for you."

Kojak lengthened his pacing to reach the door and barked again.

"You know—"

"Shh," Kelli said, holding out her hand. "Be quiet a sec." Kojak stopped at the door and began scratching at the bottom of it. The evidence of claw marks on the bottom of the wood told Kelli it wasn't the first time. She rolled her eyes.

"What is it?" Bronte said in a stage whisper.

Kelli waved her away. "I think someone's outside."

Her friend's blue eyes twinkled. "The landlord?"

She threw an embroidered pillow at Bronte. The landlord, indeed. Bronte knew exactly who had written the note without her having said anything. Not that it would take a genius to figure it out. She'd been back in town a whole five days, and two of those she'd spent moving in. The other three had included a maddeningly sexy, egotistical, insufferable man named David McCoy. Sometimes it stunk having a friend who knew everything about you.

Kojak barked, making Kelli jump. Then his stumpy tail

started wagging like crazy. She watched as something small and round rolled under the door—something the dog happily gobbled up.

"I can't believe it!" she whispered. "You little traitor." She had trouble enough getting him to eat his special diet food now. With a certain conniving someone feeding him treats under the door, he'd be impossible to live with.

A quick, clear knock, then, "Kelli?" filtered through the door. "I know you're in there, so you might as well just open up."

Ignoring the two males that occupied more of her time than she liked, Kelli started unpacking the bags on the couch next to her. Black leather-like pants. Low-cut vests. Clingy tops in various rich gemstone shades began piling up next to her. "You know, I'm still not really sure about this one," she said, holding up a dress for Bronte to see. "Do you think it suits me?"

"I think it makes you look like a ten-dollar whore." She smiled. "It's perfect."

"Yeah, well, the only reason I bought it was because you insisted."

"And now I'm insisting you keep it." Bronte stood up and molded the decadent scrap of material against herself. "If only so I can borrow it." She draped the dress alongside the rest of the clothes.

Another brief rap on the door. "Just so you know, Kell, I'm going to stay out here until you talk to me."

Kelli avoided Bronte's curious gaze. She picked up a pair of black platform shoes, then slid her feet out of her practical loafers. "God, I don't even know if I can walk in these, much less run."

"Kel-li," David dragged her name out.

Bronte laughed. "Are you going to let the sad sack of lust in, or leave him hanging out there all day?"

"Leave him hanging?"

"Oooo, who'd have thought you'd be so shamelessly… wicked?"

"Oh, shut up, Bronte." She glanced at her watch. "Give him twenty minutes. He'll go away. He always does."

Bronte flopped back down in the chair. "Always? For God's sake, Kell, how long has this been going on?"

She shrugged. "Since last night." More specifically, three times last night, then two times this morning before she'd even gotten up. She hadn't been pleased when he'd awoken her from the first good sleep she'd had since the night they'd spent together. Especially since that sleep had included decadent images of them doing everything but sleeping. His mouth planted on hers. His toned, hot body stretched out alongside hers. The evidence of his desire for her pressed against the soft, sensitive skin of her belly. Images she could at least enjoy while sleeping, but fantasies she didn't dare indulge in in the real world.

"Uh-huh." Bronte thoughtfully stroked the material of a silky teddy, then dangled the wicked slip of material from her index finger. "This for work? Or for more…depraved purposes?"

Kelli snatched the most self-indulgent of her purchases from her friend's hand. "If you're asking if I'm going to charge the department for it…no."

"That's not what I'm asking and you know it."

"I'm tired of sleeping in old, torn T-shirts. Is that all right with you?"

They both heard the shuffle of feet outside the door. "What? What did you buy?"

Both women looked at each other then burst out laughing.

"Just so long as you're in bed…alone, I don't see a problem with the purchase. I have a dresser full just like it." Bronte frowned. "Though I've come to prefer the old, tattered T-shirts, myself."

"See, that's just what I mean. You're no fun anymore," Kelli told her. "Speaking of which. Since you now know the identity of my...secret admirer—" she heard a sharp curse from the other side of the door "—that means you have to answer my question. Why the dull love life lately?"

"I'd have to have a love life for it to qualify as dull," Bronte corrected. "No, I'd say my love life is pretty much nonexistent right now."

"Which is a nonanswer. Come on, Bron. What gives? In the entire history of our friendship, I don't think I've ever seen you go without a man for more than a few days at a stretch. What gives?"

She shrugged, but there was nothing remotely nonchalant about the gesture. "I don't know. Maybe I thought it was time I finally started to see myself outside the confining bonds of a relationship. Get to know who I was, rather than who I was pretending to be for a man's sake."

She shook her head. "Uh-uh. Too philosophical for you. Come on, Bron, you've always known who you are. You may have come to the conclusions you've just cited since you stopped dating, but what I want to know is the main catalyst. Something had to have happened."

"Maybe."

Kelli gazed thoughtfully at her friend. Even when she lived in New York they'd remained close. Phone calls nearly every other day. Spontaneous visits. Despite the distance that separated them, they'd always maintained a closeness she treasured. Well, except when it came to men like David McCoy.

She tried to remember what was going on six months ago. The only thing she could recall was that Bronte had been steadily dating a mystery man she refused to share much about. Kelli remembered being somewhat surprised by the lack of information from her usually very talkative friend, but she hadn't thought much of it. She'd thought Bronte would share when she was ready, though she never had gotten to that point. Instead, one day she lightly said that they'd broken up and that she'd moved on to greener pastures.

Kelli wondered if they were greener, lonelier pastures.

"It's that guy, isn't it? That one you wouldn't talk about?"

Bronte's cheeks reddened and she knew that she was right. "You're wrong. This isn't just about some guy, Kelly. This is about me."

"What guy?"

The question came from the hallway, letting them know they weren't exactly alone.

Bronte rolled her eyes and laughed. "You know, you probably should talk to him. Let him get whatever he has to say off his chest so you can get on with your life without some moron sitting on your doorstep."

"I heard that," came David's muffled response.

Kelli smiled. "I already know what he has on his chest…and elsewhere," she said teasingly. She leaned forward, lowering her voice for Bronte's ears only, though she said little more than that this girl talk was probably driving him bonkers.

"Really?" Bronte asked, playing along.

Something clunked against the door, then David groaned. "What? What did she say?"

Kelli's smile widened as she began stacking her new undercover wardrobe back into one bag.

Bronte cleared her throat, then asked softly, "What's really going on, Kelli?"

"Simple. He didn't think I was a capable cop, now he thinks I'm insane for accepting this position on the task force."

"That makes two of us."

"The difference being I'm still letting you into the apartment."

Bronte raised a finger. "Important detail, that one."

Kelli started to get up. "Want some coffee?"

"I do," David said from the other side of the door.

"Tough," Kelli said, then cringed when she realized she'd spoken to him directly. And here she had been doing so well ignoring him. She stalked to the door, but rather than opening it, she curled her fingers around Kojak's collar and dragged him unwillingly toward the kitchen where she planned to close up the little traitor.

A short while later, after Bronte told Kelli about her latest case with the U.S. attorney's office and Kelli gave her some advice on effective personal protection devices, they noticed their conversation had dwindled down to the two of them.

Bronte glanced at her watch. "Took longer than twenty minutes, I think."

Kelli grimaced. "I think that's because he had an audience."

"Speaking of audiences, I have to go put in an appearance at the Senior U.S. Attorney's Christmas party tonight. And if I hope to look drop-dead gorgeous—a three-hour job at least—I'd better get running."

"You always look great."

Bronte looked her over. "Yeah, but my kind of beauty takes work. Yours…you have this girl-next-door look going on that not even a week at the Estee Lauder counter can give me."

Kelli got up with her. "I better go make sure the coast is clear first. Lord knows what'll happen if a certain somebody gets a hold of you outside the door."

"You're worried about me?"

Kelli draped an arm over her shoulders. "I'm worried about him."

They laughed as Bronte shrugged into her coat. Kelli made a production out of looking through the peephole. She firmly told herself she wasn't disappointed when she found the hall and surrounding stairs empty. She quietly unlocked the door and opened it. A quick peek found no sexy David lurking in the shadows.

Damn.

"Okay," she said, turning to Bronte. "All clear." She gave her friend a quick hug. She was about to pull away when she changed her mind and gave her a heartier one. She stood like that for long moments, just squeezing.

Bronte slowly drew away. "What was that for?"

Kelli smiled. "I don't know. You looked like maybe you needed it."

Judging by the moisture in her dear, dear friend's eyes, she suspected she'd guessed right.

Kelli straightened the lapels of Bronte's coat. "Call me, later, huh? No matter what time you get in. You know, so you can give me the full scoop on whose wife was wearing what, which husband was caught banging his secretary in the broom closet, and which idiot fell into the punch bowl."

Was it her, or was Bronte's laugh a little shaky? "Okay."

Kelli watched her walk down the steps, then she closed the door and leaned against it. She knew there was much more involved in Bronte's decision to stay seriously single, but she hadn't a clue how to go about getting her to share the information. Her friend had never kept anything from her before. The fact that she was now alerted Kelli to the seriousness of the situation. But until she knew what had happened there was very little she could do beyond letting Bronte know that she was there for her. And she intended to do that at least twice a day now that she was back in town and long distance carriers weren't involved.

The sound of scratching came from behind the kitchen door. Kelli sighed and figured she'd better let Kojak loose before she ended up either staying in the apartment for the rest of her life, or replacing all the doors when she eventually moved out.

She propped open the swinging door and stared down at the little criminal. "You're in big trouble, mister."

Kojak comically backed up, then plopped his full-size behind on the floor, his pitiful whine combined with a bored yawn. She laughed, then bent over and gave him a playful tousle. She waggled a finger in front of his watery eyes. "No more treats for you. One year," she said.

He barked, then played nip-the-ankle while she washed the coffee cups. Afterward she went back into the living room to attack a few of the easier boxes. And seeing as Christmas was less than a week away, she should probably think about decorating a bit. She considered the far corner. A small tree would be nice.

But first she felt an inexplicable need to get her life back into some sort of order and that meant unpacking essentials. Like her neon purple sports water bottle.

The only problem was that an hour and six boxes later she felt no more at peace than she did before she started, water bottle notwithstanding. Plunging her hands deep into box seven, with Kojak attacking pieces of crumpled old packing newspaper like they were small, predatory animals, she wondered just how she had accumulated so much stuff, and how she could go about getting rid of it all.

She drew her finger along an antique frame that held an old, professional shot of her and her parents taken when she was five.

A knock at the door startled her.

Kojak looked up and made a Scooby-Doo-style sound of inquiry, then ran, barking, to the door.

"Oh, no, you don't," Kelli said, hurrying after him.

After several unsuccessful attempts to stop him from scratching at the bottom of the door to get at his new friend, Kelli snapped upright, sighed, then yanked the door open wide.

"I've had just about as much of this as I'm going to take,

McCoy. Get this through your thick, stubborn head right now. I am not going to sl—"

The word died halfway out of her mouth, leaving her feeling like she'd just choked on something very bitter indeed. Because rather than staring into the too-handsome features of one yummy David McCoy, she instead gaped at the very familiar face of her father. He was definitely as startled as she was. And he was dressed to the nines in his complete police uniform.

WHOA. THAT COULDN'T be who he thought it was…could it?

David crouched down lower in the front seat of his old Mustang, eyeing the familiar figure leaving Kelli's apartment building. There was no mistaking Assistant Chief Garth Hatfield, or ignoring the glowering expression he wore as he looked both ways down the street. David slid down a little lower and cringed. The action made him feel like he'd just been caught sneaking a peek under Little Miss Muffet's tuffet.

Hatfield walked to a four-door sedan, then got in, his movements quick and precise. Within moments he was driving away.

David expelled a long breath. Boy, if he thought yesterday was a bad day, today was turning out even worse. He'd sunk to a new low hanging around outside Kelli's apartment, but he didn't see that he had any choice. He'd reasoned that things had to improve for him sooner or later, right?

Wrong.

He brought his forehead down on the steering wheel with a clunk, ignoring the spicy Mexican food that sat in a large bag on the passenger seat. Given all the trouble he was having with someone by the name of Hatfield, he should have quickly connected the dots and brought her together with one Garth Hatfield, Regional Assistant Chief for the East. But ever since meeting Kelli that night at the bar, his entire equilibrium seemed to be off-kilter. Hell, who was he kidding? He was having a hard enough time keeping upright with all that was going on.

Despite all that, he wasn't about to delude himself into thinking Garth Hatfield had been visiting someone else in the apartment building.

He didn't know what he'd done in this lifetime or any other to deserve this abuse, but whatever it was, it must have been a doozy.

"Pops is going to have a fit," he muttered.

Pulling back from the steering wheel, he stared through the now fogged windshield at the empty street blanketed with a moderate covering of snow. Oh, he knew of the feud between Sean McCoy and Garth Hatfield. It was impossible to be anywhere on the M.P.D. and not know of it. Not that he'd ever discovered what the feud was about. Pops had got so worked up when he'd brought it up over dinner one night, David was afraid he might choke on his mashed potatoes. But in the years since, he'd unearthed a few small, insignificant details. Such as the two men had been best friends when they went through the academy together. They were from the same neighborhood in north D.C., having grown up no more than two blocks apart. And that if time and circumstances ever found them in the same room together now, they'd likely do each other bodily harm.

The revelation had amused him in the beginning. Pops was so levelheaded about everything else that this little feud had been his own personal ace in the hole. The card he used whenever he wanted to change the subject.

Thankfully he'd only had one run-in with Sean's adversary. And it hadn't been pretty. It was his first year on the force and after the successful collaring of three armed robbery suspects he'd been barreling into the station at the same time Hatfield had been coming out. Damned if he didn't plow straight into the old man. He hadn't yet learned to distinguish between the stars and bars on a uniform. Not that it mattered, because Hatfield hadn't been wearing his full "u." He'd been in plain shirtsleeves and dark slacks and looked about as cocky as David had felt at that particular moment. David had none too politely suggested he watch where he was going. It was then his partner at the time had pointed out the error of his ways and respectfully acknowledged the chief. Hatfield had asked them to introduce themselves. And when he'd heard the name McCoy, he looked…well, pretty much how Pops had looked that night when he'd first mentioned Hatfield's name.

No, it definitely hadn't been pretty.

Someone rapped on the window. David jumped, half expecting Garth Hatfield to be standing outside, palming the revolver in his weapons belt. Instead he found a beat cop pointing at the no parking sign he sat in front of. David flipped out his own ID and plastered it against the window. The officer smiled and gave him a thumbs-up.

David watched him walk on down the street. A part of the normal routine? Or did Daddy have extra protection on his baby's block?

When another squad car slowly drove by, giving him a long look, David decided firmly on the latter.

Not only was he involved, or very desperately wanted to be involved, with his own partner, that same partner was the daughter of a D.C. Metropolitan Police chief.

Could things get any worse?

He figured they couldn't.

He stared at the brightly lit third-floor window. But that didn't mean they couldn't get any better.

Grinning, he grabbed the bag of Mexican food and opened the car door.

CHAPTER SIX

KELLI SAT ON the arm of the couch staring at the opposite wall. Only a short while before she'd hung her academy certificate there, and positioned black-and-white professionally framed photos of D.C. around it. Not that she saw any of them. She could concentrate on little more than the visit she'd just suffered through with her father.

Ever since she was twenty and made her intention to join the force known, a tension had stretched between her and Garth Hatfield that strained like the steel cables holding together a suspension bridge. Over the years she'd come not only to accept the tension, she'd learned how to carefully balance her need to be a police officer with her father's need to protect his only child. Had even come to enjoy their little tugs-of-war, their endless debates over their differences of opinion, and had taken comfort in knowing that despite everything, he'd always be there for her.

But tonight...

Wow.

She'd known the instant she'd opened the door that she'd made a big time error. But she'd been completely unprepared for her father's nuclear meltdown at the knowledge that one certain David McCoy, of the hated McCoys, not only knew where she lived but was an expected visitor. She'd been unable to do anything more than blink at him as his handsome face had turned an unhealthy shade of red while he'd stood in her hallway and lit into her.

"You better get this straight, missy. I may have to put up with your being a police officer. And now your stupid notion of getting involved in that godforsaken task force, but this... Are you seeing that uncivilized slug?"

"Slug?" she'd practically coughed, slightly amused at that point, though still stinging at her blunder.

"You heard me, girl."

His penchant for calling her "girl" had really never bothered her. Up until that point he'd used it as an endearment like honey or darling. But this time it came out sounding condescending and derogatory, and something within her bristled. She'd stubbornly crossed her arms and said, "Well, excuse me if I don't answer your question, Daddy, but I don't see that my personal life is any of your business."

Now Kelli cringed as she rubbed her forehead. She supposed she really shouldn't have baited him that way, not knowing how upset he already was. But who knew he would blow a gasket over her perfectly vague statement?

Kojak whined, then stuck his head out from where he'd been cowering in her bedroom. His tongue lolled out of his mouth as he checked to see if the coast was clear.

"A cease-fire has been declared," she told him, then silently added, "for now."

The dog happily made his way across the wood floor, his nails clicking, then plopped down near the door.

Kelli considered him. "Do you want to go for a walk, K?"

If she didn't know better, she'd think he'd shaken his head. No. It was probably his version of a canine sneeze. He looked at the door then whined again.

Kelli's gaze zoomed in on the thick white wood. *Don't tell me...*

Pushing from the sofa arm, she followed Kojak's lead. Frowning, she reached over him, much to his tail-wagging delight, and pulled open the door.

Just as she suspected. David stood on the other side, hand raised to knock, his eyes as large as his badge. What she didn't expect was the rush of warmth and pleasure at seeing him.

"I didn't even knock yet," he said.

Kelli motioned toward his new buddy.

"Oh." He reached down and patted the dog, then straightened and held up a white bag. "Hungry?"

She curved her arms around her upper torso. "Not particularly." She turned and walked back into the apartment. "But you might as well come in. You can't possibly be any worse than my last visitor." She partially turned and jabbed a finger in his direction. "But no funny stuff, you hear?"

"Got it."

She heard the door close behind him and continued on into the kitchen, emerging seconds later with two bottles of beer. She handed him one, then took a long, needy pull from the other.

"That bad, huh?" he asked.

She sat back down on the sofa arm, gazing at where he was sprawled all too attractively in the chair across from her. "If you only knew."

He raised his bottle in a silent toast to her, then took a sip. "Actually, I think I do."

She eyed him. She wasn't exactly sure why she'd let him in. Perhaps in childish rebellion against her father. Maybe because she felt somewhat guilty about making him sit outside her apartment all afternoon. Whatever the reason, she'd be well served to remember he was still her sexual enemy.

But she couldn't ignore the part of her that wanted him to be her friend. "How so?" she asked.

He grimaced as he put his bottle down on the coffee

table. "I don't know if I should admit it because I'm feeling a little stupid that I didn't put two and two together before now."

Kelli closed her eyes and groaned. "You saw my father, didn't you?"

He sighed and grabbed the bag. "Yeah."

Oh, no. "You didn't run into him or anything, did you?" She searched his face, looking for physical evidence that Garth Hatfield had done as he promised he would do, which was show that lover boy McCoy that he shouldn't be messing where he didn't belong. As angry as he was, she was half afraid he would pull David's address from department personnel records and head over there for a one-on-one battle tonight.

He started routing around in the paper bags. "No. I just saw him leaving. Don't worry, he didn't see me, so there's no reason to think he knows anything about us."

Kelli looked down, her cheeks flaming.

The rustle of paper stopped. Kelli looked to find him staring at her, his hands stopped midmotion. "I think this is where you're supposed to say that there is no us."

Her spine snapped straight. "There is no us."

A wrapped something or other in hand, he flopped back against the cushions, oblivious to the fact that Kojak had stuck his head into the bag. "Oh, hell, Kell, don't tell me that you told him."

"Told him what?" She snatched the bag away from Kojak. "There's nothing to tell." She rummaged around inside, finding Mexican food. She nearly groaned out loud. It had been eons since she'd had good Mexican, and this definitely smelled good. "This for me?"

"Knock yourself out." David waved a distracted hand. "So what did you tell him?"

She shrugged. "Well, I didn't exactly tell him anything. I

just kind of alluded to the fact that there might be something between us, that's all."

"Alluded?"

She glared at him. "I had to do something after I virtually called him your name when I answered the door."

She watched a grin edge across his exceptionally handsome face. "You didn't? Oh, what I would have given to be there when you did that."

She unwrapped a burrito dripping with cheese and snorted. "Be glad you weren't or else you wouldn't have any teeth left to chew with."

The grin vanished.

Kelli concentrated on her food and David did the same, silence falling between them. She rolled her eyes when he fed a taco, lettuce and all, to Kojak. At this rate the dog was going to follow him home. And then where would she be?

What a sorry life she led.

She'd moved on to a delectable fajita and pointed it at him. "You know, you could have said something about this stupid…rivalry thing going on between my dad and yours."

"You forget, I didn't know your dad was your dad until just now," he said. "And it's a feud."

"Cute. Anyway, I didn't find out anything until the other day when Dad found out you were my partner."

"I bet he was happy."

"Yeah." She took a long sip of beer, then stared at the bottle. "He mentioned something about busting one of these over your dad's head."

"You're kidding."

"Nope."

He leaned his forearms against his jean-clad knees. "He didn't happen to share what started this feud, did he?"

Her gaze flicked to his. "You mean you don't know?"

"Uh-uh. I just know that the feelings your father has for mine are returned two hundred fold—which is weird, because Pops gets along with everyone."

"So does my dad."

David hiked a dark blond brow.

"Well, most people anyway," she qualified. "At any rate, I've never heard him voice the sort of antagonism he feels for your dad before."

They continued eating in silence. It wasn't until every last morsel was gone, and Kelli had gone to fetch fresh beer, that she said, "You know, after this I might even believe you're half human."

He grinned and accepted the beer. "What do you mean?"

She sank down onto the couch across from him and rested her bare feet against the edge of the coffee table. "You've been here for what? A half an hour at least and there's a bed—" she pointed the neck of her bottle toward her bedroom door "—not twenty feet away and you haven't once tried to get me into it."

"Yet," he added.

She couldn't help her smile or the sizzling, hopeful heat that warmed her upper thighs.

"Hey, even a guy like me knows some things about women."

"You know jack."

"Your words a minute ago say differently."

She shook her head. "No, I said you might be half human. I didn't breathe one word about your sexual prowess, or lack thereof."

He groaned. "You don't know what it does to me just hearing you say the word 'sexual.'"

As she looked over at him, Kelli couldn't ignore the slow burn in her belly that had nothing to do with the spicy food she'd just devoured. The guy was better looking than any one man had a right to be. She forced her gaze away and found herself staring at the notes resting on the side of the table. "Okay, McCoy, now that you have my undivided attention, talk."

"Talk?"

She stared at the ceiling. "Isn't that the reason you've spent half the afternoon parked out in my hall? Why you've left four notes at least—"

"Three."

"Three then. Why you've left three notes on my door saying we needed to do exactly that."

"Talk?"

She nodded and smiled around her beer bottle as she took another sip. The magic golden liquid was beginning to spiral its way through her bloodstream, relaxing her, making her bolder than she should be.

He lifted himself from his semisprawled position, placed his bottle down on the table, then looked her squarely in the face. "Okay, then. I think you need to forget about this task force stuff and come back to being my partner."

Kelli nearly spewed the contents of her mouth across his serious face.

DAVID WATCHED Kelli's expression go from shock, to amusement, then melt into what it was now, somewhere between anger and disgust.

"You've got to be kidding," she said, taking her tiny, sexy feet from the table and mimicking his posture.

He shook his head. "I'm serious as a heart attack, baby."

She sprang from the couch so quickly he moved back. Strictly as a defensive maneuver, even though five feet and a coffee table separated them. She stalked over to the dining room table behind him, forcing him to turn in order to keep her in view. And, oh, what a view it was, too. Despite the topic of their conversation, he'd spent the past half hour wrestling with his libido and basically stopping himself from lunging across the way and plastering his mouth against her luscious one.

She opened a manila folder but he doubted she saw the contents. His gaze slid to her nicely rounded bottom under the loose fit of her jeans. He could just make out the high cut of her panties under the soft fabric.

He turned back to face forward, taking the quiet moment to look around the place. Since he was last there she'd somehow managed to make the place look like a home. There were still a couple of boxes stacked up in the corner of the dining area, but overall he suspected she was almost done. At his feet was a colorful area rug stretching from his chair to the sofa. On the walls were pictures and photographs artfully hung so as to complement the decor of the apartment rather than detract from it. And through the bedroom door he saw that she'd finally made the bed they'd spent so much time in the other night. A blue and white striped comforter, a white bed skirt, and a few accent rugs made the room look all too inviting.

Kelli had made the comment that not once had he tried to get her in there in the past half hour. Well, he didn't know what she'd think if he told her it had taken Herculean effort not to toss her over his shoulder and carry her off into that room. Oh sure, he suspected she initially would have fought him like a she-cat. But he had little doubt that all that restless energy would then have been channeled into some pretty sublime sex.

He ran his hand over his face. They might have been in that room right now if he hadn't gone and opened his stupid mouth. But he suspected if he tried anything now, she'd just as soon shoot him.

Speaking of which…

He gave the apartment another cursory glance but nowhere did he see evidence that she kept a revolver tucked away anywhere. Then again, what had he expected? For her to have a slew of them displayed on the wall? His own weapons belt was at his apartment hanging on the coat tree just inside the door.

He cleared his throat, growing more uncomfortable with her silent treatment. "Well, aren't you going to say anything?" he asked.

She slowly closed the file, then turned to face him. "When you say something worthy of a response, I will."

He rested his head against the back of the tan chair. "Come on, Kell, you have to know I'm saying this for your own good. You're out of your element as a uniform. But at least when you're there I can keep an eye out for you."

Uh-oh. Wrong thing to say. He could see it on her face.

She stalked back to stand directly in front of him. "You seem to forget that I got along just fine in New York for three years without you, McCoy."

"That's different."

"Oh? How so?"

"I wasn't there."

She threw her hands up in a way that made her breasts bounce under the soft wool of her green sweater. "You are just too much, you know that, McCoy?" She caught him looking at her chest and firmly crossed her arms to cover it. "Forget it."

He looked at her. "Forget what?"

"I'm not going to quit the task force."

He grimaced. "Just what do you have to prove, Hatfield?"

"I don't have to prove anything. But I am hoping to achieve something. If this works out the way I'm hoping it will, I'll have a detective's shield faster than I planned."

Detective's shield? Is that what all this was about? He opened his mouth to say the words, but she rushed on.

"So you can just take your request and stick it where the sun don't shine, McCoy, do you hear me? I don't need any macho man, station-house-hotshot lady-killer thinking he needs to look after me like I'm some simpering wimp unable to protect myself. I'll have you know I've seen my share of scrapes and hairy moments."

"Yeah?" He eyed her slender body.

"Yeah."

He couldn't help his grin. "Prove it."

She lifted her sweater to hover just below her rib cage, revealing a puckered scar. "See that? A twenty-two at close range."

"Hmm." He leaned in to get a closer look. The tiny flaw on her otherwise silky skin turned him on beyond belief.

She quickly turned around. "And this?" she said, tugging on the waist of her jeans to reveal a cute little dimple. He tore his gaze away from it and to where she pointed to a thin red line. "I took a serrated knife to the back."

"Hmm," he said again, running his fingertip along the length of it.

He felt her involuntary shiver and grinned.

Before she could object, he grasped her hips, swiveled her around, then tugged until she was sprawled across his lap. "All those scars prove, Hatfield, is that you need me to look after your cute little behind all the more." He slid a hand up the back of her leg to cup the area in question.

She gasped.

God but she flushed the most attractive shade of red when she was angry.

He braced himself for her counterattack. There were any number of defensive maneuvers she could use to free herself from his grasp. The one he hadn't counted on was her pressing her mouth hungrily against his.

David groaned and slid his hand up to cup the back of her head. It was empowering to know that while he'd been biding his time, waiting for the exact right moment to make his move, all along Kelli had wanted him as badly as he wanted her.

He thrust his tongue into her mouth with a bold, thorough stroke. It was impossible that she tasted even better than he remembered, but she did. So good, in fact, that he wondered how he had survived this long without devouring her. Her fingers pushed up the fabric of his shirt and he caught his breath, cracking his eyelids to find her watching him, her green, green eyes holding all the hunger he felt.

She hauled her mouth from his, her lips damp, her breathing ragged. "This is crazy, you know?"

He smiled and pressed his lips against the very corner of one side of her mouth, then the other. "I know."

And he kissed her again, thinking the word crazy about summed everything up. He was crazy with lust for her. Crazy with need. Crazy about her, period. Everything about her. Her prickly defensiveness. Her unpredictable passion. Her ability to cut him down to size with no more than a few words...or with a simple kiss from her delicious mouth.

Something brushed against his leg. David nearly jumped clear out of his skin as he hauled his mouth from Kelli's and stared down at where Kojak avidly watched them, his panting tongue curving up against his nose.

David threw back his head and laughed.

Kelli got up. It was all he could do not to yank her back down. "Oh, no, Jackie boy, this is not something your innocent eyes should be seeing."

David's heated gaze followed Kelli as she shut the dog into the kitchen, her words sending his pulse rate soaring off the charts. She turned, stopped, then pulled her sweater over her head, tousling her blond hair and revealing a purple satin bra that enhanced rather than concealed her breasts. She tossed the sweater to the dining room table then continued walking toward him. He nearly died when she dropped to her knees between his legs and began tugging at his leather belt. But he was nowhere near patient enough for whatever she may have had in mind. As soon as she held his throbbing shaft in her soft little palm, he hauled her back up onto his lap and with impatient tugs and pulls freed her of her own jeans, his mouth seeking the breasts swaying in front of his hungry eyes.

Then finally he was safely sheathed and was filling her. Her heat surrounded him. Her sleek muscles expanding and contracting as she adjusted to his size.

He grasped her hips, holding her there, holding her still as he gritted his teeth. "Hold up, Kell. Let a man catch his breath."

Her sexy little smile nearly toppled him right over the edge. "Oh no, McCoy. You're not the one calling the shots this time." She rocked her hips forward then drew them slowly back. She moaned then caught her bottom lip between her teeth. "I am."

And what shots they were, too. He fumbled behind her for the clasp to her bra and she followed, easily releasing hooks and allowing the material to slide from her breasts. David hungrily fastened his lips over one rosy tip, then moved impatiently to the other, unable to get enough of her.

Especially when she rocked again.

With an almost inhuman groan, he edged from the chair, and with a single sweep of his arm, cleared the coffee table. Empty beer bottles, food wrappings and candlesticks clicked to the area rug one after another. In one smooth move, he laid her across the smooth surface, sliding her down until her sweet little bottom was even with the end, all the while keeping the connection with her, reveling in the feel of her surrounding him. Taking him in. Making him hers. Her hands moved so quickly he could barely keep track of them, much less identify the myriad sensations they awakened. From his hair where she tugged on the sensitive strands, to his back where she drew her short nails down the length of his burning flesh, to his butt, where she squeezed then pulled him closer at the same time that she thrust her hips upward.

Damn. Her impatient, carnal, needy movements nearly shoved him straight over the edge.

Hooking his arm under the back of her knee, he drew her leg up, pleased with her agility, and wild with desire as she not only happily took every inch of his deep thrust, but sweetly swiveled her hips to take him in even deeper. Needing to get a handle on himself, he slowly began to withdraw. But her whimper and the answering grinding of her hips would have none of it, so instead he filled her.

And oddly felt something begin to fill him instead of the other way around. It began in his chest. More than just the pressurized building of an incredible orgasm, it seemed to spread with every beat of his heart. Heat, surety, peace…

Then Kelli cried out and that peace imploded, like a window bowing inward, then cracking and scattering into crystalline pieces on the other side. Pieces that swirled up and up until they were out of sight in the dark night sky.

"Wow," Kelli murmured, moments later, their bodies spent, their ragged breathing losing its edge.

David budged his head from where it rested against her smooth collarbone, a grin easing across his face. "Yeah. Wow."

CHAPTER SEVEN

THE FOLLOWING afternoon Kelli still felt…gob-smacked, wowed, completely out of sorts. As though the world didn't make sense anymore, somehow. As though David had gripped the proverbial rug that she had so safely stood on for the past twenty-five years and effectively yanked it out from under her feet. More than that, he held the battered old familiar rug up bullfighter style, teasing her with it, mocking her. She groaned at the image, practically hearing him say "olé."

Considering that she was in the middle of launching her undercover assignment as the new sales girl at Adult Indulgences, her mind should be everywhere else but on David. But the owner, Jeremy Price, had left her alone in his office to go find something, and her mind kept wandering back to the night before.

While things between her and David had begun on the coffee table, they certainly hadn't ended there. She'd thought the first time had been aberration. A momentary lapse of good sense brought on by the excitement of finally being home. She imagined the incredible passion had been heightened by her new sense of power, of plans nearing completion.

Oh, how very wrong she'd been.

Well, at least partially. She didn't think she was ready to grant David more than just a smidgen of credit for her reaching orgasm not once, not twice, but a whopping three times. She pressed her palm against her burning cheeks. But she had to admit that the guy was…incredible. Attentive. Pleasingly hungry. And he definitely got an A for endurance. But she was nowhere near prepared to admit that her unusual responsiveness was due solely to him.

She tucked a strand of heavily moussed, teased hair behind her ear, searching for alternative explanations. Answers that didn't include David McCoy's bragging smile.

Lack of sex. No, no, lack of really good sex. For years she had voluntarily stood back and watched Bronte conquer the sexual world, all the time wondering at its appeal. Even during her time with Jed she had distantly wondered if that was all there was. Now she knew it wasn't.

That was it. She latched on to the lame rationalization with both hands. She was a woman who had just gone too long without.

She mentally cringed. That was such a man-thing to say.

Still, she couldn't help wondering in a shadowed, cowardly corner of her mind why David sought her out. Certainly he had better things to do than hang around outside her apartment door all day. A guy didn't come by the nickname Stationhouse Casanova for pulling little stunts like that.

She forced the thought from her mind, not willing to go there just yet. She had enough emotional fodder to chew on for the next two years, at least.

Speaking of bullheaded men, her father intruded on her thoughts. She'd picked up the phone no less than four times throughout the day only to hang it back up. Once she'd gotten all the way to the last number. But ultimately she couldn't go through with it. She couldn't help thinking that her making the first call would be akin to apologizing, and she didn't think she had anything to apologize for. If anyone should be apologizing, it should be him. But her own phone—when she hadn't had it off the hook—had stayed criminally quiet.

She shifted uneasily on the simple office chair. At any rate, she really shouldn't be thinking of either of the men currently complicating her life, not when she had a job to concentrate on. She gave a secretive look around.

Who knew there were so many different sex toys?

Although it was the second time in as many days that Kelli had been in the store that catered to sexual tastes obviously far more decadent than hers, she still couldn't take in enough of everything surrounding her. Even sitting in the office chair, she craned her neck to look through the open door. One wall was covered entirely with X-rated videos. Another, with row upon row of leather paraphernalia that looked cruel even for a pet store.

An image of David slipped through her mind and she fought a decidedly naughty shiver.

"Found them," Jeremy Price, the store's owner, said breezing back into the room. And breezing was the word for it. His sexual orientation was blatantly obvious, making her decidedly more comfortable around him. "Just sign there and we're good to go." He placed a W-2 form in front of her.

Kelli smiled at him. Jeremy was an unexpected surprise. And, she hoped, a friendly ally during the time she was assigned to work undercover at Adult Indulgences. She had no cause to think otherwise. Everything else was going as planned, right to the letter. The regular girl, Ginger Olsen, had accepted a generous cash donation to her favorite foundation—herself—and had been given a two-week Jamaican cruise, just to make sure she didn't run through the money and show up at the shop looking for her job back while Kelli was still working undercover. Kelli, herself, had applied for the job the day before. Then undercover task force officers had sidetracked every woman they pegged as applying for the job the second before she could walk through the glass-paned door.

Kelli's own past experience had helped. She'd worked at

mall clothing stores during the summers when she was in high school, and had made it to manager of the juniors department in a swanky department store in the two years before she entered the academy.

Throw in a sham recently failed relationship during which she wasn't required to work, and she was probably overqualified for the position of cashier at the tawdry adult bookstore.

She signed the form with a flourish she was sure was more in fitting with her new persona, then handed it back to Jeremy across the desk of the backroom office.

"That's it then," he said with a dramatic sigh, then smiled. "Welcome to Adult Indulgences."

"Thank you. You won't be disappointed," Kelli fairly purred, barely recognizing her own voice.

Jeremy put the paperwork aside, then stood, coming around the desk. "Let me show you off, kitty cat."

Kelli had stuck with her own name, so she was sure he was merely using the nickname kindly. She managed a smile and slowly got up, wobbling on the too-high high heels, forcing herself to stop plucking at the too-short skirt, and shoving her chest out to distract any passersby from both.

She could do this. She could. If only her father's voice would get out of her head. And if only she could stop thinking about exactly what one Officer David McCoy was doing right about now.

"Jose, come over here," Jeremy called, waving to a guy in his mid-twenties who was stocking newer magazines on a rack. "I want you to meet the latest addition to our little family." The Latino fiddled with the edges of his mustache, then lumbered over, very much like a male cat on the prowl for Kelli's Kitty Cat.

"Ola, chica," he said with a sneaky grin that made Kelli's skin crawl.

"*Ola* yourself," she said, thrusting out an arm covered with beads and metal bracelets. "I'm Kelli."

Jeremy clucked his tongue, then stood back and looked her over. From the tips of her black boots, to the scalloped edge of her too-tight tank, his gaze lingered on every inch. "Not anymore you're not, babe. You've just been promoted." He took a magazine from Jose and rolled it up tightly. Tapping her lightly on the head, he said, "I now officially pronounce you to be Kitty Kat, with two k's." He laughed then slapped the magazine back into Jose's palm. "Doesn't she just look good enough to eat, Jose?"

A snort that Kelli took to mean agreement was Jose's response.

"Okay, then," Jeremy said with another long sigh, then waved his hands. "Let me show you around."

A half hour later Kelli was afraid her eyeballs would fall to the floor. Either that or she would trip over her jaw. From the viewing booths in the back of the shop, to the various classifications of video—from soft porn to hard core—to learning the names of all the sex toys, she felt like her head was going to explode. Her reaction wasn't just from having to memorize each item, but from the crowbar that had just been used to expose her mind to a completely different side of life she had no idea existed. Well, okay, she'd had an idea. She'd even worked undercover twice as a prostitute in New York. But even during those assignments, the second she got the john to name a price, she'd slapped her cuffs on faster than he could blink, so that didn't really count.

Now…well, now she would have to use words she wasn't even sure she knew the meaning of on a daily basis.

"Eighty-three percent of our clientele is from perfectly normal suburbia," Jeremy was telling her as he showed her how to work the cash register.

"And the other seventeen?"

The register bell rang and released the cash drawer. Jeremy jabbed a finger toward the back booths. "Are back there right now."

Kelli laughed, wondering what her duties were in regards to the booths. She cleared her throat. "I won't, you know, have to do any cleanup—"

"Oh, no," Jeremy said, squeezing her shoulder. "Jose gets that job." His smile widened. "We don't want one of those guys pulling you in there, now, do we?" His gaze skimmed her backside. "We want you out here to do what you're designed to do, girlfriend. Get customers to buy, buy, buy."

DAVID COMPARED the address written on his pad to the store-front across the way. Adult Indulgences. In a fashionable part of town, looking no more out of place than the locksmith next to it. Brick facade, white trimmed windows. People walking by, in and out, going about their business as if passing by or browsing through an adult bookstore were a normal part of their day. And perhaps it was. Just because it wasn't part of his lifestyle, didn't mean it wasn't the norm. What passed for normal these days was anything from tongue-piercings and purple hair to self-mutilation and tattoos.

He scratched his chin, trying to imagine his brother Jake in the leather getup the man who just walked out of the place had on. For all he knew his other brother Mitch got into his wife's lacy underwear under his jeans.

The thought made him burst out laughing. If it was one thing he was sure of, it was that he and all four of his brothers—and his father for that matter—were as arrow-straight as they came. Hell, they had a hard enough time with the normal, head-on type of stuff, let alone the strange fetishes this place catered to. None of them had a single tattoo or a piercing. And women's underwear…well, that's what women wore, not men. Certainly not men from the McCoy clan.

He got out of the car and watched a woman who looked not unlike Kelli walk into the place. Hey, to each his own. So long as it didn't hurt anyone else, more power to them. Whatever got your rocks off.

He grimaced at the nonsensical stream of clichés drifting through his mind. Who was he kidding? This stuff made him nervous as hell. He'd sooner go browse through a New Age shop, have his palm read, wear some sort of vampire-repelling crystal around his neck than go into this place.

But if anything were impetus enough, seeing that Kelli was all right certainly was. He didn't know what strings the guys in the task force had had to pull to get her in there, but if there was one place one very innocent looking Kelli Hatfield didn't belong, it was here—no matter how uninnocent her actions the night before.

It took some doing to get the address of the place. So hush-hush was this assignment, he'd had to give up Christmas Eve to work a shift for the guy who had given him the info. The information had only made him that much edgier. Who was watching Kelli? What kind of surveillance was set up on the place? Did she have on a mike? Was there video? How about backup? Even he, with his bad track record with partners, understood that you needed good backup at all times. But Jennings had refused him anything more than the name of the shop she was working at and her hours.

"Stop your stalling, McCoy, and get in there," he mumbled under his breath.

Looking both ways, he tucked his chin into his leather jacket—the only thing he had he deemed suitable for such a visit—and crossed the street.

He opened the door, setting off a digital bell that chimed

out. Then hearing the sound of the store's background music, he groaned. Was that really Rod Stewart's "Do You Think I'm Sexy"? He nearly turned tail and ran right there. It was one thing to proclaim yourself a lady-killer, quite another to have to go somewhere to study the stuff. If any of his brothers caught him in this place, he'd be dead meat.

And if Kelli *was* under surveillance, his hide would be Kowalsky's.

He dipped his chin down a little farther into his jacket, then reached up and pulled the side of his plain brown skull cap down to cover his ears.

A woman of forty-something walked by him on her way out, shooting him a furtive glance. Why was she looking at him like he was the bad guy? She was the one doing her shopping in the local S&M place.

He glanced down the left side of the shop. It looked just like a family video rental store. He began to relax a little. Until he nearly tripped over a box that held an inflatable woman and it began making moaning noises. He reached down to find the off button, but the moaning only got louder. He dropped the box back to the floor and scooted it under a rack with his foot.

Suddenly, he was altogether too hot. It was all he could do not to turn and run back outside into the cold.

"Can I help you, sir?"

David would recognize Kelli's voice anywhere. Damn. He'd wanted a few minutes to himself to case the joint, then watch her without her knowing he was there. So much for plans.

He cleared his throat and purposely lowered it, keeping his head turned away. "Just lookin'," he said gruffly.

There was a heartbeat of a silence, then she sighed. "All right then. If you need anything, I'll be right over by the cash register."

David didn't dare turn until he heard the click, click of her heels walking away. When he did finally turn, he had to do a double take.

Naw…

There was no way on God's green earth that the woman walking away from him was his partner, Kelli Hatfield. Slack-jawed, he watched feet, clad in shiny patent leather boots, lazily move one in front of the other. The tantalizing stretch of leg from the top of the boots to the bottom of her short-short hem were clad in white fishnet stockings, complete with a line down the back. And the skirt. Woooweee! It was enough to send any man to his knees begging for a chance to peek under it.

No, the woman walking away from him was definitely not his partner. But she did resemble the woman he was coming to know between the sheets.

"Jesus, Kelli, is that you?" he croaked.

KELLI TURNED so quickly, she nearly fell off her heels and straight into the edible underwear stand.

"David!"

What was *he* doing there?

Realizing she had practically shouted his name, she looked around to see who had overheard. The only one within speaking distance was a twenty-something guy looking over the latest edition of *Naked Women Weekly.* So caught up was he in the centerfold, he didn't even glance their way.

When she turned back around, she found David practically gaping at her cleavage. She felt the incredible urge to cover herself.

Funny, she'd spent the past three hours in the shop prac-ticing her sashay, working a little southern drawl into her voice, and trying not to choke at the items the customers laid on the check-out counter. But one look at David and she was ready to run screaming to the closest sporting goods store for a set of the baggiest jogging suits they sold.

Kelli descended on him. "What in the hell are you doing here, McCoy?" She grabbed his arm, ignoring the way the cool soft leather felt against her palm as she spun him toward the door. "And where did you get that ridiculous hat?"

As if in a daze, he slowly reached up and dragged it from his head. Kelli inwardly groaned, suppressing the desire to tell him to put it back on. All that golden blond hair tempted her touch even more than the soft leather under her fingertips.

His mouth worked, but no words came out. She didn't flatter herself into thinking she was the one solely responsible for his speechlessness. Kelli snatched her hand back from tempting territory, then faced him, her hands planted firmly on her leather-clad hips. "What is it, McCoy? Spit it out, man."

"You…you…"

She nodded. "I…"

"You…look…incredible."

Heat swept over Kelli from her cheeks to her toes. She'd been visibly ogled by at least a dozen men that evening, but those few, simple, choked out words made her feel sexy as all get out.

"You didn't answer my question," she pointed out.

His frown told her he wasn't following her.

"What are you, hearing impaired? I asked what…are… you…doing…here?" She slid another glance behind her to make sure Jeremy was nowhere in sight. "And you better make it good, McCoy."

"You weren't at home," he said.

"And…"

It seemed to take everything in his power to rip his gaze from her chest. He concentrated instead on a nearby rack of novels with pink labels plastered all over them warning of sexually explicit material. Kelli could virtually see every ounce of his usual cockiness reassert itself, much as mercury fills a thermometer. When he turned back to her, his big-headed grin was firmly in place, and he seemed to have undergone a demeanor transplant. Where he was awkward and gawking mere moments before, now he was downright sexy, his feet placed apart, his weight leaning on one leg, his gaze openly sweeping her. The warmth that Kelli felt moments before ignited into a full-fledged fire.

"Hey, it's fate, baby cakes." He picked up a magazine. "I happen to come in here all the time. Ask anybody."

Kelli wanted to sock him one. But when he opened the magazine and got a gander at what it held, he instantly dropped it. She laughed and bent over to sweep the magazine up, only afterward realizing how much she'd probably just revealed from behind. She tugged at the unwieldy material. "Uh-huh. Come here all the time, do you?" She showed him the cover of the magazine then slipped it back into its holder. "I happen to know that your appetite is for women, McCoy."

He said something under his breath that sounded like, "You got that right."

She crossed her arms under her breasts, very aware that the action accentuated her cleavage all the more. She refused to think about last night. Refused to remember how he had thoroughly explored every inch of the flesh he was now visually devouring. His being there was distracting enough without her mind delving into areas she had yet to make sense out of.

As expected, his gaze zoomed in immediately on her chest. So long as he talked to her breasts, she could handle him. "Tell me the truth. What are you really doing here?"

"Making sure you're okay."

The urge to pop him one returned full force. The guy was infuriating. "Officially or unofficially?"

His gaze skittered up to her face.

"That's what I thought." She started to turn him toward the door again.

"Look, Hatfield, I know I wasn't exactly…discreet just now. But we've got to talk. Promise we'll talk and I'll leave."

"You've already had your say, McCoy." In fact, he'd already had more than his say, and so had she. And the topic of discussion had nothing to do with her being assigned to the task force. "You're going to leave—"

He leaned in toward her ear, cutting off her words as efficiently as if he'd kissed her. And she found she wanted him to do just that, no matter how unbecoming. His warm breath tickled the skin of her neck. "If you promise to have this talk, I promise I'll leave without blowing your cover," he said, underscoring his point by flicking his tongue over her skin then blowing on it.

Kelli's eyes widened. "You wouldn't!" she whispered harshly.

His grin was back full force. "Try me." He crossed his own arms. "It would be all too easy, Kell. Hell, I didn't think you had what it took to wear a uniform. This whole thing…well, I don't think I have to tell you how much happier I'd be if I got your sexy little bottom fired right here and now."

Kelli could do little more than sputter, upset by his words, turned on by the feel of his mouth so very close to her skin.

"Is there something you need help with, Kitty Kat?" Jeremy asked somewhere behind her.

Kelli leaned back to stare into David's questioning face. He arched a brow and mouthed, "Kitty Kat?" She began slowly shaking her head, as much for David's sake as for Jeremy.

"No, I've got everything under control, Jeremy, thanks."

She sensed he hadn't left. A moment later, he said, "Are you sure?"

"Positive. This…gentleman was just saying how much he liked my perfume. Wants to buy some for his…um, girlfriend. I was just helping him out, that's all."

"All right. But make sure he buys something here before you go sending him off to another store, you hear?"

Kelli laughed and noticed David did, too. She almost slumped against him with relief when she heard the office door close behind her boss.

"Well," David hummed. "I guess I don't have to worry about anything going on between you and the boss now, do I?"

Kelli pushed at him with both hands. "You really take the cake, McCoy, do you know that?"

"Nope. But I'd like to." He ran his rough palm up the back of her net-clad legs and this time she did slump against him.

"You've already had a little too much cake."

"Uh-uh, Kitty Kat. I've merely sampled the icing. I plan to dig a little, um, deeper the next time we're together, so just put those claws away and stop spitting at me."

She groaned, thinking she'd have to make sure they weren't alone again together in this lifetime.

The smile hovering around his luscious lips made her lick her own. "Look at you. You're flustered. Tell me something, Hatfield? If you can't handle little ol' me, how are you going to protect yourself against a marauding murderer?"

She told him to go do something that was physically impossible, causing him to laugh. "Only if you promise to help." He let her go then looked around the place. "With everything I'm sure you'll pick up around here, I think you're just the person for the job."

Instead of her turning him toward the door, he instead swiveled her to face the cashier's desk. "Now, go on and get back to work. We wouldn't want you to get into any trouble now, would we?" He patted her firmly on the backside and she gasped and stumbled a couple of steps away. "Just remember we need to have that talk."

Talk. Why was Kelli getting the impression there wouldn't be many coherent words included in that little discussion?

She hurried back behind the counter and made busy with her hands, though she did nothing. Her gaze kept straying to where David had unzipped his coat and stepped to the opposite side of the store. She appreciated the curve of his bottom in jeans even as her own still smarted a bit from his swat. She watched him pick up something with his index finger and thumb as if it might bite. She couldn't help herself. She called out, "You break it, you buy it," causing him to nearly drop the sex toy.

She gave a husky little laugh, then smiled at a woman who approached her with her purchases. Kelli tried to concentrate on her rather than her choices. With light brown hair, thirty-ish and petite, she was similar in age, appearance, and class to the other victims. Though none of the D.C. Degenerate, now D.C. Executioner, women had actually been found to have frequented Adult Indulgences, the task force director had thought it important the shop be covered just the same. Kelli rang up the items, then completed the transaction. Sheesh, she could easily have run into the woman at any number of places. The hairdresser's. The grocery store. The doctor's office. If not for this assignment, she'd have happily lived the rest of her life not knowing what really went on behind the closed doors of these perfectly normal-looking people.

Let's face it. Who really needed bottles of flavored oils in order to have a good time? Her gaze automatically flicked back to David and her throat closed. Not her, that's for sure. Time—more specifically, two times—had proven she needed little more than privacy, fresh air and David McCoy.

"Those are on sale," the woman pointed out as Kelli rang up a pair of red silk panties edged with black lace.

"Are they?" Kelli searched them for a tag to find they were missing half the fabric. "Um, how much?"

The woman quoted a price and Kelli entered it, not up to going back there and fingering through the rack to make sure the woman was right. Not so much because she was appalled by the lingerie, but because for that price she was tempted to pick up a pair for herself.

She bagged the purchases and handed them to the customer. "Don't do anything I wouldn't do," she said with a saucy smile.

"I won't."

If you only knew...

Without someone to keep her occupied, she switched her attention again to David. Now that a bit of time separated his closeness from her highly David-sensitive nerves, her spine began to stiffen. What did he mean by her not being fit for a uniform? Sure, maybe he'd been floored when she not only showed up at the station for work the day after their encounter, but ended up being his partner, but what made him think he was capable of judging her competency as a cop? And this time it hadn't sounded as if his conclusions had been drawn on her merely being female. They sounded as though they were based on specific knowledge about her.

"How would you know what I'm capable of?" she said under her breath.

Then it hit her. There was one area that he was privy to exactly how competent she was. In bed.

Her cheeks flamed.

Oh, God...

Was he basing his judgment on how well she had...how much she knew...how good she was...?

She groaned out loud, earning her his attention. She quickly turned away. Sure, maybe she wasn't all that experienced when it came to the bedroom. But that didn't mean she was innocent, for cripe's sake. And her inexperience with sex had absolutely nothing to do with how savvy she would be on the job. She fully intended to have that detective's shield by the time she turned thirty, no two ways about it.

Her ability to do that, however, rested a whole lot on how well she performed in this assignment.

The guy who had been ogling the new issues rack of magazines sauntered up to the counter.

"Hey, sweet thing, how come I don't see any pictures of you in these?" he asked, his gaze slithering down her scantily clad body.

She was aware without even looking that David was tuned into their conversation. No matter how slimy the guy's attention made her feel, she pasted on a smile and leaned suggestively across the counter. "Do you really think I make the grade?"

"Oh, yeah, baby, you definitely make the grade." He put his choices down on the counter.

She batted her eyelashes. "Too bad I don't have a portfolio or anything, huh?" She began ringing up the magazines.

"You talking pictures?"

"Uh-huh."

His flashy grin broadened. "Well, hell, why didn't you say so? I'd be more than happy to snap a few, um, photos, you know, for good will's sake."

A hand came from out of nowhere, clutching the guy by the collar of his sheepskin coat. "If there are any pictures to be taken, you can bet I'll be the one taking 'em, slimeball," David said, fairly growling at the other man.

"And who are you?"

Kelli smiled at him innocently. She hadn't been sure how David would react, but she admitted to being slightly pleased that he had.

"I'm the guy she's going to marry."

Both of her eyebrows shot up so high they were probably lost in her hairline. Had he just said what she thought he had?

The guy held up his hands in surrender. "Whoa, buddy. I wasn't asking the girl to marry me, if you get my drift. But if she's claimed property, I don't want nothing to do with it, you know?"

"Claimed property?" Kelli repeated.

"Uh-huh," David said with a grin, finally releasing the guy.

Kelli rolled her eyes toward the ceiling. From lady-killer to old woman in one blink of an eye. Despite the beef her father had with the McCoys, she suspected he and David would get along famously. After all, they shared the exact same view on her capabilities, which lay somewhere between zip and zero.

The customer straightened his coat. "If you're ever interested in sharing some of those pictures, I'd pay a couple of bucks for them."

Kelli gasped, then leaned across the counter to where David was cocking his arm back. "Don't even think about it."

She quickly accepted the guy's money then apologized as she saw him out the door.

"Looks like you're really not interested in having that conversation you were talking about." She swiveled toward David and squashed the pads of her index finger and thumb together. "Because you just came this close to getting me fired already. And it's only my first day on the job."

"That guy was—"

"That guy was someone I could handle, thank you very much." She tilted her head to the side. "You seem to forget that we went through the same exact training at the academy, McCoy."

"Yeah, but learning something and putting it into use are two entirely different things."

"Marry?" she blurted, choosing to ignore his comment.

Rather than looking away as she expected, he had the audacity to grin. "Yeah. Pretty good comeback, don't you think?"

She groaned, rounded him, then forcefully pushed him toward the door. "Get out of here, McCoy. Before I show you just how well I can put to use what I learned at the academy."

"Academy?" a male voice echoed from behind her.

Kelli tensed, as did David's back muscles through his coat. She plucked her hands from him, then messed with her skirt while she turned to face Jeremy. *Think, Hatfield, think.* "Yes, the academy," she said around an affected smile. "You know. The Holy Mother's Academy for Girls? That's the high school I attended."

Jeremy grinned. "A Catholic girl, huh? Ooo, you're just getting more and more interesting, Kitty Kat." His gaze switched to take in David. He made no secret of his open appreciation for the prime piece of male flesh. It was all Kelli could do not to claim *him* as her property. "Well, aren't you going to introduce us?"

"Of course," Kelli said quickly. "Jeremy, this is…David McCoy."

"Well, hello and how do you do, David McCoy." The shop owner extended his hand and David hesitantly took it. "It's not often we get guys of your…caliber in here. Have you ever thought about modeling? You'd be to-die-for in one of those little leather getups over there." He tapped his finger against his pursed lips. "Without the hood, though. We wouldn't want to cover up those finely chiseled features."

Kelli recognized a smoother version of the come-on line the last customer had just tried on her, and cringed. She slanted a gaze at David, unsure of his reaction. She was surprised to find him grinning at Jeremy. "If that was a compliment, thank you."

Jeremy chuckled. "Oh, you are priceless."

"I'm also Kelli's fiancé."

Kelli yearned to stomp her high heel on top of David's foot with every ounce of energy she possessed. "*Ex*-fiancé," she said, scrambling to save the situation. Didn't the idiot know that part of her cover was that she had just come off a long relationship?

The two men fell silent, leaving her to wonder whether or not her knee-jerk reaction had been particularly wise. Or if David had completely screwed up everything before it had even begun.

"For now. But I wouldn't count on that status holding for long," David said, his voice akin to a soft hum.

Jeremy sighed, then chuckled good-naturedly. "Ah, why is it women always get the best men?" he asked, then sighed. He waved his hand dismissively. "Never mind." He eyed David one more time. "It was nice meeting you…Mr. McCoy. Given your connection to our Kitty Kat here, I hope that means we'll be seeing more of you."

David's grin was wider than she'd ever seen it. She braced herself for his response. "On that, you can count, Jeremy."

The owner nodded in agreement, then went back into his office.

Kelli glared at David.

"So," he said, "what's say we meet back at your place later?"

"No."

He quirked a brow. "My place?"

"Never." This time she made no attempt to physically remove him from the shop. She allowed her expression to speak for her. "Get this straight, McCoy. I don't need you hovering over me under the pretense of protecting me." She crossed her arms, but this time there was nothing provocative about the move. "I don't need you thinking that just because we've slept together—"

"Twice," he added.

She rolled her eyes. "It doesn't give you the right to come and go as you please. And I certainly don't need you screwing up my assignment." She had promised herself she wouldn't touch him, but she couldn't resist poking her finger into his rock solid chest. A move that may have knocked her off track a few minutes ago, but she was so angry a bulldozer probably couldn't have moved her at that moment. "And don't even joke about blowing my cover, McCoy. I'll go to the task force and Kowalsky so fast you won't know what hit you. And I think they'll be even less amused than I am with your interfering behavior." She narrowed her eyes. "And I don't think I have to remind you who my father is, now, do I?" She really hated throwing that extra bit in, but hey, all was fair, right?

"I'm—"

"Don't." She stopped him with a raised hand.

"But—"

"Stop."

"Still—"

"Forget about it, McCoy. Absolutely nothing you could say to me right now could make me think about anything else but watching your butt, no matter how cute, walk straight through that door forever."

He heaved a sigh. "You'd really make me lose my job?"

She winced but held herself straight. "Let's put it this way. I care as much about your job security as you care about mine."

"Ouch."

She pointed to the door. "Now get out of here."

CHAPTER EIGHT

DAVID DRIBBLED the basketball the length of the indoor court, weaving in and out, skirting around the teenagers he coached at the youth center downtown. Several of them were already taller than he was, and far more talented, but tonight he had an edge they couldn't hope to challenge. Tonight wasn't normal practice or game night, but he'd been restless and distracted and had come anyway to find most of his team there, preferring the warmth and companionship of the center to the bitter December cold outside. Sneakers squealed against the waxed old wood, sweat dripped from his chin, and thankfully for the first time in days he wasn't focused solely on one sexy Kelli Hatfield.

He drew to a quick stop and set up his shot…and missed the hoop by a mile.

So much for focusing on something other than that maddeningly sensual woman. Even when he didn't want her to be, she was there on the fringes of his thoughts, her luscious mouth smiling, her green eyes snapping, her bare back arching. It had been even worse recently, since all attempts to see her in the past two days had been effectively blocked.

He'd known his showing up at the shop the other night had irritated her, but he hadn't known he'd so thoroughly pissed her off. He was still trying to figure that one out. Why did his wanting to protect her send her off the mental deep end? Hell, his experience with women was that he didn't pay enough attention to them. Essentially Kelli was accusing him of paying her too much attention.

It didn't make any sense.

After she'd hung up in his ear the day before, he thought it prudent to give her a little time to cool off. While thoughts of her at that damn store, unprotected, drove him up the wall, thoughts of her slamming the door on any further contact between them were even more frustrating.

Yeah. He'd lay low for a couple of days, wait for everything to blow over, then show up at her place begging for forgiveness.

If only he knew what he would be apologizing for.

Chris Tucker, a fifteen-year-old who was already a foot taller than he was, lumbered up to walk him to the mostly empty bleachers. "That one should have been all yours, coach. What happened?"

David fished a towel from his gym bag and dragged it across his face. "Wasn't focusing, Tuck. It's as simple as that."

The kid grinned, likely finding it funny that he could use some of his own coaching advice. "Yeah."

David waved him away. "You go on and I'll watch. This old guy has had enough for one night."

Chris didn't believe him for a minute, but thankfully he didn't say anything. He rejoined the other kids on the court, which included two females, and then continued play.

Normally David made it a point to keep up with the teens. It was a good way to keep in shape, burn off the excess energy usually left after a long and frustrating day, as well as help some neighborhood kids keep off the corner. Not just one specific corner, but all of them. Everywhere where deals were made, drugs sold, young flesh peddled. He'd started coaching five years ago and planned to continue doing it until he could no longer physically keep up. He was determined that would be never.

He dropped to the first bench and watched the kids work their way to the opposite end of the court. Even as he did, their images faded to be superimposed with the mental image of Kelli Hatfield. He grimaced. The mere thought of her working in that place, with all those losers slobbering all over her, dressed like… He went brain dead just thinking about the close-fitting, downright sexy clothes she'd had on. The boots alone filled his mind with fantasies of seeing her wearing them, and nothing else, standing over him as he lay stretched out on her bed.

"Hey, little bro, how's it hanging?"

David turned to where the spot on the bleachers one up from him was no longer vacant. "Fine, couldn't be better," he said by rote, his token response for the past couple of days when he was everything but fine.

Marc McCoy hiked a skeptical brow as he laid his coat on the bench beside him.

David chugged down a swallow of bottled water, the cold liquid barely sliding its way past his tight throat. "How did you know to find me here?"

Marc shrugged. "Lucky guess. If you weren't at home or in Manchester, it was a pretty good bet that you'd be here."

David gave him a meaningful glance. "With Melanie about to pop that baby of yours, I would have thought you'd be chained to her side."

He had to do a double take. Had his brother actually just frowned? Uh-oh, was there trouble in paradise?

"Haven't you heard? She's staying out at the house. What with the lame duck still on Penn Ave, and the president-elect primed to take over next month, we've all been putting in double shifts. Mel's fit to be tied."

"Ah, life in the Secret Service." David messed around with the valve on his bottle. Maybe this women-problems thing was due to something in the water. "You think hanging out with me is going to help matters any?" he asked.

Marc shrugged. "What Mel doesn't know, won't hurt her. Besides, I need to unwind a little before making the long drive out to Manchester." He grabbed the water bottle and took a swallow. "Don't tell her I said this, but I personally think she's jealous. She just wishes she could be out there scoping out potentials right along with me. This baby thing has her wound up just as tight as I am."

David smiled. "Yeah, you're probably right."

"So what's up with you?"

He shrugged. "Not much. Same old same old."

Marc stared at him. "Uh-huh."

"What?"

His brother shook his dark head. "Oh nothing."

From the door in the corner a couple of teenage girls walked in dressed to the neighborhood nines, shaking their heads to rid themselves of the light snow that started falling about an hour ago. Marc sat up a little straighter. "Woooweee, will you get a load of that," he said appreciatively. "They didn't make them that way when I was a teen."

"Yeah, they did. It was just so long ago you can't remember."

Marc slugged him playfully in the arm.

"You just make sure you keep your hands to yourself, you hear? Aside from them being jailbait, there's Mel to think about. You might be able to handle her, but I'm not even going to chance facing her wrath."

Marc rubbed the back of his neck. "Hey, it's just eye candy. You know I'd never act on it."

"Yeah, well, normally you wouldn't even notice."

"A month without some Grade-A sex will do that to a guy.

But as soon as the doc gives the thumbs-up, Mel and I are leaving the baby with Michelle and taking off for the weekend to make up for lost time."

David barely heard him.

"That's my story, little bro. Now what's yours?"

"Huh?"

Marc nodded toward the girls who had taken seats down the way. "You're the loverboy with the sweet tooth and you've barely even looked at them. No matter the age, there's just something in your genes that makes you want to win every woman over."

"Yeah, I must have inherited all the charm you guys didn't," he mumbled even as he grimaced at the description. "Not in the mood tonight, I guess."

"You guess." Marc leaned his forearms against his thighs. "Oooh, I recognize that expression."

"What expression?"

Marc pointed at him. "That expression. The one that says you expect the world to end at any minute. Oh, boy, you've got it bad."

He looked away.

"Okay, who is she, and why aren't you with her tonight?"

David blinked at him. Of the five of them, it could never be said that Marc was the most observant. Not when it came to relationships anyway. In fact, Connor relished calling him dumber than a doornail when it came to women. He grimaced. He wondered if they all had been wrong. Marc had been the first of them to marry. It may have taken a baby and an assassin to get him to come around, but he had long before the rest of them.

He considered lying to Marc, telling him that the last thing he had was woman problems, but he figured his brother deserved some credit for his powers of observation, however dubious. "Kelli."

"Kelli," Marc drew out, coaxing him into sharing more.

"Kelli Hatfield. She's my new partner. Well, she was anyway, until she got this special undercover assignment with the Executioner task force."

"Hatfield…Hatfield." Marc pondered along with the kids still playing in front of them. His eyes widened. "Not as in Garth Hatfield?"

David visibly winced. Trust Marc to put two and two together when it had taken him days to add up the sum. "One and the same. She's his only kid."

"Does Pops know?"

David leaned back. "As of right now, there's nothing to know, because nothing's going on."

"But there was."

Was there? David couldn't be sure anymore. If his brother had asked him a couple of days ago, he'd have answered with an unqualified yes. But now… Well, now he wasn't all too sure where he stood with the frustrating woman. She was all soft and sexy on the outside, but inside he was coming to suspect that she was impenetrable steel.

When Marc had said he had it bad, he put his finger directly on his dilemma. He did have it bad for Kelli Hatfield. Which was totally baffling, because he'd never felt quite like this before. And without previous experience under his belt, he had no idea what to do about it. He felt like a mouse running around an unfamiliar maze. He could smell the cheese, he wanted the cheese, but he couldn't find the damn cheese.

Marc chuckled and shook his head. "I never thought I'd live to see the day when a woman would get to you, Casanova."

David bristled. "And why not? I'm human, aren't I? If you cut me, don't I bleed red?"

"Yeah, but up 'til now it was red roses."

"Cute, McCoy, real cute."

Marc stretched his long legs out to rest against the bleacher below him and crossed them at the ankle. "So a woman has gotten the better of the infamous David McCoy, huh?"

"Infamous?" David hiked a brow.

"Come on. Don't tell me you didn't purposely build that naughty reputation you have. Forget Manchester. Forget the M.P.D. You're now a citywide bad boy."

"And you're making much more out of this than there is."

"Am I?" He reached over and picked up his coat, slipping something out of the inside pocket. "Normally I don't read this garbage, but Mel called this morning practically shrieking with the news." He slapped a folded back weekly magazine into David's stomach. "Read it and weep, Casanova Cop."

David stared at the glossy paper, afraid to touch it. Is that how everyone and his brothers really saw him? As some sort of love-'em-and-leave-'em renegade? He groaned and forced himself to pick up the magazine. Spread across the left-hand page was a picture of him in full uniform grinning with his arms crossed. He recognized the background as being just after the hostage situation the other day. On the other page written in bold letters was "Casanova Cop: What D.C. Woman Wouldn't Want to Find Him Under Her Christmas Tree?"

Yeah, every woman but Kelli Hatfield. Especially after she got a look at this story.

He closed his eyes and groaned. He vaguely recognized the reporter's name as someone he talked to after the hubbub. He'd had no idea she'd planned to run this kind of story on him. Then again he hadn't bargained on the news media jumping all over the hostage story either. He'd taken his share of ribbing from fellow officers over the past week, and even the kids had mentioned it before he told them to can it.

Marc pointed to a highlighted part of the story. "I like this part the best. She talks about your being a bad boy in need of a woman's good loving to turn you around."

David groaned even louder, then threw the magazine back at Marc with more force than was necessary.

"Hey, I thought you'd eat up coverage like this."

"A week ago, maybe I would have. But that damn fluff piece probably just cut my chances of getting through to Kelli in half."

Marc laughed and tossed the magazine onto David's gym bag. "I know I'm repeating myself, but I can't help it. I never thought I'd live to see the day when a woman would get the better of you."

David dropped his head into his hands and rubbed his eyes. "I didn't either."

Marc fell silent, leaving only the sounds of the sneakers squeaking against the basketball court, and the good-natured jests of the players.

What was he going to do?

"You'll figure it out," Marc said, as if he'd asked the question aloud. "You're a McCoy and McCoys always get their man. Or woman, in this case." Marc thumped him on the back.

"We're not talking about a fugitive here, Marc."

"Worse. We're talking about the opposite sex." He sat up. "You know, I still have all those, um, women's magazines at home if you want to take a look through them. Not that they ever helped me, but you never know. They have all kinds of crap in there on what a woman really wants from a man." He grinned. "Although given that Casanova Cop piece, apparently you've already got it."

David groaned again. "Shut up, Marc. Just shut up."

KELLI PACED the length of the reversible bulletin board she'd set up in the corner of her dining room, right next to her three-foot live Christmas tree. She methodically searched pictures, diagrams and information posted on nearly every square inch of this side of the board, seeking out something, anything, new, while Kojak alternately watched her and the flashing lights on the tree. Lying a safe distance away so as not to get stepped on, his head resting on his meaty paws, only his eyes shifted. An occasional yawn told her how bored he was with the entire routine.

There had to be something here, something she'd missed three years ago, the last time she'd gone through the copy of the inactive file on her mother's murder. Finding a spot for the slip she held, she pulled out a green pushpin, then fastened the phone message to the corkboard between a studio photograph of her mother taken eighteen years ago, and the media shot of her body being carried out of the house, Kelli's own image as she ran after the sheeted figure carefully cut out.

She tapped the board, causing it to rotate and reveal the side she had mapped out on the D.C. Executioner's crimes, then flipped it back again, the images beginning to swim before her eyes.

"There has to be something…."

Kojak snapped his head up and whined hopefully. She slowly turned her head and zoomed in on him. He seemed to sense that she wasn't really looking at him, rather was looking past him for the answer that always seemed on the edge of her mind. Kojak barked.

"What is it, boy? You think I'm heading in the wrong direction?"

His stubby little tail moved frantically back and forth, indicating his answer in the affirmative.

Kelli flopped down in the dining room chair and fingered through the other material strewn across the surface. Kojak came to her side and she absently dropped her hand and petted him.

"Maybe you're right. Maybe this burning the candle at both ends stuff is finally catching up with me."

She rested her other elbow on the table, then propped up her head with her hand. The past couple of days had been grueling. She began each morning down at task force headquarters, reviewing new information that had come in on the suspect—today it had been two different character profiles and a hazy almost unusable suspect sketch—and turning in her own detailed notes on the case. Then came changing and checking in for the job within a job itself. She'd forgotten how much of a physical drain working the sales floor could be. Heap on top of that her need to note every suspicious character and scope out each potential victim, and by the end of her shift her brain was about ready to explode with details she had to retain until she got home and could make her notes.

Kojak got up and lumbered toward the kitchen. She wearily eyed the files littering the table. She'd finally gone through them when she couldn't sleep two nights ago because images of a certain someone kept slipping through her mind. Since then, she'd spent every free moment following up leads long dropped and dogging trails long gone cold.

She glanced at her watch. She listlessly toyed with the files, then looked at her watch again. It was after ten. As tired as she was, a nice long hot bath, bed and the book lying half open on the nightstand should have sounded awfully tempting. But it didn't. Not when she knew that long periods of time without something to occupy her attention were just inviting trouble in the image of David McCoy. And the romance she was currently reading would only further exacerbate the situation.

She reached for the phone, then pulled her hand back. Bronte had left for New Hampshire that morning to visit her folks for Christmas.

Christmas. Was it really only three days away?

She rubbed her forehead. David wasn't the only man she hadn't talked to recently. Garth Hatfield was proving even more stubborn than she was. She'd given in and called his office phone yesterday and left a brief message. He'd never called back.

Why was life so damn complicated?

Kojak wandered over to sit practically on her foot, making his usual postfeeding sounds.

"That good, huh?" she sighed. "Ah, to have your uncomplicated life."

He barked then began gnawing at something near his back end. Kelli laughed. "Then again…no."

Her thoughts drifted and she was convinced she'd fallen asleep with her eyes open until Kojak whined. She looked down, having to see that her hand rested idly against his ribcage before she realized she'd stopped petting him. She scratched him behind the ears. "What's the matter, Jackie boy? Feeling a little neglected lately?" His panting seemed to increase in intensity. "Yeah. Me, too."

She pushed back from the table and Kojak instantly got up, too. She eyed him and his bulky frame. "All right, all right, enough with the guilt trip. I'll give you a treat, okay?" He barked, doing the canine equivalent of the rumba as he followed her into the kitchen. "That's treat. Singular. As in one. You got it? And I don't want to hear any complaints. You just ate."

She reached on top of the refrigerator where she had his goodie box stashed and thrust her hand into it. Nothing. The box was empty.

Talk about guilt trips.

"Sorry, buddy, but we're all out of comfort food." He barked. "What? You don't believe me? Take a look for yourself." She held the box out. He sniffed, and sniffed again, then began whining.

"I know how you feel." Boy, did she ever. She was so desperate for the sound of a friendly human voice she was making do by talking to an animal who couldn't answer her.

She dropped the empty box into the garbage, then turned toward the refrigerator itself. Not one thing edible for a human, much less a dog.

She closed the kitchen door, trying to figure out a way to break the news to him. She highly doubted there was a pet supply store open at ten, and that was the only place she could get the brand of special diet treats he would touch.

Then it occurred to her that she knew exactly where she could come by some treats on such short notice. There was this certain someone who took great pride in wooing her dog away from her. She plucked a Post-it Note attached to the refrigerator door with a handcuff magnet, then forced herself to put it back where it was. If she was any kind of modern woman, she'd crumple it up and throw it into the garbage along with the empty treat box. But she wasn't quite ready to do that yet.

She eyed where Kojak had dropped to the floor, the epitome of canine disappointment and depression. Then ignoring the voice telling her it was a big mistake, she said, "Hey, Jack, you wanna go for a walk, boy?"

DAVID EMERGED from the bathroom fastening a towel around his hips. The workout at the basketball court had nicely tired out his muscles but his mind continued irritatingly along on its Kelli Hatfield track. Grimacing, he grabbed the remote, flipping through the channels until he came across a rerun of *The Simpsons*. Recognizing the episode as one of his favorites, he tossed the remote to the two milk crates that served as his coffee table, trying to forget another coffee table he'd recently become very familiar with. Forcing his gaze away, he stalked into the kitchen and grabbed a beer.

Of course whatever physical release of tension he'd gained from the workout on the court was obliterated by his stress-inducing conversation with Marc. Trust his brother to further complicate a situation that was probably pretty simple once you cleared away all the garbage. Standing in front of the open refrigerator door, he gulped down half a beer, then grabbed a half deli sandwich he'd tossed in there when he got home from work.

Ignoring that the towel had slipped a little lower on his hips, he sauntered back into the living room and stared at the television screen. He grinned at something Homer said, then idly wondered if Kelli had ever watched the show. His grin vanished as he took another bite of ham on rye. Kelli probably scoured the proliferation of news shows cramming the network stations, absorbing every byte should she need it to solve a case somewhere down the road.

He reached out and poked a button on the remote, but the talking head failed to keep his interest and he hit the last channel button, instantly relaxing as the cartoon again filled the screen. He took another bite of his sandwich, feeling mustard trickle down the side of his mouth.

A brief knock sounded at the door. He glanced at his waterproof watch, then swiped at the spot of mustard. "Jeff's one door down," he called out.

On his worst days, he was tempted to run his neighbor in for disturbing the peace. But he never did. Jeff was a popular guy who had a lot of friends who just happened to stop by at all times of the day and night. He was used to it. That didn't mean, however, that he couldn't be a wee bit envious.

Another knock.

Sighing, David walked to the door, slid his beer into the crook of his arm, then opened it. "I said that Jeff's—" His eyes widened as he stared at the pair waiting in the hall. He couldn't have been more shocked had he opened the door to find Homer Simpson standing there.

Kojak barked, barely contained by the short leash Kelli had him on. He looked at the dog, then back to his owner, certain he was seeing things.

"I know it's late, but Kojak and I were out walking, and, well…" Her words trailed off as her gaze slid the length of his unclothed body. "Oh, God," she said softly, her cheeks blazing the most amazing shade of red.

David stared down at where his towel was barely hanging on, looked at the beer still in the crook of his arm, and the mess of a sandwich in his hand. Remembering the mustard that had dripped down his chin, he swiped at it with the back of his hand, hoping he was rubbing in the right place.

"Hi," he said. "Come in."

"No, I…we're interrupting you. I think we should just go—"

"No!" he fairly shouted, causing her to jump and the towel around his hips to dip even lower. When it would have slid off altogether, he grabbed at the front, holding it tight. "I just got out of the shower and was catching a bite." He grimaced, wondering if he could waste anymore time stating the obvious. "Why don't you two come in so I can go, um, put something on?"

He turned and led the way in, kicking a pile of sports magazines out of the way as he went. He saw his apartment as she would and mentally cursed himself. Then he mildly cursed her. What was it with this woman? He tries to contact her, she ignores him. The instant he gives up, she pops up on his doorstep when he's at his absolute worst.

The door quietly clicked closed behind her. "K, would you just settle down."

"You can let him loose if you want," he said, setting his

beer down on one of the crates. He stopped himself from shoving what was left of the sandwich into his mouth and put it next to the bottle instead. "I'm, um, just going to go put something on. Make yourself at home."

He stepped toward the door to his bedroom. He had it half closed behind him when Kojak darted in.

"Kojak! Get back here."

David popped his head around the door. "I've got him."

Then he closed the door and softly uttered every curse word he'd learned in his thirty-year existence. The dog plunked his rump down on the floor and sat looking at him, his head cocked slightly to the side. "You think this is funny, huh?" He grabbed the blue flannel shirt hanging on the doorknob. He sniffed the underarms, then slipped into it. "Just see if you get any more treats from me."

At the word treat, Kojak barked, causing David to cringe. The building didn't allow pets. All he needed now was a call from the building manager who lived below him to round out a perfectly awful night. "Okay, okay. I was just joking. Give me a second, will ya?"

He reached past the pooch and grabbed the jeans on the bed and hopped into them, only as he began zipping them remembering he hadn't put briefs on. Oh, well. If things were finally going to take an upward turn he wouldn't have his jeans on for long anyway. He carefully zipped them up then craned his neck to see his hair in the mirror across the room. He'd just towel-dried it after his shower and it was sticking up at odd angles all over his head.

"Damn."

A couple of minutes later he walked into the other room, still barefoot, his shirt hanging open, but as presentable as he could swing in five minutes. Kojak followed him out.

Kelli was perched on the arm of the futon. She looked at

him, then back at the television, an amused sparkle in her green eyes. David groaned and reached out to shut off *The Simpsons* midjoke. "I, um, just turned it on. I don't watch that stuff," he said.

She smiled. "Uh-huh."

He started to walk toward the kitchen. "Can I get you something? A beer? A soda?"

Her gaze dropped to his chest and the smile faded from her face. "Um, no thanks. I really shouldn't drink and walk and it's kind of late for a sugar and caffeine buzz."

He frowned at her. "Water?"

Her gaze skittered away from him as she nodded. "Okay."

Kojak nudged his head against his knee. "All right then. One water and one treat coming up."

Get it together, man, he told himself once he was out of view in the kitchen. You can handle this.

It wasn't often that he had a woman in his apartment. He rarely gave out his address. But he hadn't thought twice when he'd fastened both his address and his phone number to Kelli's refrigerator a couple of days back. Perhaps because he'd never thought she'd use it. Or maybe because he'd hoped she would.

Either way he felt out of his element here. He'd never once given a second thought about his lifestyle. Never, that is, until Kelli came a-knocking at his door. Now he was wondering if the low pile gray carpet could do with a vacuum, wished he had thought to do the dishes piled up in the sink, and wondered if there was some way to order a new couch and have it delivered in the next half hour.

"Way to impress the woman, McCoy," he said under his breath as he washed out a glass then filled it with ice and tap water. Only as he was walking back into the other room did he manage to remember to grab the box of treats sitting on the counter.

Kojak came running up and he tossed him one. All he needed now was for the overgrown pooch to jump on him and cause him to drop the water.

"There we are," he said, holding the glass out to her where she was still perched anxiously on the arm of his futon.

Was it him or had Kelli just jumped?

He frowned as she took the glass and offered up a soft thanks.

He dropped down to sit on the other side of the sofa. "You can sit down. I won't bite."

She smiled and slowly shifted to sit next to him. "I don't know if I'm convinced of that."

He held up his hands. "Have I ever done anything you didn't want me to?"

She shook her blond head. "No. But this place…well, it's just what I'd expect from the Casanova Cop."

"Saw that, did you?"

"Not that it matters. That's your nickname anyway. I hear it every time I walk into the station. 'Hey, Hatfield, how's that Casanova Cop of yours doing?' I don't even want to know how they found out. Not that I'm claiming you, by the way. And the piece…well, let's just say it's hard to miss. By now they probably have copies posted all over the station."

He groaned inwardly.

"Nice choice of a color for the walls."

He stared at the black paint. "They were that way when I moved in." He shrugged. "Matched the futon, so I left 'em."

"Um-hmm. I especially like your tree."

He winced at the tiny, deformed silver Christmas tree he'd put up on top of the television. It bore a total of four bulbs and half the lights were missing. "What's the matter with it? It's…Christmasy."

He thought about picking up his beer bottle, then dismissed

it, instead stretching his arm across the back of the futon. "So…" he said, "you and Kojak were just out for a walk, huh?"

She seemed inordinately fixated on the close proximity of his arm. "What?"

He pulled his arm back. "Okay, Kelli, spill it. What's really going on here?"

CHAPTER NINE

KELLI BLINKED at him several times. It was a valid question. What *was* she doing there? The problem was, she really didn't have an answer. Unusual, since she usually had an answer for everything, even if sometimes it didn't make much sense.

She shrugged. "I was out of treats and Kojak looked so miserable…"

That was lame.

"So you walked a mile and a half in the dead of winter in the middle of the night to come over here so your dog could have a treat?"

She smiled at him. "Yeah. Got a problem with that?"

"Hey, if it works for you." He grinned at her, again stretching that arm of his across the back of the sofa. Her gaze flicked to where the action further opened the unbuttoned flaps of his soft flannel shirt. She'd half expected to find his apartment filled to the rim with weights, but as far as she could tell there wasn't even a dumbbell in the place. She idly wondered how he managed to keep in such great shape. He didn't strike her as the fitness club type.

And she was spending far too much time staring at his six-pack abs.

She cleared her throat and sipped at her water when all she really wanted to do was grab his beer bottle and guzzle the rest of the contents down.

"How are things at the station?" she asked idly, cringing at the small talk.

"They're okay. Johnson and I have settled into a pretty good routine."

"And you got a guy this time around. Good for you." She tried to translate his suddenly dark expression.

"How are things at Adult Indulgences?"

She averted her gaze and ran her fingertip along the rim of her glass. "Okay. A little more grueling than I thought."

"Any progress?"

"On what? Catching the D.C. Executioner?" She shook her head. "No. The heads of the task force are starting to get edgy. The deadline between the timing of his previous crimes is coming up and they want to get him before he can strike again."

"Isn't that a bit optimistic?"

"That's what I thought. I mean, they just set up the task force and already they're leaning on the undercover cops to come up with something. This guy has been lurking out there for over three years and they don't have one solid piece of evidence against him, aside from a couple of Average Joe sketches that could be anybody and a DNA workup that doesn't help us until we actually have a suspect." She sighed and put her glass down on the table. "And they expect us to come waltzing in with him in cuffs yesterday."

"It probably doesn't help that the first murder victim was a cousin twice removed of a senator."

She jerked to look at him. "How do you know that?"

He shrugged a little too nonchalantly. "Word gets around the division. You know that."

"Yeah, but that little piece of info was being kept hush-hush."

David grinned. "There's no such thing as hush-hush in this city, Kelli. If information can be used, it will be. I've heard of guys who make a living out of selling bits to the local news media."

She shook her head and tried to settle back into the cushion, then immediately sat back up when her back made contact with the crook of his arm. She nearly leapt off the couch when he touched her shoulder.

"You're wound up tighter than a fishing reel."

She tried to shrug him off. "I came over here because I needed some human company, McCoy, not because I was looking to get laid."

"It might be a good outlet for the tension radiating from you."

"So might a good sock in the kisser."

He threw his handsome head back and laughed. "Good point." While his mouth said one thing, his fingers were still kneading the tight muscles of her shoulders. She tried to shrug him away again.

"Would you just relax?"

"I can't," she blurted.

He narrowed his eyes. "Hey, Hatfield, even I know the meaning of the word no. This isn't an attempt to get you out of those jeans, no matter how good the wares underneath look. This is just a friend helping a friend."

"A friend helping a friend," she whispered. How much she wanted that now. A friend. Someone to talk about all her worries to.

Kelli drew in a deep breath and closed her eyes, trying to imagine Bronte's innocent touch affecting her this way.

Taking her response as a go-ahead, David slightly shifted her so her back was to him. Then he eased a path down her back with both hands as if testing the muscles there.

"Ouch," she said when he probed a little too thoroughly near her neck.

"Shhh."

She obeyed, noticing as his probing touch changed into a soft, relaxing one. She heard Kojak yawn and cracked open her eyes to find him curling into prime sleep position near the door, either bored stiff by the lack of action, or tired out from the long walk. She smiled, somewhere in the recesses of her mind thinking it interesting he should be so comfortable here, in David's apartment.

"Kelli?"

She hummed her response, finding it amazing that a man as rough and tough as David McCoy could have hands so incredibly gentle.

"What's really bothering you?"

She snapped upright.

"Don't do that. You just undid five minutes of work."

She immediately tried to make herself relax again, but her muscles weren't having any of it.

She shrugged as he kneaded a particularly nasty knot in her right shoulder. "I don't know. Are there ever times when you think that if just one more thing happens you're afraid you'll run screaming into the woods never to be heard from again?"

"It depends."

She snuck a look at him. "On what?"

"On whether either of us are naked when we do it."

She laughed softly, finding the release relaxed her even further. "You have a one-track mind."

"I never said I didn't." His thumbs pressed on the back of her neck and he slowly, deliberately drew them down the length of her spine. She couldn't help a delicious shiver.

"So tell me, Kell, what else is worrying you?"

You, she wanted to say, but didn't dare. To do so would reveal more than she was ready to at this point. "How much do you know about my father?" she asked.

"You mean aside from the fact that he'd like to have my head served up on a platter?"

She caught herself smiling. "Yeah."

"Not much, really. I know he's been on the force for a long time. Why?"

She ignored his question. "Do you know anything about my mother?"

His hands stilled on her back and he didn't say anything for a long moment. After a couple of heartbeats, Kelli regretted asking the question.

She didn't talk to anyone about her mother, not even Bronte. And on the occasions when she'd tried to talk to her father about her, he'd frozen her out—a reaction she still couldn't quite comprehend. Holidays, birthdays and Mother's Day went by without even a passing mention by her father. It was almost as if Loretta Jane Hatfield had never existed, even though Kelli's own existence was proof positive she had.

David cleared his throat. "Should I know something about your mother?" he asked.

She peeked at him over her shoulder. "No. Like you said, things tend to make the rounds at the station."

"Some things," he clarified.

She turned back around and bit thoughtfully on her bottom lip.

"Tell me about her," David said softly, coaxing her to drop her head forward.

Kelli closed her eyes again, envisioning the picture of the woman on her bulletin board at home. But she remembered more than that. She recalled Sunday afternoons making brownies in their Georgetown kitchen, of licking the spoon and getting more of the chocolaty mix on herself than in the pan. She remembered stringing long garlands of cranberries and popcorn, then hanging them on the tree next to handmade ornaments. She recollected cuddling up on her twin bed with her mother on cold nights like these. She'd pull the quilt up to her chin as her mother read her *Heidi* or *Little Women* or *Wuthering Heights,* books her father had thought were too old for her but she had loved just the same. It had made her feel like an adult. Later she'd since figured out her mother had left out some of the racier passages, tailoring the stories for her young ears.

She smiled softly. It had been so long since she'd thought of her mother as more than a lifeless shape under a white sheet. It felt good to remember the loving person she'd been.

"Kelli?" David said softly, his words closer to her ear than she expected. "You aren't falling asleep on me, are you?"

She shook her head. "No. Sorry. I was just remembering my mom."

His fingers shifted from her shoulders to trace soft lines against her scalp. She hummed her approval and dropped her head back.

"She died when I was seven years old."

His hands slowed. "I'm sorry."

"Don't be. You're not the one who did it."

"Does that mean she was—"

"She was murdered."

"Was her killer caught?"

She swallowed. "No." She absently curved her arms around her torso.

"That's got to be tough."

"What's tougher is trying to find leads left dangling for over eighteen years."

He removed his hands altogether. "You're not saying what I think you are."

"What? That I've been working on the case on and off for the past four years? Yes, I guess I am."

She had no idea why she was sharing all of this with him. No one else knew about her covert activities except the detective she'd talked into copying her mother's case files for her—and he'd only agreed because he was the older brother of one of her academy partners. She'd tried to tell her father once. But it was so obvious he wasn't ready to hear the information that she'd stopped just short of blurting it out.

That she was telling David everything now was puzzling at best, disturbing at worst.

She prided herself on her independence. Despite her and her father's closeness over the years, when it came to her mother, she'd always been on her own.

She gave a small shiver.

"Are you cold?"

She shook her head. "No." Truth be told, she was feeling a bit warm. His older apartment was like hers in that it had radiant heat, making it nearly unbearably warm.

She gave a tiny gasp when she felt his fingers edging up under the back of her shirt, touching the flesh there.

"With all you've taken on, no wonder you look like you're about to drop," he said.

Thick tendrils of awareness curled through her belly. "I always said you were a flatterer."

"You know what I mean."

"Yeah, I do." And she did. That he glimpsed just a bit of the pressure she was under was comforting somehow. Almost as comforting as the fingers sliding against her bare back. "You have to promise me, you know, that you won't tell anyone that I'm investigating my mother's case on my own."

"It never crossed my mind. But…" His words trailed off.

"But?"

"But do you think you should really be doing that? I mean, with all you've already got going on, investigating your mother's death on the side…well, isn't it too much?"

"Sometimes. It's just that it's something I have to do. The three years I was in New York I barely opened the files because there wasn't much I could do there."

"So the instant you got back here you started up again."

"Yes."

His fingers edged upward to where the strap of her bra should have been. It was only then that she remembered she wasn't wearing one. And the halting of his hands in the area in question told her he just figured it out, as well.

"Uh, Hatfield? Aren't you missing some…underwear?"

"Missing is a funny word to use, don't you think?" She smiled. "I usually don't wear one this late."

"Uh-huh. I'll have to remember that."

She lightly drove her elbow back, catching him in the ribs.

"Ooof. Hey, I'm just making conversation."

"Uh-huh." It was then Kelli realized just how very close he was. When he'd turned her on the couch, he must have shifted himself, and she was cradled in the vee of his thighs. His chest was mere inches away from her back, leaving just enough room for him to work his magic with his fingertips. His mouth when he spoke to her was close enough to stir the hair over her right ear.

All she had to do was lean back and she'd be ensconced in the warmth of his arms.

She found the prospect very tempting indeed.

DAVID WASN'T SURE exactly when the mood had shifted, but he grew very aware of the charge in the air between him and Kelli. Telltale signs were the way she wriggled her behind backward until she was nearly pressing against his groin, the new shallowness of her breathing, the slight arch in her back as he slid his hands up the silky expanse of skin.

He didn't know a woman could be so soft. He remembered thinking recently that under Kelli's innocent exterior was steel. How wrong he'd been. While she was one of the strongest women he'd ever met, the reasons behind her prickly demeanor and steadfast ambition were as soft as they came.

Her sweet-smelling hair tickled his nose and he fought the desire to close his eyes and groan. He knew without asking that her sharing what she had marked a milestone of sorts in their relationship, even if she refused to admit that they had one. And her talking about her mother made him think of the lack of a mother in his own life.

Up and down, back and forth, he methodically moved his fingers along the now pliable muscles of her back, trying to ignore how damn good she felt.

He hadn't given much thought to his own mother except when he and his brothers and Pops trudged out to her burial site once a year on the anniversary of her death. He supposed it was because he'd never known her. He was two when she'd died. Too young to remember anything. And his brothers and his father hadn't been much good at filling in the gaps. Not that he'd ever asked them to. His not having a mother was just a fact that he'd lived with. An unquestionable reality that was part of his life.

But the way Kelli had smiled when remembering hers made him wonder how things might have been different had his mother lived. What it would have been like to have a woman around the house when he was growing up.

"My mother died when I was very young," he found himself saying.

Kelli looked at him over her shoulder, her eyes curious. "I'm sorry."

He'd said the same thing to her a short while ago. Why was it that you always felt the need to apologize for something you had no control over when someone mentioned the death of a loved one? Maybe it was the need to say something, anything, to let the other person know you cared. And that Kelli cared made his stomach feel oddly weightless.

"Don't be. You couldn't have stopped the cancer any sooner than I could." He raised his hand to her neck, forcing her to face forward again. "It never really bothered me, you know, her not being there. Maybe because I was too young to remember anything. But my brothers and Pops keep telling me that when I was six or so I ran away to a neighboring ranch to live with a family that had both parents intact."

She reached around and caught his wrist, neither squeezing nor pulling. Just holding.

"I don't remember that either, but they say I fought like a bear when they tried to take me back home." He chuckled softly. "I don't know, I sometimes think they're just pulling my leg, getting back at me for pulling the pranks I have. Only they always use the same story."

Kelli's voice dropped to a whisper. "Which means it's probably true."

He smiled. "Yeah. That's what I thought. Then again, knowing my brothers, I wouldn't put it past them to make up something like that."

"Sounds like they're just like you."

David squinted his eyes. "Yeah. I guess they are."

He'd never really thought of the similarities that connected him to his brothers, only the differences. And it made him feel good to realize that they were bonded together in some important way.

Kelli released his hand, then scooted back a little farther, putting her curvy little bottom in direct contact with him.

He'd been semierect since the moment he first began massaging her back, but now he pulsed rock hard. His breath caught in his throat. "Um, Kelli, I think you'd better move a little bit in the other direction."

"Oh, I don't know. I think I like it right where I am." Her quiet laugh told him the evil little wench knew exactly what effect she was having on him.

He tunneled his nose through her hair until it was right next to her ear. "Here I am trying to have a serious conversation and all you can think about is sex."

She started to pull away from him, the alarm on her face evident, but he refused her escape, instead tugging his hands out from under her shirt and hauling her until her back was flush against his front. "I'm just kidding, Kell. Hell, I'd be the last one to object if you wanted to get naked right this minute."

"You're intolerable."

"And you're a tease."

"I am not," she said indignantly.

"Uh-huh. And I suppose your pressing that cute little bottom of yours against me was completely innocent."

He caught her devilish smile. "Well…no."

"Just as I thought. Can you shift a little bit? Good." He moved his left leg from where it was bent at the knee and stretched it out on the other side of her. "There."

He curved his arms around her rib cage, then folded his fingers on top of her flat stomach.

"You know, I really should be getting back home," she said quietly.

"You think so, huh?"

"I have to get up early tomorrow and put in another full day."

David rested his chin against the top of her head. "No rest for the weary and all that."

She placed her hands on top of his and he noticed she was

getting more comfortable rather than making any real attempt to move.

"Kojak might have something to say about your leaving, don't you think?"

They both looked over at where the pooch was lying on the sports magazines David had kicked out of the hall. A loud snore that was more like a snort made them both laugh.

For long, quiet moments David just stayed there like that, taking comfort in holding Kelli and reveling in her letting him hold her.

She wriggled slightly, reminding him of his aroused state. "Stop it, Hatfield," he murmured as he closed his eyes.

"What? I'm just trying to get more comfortable."

"Uh-huh."

Silence, then, "David?"

"Shhh."

"Don't shush me," she said, though her whisper took the bite out of her words. She quietly cleared her throat. "I just wanted to tell you…I mean, I want to say…"

"What?"

"Thank you."

He tightened his arms around her and pressed his lips against her hair. He wasn't sure what she was thanking him for. Wasn't sure if he wanted to know. All he wanted to do was lie there and hold her. "You're welcome, Kell. You're very, very welcome."

CHAPTER TEN

KELLI CLOSED the cash register drawer, then gave a brief glance around the shop. It was hard to believe that around this time last night she was dead on her feet. It was four o'clock and, well, she felt refreshed somehow. Happy. Ready to go another shift with no problem.

She supposed a portion of her mind-set might have something to do with waking up next to David this morning. Somewhere during the night he must have taken off her shoes and her jeans and carried her into his bedroom, but damned if she could remember any of it. She'd briefly wondered what else had happened, then realized she would have remembered if she and David had made love. That wasn't something easily forgotten. So she had snuggled farther into his arms and dozed off again, taking comfort in Kojak's weight at the foot of the bed.

She'd never spent the entire night with a man before. And to think that sex hadn't even played a role was doubly astonishing.

She'd awakened an hour or so later to find a note on David's pillow telling her he'd gone to work, but that she should stay put for as long as she wanted. He'd also left a bowl of Cocoa Puffs, a small pitcher of milk and cold toast on the nightstand next to the bed, and when she went into the kitchen she'd found a bowl of dog food and water put out for Kojak. She'd been surprised to find he'd even bought the right diet brand.

Who'd have thought hotshot David McCoy could be so thoughtful?

Kelli caught herself smiling, as she had often throughout the day and made an effort to banish it. If she kept mooning after David every spare moment, she wouldn't be able to catch a shoplifter much less a murderer.

She looked around the place. Not a person in sight. Jose was probably tending to the mostly empty booths in the back, while Jeremy was off on one of his errands, his office door closed.

Biting down on her bottom lip, she looked toward the door again, then inched toward the office. A try of the knob proved it was unlocked. Before she had a chance to second-guess herself, she ducked inside, leaving the door open in case Jeremy came back. It would be bad enough to be caught in the office with him there, much less with the door closed behind her.

With one eye on the shop's activity, or lack thereof, she fingered through the papers on his desk. She'd snooped through the room twice before. There was nothing there but normal business stuff: receipts, purchase orders, a payables ledger. She opened the drawers one by one. Nothing out of the ordinary. Not that she had expected to find anything. Despite his unconventional lifestyle, Jeremy was as conventional as they came.

She picked up a couple of receipts. One was from an adult bookstore on the edge of the city, the other from a racy lingerie shop a mile or two down the street. She frowned. Checking out the competition, maybe?

Most likely.

She put the receipts back down, checked out the video recorder in the corner, flipped through his address book to see if he'd added any names, then let herself back out of the office, closing the door after herself.

Well, that had certainly gotten her far, hadn't it?

She stepped back to the relative safety of the counter. Tugging her small notepad from where she had it stashed inside her bra, she jotted down the names of the last two customers. Thank God for credit cards, was all she had to say. Made her task of keeping track of people that much easier.

"Making your list and checking it twice?"

Kelli froze. Without her even being aware of it, Jeremy had come back and was grinning at her from the end of the counter. She managed a shaky smile in return. "Yeah, I'm one of those dreaded last-minute shoppers. They'll probably have to kick me out of the stores Christmas Eve." She snapped her notepad closed, then tucked it back into her bra. Jeremy watched her, his gaze lingering on her breasts. "How about you?" she asked. "Have all your Christmas shopping done?"

He sighed and leaned against the counter. "Unfortunately, I don't have that many people to buy for."

"Some would say that's fortunate."

"Yeah, but that also means I don't get very many presents either."

"A definite drawback," Kelli agreed, straightening her skirt. "Look, Jeremy, I really want to thank you for reworking my shift so I could get off early this afternoon. I usually don't do these family things, but this year…I thought it was time to make amends, if you know what I mean."

What she was really hoping was that she could talk to her father at the annual station Christmas party. That is, if he showed up. She felt it somehow important she try to smooth things over between them and move on to neutral territory before Christmas dinner at her aunt Beryl's. She could barely choke down Aunt B's cornbread dressing as it was. With her father glaring at her from across the table, she was afraid she'd choke and require the Heimlich performed on her.

"*De nada,* sweet thing. As you can see, business gets light around this time of year anyway. Everybody getting religion and all that." He grinned. "Not to worry, though, the day after the major event, they flock in here all set to party down for New Year's."

She laughed, then drawled wryly, "Gives a whole new meaning to New Year's resolutions, doesn't it?"

She wasn't sure if it was the lights or the way he was looking at her, but somehow Kelli thought he looked older than she initially pegged him to be. Rather than in his mid-forties, she guessed he was closer to sixty, his light hair camouflaging the patches of gray. Either that or he was in need of a new dye job. She'd pretty much figured out that outside of the shop, he didn't seem to have much of a life. He sat in his office most of the time, reviewing product catalogs and spending a lot of time on his computer. A check of his hard drive and Internet files a couple of nights ago had proved he was as clean with his computer as he was in the store.

"So tell me, Kitty Kat," he said slowly, "you any relation to Loretta Jane Hatfield?"

Kelli's stomach did a double flip that seemed to sit at an uncomfortable angle in her belly. She turned toward the cash register and opened it. "She was my mother." She carefully controlled the pitch of her voice. "Did you know her?"

He crossed his arms and sighed. "Naw. I'm a crime buff and was just doing some run-of-the-mill web surfing a few months ago and came up with the articles related to her death, what was it, twenty years ago?"

"Eighteen." She tossed a smile over her shoulder, wondering why she hadn't come across his interest in crime either in his office or his computer. Good thing she hadn't been in town long, or he might have stumbled across some information on her. As luck would have it, she wasn't even mentioned in any of the pieces run on David recently. "What were you doing? Spying on me, Jeremy?"

"No. Just curious. You looked familiar to me somehow and I was curious as to why." He scanned her. "You look just like her, you know."

Her throat threatened to close up.

"From what I can tell from the pictures, I mean. Quite a looker. And so are you."

"Thanks."

"No need for thanks. I should be thanking you for coming to work for me. You've really brightened things up around here."

"Well, thanks for hiring me."

He reached out and picked up a returned box of scented oils a customer claimed irritated her skin. "Well, now that we've established the mutual appreciation society, I'd better let you go. What time did you say that party started?"

Kelli looked at her watch, then gasped. "Five. And it's a quarter to." She closed the cash drawer, then grabbed her coat where she'd stashed it under the closed counter. "I guess I'll see you tomorrow morning." She smiled. "Can you believe it'll be Christmas Eve?"

"At this point in my life I can believe just about anything. Have a good time, ya hear? I expect you to share every juicy detail when you come in tomorrow."

"You got it." Boy, she was going to have to make a note of his interest in crime and pass it on to the task force. Not that she even remotely believed Jeremy a suspect, but anything crime-related was worth mentioning. She was certain there were things about the case the task force leaders knew and weren't sharing.

She began to pass Jeremy, noticing how sad he looked suddenly. Impulsively, she kissed him on the cheek, then pulled back to look at the surprise on his face. "Thanks again, Jeremy. You're a prince among men."

"Ah, I've always fancied myself a royal."

Kelli waggled her fingers at him, then hurried out the door.

DAVID SAUNTERED into the decorated lobby of the station, immediately hit by the sound of Christmas carols being played on a giant boom box on the counter, and cringing at the garland some of the guys had on around their necks. The majority of the festivities were scheduled to take place in the briefing room where the chairs had been folded up and put away, making room for the fifty-some officers and their spouses who were expected for the party.

David usually breezed through the rooms, wishing everyone a Merry Christmas, then moving on to whatever plans he had on tap. This was the first year he'd actually looked forward to the event. Solely because he had no doubt Kelli would be there.

"It's the Casanova Cop!" O'Leary called out from the front desk. "Hey, everyone, hold on to your wives and girlfriends. D.C.'s most eligible bachelor has just entered the building."

David grinned. "Cute, O'L, real cute. But don't you have to be rich or something to make the most eligible list?"

Janesha in records walked by on her way to the briefing room. "Take it from me, honey, money ain't everything." She kissed him loudly on the cheek. "Oh, no. Sugar like that beats money any day."

Those in the lobby burst into laughter along with David as the woman old enough to be his mother made a play at licking her lips then sashayed from the room. "Mmmm, mmmm."

David raised his hands. "I have it on good authority that Jan is prejudiced. Three years ago I threatened to arrest her landlord when he wanted to evict her for having a cat."

"Always were a sucker for the ladies, weren't you, McCoy?" O'Leary called back.

"I don't have to stand here and take this abuse, you know. In fact, I won't. I'm going to the locker room to change. Anyone have any objections?"

There were a couple of colorful responses, then David shook his head and stepped down the hall toward the showers. He was halfway there when Lieutenant Kowalsky stepped from out of one of the offices and blocked his way.

David's smile melted into a grimace. At least this time he hadn't literally run into the man. "Hey, Kow, you officially off the clock yet?" He realized his mistake even before his superior's eyeballs nearly popped out of his head in surprise. "Oh, geez, sir, I'm sorry. I didn't mean any disrespect—"

"Unlike some people that'll go unmentioned, I'm never off the clock, Officer McCoy."

"Of course, sir."

Kowalsky's sudden warm grin nearly knocked him backward. "And it's quite all right to call me Kow, David. That was my nickname in the service. Been a while since anyone's had the guts to use it, though. Brings back some memories."

David released a long sigh of relief. "For a minute there I was afraid you were going to knock me into the middle of next week."

"For a minute there, I thought I was, too." Kow put his arm across his shoulders. "Come on, I'll walk you to the locker room."

David watched the man he'd declared enemy long ago out of the corner of his eye. If he didn't know better, he'd think Kow was getting sentimental on him. Must be something in the punch. Then again, he doubted the six foot five man ever touched liquor. Or if he did, it would probably take the entire contents of two heavily spiked punch bowls to even begin to intoxicate him.

Kowalsky cleared his throat. "I heard what you did down

on V Street this morning, McCoy. Good job. I just want you to know that I'm making a special note of it in my report."

"Sir?"

"The way you pulled in all the kids from the youth center to work the soup kitchen. I hear it was a great success."

David felt the tips of his ears heat. "Oh, that." He cast a wary glance down the hall. "Don't let word get around. I'm having a hard enough time taking the teasing now, sir."

Kow laughed and gave his shoulder a brief squeeze before releasing him. "Don't let 'em bust your balls, McCoy. You know what you're doing. That's all that matters."

"How about you, sir? You ever play sports?"

"Sports?"

David reveled in his ability to catch his superior off guard. "Yeah, you know. Basketball? Football?"

"I used to be pretty damn good in the boxing ring."

David tried to imagine climbing into a ring and facing him. The image would probably give him nightmares for days. "We could probably use someone with your experience down at the center. You know, if you have the time and all."

Kow's smile widened into a grin. "I'll give it some thought, boy. I'll give it some thought." His gazed flicked over him as if reassessing an earlier opinion. "Now go on, get changed and get back out here and join the party."

The lieutenant did a military style turnabout then marched back down the hall, leaving David staring after him completely dumbfounded.

For the second time in the past half hour, David found himself shaking his head. What else could possibly happen today? First he'd awakened to find Kelli's sweet little body snuggled against him in his own bed, her dog whining at him from where he had his head resting against his feet. Now this.

He didn't know what it was, but he mentally braced himself

for a fall. If there was one thing he'd learned early on, it was that with every good eventually came bad.

He caught sight of someone sitting across from his locker. Only it usually took the bad a little time to catch up.

"Hey, Pops," he called out, noticing the wariness laced through his voice.

Ever since he'd learned exactly who Kelli's father was he'd been avoiding Manchester and his father, not looking forward to having a conversation that was sure to get ugly. Too late, he realized that Marc must have spilled the beans.

Damn. It would have been nice to have a few more minutes to glow following Kow's unheard of praise. By the look on his father's face as he got up from the wood bench, it was going to be all downhill from there.

"Hey, yourself." He was still in uniform, still every bit the young cop David had a picture of on the wall at his apartment. He'd never gotten thicker around the middle. If anything, he looked in better shape now than he ever had. Of course, part of the reason for that might be his recent relationship with Melanie's mom, Wilhemenia.

He picked up his step, tossing his cap onto the top shelf of the locker, then hanging his coat. "Got something on your mind, Pops?"

"Yeah, actually I do."

David grimaced. "Figured it had to be something. You know, to bring you downtown and all."

"Yeah."

David glanced at him, curious as to why the old man hadn't gotten to the point yet. No one could say that Sean McCoy was at a loss for words when it came to something important to him. Lord knew he and his brothers had taken their share of tongue-lashings that could rival the world's best over the years. He turned back to his locker and took out his jeans and a green-and-red sweater that one of the women he had dated a couple years back had given him. It was hideous, but it fit the occasion. He held it up, thought of Kelli, and fought the urge to toss it into the garbage. He would have had he something else to wear.

"Can it wait until I catch a quick shower?"

Sean nodded, but his gaze was concentrated on his shoes. "I suppose."

It made him uncomfortable to see his father at a loss. "Okay. See you in a couple."

He stepped off to the showers, wondering exactly what his father had to say. And exactly when he'd get around to saying it.

KELLI STOOD sipping on the bitter punch, idly wondering how many guys had spiked it and just how potent the tepid liquid was. Someone should have a Breathalyzer waiting outside the station along with a row of taxis if the quick evaporation level of the bowl was anything to go by. Wrinkling her nose, she stepped to the soft drink table, tossed the contents of her plastic cup into the garbage then filled it with clear soda.

She turned and surveyed the room over the rim. She had hoped her father would be hanging around somewhere, but she'd been there for ten minutes and had yet to spot him. Given her lateness, she'd barely had time to stop off at the apartment and change. Having spent all day tottering on stiletto heels and confined in tight clothes she'd opted for a simple pair of dark green slacks with loafers and a cream colored blouse. While she wasn't as dressed up as some of the women there, at least she wasn't wearing anything that was blinking, flashing, or otherwise capturing attention. Right now she preferred just to blend into the background.

As she scanned the room again, she realized her father

wasn't the only one she was looking for. Somewhere David McCoy was probably wowing his coworkers with stories of his latest escapades. She had heard what he'd done at the soup kitchen already. Twice.

How in the hell was she supposed to guard her heart against a hotshot cop who could hold her all night without making a move, fix her breakfast and help neighborhood kids and the homeless? She picked up an overiced Christmas cookie and crunched off a bite. She'd initially been appalled by the magazine piece. Casanova Cop, indeed. But the more she thought about it, the more she sincerely believed that David McCoy deserved the better part of the attention he was getting.

Of course, she'd never tell *him* that. The guy already had an ego the size of the Capitol building.

Besides, she didn't think she needed to tell him anything. What he did, he did because he enjoyed doing it, not because he got off on the publicity. If anything, he seemed somewhat embarrassed by the attention. At least when you looked past the grin and paid attention to his ears, which had a tendency to redden when he was embarrassed—yet another endearing detail she had come to learn about him.

Of course if it were up to Kojak, who she'd had to drag from David's apartment that morning, she'd be marrying the guy next week.

She nearly choked on the dry cookie. Turning away from the group next to her, she coughed her way through it, then took a long sip of soda.

Where had *that* thought come from?

"Wrong pipe?"

She swiveled around to find none other than her father standing next to her, looking everywhere but at her. Had he said anything else she might have thought he'd spoken to someone else.

"Yeah. Cookies are, um, a little dry." She gave another glance around, this time furtively. If David *was* around somewhere, she hoped he didn't choose now to pop up. She'd asked her father to come to the party before she'd spent last night with David and hadn't exactly expected to be on speaking terms with the Casanova Cop tonight, much less… What terms *were* they on?

Her father nodded in a stiff way that made her want to groan. Either that or whack him in the arm until he stopped being such a mule.

"Glad you could make it," she said quietly.

He finally looked at her. "Glad you invited me. Even if it was via my answering service."

She grimaced. "Yeah, well, I'd have done it directly if you'd have returned any of my phone calls." She bit down hard on her tongue. This line of conversation wasn't going to get them anywhere. "Sorry," she said quietly.

His eyes softened briefly. "Me, too."

The tension in her shoulders melted away so quickly she nearly slouched in relief. "If that was an apology, then I accept."

His gaze flicked over her smiling face. "I don't want you to get me wrong, Kelli Marie. I am apologizing, but not for what you think I am."

She considered him. "I'm not sure I get you. What *are* you apologizing for, then?"

"For not returning your calls. No matter what happens, it's important to remember that…well, you know."

You and me against the world, kid. It's just you and me against the world.

How was she supposed to argue with that?

She looked away, covertly blinking back tears. He hated it when she cried. She'd learned that very young. Then again, maybe it was time she stopped hiding things from him. She purposefully tipped her chin up, letting him see the tears in her eyes.

He stubbornly looked away.

She took a long sip of her soda then cleared her throat, silent until she'd regained control over her emotions. "Just so I'm straight on this, what you're not apologizing for is everything else."

That drew his gaze back.

"You're still against my working on the task force," she clarified.

He sighed. "Yes."

"You still want to see David McCoy banished from the face of the earth."

His jaw tightened. "Along with that low-down, no-good father of his."

"And you don't think there was anything wrong with your calling me 'girl.'"

He looked suddenly exasperated. "I've called you 'girl' for years, Kelli. Why does it bother you now?"

"Because you said it differently, that's why."

"What?"

"You know what I mean. And if you don't, you need to figure it out." She held her hand up. "Okay, I'll indulge you. Do you want an example of what I mean?"

His eyes narrowed. "It looks like you're going to give it to me whether I want you to or not."

She ignored that. "Repeat after me. 'I only want the best for you, girl.' Then say it again substituting the word 'honey.'"

He didn't utter a word.

"Dad—"

"Okay, okay." Lowering his voice, he repeated the sentence.

"See how the two words 'girl' and 'honey' are interchangeable? Good. Now repeat this one. 'You don't know what you're talking about, girl.' And do the same thing with the word 'honey.'"

He didn't do it.

"You can't, can you? Because the meaning isn't the same."

He released a long-suffering sigh. "God, I've raised a monster."

She cracked a smile. "No, Dad, you didn't. You raised a person who expects respect. Even from you."

An unfamiliar something shone from his eyes. For a moment she thought it was the very respect she'd been after.

"Now, about the other issue…"

He quickly held up a hand. "Can it hold? I'm really not up to discussing that now…honey."

She laughed. "Sure. We can discuss it later. Just so long as we agree to discuss it."

"Good."

"Great."

She hooked her arm through his, giving it a squeeze. Lowering her voice, she said, "Does this mean you're going to go back to calling me every hour on the hour?"

He gave her a warning glance.

"Good. I've missed those calls."

BACK IN THE locker room, David sat forward on the bench, trying to absorb everything his father had just entrusted to him. Twenty minutes of detail-loaded monologue that left his head swimming. He frowned at his father where he sat next to him. "That's what all this is about? This whole feud thing between you and Garth Hatfield? Because he used to date Mom?"

Sean's face grew unbelievably red. "He didn't just used to date her. He tried to steal her from me."

"While you two were partners."

"Yeah."

David scratched his head, then ran his fingers through his still damp hair. "I don't get it. You and Mom got married despite what you think Hatfield did, right? So why still the bad blood?"

"Because Garth tried—"

"Yeah, yeah, I got it the first time, Pops. Because Garth tried to steal her from you." He leaned back and studied the ceiling. "Let's see, here it is thirty-something years—"

"Thirty-eight."

"Okay, thirty-eight years and five kids later in your case, and a marriage and another kid in his, and you're still holding this grudge." He threw up his hands in exasperation. "Hey, makes perfect sense to me."

"I knew you'd understand once I explained everything."

David grimaced. "That was said tongue-in-cheek, Pops. It doesn't make *any* sense, especially considering how close it looks like you two might have been."

"We were never close," he said vehemently.

"Yeah, right. That's why you're still upset about all of this."

Sean looked at him, a very familiar shadow of sadness, of grief, coloring his eyes. "You just don't understand."

David sat forward again. "I want to, Pops. I really do." He sighed. "Look, maybe I...we both need some time to think this through. It was dumb of me to think a thirty-something—"

"Thirty-eight."

"Yeah. It was stupid of me to think I could undo in a half hour conversation what has been years in the making." He patted his father on the back. "Let's say we go out and have a drink, huh? I don't know about you, but after all this I sure could use one."

Sean smiled for the first time since David spotted him in the locker room. "So could I."

KELLI LAUGHED at a particularly ribald joke one of her fellow officers had just shared with her and her father, feeling completely at ease for the first time in far too long. She and her father were not only talking again, they were talking at the station, a place she had never dared talk about to her father before, simply because he wanted to forget where she worked. That he was here, that he was treating her like a work equal was saying a lot.

Then there was David. She and he…well, they were doing *something* again, and even if she didn't know exactly what that meant, that felt good, too.

"Merry Christmas, Chief Hatfield."

Kelli nearly dropped her soda at the sound of the familiar voice. In one split second it appeared everything was going to change.

She turned toward where David was addressing her father, his hand outstretched, a congenial smile on his face. "I don't know if you recall, but we have met before, however unofficially. I want to say what a pleasure it is to see you again."

Oh, God.

Kelli didn't know quite what to do. She was caught between wanting to launch herself at David, get him away from the immediate area ASAP and grabbing her father to keep him from doing anything rash. It didn't surprise her that her father completely ignored David's hand. It didn't shock her that the entire room had just fallen completely silent. What did amaze her was that cool, calm and in control Garth Hatfield pulled back his arm as if in slow motion, then hauled off and punched David right in the jaw.

CHAPTER ELEVEN

IN THE MIDDLE of the briefing room floor, David propped himself up on his elbows, staring at the huge man who had just clocked him. Wow. Garth Hatfield might be an old guy, but he still packed a helluva wallop. Maybe he'd have to rethink his entire approach to this whole Hatfield and McCoy feud, because there was obviously more bad blood here than he'd realized.

"Why you…" Pops emerged from the crowd that had gathered, zooming in on his archenemy like a gang member out for blood. A unified gasp went up as Kelli stepped in front of her father and David scrambled to his feet to stop his father. As much as he'd like to see Pops get some payback, this thing had already gone far enough already. And two days before Christmas even.

David noticed several of his closer coworkers, including Kow, step up ready to provide reinforcements.

Pops struggled against him. "Let me at 'im, David. Nobody sucker punches a son of mine and lives to tell the story."

Garth strained against Kelli's blocking arm. David looked down to where she had her leg ready to trip him up should he try to go any further. "No son of yours touches my little girl without paying the price."

David slanted a glance at Kow who raised a brow and looked between him and Kelli. Damn. So much for keeping that little detail a secret.

Sean McCoy looked ready to pop his lid. He jabbed a finger in Garth's direction. "You've been angling for this for a long time, Hatfield. And I'm only too happy to give it to you."

"*I've* been angling for this? What about you, McCoy? I wouldn't be surprised if you put your son up to this just to get back at me."

"Yeah, well, maybe I did. Lord knows it would serve you right, you pigheaded, self-absorbed, sorry excuse for a chief."

This time it was Kelli's brows that rose. David groaned. "That's enough, Pops. This isn't the time or the place for this." He stumbled a couple of steps backward, his father's strength and determination proving more of a match for him than he thought possible. "Now tell the good man here that you didn't put me up to anything."

Sean finally stopped struggling and stepped back. He pulled the ends of his uniform jacket down to straighten it. "I'll do no such thing."

"Now, Pops—"

"Let the man speak, boy," Hatfield ordered.

David grimaced as Kelli released her father and stood stiffly between the two men. "I think there's been enough talking done around here already. All those who agree with me, say 'aye,'" she called out.

A series of in sync "ayes" echoed through the suddenly quiet room, though David made out a couple wanting to see a fight.

Kelli grimaced. "Okay, I think it's time for you to go, Daddy."

Garth Hatfield first appeared ready to plow right through his own daughter, then dropped his gaze, his face flushing an even deeper shade of red. "I don't see why I have to go first," he mumbled under his breath, much like a five-year-old who'd just been involved in his first scuffle.

"You have to go first because I invited you here and you've just embarrassed me beyond belief so I am officially uninviting you." She lifted her hand and pointed at the door as if addressing that sulky five-year-old. "Go. Now."

Garth appeared ready to do exactly as she requested. With that done Kelli turned toward David and his father. David blinked at her, impressed, proud, and disgustingly turned on. "If you wish to press charges, Officer McCoy, I'd be more than happy to take the report."

"Report!" Garth shouted.

Without even turning, Kelli stomped her foot and pointed to the door.

David eyed his father. "Pops? Is it safe for me to let you go now?"

Sean McCoy stared after his adversary as he stormed from the room.

"It would be nice if you answered me, like, sometime today," David prompted.

As soon as Garth was gone, Sean seemed to deflate. He dragged in a deep breath then exhaled gustily. For the first time, it seemed, he looked at Kelli. And to David's disbelief, he smiled, however shyly. "I don't think my son will press charges Officer Hatfield. If it's all the same to you, this is something your father and I have to work out outside official channels."

"I think you both need to have your heads examined," David said under his breath, then grinned at Kelli's glare.

He made a production out of rubbing his throbbing jaw. "What?" he asked innocently enough.

Kow stepped up and faced the crowd. "Okay, folks, the fun's all over now. Go back about your business," he said. "And Merry Christmas."

David felt the most absurd need to laugh. Not a brief chuckle, but a side-clutching, hysterical kind of laugh that would leave him back on the floor, rolling to catch his breath.

"Come on, Pops," he said, putting his arm over Sean's shoulders. "I think that's our cue to get you out of here, too."

"McCoy!" Kow barked. "I think your father is capable of seeing himself home. You, Hatfield and I have some unfinished business."

TWO DAYS LATER, Kelli let herself into her apartment, closed the door, then stripped out of her shoes, stockings and dress as she made her way to her bedroom. Overjoyed that his daylong sentence to solitary confinement was at its end, Kojak followed her around, barking, bounding and sniffing after each item as she dropped it to the floor.

"Merry Christmas, Jack," she murmured, giving him a playful wrestle. "But if it's all the same to you, I'd prefer to stick with 'bah, humbug.'"

The two days since the humiliating incident at the stationhouse Christmas party felt like two weeks. Her head ached, her muscles twitched and she basically just wished the whole blasted holiday season were over so she would stop having to be so nice to everyone when she felt like growling.

First there had been the lecture on proper conduct by Kow that she and David had sat through in his office, away from the party crowd. He'd given it to them good, getting them to spill that they'd not only known each other before they were paired together, but that they'd been, um, somewhat intimately involved. Given Kelli's task force assignment, he'd said he'd let the situation slide for now, but that they had better be on their best behavior at the station for the next six months at least. So thorough had the lieutenant stripped a piece off of them that David had whispered that he didn't think it was a good idea if they left together, so they hadn't. And he hadn't shown up later at her place, either, as she'd hoped he would.

Speaking of the task force, everyone was fearful that the

D.C. Executioner had plans to play the Grinch—his own little gruesome Christmas gift to the citizens of D.C.—so they had instructed her and the other female officers working under-cover at area adult bookstores to request double shifts, and the survellience teams were put on extra alert. So yesterday, on Christmas Eve, she'd worked from 9:00 a.m. until 7:00 p.m., when Jeremy had shooed her home. That had been fine with her. Despite the fears she shared with the task force com-mander, she'd been bushed. She'd dragged herself home and straight to bed and hadn't even woken up again until after nine this morning. That meant she'd been late getting to her aunt's in Baltimore. And she hadn't had a chance to talk to either her father or David since the socking-in-the-jaw incident.

She sank down onto her bed and worked all the pins from her hair, sighing in relief. Sitting across from her sour-faced father all day had been a lesson in patience. No matter where she went, there he was, smack-dab across from her. Gift giving, across from her. Dinner, across from her. In the kitchen helping to clean up…the stylish island where the sink was located allowed him to sit across from her even then.

It would have been okay had he had something nice to say. But every time he'd opened his mouth some kind of under-handed jab was sent flying her way. From "I can't believe you'd side with that pissant over me," to "the way you're acting, you're no daughter of mine." Even her aunt had reached the bottom of her infinite well of patience and whacked him in the arm as they were leaving.

Yes, this was certainly one Christmas for the picture albums. There she would be rolling her eyes toward the ceiling with her father hovering somewhere on the fringes glowering at her.

Kojak whined and thrust his cold, slimy nose in the valley between her toes and the ball of her foot. She jerked back and laughed. "Oh, Kojak, you certainly know how to put things back into perspective, don't you, boy. Thank God I always have you." She rubbed him behind the ears, enjoying his soft murmurs of satisfaction. "Easy to please, you are. I can leave you alone all day and you'll still rush to the door, happy to see me. You couldn't give a hoot who I spent the time away with, or whether or not I worked at a brewery or on the force. Just so long as I throw a treat your way every now and again, you're putty in my hands."

She plopped back on the mattress and patted the comforter beside her. Kojak immediately jumped up, laying his head against her belly. She closed her eyes and patted him, wondering if this was how she was destined to lead her life. An old maid with a dedicated dog instead of a house full of cats.

Unbidden, an image of David McCoy unfurled in her mind, as handsome as all get out and larger than life. She smiled. She couldn't help herself. Whenever she thought of him hitting the floor and blinking at her father in undisguised shock, she felt like laughing. He'd been so damn cute. And so magnanimous. He'd taken the knock and gotten right back up. If his father hadn't lunged for hers, she wouldn't have been surprised if David had turned the other cheek then offered up his hand to her father again.

She had no idea what he had on tap for today. She knew he was scheduled to work last night, something about a favor for a friend. But he'd likely spent today at his family's.

She groaned and rubbed her nose. "You probably made a helluva first impression on Sean McCoy, Kell."

She wondered if the day had been as torturous for David as it had been for her. But she doubted it. She still couldn't believe Sean hadn't wanted his son to press charges. If the roles had been reversed, her father would have stopped at nothing to see that both McCoys were locked up well into the new year.

If she knew more about what had happened so many years

ago, maybe she could understand why these two men wanted to dance around a room like it was a boxing ring saying "put up your dukes, put up your dukes." But she knew no more now than she had a few days ago when her father first voiced his disapproval of David simply because of his relationship to a man he didn't like.

The sound of someone knocking at the front door snagged her attention. Kojak lifted his head and gave an experimental sniff. "What do you say, Jackie boy? Do we see if there's any Christmas spirit to be had and open it, or just lie here and pretend this is just like every other day and ignore it?"

Another sniff, then Kojak barked and ran toward the door. Kelli sighed. "I guess that means we open it."

Clad in only her black slip, she padded through the living room then peeked through her peephole.

Nothing.

Frowning, she leaned back, nearly tripping over Kojak. She looked down and watched a treat roll from under the door and stop right in front of the expectant pooch. Shaking her head, Kelli looked through the peephole again. Sure enough, David unfolded himself and grinned at her through the hole.

She unlocked the door, then opened it. "I hope he's not the only one you brought a treat for," she said, leaning against the jamb.

He held up his hands. "Guess you're going to have to settle for the package in front of you."

She grabbed his shirtfront and pulled him into the apartment. "You'll do."

He chuckled. "Wait a second. I was just joking."

She blinked at him as he ducked back into the hall and produced a red foil-wrapped package about the size of a shoebox.

"Oh, David, why did you have to go and do that? I didn't even think to buy you—"

He leaned forward and stole the words from her mouth with a searing kiss. "Don't worry, darlin'. This gift is for both of us."

"Ooo, chocolate?"

His gaze burned a trail down her exposed skin, reminding her of what she had on, which was not much. "No, but it's something almost as good." He pushed the door shut with his foot and came inside, shrugging out of his coat. "Though I'm more interested in exploring what's in your nicely dressed package."

She crossed her arms, deciding she was decently covered despite the indecent expression on his face. "I just got home."

"I know. I've been waiting outside for the past half hour."

"I'm impressed."

"Don't be. I used the time to catch a much-needed catnap." She headed toward the kitchen. "Can I get you something?"

"You got any nog?"

"As in eggnog?"

He grinned. "Yeah."

"No."

"Okay, a beer will do then."

"Well, since you didn't bring any, how do you feel about homemade hot chocolate?"

"Homemade? This, I've got to see."

She padded into the kitchen, unsurprised when he followed her. "So how did it go last night?" she asked.

"On the streets of D.C. on Christmas Eve? Let's just say a lot of creatures were stirring. Somehow I never get used to putting a Santa Claus behind bars."

She clucked her tongue. "Just think of all the kids that didn't get their presents this morning."

"I was more concerned with getting the drunk and disorderly Santa off the street before he completely ruined his reputation."

She laughed, then smacked his hand away from the

gourmet chocolate bar she'd taken from the cupboard. "There won't be enough for the hot chocolate."

"Looks like there's plenty there to me."

She popped a square into her own mouth. "Yeah, but that's for the cook."

He leaned forward. "You've got—" he kissed the corner of her mouth "—a little bit—" he drew his tongue the length of her lower lip "—right here." He kissed her fully, causing Kelli's knees to go as soft as the marshmallows on the counter. "Mmm. It tastes better on you."

She worked her fingers between their mouths then slid a chocolate square between his lips. "Yeah, and if you don't stop, I'm going to burn the milk and ruin my best pan."

He chuckled and munched on the treat. "Okay, I'll wait."

She narrowed her gaze playfully. "Just what do you have planned, Officer McCoy?"

He shrugged. "Not much."

He wandered out of the kitchen, Kojak following on his heels. Moments later the strains of Bing Crosby Christmas carols filled the interior of the apartment. She grimaced, remembering the frightful day spent at her aunt's where they'd been playing the same music. Then she realized he'd changed the channel, scanning for something else. Judging the milk warm enough, she dropped the chocolate squares in one at a time, finishing as a bass thrumming, bluesy song reached her ears. It took her a minute to recognize the same Christmas carol played in a completely different way. A tiny thrill shimmied down her spine. Trust David to somehow make even Christmas Day sexy.

She smiled, then dipped her finger into the pan. She started to pop it into her mouth when David curled his fingers around her wrist and slid it into his mouth instead. "Mmm. This just might be worth waiting for," he said, drawing her finger into the depths of his mouth again.

Kelli watched his decadent lips curve around her knuckle. She was mesmerized, not just by the action itself, but by the man.

As she licked her own suddenly scorched lips, she wondered at everything that went into making one certain David McCoy. She just wasn't the type to fall into such an intimate relationship. It had taken her and Jed six weeks before they made it to bed the first time, then the second had come a month after that. She wasn't exactly sure why she was overprotective when it came to matters of intimacy. It could be Brontë's poor track record. Or it could be that somehow the lack of closure in her own mother's death made her overly wary of opening her heart to anyone. But she realized that with David, all her defenses melted on command. More specifically *his* command.

He dragged his mouth from her finger. "I, um, think something's burning."

She swallowed hard. "Yeah, me."

Her hands trembling, she removed the pan from the heat then poured the contents into two extra large mugs. Then came a handful of tiny marshmallows, whipped cream, and chocolate shavings.

She picked up both mugs.

"What, no cherries?" David asked.

"This is hot chocolate, not an ice-cream sundae." She couldn't help smiling. "But if you want, there's a jar in the cupboard next to the fridge."

He followed her into the living room, palming the extra large jar of maraschinos. "I knew you were my kind of gal."

Kelli laughed softly. "They, um, were on sale."

"Uh-huh."

He plopped down on the oversize couch next to her after she had placed the overflowing mugs down on the table. She tucked her legs under her, then picked up her mug, motioning for him to do the same. She noticed with interest that he left the cherries untouched. Once he was facing her, mug raised, she gently touched hers against his and said, "Here's to Christmas being over this year."

David's blue eyes twinkled. "Here's to the real festivities beginning."

She sipped hers and he did the same, licking the cream from his lips with heavenly abandon. "Now that's what I call hot chocolate."

Kojak whined at her feet. Kelli curved the fingers of her other hand around her mug then reached down to pat him. "What is it, K? Feeling a little left out?" She glanced toward David. "Watch this." She cleared her throat, then removed her hand. "Okay, you can open your gift now."

She had barely finished her sentence when Kojak charged the tree in the corner at full speed, his skid pushing in the tree skirt. He nosed through the few gifts left there, then came up with his. Growling, he locked his meaty jaws around it, then whipped it back and forth, sending the loose wrapping flying. In no time at all he was stretched across the floor chomping down on his own pooch chocolate chew.

Kelli smiled at David who was chuckling. "Quite a kid you've got there, Hatfield."

"Yeah, I'm pretty proud." Despite her guilt at not having bought him anything, her gaze kept trailing to the present sitting on the edge of the coffee table nearer to him. "So are you planning on letting me open that or not?"

"It's not that type of gift."

"And what type is that?"

"The kind you unwrap and display on your mantel for all to see."

"Ah, so it's something you wear?"

"Well, kind of."

She squinted at him. "Either it is or it isn't."

"Okay, then, it isn't."

She stretched her legs out, tucking her feet under his muscular thigh. "I think that deserves some explanation."

He followed the curve of her leg up from heel to knee to the hem of her black slip. "Let's just say it's the kind of gift better experienced."

Kelli closed her eyes and groaned. "Considering where I'm assigned, I'd suggest you not leave things to my imagination."

He grinned. "Then I won't. Go take a shower."

She wrinkled her nose. "Huh?"

"I said go take a shower." He dropped a kiss to her bare knee, then swirled his tongue along her skin and kissed her again. "Not that you need one, mind you. I just need to buy some set-up time."

"Set-up time—"

He slid his hand up the inside of her leg until his fingertips were mere millimeters away from her panties. "Has anyone ever told you that you ask too many questions?"

"Yeah," she whispered. "You."

He swept her feet down until they were resting on the rug. "Uh-uh. No matter how incredibly sexy you are, you are not going to sidetrack me. Now go on. I need at least fifteen minutes."

She got up and slowly began making her way toward the bathroom. "Fifteen minutes, huh?"

"Yep."

"Should I wash my hair?"

"Nope."

"Then I can be done in five."

He eyed her over the rim of his mug of hot chocolate. "Ten."

"Deal."

She rushed to the bathroom and closed the door. She hadn't felt this giddy since...well, since she couldn't remember when. Maybe when she was about five and still believed in Santa Claus. She stripped down and climbed into the shower, only to reach out a minute later dripping wet to fumble for the fragranced soaps Bronte had given her for her birthday that she'd used only for decoration until now.

She was quickly blotting herself dry in a cloud of steam when a knock sounded at the door. It opened a crack and David's hand appeared through it. "Here. Put this on."

She took the scrap of black silk and turned it one way then the next. "Uh, David, I don't think this is going to cover me."

His chuckle reminded her that he had yet to close the door. "I hope not. It's a blindfold."

"Oh." Then it hit her. "A blindfold. David, I don't—"

"Just put it on, Hatfield. Oh, and as sexy as the little slip is, leave it, okay?"

A delicious shiver of anticipation slithered down her back. What exactly did he have planned?

"Is it on yet?"

She hurriedly tucked the towel, and nothing but the towel, around herself, then smiled. "No."

"Well, get hopping already, Hatfield. Sheesh."

She carefully tied the blindfold around her head, leaving just a slit to look out of. "Okay."

She heard the door open completely, then saw his bare feet as he entered the room, though the hem of his jeans told her he was at least still partially dressed. "Nice try," he said. "Turn around."

She played at a groan as he fastened the blindfold more securely. No matter how hard she tried, she couldn't make out a thing through the dark fabric.

"There." He grasped her shoulders and swiveled her back around. "God, you smell good."

Kelli fought the need to put her hands out in front of her

as he led her back out into the living room. It was so odd to move through her apartment, knowing it was her apartment, but still not knowing exactly where everything was with her eyes closed. She felt something warm on the back of her leg, then that same something swept up and cupped her bottom. She gasped, realizing it was David's hand.

His chuckle sounded above her ear. "Sorry. I couldn't resist."

"Just don't do it again," she whispered. "I thought it was Kojak for crying out loud."

"K's in the kitchen for the duration."

"Oh."

Funny how everything smelled differently with the blind-fold on. Scents she normally didn't pay any attention to now stood out in stark relief. She picked up the tang of lemon fur-niture polish. The pine of the small tree. She swore she could even make out the chocolate in the mugs probably still on the coffee table.

"Hold up," he told her.

She stopped, then put her foot out, feeling that same coffee table. Only it wasn't where it was supposed to be. He'd ob-viously moved it.

"This way," he said, gently gripping her elbow.

The scent of something strong and pungent reached her nose and she wrinkled it. "What's that?"

"What's what?"

"That smell."

He tugged on the bottom of her towel. She gasped and grabbed the top. "You'll find out soon enough." He maneu-vered her so she was facing him. "Now, feel the cushion behind you? I want you to sit down on it."

What was her sofa cushion doing on the floor? And what was it covered with? She slowly did as he asked, trying to keep the towel wrapped around her.

"Oh, and you won't be needing that."

With a quick swoosh, he took the towel from around her.

Kelli blindly groped for it, feeling more than naked. She felt suddenly very, very vulnerable. She reached for the blindfold.

"Uh-uh." David caught her hands, coming to sit beside her. "You're beautiful, Kell. Just trust me, will you?"

"Trust you? First you blindfold me like some—"

His mouth, sizzling and wet, trapped the rest of her words in her mouth. She tried to protest, then his tongue flicked out, played along her lips, then plunged into the depths of her mouth. She groaned and collapsed, boneless and towel-less, against him.

After long moments, he dragged his mouth from hers, his breathing ragged. "If we keep on like that, I'll never see this through."

"See what through?" she whispered. "David, let me take off—"

"Here," he said, ignoring her and pressing her back on the cushion. Only she realized it wasn't just one cushion, but probably every cushion and pillow in the apartment, covered by some sort of silky fabric. She tried to peek out from under the blindfold but it was still very much in place.

"You have the most incredible mouth," David murmured, then kissed the side of it. Kelli turned her head to meet him straight on, then felt his breath on the other side. Frustrated, she trapped his head between her hands and brought him down for a deep, soul-searching kiss.

He chuckled softly as he drew back. "I knew I should have tied your hands."

She started to lift herself up. "David, I'm not sure I like—"

"Shhh." Then his mouth was on her breast. She gasped as he swirled his tongue around the instantly hard tip then pulled it deep into his mouth, seeming to manipulate cords that stretched down to between her legs. She lay against the cushions and arched her back. He drew away, then ran his hands the length of her arms, lifting them above her head. "Now that's more like it. Stay just…like that."

His weight shifted away from her. There was that smell again. Kelli curled her hands into the sleek material above her head.

"Now this may be a little cold," he murmured.

"What may—" She drew in a ragged breath as something brushed against her other breast. A tiny little flick of something…wet. Something cold and wet. Definitely not his mouth. Her nipple instantly responded, growing hard and achy even as the first flick was followed by another. Then another. Then the flicks turned into curved swirls.

Kelli clutched the fabric above her head for dear life, feeling the growing heat between her legs compensate for the cold of the substance. David moved to the other breast, doing the same there, not satisfied until she was trying to force a more solid contact. Then he shifted and moved in ever-widening circles until her entire chest was covered with the cold matter. Kelli thought she would go insane with pleasure. She went from being completely relaxed to wondrously excited as he painted her—somewhere in the thick cloud of desire that fogged up her mind she had realized that's what he was doing.

He drew a slow, cold, languid trail down the middle of her stomach. She sucked in air as he circled her navel, then filled it with the cold, wet substance.

"What…what is that?" she whispered.

Then that something wet flicked against her most sensitive part and she gasped.

David's mouth was against her ear. "No questions."

An almost unbearable ache filled her belly, threatening to consume her with need. She quickly nodded. "Okay…okay. No questions."

Another flick and she nearly climaxed right then and there. "No words either."

Kelli pressed her lips tightly together, drawing quick, rapid breaths in from her nose until her need for air demanded she open her mouth.

Again, he was on her stomach, drawing long, languorous lines down to her hips. The mere movement alone seemed to concentrate all her thoughts there, all her heat, until she was afraid she would cry out from the exquisite pleasure of it all.

He drew the wetness down the inside of one thigh, then up the other, then down again, until her legs were covered. The wanton that apparently dwelled deep within her emerged, and she inched her legs open.

"Good...girl." David's voice was husky and his own breathing sounded nearly as irregular as hers.

Questions filled Kelli's mind, but she was rendered completely speechless, trapped as she was in her black world of pure, sensual sensation. Of smell, of touch, of sound.

Earlier, he'd asked her to trust him. And in that telling moment, she realized she did. Completely. Utterly. Irreversibly. With every flick of his brush, he did away with another of the sexual walls she'd spent so much of her adult life erecting. With each skillful touch, he prepared her for an ecstasy she could only wonder at. She was his to do with what he pleased and she had faith that he would do only that which would bring her joy.

The brush swiped across the bud nestled between her thighs again. She cried out, instantly climaxing. Pleasure rippled along her taut muscles, surprising her with their intensity as she clasped her thighs together. Long moments later, she sank back against the cushions as the golden sensations subsided, the sound of her panting filling her ears.

David's voice was low and gravelly as he tsked at her. "Now

look what you've gone and done. You've, um, gotten my...work all wet. I'll just have to clean up and start all over again."

She knew instantly that the something touching her now was David's mouth lapping up the edible paint. Her back came up off the pillows. His tongue burrowed through her damp curls. He followed the shallow crevice of throbbing flesh, each touch of his tongue like the flick of flames. Then his fingers were spreading her and he swirled his tongue around her swollen core. She whimpered uncontrollably, breathlessly begging him to come to her, to end the exquisite torture. Then he took a more intense taste, pulling her deep into his mouth. Another climax threatened to follow quickly after the last. She went rigid in preparation when all too abruptly, his heat was gone.

Kelli's panting sounded foreign to her own ears as she sank back, utterly boneless against the makeshift bed.

"You even taste like a peach," David said so softly she nearly didn't hear him. He ran his finger along the length of her. "There. All clean."

She blindly reached out, desperate to feel him inside her, filling her, needing to share her pleasure with him. But he hovered just beyond reach.

"Shhh," he murmured. Something rested against her lower lip. She opened her mouth and she immediately recognized the smooth skin and sharp tang of a cherry. She chewed slowly, then turned into David's kiss.

"I'll be there soon enough, Kell," he whispered. "Just relax."

The brush again flicked against the crux of her heat. She shuddered from the contrast between hot and cold.

"Please," she whimpered, her legs thrashing wildly even as he tried to hold them in place.

"Almost done," he whispered, giving another feather-light flick. "There."

For long moments Kelli lay there, hearing nothing but the sound of her own breathing. In and out. In and out. Where was he? She hadn't heard him leave. And he wasn't touching her anymore. Where was he?

"David?" She anxiously licked her parched, swollen lips.

Then his mouth was on hers and he was kissing her. Madly. Deeply. Completely. Instinctively, Kelli tilted her hips up, seeking contact with his body, but she found nothing but air.

"Lie still," he commanded softly.

She immediately did as he asked. Then she was rewarded a moment later with the feel of his fingers on the blazing, hungry flesh between her legs, the unmistakable sound of a foil packet being torn open, followed by a deep thrust that found him inside her.

She cried out and reached out to clutch him. Either he had forgotten his command, or he was as out of his mind with pleasure as she was, but he didn't fight her when she clutched his back, pulling him full against her, grinding her hips upward against him.

She didn't think she'd ever feel this kind of excruciating bliss ever again.

Then he began to move in and out of her with long, powerful thrusts and she was proved a liar.

"You feel so damned good," David groaned.

And she was a goner. The world behind her blindfold exploded into a million different colors. David increased the pace of his rhythm, driving deeply into her again and again and again, drawing out her orgasm to unbelievable proportions, until he, too, went rigid and shouted out her name.

It could have been minutes later. It could have been hours. But as Kelli lay there flesh on flesh, flesh in flesh with David, she knew one thing for certain. She'd never be the same woman again.

She felt David shift. "Turn your head," he whispered into her ear. She did so, and he untied the blindfold, slipping it from in front of her eyes. She blinked, finding the room awash in candlelight and the colored lights from the tree. And to find herself painted from neck to toes in black and red paint. He'd traced licking red flames from the tips of her breasts down to the apex of her thighs.

"Merry Christmas, Kell," he murmured, kissing the side of her mouth. "And it's not over yet. Just think…now it's time to do the other side." He withdrew from her, then cupped her womanhood almost roughly in his hand. "Do you have any idea how much you make me want you?"

She reached out and curled her fingers around his already hardening erection. "If it's anything like the way you make me want you, then I think I have a clue."

He groaned, tightened his hand over hers, then gently removed them both. He began to turn her over. Kelli only too willingly helped, reveling in the satiny feel of the fabric and paint against her breasts, then blindly, insatiably thrusting her bottom into the air, longing for him to be back inside her…*now.*

The sharp chirp of ringing sliced through the intoxicating atmosphere. It took two full rings before Kelli realized that it, indeed, was the telephone. To think, somewhere out there beyond the windows, the world continued to turn. It seemed impossible.

"Ignore it," David ordered. He pulled her down on the cushions so that her legs were on either side of his where he knelt behind her.

Then another ringing acted as a shrill counterpoint to the ringing of her phone. She slowly came to understand that it was his cell phone.

David groaned, his hands still against her ankles.

"Ignore it," she told him.

She felt his absence before she saw it, and instantly wanted to pull him closer. She looked over her shoulder to find him fishing his cell phone out of his coat pocket. He closed his eyes and muttered a curse. "Sorry, Kell, I can't. My sister-in-law Mel is on labor watch."

Kelli slowly got up onto her knees, reluctantly dragging the towel to cover herself.

"Hello?" A moment later, David covered the mouthpiece. "It's her. They're taking her to the hospital right now." Into the phone, he said, "You guys have impeccable timing, you know?"

Kelli moved to pick up her own phone, which was on something like its tenth ring. "Hello?"

Her father's voice rang out loud and clear. "What the hell is McCoy doing up there?"

Kelli started and pulled her towel closer, feeling suddenly all too exposed, too vulnerable. "Where are you?" She turned around as if half-expecting to find him in the room.

"Parked on the street."

David hopped into his jeans, then put his boots on. He came up behind her and put his hand over the mouthpiece. "Put your clothes on, you're coming with me."

"Daddy? You and I are going to have to talk about this later. We're going to the hospital."

CHAPTER TWELVE

DAVID RUSHED into the hospital waiting room that was filled to the rim with McCoys, then realized he was missing something. Ducking back into the hall, he grasped Kelli's hand then tugged her in along with him.

"David!" Little Lili called, flinging her four-year-old body into his arms.

"Whoa there, Princess," he said, sweeping her up into his embrace. He was aware of a sudden silence as his brothers Connor, Jake and Mitch and his two sisters-in-law Michelle and Liz stared openmouthed at Kelli, but he chose to ignore it. He instead focused on his blond niece, Jake's adopted daughter. She was by far the easiest to deal with. She wouldn't look at him like he'd grown two heads just because he'd brought a woman along with him. "Lili, I'd like you to meet Kelli. Kelli, this is Lili."

"Hi, Kelli," his niece said, bestowing her with one of her urchin grins. Kelli returned the greeting. "Uncle David, you should have seen Aunt Melanie." She cupped her hands over his ears then said in a loud stage whisper, "She said all kinds of bad words in the car that Papa says she shouldn't have said, but that she was hurting real bad, 'cause my cousin is trying really, really hard to come out, and Aunt Liz said it's like trying to fit a watermelon through a mouse hole."

In the corner, Liz reddened, and the rest of them burst out

laughing. David looked back down at his niece, tucking strands of her near-white hair behind a tiny ear. "Actually, I like the stork story a little better. Don't you?"

Michelle, Lili's mother, moved to stand before Kelli. "Hello," she said in her nicely Americanized French accent. "My name is Michelle."

"Um, hi," Kelli said, clearly uncomfortable.

"Why don't you come with me, Lili," Michelle said. "You still have that picture to finish for Aunt Melanie."

"Oh, yeah!" The energetic little girl wriggled to be let down. "You think she'll like it?"

Michelle smiled. "Sure, why not? Everyone likes to see a picture of themselves caught at their red-faced worst."

"Speaking of red-faced." Liz got up from where she was sitting and introduced herself to Kelli, as did Connor, Jake and Mitch. David noticed that Pops stayed off to the side, not needing introductions, but not appearing upset by the surprise addition to the group.

Kelli smiled somewhat nervously. "There are so many of you."

David curved his neck to look out into the hall. "And Marc?"

Mitch hooked his thumb toward the window. "I'm surprised you didn't see him when you came in."

David stepped to the wall-long stretch of glass to look outside. Three floors down, Marc's gaze was plastered to the window as he paced about ten feet, then paced back again, his hands thrust into his jeans pockets as light snow swirled around him.

"The expectant father?" Kelli asked softly.

David grinned. "Yeah."

"What's he doing down there?"

"Long story. You see Marc has a bit of trouble with hospitals." David shook his head then turned back toward his family. "Melanie must be fit to be tied."

Connor grimaced. "You don't want to know. Marc will be lucky if she doesn't toss his cowardly butt into the street after all is said and done."

"Ouch."

"Yeah."

KELLI'S MUSCLES were pulled tighter than a towrope. She didn't belong here. Not in this room with this incredibly warm, incredibly *large* family who were sharing a very special time in their lives. She'd known David had four brothers and that three of them had just recently married, but she hadn't thought ahead to when she might actually meet them. Her gaze flicked to where Sean McCoy was awfully quiet in the corner. No, she didn't belong here at all.

She tugged on David's shirtsleeve. "Um, can I talk to you…in the hall?"

He seemed to understand the seriousness of her request. "Sure."

She led the way out as David excused them, then turned as soon as they were out of sight. "I don't belong here," she blurted. "I think…well, don't you think it would be a good idea if I left?"

He skimmed her arm with his hand, reminding her that just underneath her heavy burgundy wool turtleneck sweater and jeans the entire front of her body was covered with body paint. "Kelli, you belong here because I want you here."

"Yeah, but—"

"Kelli Marie, I demand to know what's going on here this very minute."

Kelli's heart leapt up into her throat at the sound of the commanding voice booming down the hall. She didn't have to turn to know that her father must have followed them from her apartment and was even now bearing down on them. She could read it all in David's shocked expression. Could feel it in the dread lining her stomach.

He drew to a halt next to her. "Are you planning on answering me, girl?"

She rolled her eyes toward the ceiling. "David…could you…I mean, would you mind waiting for me in the other room?"

His gaze scanned her face, looking more concerned than she could deal with right now. Finally, he nodded. "I'll be in there. You know, if you need anything."

"What could she possibly need from you, McCoy?"

Kelli planted her palms against David's chest. "Just go. I'll be okay."

He reluctantly did as she asked. As soon as he had rounded the corner, she turned on her father. "How dare you follow me here!"

"How dare I? What did you expect me to do after you tell me you're going to the hospital, then hang up in my ear? Good God, girl, I thought there was something wrong. I spent the past fifteen minutes stalking the emergency room and grilling the nurses there, but no sign of you. Then it occurred to me that since you came with…with that McCoy that it might be something related to him. That's when I found out that one of…them is delivering a baby."

Kelli kept her gaze steady on him. "David's sister-in-law is having the baby, Dad. And it's Sean's first biological grandchild."

His gaze dropped to the floor. "I don't care if Sean himself is giving birth, Kelli."

She curved her hands into tight fists, willing the growing tension in her muscles away. "So then what do you want?"

"I just told you—"

"No, Dad. You explained why you followed me—us—to the hospital. You didn't say anything about what you were doing sitting outside my apartment at ten o'clock at night."

She didn't think it was possible, but his reddened face flushed even further. He mumbled something under his breath.

She crossed her arms over her chest. She nearly had a coronary when her sleeve budged up, revealing the paint there. She tugged at the woolen material, thinking that if she did have a heart attack, at least she'd have a valid reason for being there.

"Dad?"

He expelled a deep breath. "I came to apologize."

Kelli's brows shot up high. "What?" she whispered.

"I said I came to apologize, damn it. Don't act so surprised. It's not like I haven't apologized before, you know."

She nodded stupidly. "Right." She scratched her nose, regarding him cautiously. "Do you want to share exactly what you're apologizing for?"

"For God's sake, can't you figure that one out for yourself?"

She twisted her lips, standing firm.

"All right. I'm apologizing for giving you such hell for...well, you know, getting involved with that McCoy."

"David," she reminded him.

"Yeah, with David."

Kelli was surprised to find that as soon as the words were out, he seemed to relax. "I don't know. After the other night I've been doing a lot of thinking. I would have told you earlier, at your aunt's, but you kept avoiding me and, well, I didn't know quite how to say it. But I think I finally have it all figured out."

He paced a short ways away, then came back again. "All this, this feud with Sean...it's about more than just that we dated the same woman, David's mother. Much more." He violently thrust his fingers through his hair. "Aw, hell, Kelli, I don't know any other way to say this except to just say it. I'm responsible for your mother's death."

Kelli felt all the blood drain from her face. "What?" she whispered.

"Don't look at me that way. I wasn't the one who threw the blow that took her life…but I might as well have been." He dragged a shaking hand through his short-cropped hair then stared at the ceiling. "I don't even know how to put this so it makes some kind of sense." He looked directly at her. "I know it sounds stupid, but…well, in retrospect, doesn't everything? Even after all those years with your mother, I was still convinced in some juvenile, twisted way that I loved Kathryn Connor, David's mother. And I think your mother knew it. If she didn't know it, she suspected it. Not that she said anything. But I think that's what chased her into another man's arms."

Kelli's mind battled against the information. No. It couldn't be true. She remembered a delicate woman dedicated to her family, nurturing to her daughter, true to her husband. She pressed her fingertips against her temple. "Mom was having an affair when she was killed?" she whispered.

Garth Hatfield looked as though the weight of two worlds rested on his shoulders as he stepped toward a row of connected chairs and collapsed into one. He bent forward, cradling his head in his hands. When he spoke again, it was so softly she had to strain to hear him. "This is all so complicated, Kelli. I think it's why I never said anything, never talked about your mother until now. I always blamed myself, you know? It wasn't until after she was gone that I…" His voice broke and Kelli realized the big strong rock of a policeman that had always been her father was on the verge of breaking down.

She stood frozen to the spot, trying to make sense of what he was saying. Trying to make sense of how she felt about it. She slowly moved to sit next to him and gently put her arm around him.

He looked at her, his face filled with anguish. "It wasn't until after she was gone that I realized how damn much I really loved her. That focusing my attention on a woman I couldn't have was a way to protect myself from getting hurt by another woman. To keep her from leaving me. Ironic that my defense should be the very thing that chased her away."

She drew her hand down his back then up again. Emotionally, Kelli was ill-equipped to handle the upheaval of everything she'd believed was true about her family. About her father, her mother. So it was with a monumental force of will that she put the personal part of it aside and attempted to focus instead on the facts. If her mother had been having an affair, then her…lover was a suspect in her murder.

She swallowed hard against the bile rising in her throat. She'd lived with the facts surrounding her mother's death for so long that it was altogether difficult to fit the new, shiny piece into the puzzle. Though once she found the hole, it slid in easily. Her mind raced with the possibilities. Her heart pumped with the need to follow each and every one of them. To find the man who had so brutally taken her mother from her. To find the man who had robbed his father of his wife.

She bit down hard on her bottom lip, then released it. "Dad…did you know who she was…involved with?"

He shook his head. Though physically he sat right next to her, his face held a faraway expression as he stared off into a past she couldn't see. "No. And I never told anyone either." He fisted the hands resting in his lap. "In fact, I made sure that the guys at the station, and in homicide, never found out anything about the affair."

"But why?" she whispered. Doing so would have brought about a closure Kelli hadn't even dared dream of.

He looked at her pleadingly, the whites of his eyes strained and red. "Don't you see, Kelli? Even though I couldn't protect your mother in life, I could in death. It was better for it to have appeared that she was killed by a random attacker than everyone to know that she was murdered by her lover."

"Oh my God," Kelli whispered, slowly standing up. What he'd said made a perfect, demented kind of sense.

And turned everything she'd ever believed upside down.

"Oh my God," she said again.

They stayed that way for long minutes, staring at each other, coming to terms with what had just been revealed.

Garth shakily rose to his feet and moved toward the waiting room that held what seemed like a ton of McCoy muscle.

"Where are you going?" she asked, panic trying to wriggle through the shock engulfing her.

He looked at her, his face drawn into grim lines, as though he'd lost his wife now instead of eighteen years ago. "I'm going to do what I should have done a very long time ago. I'm going to apologize to the best friend I ever had. I only hope he'll forgive me."

Kelli watched him disappear into the room, her eyes brimming with tears. "He will, Dad," she whispered. "He will."

A SHORT TIME later, David slid his gaze from where Garth Hatfield stood talking to Pops quietly in the corner, to Kelli, who looked more pale than he'd ever seen her. He didn't know what had gone down in the hall, but whatever it was, Garth was talking to Pops and not threatening to take him out back and have at him. He scratched his head, still trying to figure that one out.

He leaned over to Kelli and whispered, "Are you all right?"

She looked a million miles away. Then his words seemed to register and she nodded her head. "I will be."

He began to ask what she meant by that when a resident dressed in blue scrubs poked her head in through the door. "Mr. McCoy?"

All five of the McCoys in the room answered, confusing her.

"Um, we're moving Mrs. McCoy to the delivery room now."

"Thanks," Mitch said. He pulled a cell phone out of an inside jacket pocket and pressed a speed dial number. David looked out the window to see Marc fumbling to answer his. "The time has arrived, Daddy. If you hope to be there for the blessed event, and I highly recommend that you are, then you'll conquer that stupid fear of yours and get up here now."

David could hear Marc shouting over the line before Mitch hit the disconnect button. In the parking lot below, he watched Marc nearly throw his cell phone into a snow bank, then shake his fist at the window. Then he stalked toward the building.

"I'll be damned. I think he's coming."

Connor grumbled. "Don't hold your breath. He's been coming for the past hour. Always chickens out at the last minute."

Jake chuckled. "He'll be lucky if he makes it for the next child born."

David stared at his older brother. This new, chatty, wise-cracking Jake was taking some getting used to. Michelle threaded her arm through his and took his hand, reminding David exactly why his brother had changed. He looked at Kelli and smiled, wondering at the changes she'd wrought in him. But given the anxious expression on her face, he didn't think now was the time to bring it up.

"You want to go get some coffee?" he asked instead.

She quickly nodded.

"Okay." His gaze swept the room. "Anybody else want anything?" He committed the large order to memory, then took Kelli's hand and began leading her from the room—only to be nearly mowed down by a frantic Marc.

"Where is she?" he demanded, looking like a caged animal. His gaze darted from wall to wall as if expecting them to close in on him at any second. Liz rushed forward to show him the way.

"Well, I'll be damned," Pops said from the corner.

KELLI WRAPPED her fingers around the steamy foam cup, willing the warmth to seep through to her bones. She'd never felt so cold in her life. It didn't help matters any that she shouldn't even be here. She longed instead to be home where she could slip into bed and pull the covers over her head until the world started making some sort of sense again.

David motioned toward a free table near the corner. "What about the stuff the others wanted?" she asked.

"They can wait a few minutes. I want to talk to you."

She frowned and slid into a chair he held out for her. He took the one across the table. It slowly began to dawn on her that he was acting a tad…odd. Ever since they left the waiting room, he'd looked a little preoccupied. As though he was nervous about something.

She blew on her coffee then took a long sip. "If you're going to ask what's going on between my father and yours—"

He shook his head. "No. Right now that's the last thing on my mind."

She set her cup on the table, though she didn't release it. "Then what is?"

There it was. That anxious expression again. The one that made him look like he was the expectant father rather than his brother Marc. And considering how manic Marc had appeared a few minutes ago, that was saying a whole lot.

He drew in a deep breath and sat back. "This isn't really what I had in mind when I planned to do this," he said softly. "But now that we're here…" He looked at his watch, causing Kelli to do the same. It was eleven-thirty. "Good. It's still officially Christmas."

Kelli grimaced. "David, what are you talking about?"

She watched as he reached into one side of his leather jacket, then the other. "I was supposed to do this after we'd, um, well, you know…at your place…" He extracted something. More specifically, a box. In particular, a ring-size box. He set it on the table between them.

Kelli's heart contracted painfully in her chest, making it impossible to breathe. Please…no. She was filled with an instant, incredible urge to run.

David got up and rounded the table. She could do little more than watch him wide-eyed, paralyzed, as he dropped to one knee beside her and placed his hands over hers that were nearly crushing the flimsy coffee cup. "Kelli Marie Hatfield, will you do me the honor of being my wife?"

She heard hushed murmurs from neighboring tables. Felt the leap of her own stomach. The warmth of his hands covering hers. And the undeniable swell of panic rush up into her throat.

She jerked her hands away from his and ran for the door.

"Kelli!" he called after her.

She was almost there.

He caught her arm and hauled her to face him.

She frantically searched his eyes. "What are you crazy, McCoy? I can't marry you." She realized her voice was near a shriek and fought to control it. "For God's sake, I hardly even know you."

His expression moved from confusion, to worry, then amusement. "Not exactly the response I was hoping for."

She shrugged his hand off her arm. "I really can't deal with this right now, David! In fact, with everything going on, I don't know if I'll ever be up to dealing with this. Certainly not tomorrow. Maybe not ever. Don't take it personally, okay?"

She turned and began walking away again, when he hurried

past to stop in front of her. "Don't take it personally? Did you really just say that. And just what exactly is that supposed to mean? Of course I'm taking it personally, Kelli. You just essentially ripped my heart out and stomped on it in front of God and everyone. Just how in the hell am I supposed to take it?"

She held up her hand, her head swimming with everything that had happened that night and was continuing to happen. "Everything is…I mean, this is…everything's just moving too fast, David. You're moving too fast."

He grinned. "All right then. So we'll set our wedding date for next year. Two years from now. I don't care."

She stared at him, openmouthed. "Are you paying attention, McCoy? I said I can't deal with this right now. Do you understand?" She began to maneuver her way around him, a sob welling up in her throat. "Why couldn't you just leave things the way they were?"

"Because I couldn't," he said softly, his words halting her more effectively than any physical touch. "I love you, Kelli Hatfield. And I want to spend the rest of my life with you. Another month together, another six months together, won't make that any clearer for me. In fact, I knew it the first moment I laid eyes on you back at that bar."

She blinked at him, hating him for saying what he was, hating her heart for responding so fully. She quickly erected an invisible defense against him, against his words, no matter how shoddily built the wall. "That's the trouble with you, David McCoy. You're so full of yourself not even you can see past your own ego. You make a decision, see something you want, and you charge in with your battle flag, intent on victory by any means necessary. You always have to be the best. The first man in. The one who saves the day." Her voice cracked. "You have to learn to see that second place doesn't always mean defeat. That every so often you have to step back in order to be the champion. That sometimes being the hero means letting someone else take the lead." Her gaze faltered and she looked down at her hands. "Life is not always about being a hotshot, David."

He looked at her as if he wasn't following her. "I don't get it, Kell. Is it so wrong for me to want you to love me in return? To need you to put me first? Above your assignment? Above the department? Above your damn career?"

"Yes," she murmured through a well of tears. "Yes, it is."

This time when she walked away, he let her.

CHAPTER THIRTEEN

"WHERE'S KELLI?

David had stumbled back to the waiting room on wooden legs, the ring box in his jacket pocket feeling like it weighed a ton. "Hmm?" He turned toward Garth Hatfield. It took him a moment to realize who he was looking at, and his immediate reaction was one of defense.

He forced himself to relax, finding nothing malevolent on the man's granite features as he asked again, "Where's Kelli? She stop off at the little girls' room?"

David looked down, unable to meet his eyes. Funny that, after all this, Garth Hatfield was now talking to him as though he accepted that he and Kelli were a couple. He could have gone without knowing that fate had a perverse sense of humor. "No. She, um, went home."

Garth cleared his throat. "Yeah, well, I had better get going, too." He said something to Sean about meeting for lunch tomorrow, then began to walk away. "Oh, and David? About the other night...I'm sorry, you hear?"

David could do little more than stare at him as Connor came up on his other side. "Apology accepted, Mr. Hatfield. Thanks for stopping by."

Garth frowned at David, then walked from the room. David became all too aware of his older brother hovering at his side, his gaze a little too watchful, a little too probing. "You all right?" he asked.

David blinked at him. "All right? Yeah, I'm fine. Never been better," he said, though he had never felt worse.

Connor's expression told him he wasn't buying a word, but David took advantage of the lapse in conversation and stepped to the corner of the room where Pops was now standing alone. If his gaze was a little intent on Mel's mom, Wilhemenia, who had apparently come in from Maryland and was standing just outside in the hall, David wasn't going to say anything. As he leaned against the wall next to his father, the old saying that misery loved company popped into his mind.

Sean's sigh caught his attention. "You look about as awful as I feel, kid."

David rubbed his hand over his face, the lack of sleep and the strange twist of circumstances catching up to him. "Ditto."

"You and that pretty young Hatfield hit a rough patch?"

David grimaced. "More like we just slammed into a dead end at full throttle." He dropped his hand to his side. "It wasn't pretty."

"What happened?"

"I asked her to marry me." He shrugged. "She said no."

Sean nodded as if what he'd just said made perfect sense. "I see."

The problem was that none of what had just happened made any kind of sense. Yesterday he'd wondered what the perfect Christmas gift would be for Kelli, and he hadn't hesitated when he thought of buying the emerald engagement ring now burning a hole in his pocket. Not even when the jeweler quoted him a price that normally would have sent him stumbling from the store. He wanted Kelli to be his wife. He wanted to propose to her on Christmas so that the day would be doubly special for them both from here on out. It was as simple as that.

Life is not always about being a hotshot, David.

Now what the hell was that supposed to mean? How did his proposing to her translate into his being a hotshot?

Michelle, sitting nearby, must have overheard what he and Pops were talking about because her head snapped in their direction.

Sean leaned closer. "You know, if you want to leave, everybody will probably understand." Pops cleared his throat and nodded to where Michelle was whispering something to Liz, who then grabbed Mitch's arm. David suppressed a groan. In thirty seconds everyone in the room would know what just happened. He didn't think he could deal with that right now.

"Thanks, Pops."

He began to step away when Sean caught his arm. "You know, it might be a good idea if, you know, you stopped off someplace on the way home. See if there's not something salvageable out of that wreck."

David frowned. "No way." He shrugged his shoulders. "I don't know." He sighed. "We'll see."

For the second time that night he walked out of the room and straight into his brother Marc. It was almost unbearable, the huge grin his brother wore. There was no indication of his deathly fear of hospitals, no sign of discomfort, no hint of his intense hatred for all things antiseptic. Instead he looked like a man who had just experienced one of the happiest moments of his life.

"It's a boy!" he shouted.

KELLI WAS completely numb by the time she finally returned home. Emotionally and physically drained. It had taken her half an hour to get a taxi back to her apartment, and the drive had seemed to take forever. The light, flaky snow that had been falling earlier had turned to rain, making the roads treacherous; the clouds and their seeping wetness mirroring the heaviness of her heart and the tears that slipped down her cheeks. Tears lost in the rain when she'd rushed from the cab to her doorway and gotten caught in the downpour. She didn't think she was capable of doing anything more than climbing into the bathtub, drinking the half bottle of cooking sherry she had left in the kitchen, then passing out with a prayer that the world would make more sense somehow when she finally woke up. Say, sometime next year.

She closed and triple bolted the door behind her, then leaned against the cold wood. Breathe, she ordered herself. Just breathe. Because each breath she dragged in took her farther and farther away from the scenes at the hospital. Because each breath brought her nearer to normalcy.

Her voice choked, she realized that same normalcy had been disrupted. "Kojak?" she said softly. The kitchen door was open, which meant he should be around there somewhere. She visually swept the place. Her gaze passed the bulletin board in the corner, then faltered and went back to it. Hadn't she turned it to the D.C. Executioner case before David had showed up? She could have sworn—

The wood behind her back shook as someone knocked on it from the other side. Putting a hand over her erratically beating heart, she stepped away, turned and stared at it. Only after she'd gotten a hold of herself did she lean in and look through the peephole. Nothing. Then a treat skittered from under the door, rolling until it landed almost under the Christmas tree.

Kelli closed her eyes and rested her forehead against the smooth wood. "Go away, David," she murmured.

He didn't say anything.

Kelli sucked in the salty moisture coating her lips. "I'm not going to let you in, so you can just forget about it and go home."

Nothing. Then finally, "I have to talk to you, Kell. I…we can't just leave everything like this. It's driving me crazy."

She laughed humorlessly. "Yeah, well, maybe you now know what it feels like to be me." She turned around and slid to the floor, her back to the door. "I'm sorry I hurt you, but nothing you can say is going to change things."

"Maybe I don't want to change things."

She listlessly swiped at the tears covering her cheeks. "Yeah, right. I'll buy that along with last week's bread."

"I'm serious, Kell." The sound of something running the length of the door sent a shiver skittering down her back. She imagined it was his hand. "Just let me in. I want to make sure you're okay."

"I'm fine. There, are you happy?"

"Okay, then, I want to *see* that you're okay."

"I'll send you a Polaroid first thing tomorrow."

There was a long silence. She didn't fool herself into thinking he had left. That would be too easy. And David never did things the easy way. "Marc and Mel had a boy," he said quietly.

She squeezed her eyes shut. She didn't want to know that. Didn't want to know anything more about David and his large, warm family. Her head was about to explode as it was. "Congratulations," she said softly.

"Your father and mine are going out to lunch tomorrow."

She ignored that one, recognizing the attempts at normal conversation as being straight out of the Metropolitan Police Department's Procedural Handbook, under the heading "How to Deal With a Nutcase."

He lightly hit the door, vibrating the wood and her head along with it. "Damn it, Kelli, why don't you just open the door so we can talk this out like the adults that we are? Your behavior now is nothing if not childish. I asked you a simple question, you gave me a simple answer. That doesn't have to change anything."

You told me you loved me. After what I just learned about my mother…my father…that changes everything.

"David, there was nothing simple about what you asked me at the hospital." She sniffed and ran the heel of her hand over her nose.

"You have got to be the most stubborn woman I've ever met. No. Let's not bring gender into this. You are the most stubborn *person* I've ever met. Now open this door."

She threw her head back to bang it against the door. "And you're the pushiest! Just go away, David. I need…time. Alone."

She heard him walk away from the door, then back again. He sighed heavily. "Okay."

"Okay?"

"Yeah, okay. I'm leaving. But I'll be back tomorrow, do you hear me? And the day after that. Then the day after that until you agree to talk to me."

She nodded her head, but didn't say anything. Tomorrow seemed so very far away.

"Try to get some sleep, okay?"

She didn't hear anything for a long time, then finally the sound of his footsteps going down the steps echoed through the hall and the aching chambers of her heart. She closed her eyes and sat there, wrapping her pain around herself along with her arms. It hurt her even more to know that she was hurting him, but she didn't know what else she could do right then: Everything she had ever believed about her mother and father had been shattered within a few precious minutes of conversation with her father. Then David's proposal had come from so far out that she responded the only way she knew how: she ran.

She lethargically pushed herself up with the help of the door, peeled off her coat, kicked off her shoes, then dragged herself toward the kitchen.

"You should have let your boyfriend in, Kitty Kat."

Kelli swung toward the voice. Jeremy Price was leaning

against the jamb of her bedroom door, regarding her with a wry grin.

It took a full minute for her to register that he was really there. To work out that she hadn't, in fact, let him in. To understand that he must have gained entrance to her apartment some other way. She pushed her damp hair back from her face. "God, Jeremy, you scared the hell out of me." His expression wavered, edging her closer to the precipice leading to all-out fear. She crossed her arms. "How did you get in?"

Removing a hand from his pocket, he held up a set of keys. "A complete copy of the keys you use to let yourself in."

Her throat tightened. He must have swiped her house keys while she was at work and had a copy made at the locksmith's next door to the shop.

Her overworked mind slowly clicked into gear. Her gun. Her gun was in her nightstand table away from where Kojak could get at it and accidentally set it off with his beefy paws and curious nature. And Jeremy was blocking the door to the bedroom.

"So, there's trouble between you and the Casanova Cop, huh? Tsk-tsk. And you two made such a cute little couple." The flagrant effeminate drawl he spoke with now made her realize that up until this moment he'd been talking in an unaffected voice tonight. She followed the realization through again.

"So you know who I am," she asked absently.

He nodded. "Uh-huh. One Kelli Marie Hatfield. Officer Hatfield up until a short time ago. Until you volunteered for a special task force undercover assignment, namely, as a floor girl at my shop."

He stepped away from the doorway, his gait more confident than she'd ever seen it at the shop. She put the fact together with the difference in his speech patterns and realized he wasn't gay at all. Had only pretended to be gay. Likely as a cover-up for other activities. Such as his role as the D.C. Executioner.

She suppressed the urge to nervously rub her neck even as she covertly scanned the apartment for something she could use as a weapon. It was then she saw that all the playtime paraphernalia that she and David had indulged in was still spread out between the sofa and two chairs. And that even now, under her respectable clothes, she was painted nearly head to foot.

He stepped to her bulletin board, still close enough to stop her from making a run for the door. He tapped the board until it rotated to the other side, the side that outlined his own crimes. "You know, I couldn't believe my luck when you first walked into my place. Since you're working the case, you must know that you fit all the major profiles of my victims."

There. He had just as good as admitted he was the Executioner. Adrenaline surged through her veins. Then the reality that she was likely his next victim stopped her blood altogether.

"But it's more than that." He waved a hand toward the ceiling. "It's almost like Fate had intervened, providing me with the one woman who would tie everything up for me."

She squinted at him, trying to make sense out of what he was saying. She shook her head, eyeing the marble candlesticks on the coffee table. "I don't follow you."

He tapped the board so it rotated again, displaying the details of her mother's case. He gazed almost lovingly at the photo of her mother, drawing the tip of his index finger down the studio shot. "You really do look like her, you know. For a second when you first walked into my shop, I thought you were her." He slanted her a disapproving gaze. "But Loretta would never have dressed to look sleazy."

Kelli shuddered.

He shoved his hands in his pockets then turned his back on the board. "I thought I gave myself away the other day. You know, when I spoke of your resemblance. But it was obvious your mind was on something else."

She looked at the bolted door. She'd been thinking about David. About the wonderful night they had spent together.

David.

Could he somehow still be out in the hall? Was it possible that he would come back again tonight?

"Oh, don't worry about C.C." He gave a chilling chuckle. "That's what I call him. You know, short for—"

"Casanova Cop," she said quietly.

"Yes." He flipped his hand in a loose-wristed way and sighed dramatically. "It's much simpler, don't you think, Kitty Kat?" He dropped his hand back to his side. "Anyway, I watched him drive away from your bedroom window. I trust he won't be coming back again soon."

Kelli looked down at her stocking feet and walked a couple of steps then stopped, pretending she was pacing when she was really angling for a better view into her bedroom. If she could reach the nightstand....

She cleared her throat and looked up, finding him overly interested in her movements, as she suspected he would be. "Are you saying you knew my mother, Jeremy?"

His grin was altogether malicious. "Knew her? Oh, yes. In the most biblical of senses, Kitty Kat."

Kelli's stomach churned. "I don't believe you," she whispered.

"Believe what? That your sweet, innocent mother would have broken her marriage vows to your father? Or that she would deign to become involved with a disgusting porn peddler like me?"

She battled back the acidic bile that rushed up her throat. She closed her eyes and tucked her chin toward her chest to ward off the rush. When she opened her eyes again, she had a clear view around the back of the chairs. She spotted Kojak's motionless legs near the corner of the one farthest from her. A sob welled up in her throat.

Jeremy went on. "I wasn't then what I am now, Kelli. I owned a legitimate bookstore then, a small place in Georgetown not far from where your family lived. In fact it was when Loretta came in to buy books for you that we met."

Kelli fought the desire to clap her hands over her ears. She had yet to fully accept what her father had told her earlier. She didn't want to hear that Jeremy was the man with whom her mother had been having an affair. Wasn't ready to face the man who had… She swung toward him. "You're the one who killed her."

The thunderous expression on his face almost made her step back, though ten feet separated them. "I *loved* her."

Anger, pure and strong, washed through her body. Forgetting her plan to zip into the bedroom for the gun there, she stalked instead toward the bulletin board. "You killed her, Jeremy. The evidence is all here." She smacked the board, causing it to vibrate, then pointed to the crime scene photo detailing the bloody blow her mother had taken to the back of the head. "You beat her to death."

He started toward her, appearing suddenly anxious. He stopped just short of touching distance. "Yes, I hit her. What was I supposed to do? She was breaking off our relationship. Said she loved your father. That she wanted to be the kind of mother you deserved. She was *leaving* me."

"So that's why you had to kill her? Because she didn't want to have sex with you anymore?"

"It was more than sex, damn you! It was love." He pressed his fingers to his temples as if pain had just shot through his head. "And I didn't kill her. It was an accident. We were fighting…" He trailed off, then turned and paced a short ways away. "And I had hit her. Once. Twice. She ran for the bathroom. The only door with a lock in your house. Only I got to her first. Then she…then she…" He looked at her. "Then she slipped on something on the bathroom floor. A tub toy. A duck! It was a duck. I couldn't stop her. She fell and hit her head on that old ceramic bathtub. Oh, God, the blood…"

Kelli's heart beat loudly in her ears. She didn't want to hear this from him. Didn't want to hear how her mother had spent her last moments. Didn't want to hear that it may have been her bath toy that had caused her mother to take that fatal fall. But she *needed* to hear all of it. She'd spent two-thirds of her life needing to hear it.

She had to force the words through her throat. "Okay, Jeremy. I believe you." She swallowed hard. "Even so, how does one go from an accidental death to the types of horrible crimes you're committing now? From depraved sex acts to rape then…murder?"

His gaze cut her to the bone. "I didn't want to do it. I never loved anyone the way I loved your mother. I sought out women who looked just like her but was never able to recreate the same…passion we shared." He whipped his hand back angrily as though lashing out at an unseen something. Kelli winced. "Don't you see? I had to punish her in some way. Had to make her pay for what she had done to me."

"By terrorizing women who resembled her," she whispered.

Jeremy pressed his palms to his temples as if unable to hold everything inside his head. He turned his back to her and paced a couple of steps away. Emboldened by his lack of alertness, Kelli desperately searched the area immediately surrounding her for something she could use as a weapon. Her new vantage point allowed her a full view of Kojak. There were bloodstains on his head and his left back leg. But it was his gentle, almost unconscious panting, the sight of his tongue as it lolled out from the side of his mouth, that made tears collect in her throat.

Oh, Jackie boy.

Spotting the heavy iron lamp on the sideboard next to her, she picked it up, yanking on it to pull the plug from the outlet. It wouldn't give. Hoping the cord was long enough, she raised the heavy lamp above her head then brought it down full force across Jeremy Price's shoulders. She heard the crack of bone, then lifted the lamp to hit him again. But he was quicker than she was. He turned, then charged her. An animal-like yell threatened to break her eardrums as he slammed her against the wall under the entire force of his larger body. The breath rushed from her lungs in a frightening gush and no air quickly followed. She wheezed and dropped to sit on the floor, slumping forward. She was afraid she'd never be able to draw a breath again when finally a small amount of air inflated her lungs.

"You little witch!" Jeremy yelled, hunched over as he picked up the lamp. He hurled it at her, causing the old, frayed, fabric-covered cord to snap, throwing sparks everywhere. Kelli flinched as the base of the lamp landed mere inches away from her leg. She tried to move, but a piercing pain ripped through her rib cage, effectively pinning her in place. She tried to pull in more air and the same pain spread like a thunderbolt through her entire chest. She realized that the impact of hitting the wall must have cracked a rib.

The smell of something burning brought her head up. She looked over to where the still plugged in half of the lamp cord had landed near the paint-smeared fabric David had laid out earlier. Her gaze darted to Jeremy to find him bent over double, trying to assess his own injuries, then back to the makeshift bed. Tiny blue flames licked across the paint-covered surface.

"Oh, God." Tightly holding the side of her rib cage that hurt the worst, Kelli rocked herself to her knees. But every time she drew in air, it felt like fire was burning its way down into her lungs. She leaned forward until her forehead was touching the floor, then fell over onto her side. She blinked, surprised to find the apartment already filling with thick, acrid smoke.

Panic welled in her stomach. She had to get out of there. She tried to bring herself to all fours again. The sound of a low whine filled her ears.

"Where in the hell are you?" Jeremy shouted.

Kelli found she couldn't make him out either, though he was probably no more than ten feet away from her.

Something touched her shoulder and she flinched, until she realized that Kojak had fastened his teeth to the fabric of her turtleneck and was trying to drag her across the room. A sob caught in her throat as she helped him, finding footholds against nearby furniture and propelled herself along the wood floor.

Kojak released her. Kelli looked up to find they were in her bedroom. The smoke wasn't as bad in here. She reached out and drew her hand carefully along the uninjured side of Kojak's face, then realized she was still a bed-length away from the nightstand that held her gun.

With the help of the mattresses, she brought herself to a standing position, every movement sending chilling shards of pain through her chest. She slowly edged her way around the bed, fighting the urge to cough, afraid that if she started she wouldn't be able to stop.

"Oh, no you don't," Jeremy said from behind her.

She swiveled around just as he grabbed her arm and sent her sprawling back in the direction of the door. She hit the door at an angle, slamming it shut as she slipped back down to sit on the floor.

She was never going to make it out alive.

But that had been Jeremy's intention all along, hadn't it?

While fire might not have been his preferred weapon of choice, dead was dead no matter which way you cut it.

The windows to his back, Jeremy stood watching her, still slightly slumped over. "What were you going for, Kitty Kat?" He reached behind him and pulled her service revolver out from the waist of his slacks. "Were you looking for this?"

Kelli slid farther toward the floor. Even if she had made it to her nightstand, it would have been for nothing. He'd had her gun all along.

Jeremy ran his hand along the back of his head, then looked at it where it was covered with blood. His breath came in long, ragged gasps. "I had planned to take my time with you, Kitty Kat. Find out if making love with the daughter is as good as with the mother. But you screwed all that up, didn't you?"

"You're the one who started the damn fire, you moron." Kelli didn't quite know what she had hoped to accomplish by egging him on, but at this point she was beyond caring, beyond playing it safe. If she was going to die, she was going to die having had the last word.

He lifted the gun and pointed it at her.

She held her chin up high. "Go ahead, Jeremy. Shoot me."

In the other room, she heard the whoosh of the fire as it devoured something else. She looked toward the windows, even now trying to figure a way out of the mess. She noticed that the one to the right was halfway open. It was also the reason there wasn't much smoke in the room. The bulk of it billowed out into the rainy, frigid night air.

She swung her gaze back to Jeremy. "What's the matter? So long as you can beat a woman into submission, rape her, you're A-number one. Macho sick-o of the year. But put a gun in your hand and you turn into an impotent wimp."

"Impotent?" he cried. "Impotent?"

Something behind Jeremy moved. Not something, she

realized, but someone. Hope poured over Kelli as surely as the rain had a short while ago.

David.

When she'd refused to let him in the apartment, he must have climbed up her fire escape, determined to gain entrance that way.

God bless his pushy, hotshot heart.

Jeremy squeezed off a round just as David slammed his arm hard down on Jeremy's. The bullet hit the wall a foot away from Kelli, spitting plaster against her turned away face.

"You heard the lady," David said, pulling on Jeremy's shoulders and yanking him back against his raised knee. "Impotent."

He easily twisted the gun out of Jeremy's hand, then stepped away from him.

For long moments Kelli concentrated strictly on breathing in and out with as little movement as possible, gazing at David like the knight in shining armor that he was. Then he grinned at her.

"I'm still not all that clear on what you meant by the second place stuff you said at the hospital," he told her quietly. "But…catch, Hatfield."

He tossed the gun in her direction. She held out both hands in her lap and it landed in them cleanly.

She jerked her head up, finding Jeremy coughing up blood and regaining his bearings even as David crossed his arms and backed away. "Do what you have to, Kell," he told her. "I'll back you up one hundred percent."

Kelli fumbled with the gun, then lifted it, setting her sights straight for Jeremy's heartless chest. At the last minute, she lowered her aim and shot him in the knee.

KELLI HAD THREE broken ribs, one of which had punctured her left lung, laying her up in the hospital. Still, her physical injuries couldn't come close to the pain caused by her emotional distress.

She turned her head on the pillow and looked toward the window. Outside the rain had moved on and the sun was beginning to set. She didn't know what kind of pain pills they'd given her but they had knocked her out cold for hours. It was hard to believe that almost a full day had passed since David had carried first her, then Kojak, out to the fire escape, where they had waited until help arrived. Harder still to believe that Jeremy Price was behind bars, likely facing life imprisonment for his actions as the D.C. Executioner.

Kelli looked down at the unappealing green of her hospital gown. Nowhere in the reports she'd given had she said anything about Jeremy's connection to her mother. And the fire had effectively burned all evidence that she'd been secretly working on the case. She hadn't even told her father about Jeremy…yet. She was sure she would, eventually. But he was in bad enough shape knowing she had been targeted by the D.C. Executioner. Anyway, right now *she* was having a hard enough time coming to terms with everything. Coming to terms with the huge mistake she had made in pushing one dashing Casanova Cop away when he had offered her the world.

Groaning, she swiped at her damp cheeks. She'd never cried so damn much in her life as she had in the past twenty hours. You would think she'd be dehydrated by now. Long cried out. But no. Every time she thought of David slipping that ring box out of his jacket pocket…remembered him standing outside her apartment door…recalled spotting him behind Jeremy at the moment she needed him most, her eyes began leaking all over again.

She'd spent the entirety of her adult life trying to solve the mystery of her mother's death. Striving to be the best cop she could be. Yearning for that detective's badge that would allow her to prevent others from suffering as she had since she was seven.

And now that her mother's murderer had been caught? Now that all the mysteries she had been obsessed with were solved?

Well, now she realized she wasn't any more ready for that detective's badge than it was ready for her.

Oh, the time would come. She was sure of that. Catching the D.C. Degenerate-Executioner wouldn't look bad on her résumé, either. But she no longer felt the desire to let her career ambitions rule her life.

No.

Instead, every time she closed her eyes, she saw David. Dear, sweet, exasperating, pushy, sexy David. Which was the only place she saw him because he'd disappeared right after they'd been brought down from the fire escape last night.

She didn't particularly appreciate the irony of the situation. When she'd wanted him to disappear, he'd stuck like glue, not giving up until he got her to give in. Now that she wanted him there, he was nowhere to be found.

The door opened. Kelli hopefully turned her head toward it, then sighed when a nurse entered.

"Good, you're up."

Kelli frowned at her as she kept the door open with one hip, then reached out into the hall. She wheeled what looked like a…was that a baby buggy? With much pain and effort, she lifted herself up onto her elbows.

"Nurse, I think you have the wrong room."

The woman eyed her. "You're Kelli Hatfield, aren't you?"

"Yes, but—"

"Then trust me, this is the right room." Ignoring her protests, she turned the buggy around. Kelli looked down but could see nothing but a large, bulky blue blanket. The nurse smiled at her. "This is breaking every last hospital rule, and could cost me my job if my supervisor found out, but…let it never be said I can't be swayed by a terrific grin and a great pair of buns."

Kelli stared at her, wondering how much medication *she'd* had.

"Are you ready?"

"Ready for what?"

The nurse swept back the blanket. Kelli's eyes opened wide as Kojak gave a plaintive bark, his short tail going a million miles a minute.

"Oh, baby!" At risk of pulling the fifteen stitches in her side, Kelli kicked her own blanket off and put her feet over the side of the bed. Through her tears, she scanned her canine hero from the tips of his ears to his back paws. His sweet little head was swathed in bandages but it didn't keep his juicy tongue from lolling out as he panted happily. But it was the splint on his back leg that concerned her most and was obviously what kept him still when he'd otherwise be loping about looking for treats. She ran her hand down the length of him, laughing with joy when he lapped enthusiastically at her hand.

"But how did you…I mean, who asked you…?" She looked up to find the nurse was gone and that in her place stood one very handsome, grinning David McCoy.

"I won't even tell you what the vet bill looks like," he said, standing with his hands stuffed into the pockets of his jeans, his black leather jacked unzipped to reveal a soft red, chambray shirt. "It wasn't pretty. And we won't even talk about your apartment."

Kelli's smile widened so far it nearly hurt her face. "Well, it's a good thing you two are a sight for sore eyes, then, isn't it?"

"Not to mention broken ribs." He glanced toward where her hospital gown was bunched up around her thighs. "How are you, um, doing?"

"Aside from feeling like I just got run over by a train? Fine." She continued patting Kojak. "I, um, can't thank you enough for this. I was just lying here feeling lonely and sorry for myself. Kojak…and you were just what the doctor ordered."

"Me?"

She held up the hand she'd been using to pet Kojak. "Before you start, McCoy, there are a few things I'd like to say."

His grin slipped. "If it's something I've already heard before, don't bother."

She shook her head and leaned back on her hands to take the pressure off her ribs. "Trust me, this is probably the last thing you're planning to hear."

His brows budged up on his handsome forehead. "Well, then, please, don't let me stop you."

She laughed, then groaned when pain shot through her chest. "Oh, please, don't make me laugh."

He stepped closer to her, helping her to lie back down. His touch was meant to be helpful, nurse-like, but she was coming to learn that the most innocuous of touches from him set her body on fire. If she was in any kind of shape to, she'd have pulled him down on top of her right that minute and prayed no one walked in while she molested him.

"So…" he prompted.

She rolled her eyes toward the ceiling. "You can't even wait for a lady to catch her breath, can you? Pushy 'til the end."

He brushed her hair back from her face. The sensitive gesture sent her eyes back to watering.

"Kell?" he said softly. "We can talk about this later if you want to."

She gave him a watery smile. "Now he wants to talk later." She caught her bottom lip between her teeth. "All I wanted to say is that…well, what I mean is…oh, hell." She gathered up her courage, then blurted, "Yes."

His grimace was so endearing she wanted to laugh, but didn't dare. "Yes?" he said, puzzled. She narrowed her eyes. "Yes," he repeated again, apparently searching his mind for the question. She knew the instant it hit him because his blue,

blue eyes virtually shot sparks, and his face lit up like the Christmas tree on the White House lawn. "Yes!"

His kiss was wonderful and wet and hot and sent her senses spiraling. She moaned when he pulled away.

"I, um, do have a condition, though," she said softly.

"Name it. Whatever it is, I'll live with it without pestering you. I promise."

"I need some time to get used to the idea. That means we don't get married right away."

His gaze was weighty as he looked at her. "That's okay. I meant what I said last night, Kelli. Next month, next year. It's all the same to me. Just so long as I know that eventually you'll be my wife." He waggled his eyebrows at her. "We are going to live in sin, though, aren't we?"

She laughed before she could stop herself, then coughed from the pain. "No, we are not going to live in sin. You think my father was bad before, let him get wind of you even suggesting such a thing and I'll be a widow before I'm a bride."

"So where are you going to live then? I mean, you can't exactly go back to your apartment. I'm sorry to be the one to tell you this, Kell, but there's nothing there to go back to."

That left her father. She cringed. Or Bronte, who had called that morning to say she was catching the first flight back into town to see her. Still… "Maybe this living in sin thing isn't such a bad idea. And we can always get married in the spring."

"Spring? As in next year?"

She hit him in the arm. "As in this year, silly. Three months away." She closed her eyes and smiled. "When the cherry blossoms are blossoming. There's something about cherries that will probably always make me think of you."

He gently slanted his mouth across hers and she languidly returned his kiss. "Does this mean you love me, Kelli Hatfield?"

She sighed and searched his eyes. "I always thought I liked

working…living solo, you know? But after you… Well, all work and no play make Kelli a very dull girl."

"There's not one thing dull about you, sweetheart. Not a single thing." He drew the tip of his nose down her cheek then over to her ear. "But you didn't answer my question, Kell."

She closed her eyes and turned her face so it lay against his, breathing in everything that was him. "I love you, David McCoy. More than the air that I almost breathe."

There was a hesitant knock at the door. Kelli ignored it as she threaded her fingers through his thick blond hair, holding him against her. He shifted his head then a quiet chuckle vibrated his chest. She pulled back to gaze at him.

"Looks like you have visitors," he said.

Kelli's heart skipped a beat as she looked toward the door. Through the long, narrow window stood not one, not two, but all five of the other McCoy men and two of the McCoy women, along with a sheepish-looking Garth Hatfield. She managed a shaky smile, then lifted a hand to wave at them.

David got up off the bed and swung the door open. "We're getting married," he blurted.

But rather than letting his and her family in as she suspected he would, he closed the door in their shocked faces, yanked the privacy panel to conceal them from view, then carefully climbed into the narrow bed next to her.

"Now…where were we?" he asked, grinning that naughty grin that made her want to surrender to him completely. It was pure heaven to finally let herself….

NEVER SAY NEVER AGAIN

To our editor, Brenda Chin,
who took one look at *License To Thrill* and saw
THE MAGNIFICENT McCOY MEN miniseries.
This one's for you!

CHAPTER ONE

CONNOR MCCOY CAUGHT A glimpse of himself in the mirror and nearly choked. Yes, he recalled agreeing to be his youngest brother David's best man, though he still couldn't quite figure that one out. Yes, he remembered putting the tuxedo on, every agonizing moment of the ordeal, from fastening the cummerbund to nearly strangling himself with the bow tie. But as he walked through David's bedroom to get his brother's wallet, he was startled by his own reflection in the mirror above the dresser.

The guy looking back at him was a stranger, as was just about everyone in his life right now. He puffed his chest out, and turned his head slightly, considering the dark-haired guy in his late thirties looking back at him. Not bad, if he did say so himself. He never spent much time grooming, which explained his startled reaction to spotting his own reflection. He made a monthly visit to the Manchester barber for a trim to the close-cropped cut he'd taken to back at the U.S. Marshal's Service Training Academy in Glynco, Georgia, over a decade ago. A supply of good, ol' Ivory soap, deodorant, shaving cream, a straight edge razor and a bottle of aspirin were the total contents of his medicine cabinet at his apartment. Completely low maintenance. Unlike some people he could name but wouldn't. His gaze dropped to the dresser in front of him and he frowned, eyeing the variety of colognes there. He picked one up. *Sex Bomb?*

"What's the holdup?" David asked, popping his head in the doorway.

Connor held up the bottle. "Do you really wear this stuff?"

His younger brother entered the room then leaned against the doorjamb. "Every chance I get. Drives the women crazy." He winked.

Connor put the bottle down, nearly knocking the rest of them over as he did so. "I think I'll pass."

David collected his wallet from the night table on the other side of the bed. Connor watched him, trying to pinpoint some sort of visible difference. Aside from the monkey suit he wore, he looked the same. His hair was a little neater, maybe, but that was about it. For all intents and purposes, David McCoy was the same smart-ass kid he'd always been.

Why, then, the sudden need to get married?

Connor cleared his throat. "Are you nervous?"

"Who? Me?" David said, jabbing his thumb into his chest. "Hell, yeah, I'm nervous."

Connor relaxed. Perhaps it wasn't too late to talk his brother out of making the biggest mistake of his life. Where there were nerves, there were good, solid reasons.

David slipped his wallet into his back pocket, then straightened his tuxedo jacket. "After all, it's not every day a man has to stand in front of half the D.C. law enforcement community and profess his love for a fellow police officer." He grinned.

Connor grimaced.

His brother whacked him in the stomach. "What's the matter, Con? You're looking a little green there. Don't tell me you're nervous?"

"Me? Hell, no." He stiffened. "I just want to make sure that…you know, that you're doing the right thing here."

"Are you kidding? Oh, I'm definitely doing the right thing. Marrying Kelli Hatfield's the smartest thing I'll have done in my life up 'til this point." He smoothed down the front of his shirt, his expression slanting toward the serious. He slowly shook his head. "You know, I thought I had it all figured out before. Life. Career. Love. Then came Kelli and she…well, she proved I didn't know diddly."

This wasn't going anything like the way Connor had planned. He took a deep breath and fought the urge to shake his own head in disbelief and pity for the youngest of the McCoy clan.

"Do you know what that's like?"

Connor snapped his head up. "What?"

"You know…loving someone. Falling in love with someone. Meeting that one person who makes the whole world look different. Like opening your eyes for the first time."

Oh, boy, was his brother really in sorry shape. "I like the way the world looks right now."

David laughed. "I knew you'd say that." He slapped his hand across Connor's shoulders, meeting his gaze in the mirror. "I hope I'm around when it happens to you, big bro. Now *that's* going to be something to sell tickets to."

"Yeah, well, I wouldn't go reserving a forum just yet, David. Because you'd lose every stinking cent you'd put down."

David waggled a finger at him. "You just watch and see if it doesn't happen to you."

"Never." He checked each of his cuff links and sighed, realizing he wasn't going to get anywhere talking to his brother now. And if they didn't get out of there soon, he was afraid David would put on a teapot to boil and suggest they reminisce about old times. "You ready?"

"For the past thirty years of my life."

Connor cringed, thinking that out of the four weddings he'd attended in the past year, this one was going to be the most nauseating yet.

SIX HOURS LATER, OUTSIDE the swanky downtown D.C. hotel, the warm spring sun was setting, birds were singing, cherry blossoms were blossoming. Inside, in a lavishly laid-out ballroom, under artfully painted ceilings and curving archways, a dark cloud hunched around Connor McCoy's shoulders, threatening to unleash a storm he wasn't sure he knew how to deal with.

He leaned against the bar and eyed the happy couple across the hall as they engaged in the traditional first dance of the night. David's blond head angled closer to his bride's ear, murmuring something that made Kelli blush then turn into his kiss. The sight was so intimate, so private, Connor couldn't help but feel like he was somehow intruding on the moment, despite the very public display, even though two hundred others looked on with him.

He swore under his breath then turned away.

Who'd have thought that one year could make so much of a difference? Twelve months? Three-hundred-and-sixty-five days? He sure wouldn't have guessed at the same time last year that he would be standing at David's wedding reception, the only McCoy male still single.

"You look like an accident waiting to happen," Sean said, coming to stand next to him.

Connor's grimace deepened. Well, okay, he was the second single McCoy male left. Pops was the first. Though he'd never really considered Pops just a male. He was a widower. His father. Not exactly prime bachelor meat up for grabs to the first bidder.

He looked down at his suit. "This is the fourth time I've had to rent a tux in a year. The rental-shop girl asked if maybe I wanted to buy the sucker. How do you expect me to look?" He tugged on the sleeves of the jacket, feeling as if the material had somehow grown snugger since he'd had it on earlier that day. Leave it to David to schedule his wedding ceremony at noon, his reception at seven, making him have to wear the suit not once, but twice in the same day.

Sean ordered a brew, then straightened the lapels of his own tailored suit. With his white hair neatly combed, his shoulders wide, he was, in fact, looking very much like an older bachelor up for auction. He said, "Oh, I don't know. I suppose I was expecting you to look happy for your brothers, maybe? Proud?"

Connor nearly choked on his own beer. "Proud?"

Pops grinned, though his gray eyes were watchful. "Yeah. I know I'm biased, but I think our boys have picked themselves a great bunch of women. Don't you think?"

Connor glanced away. There was something about the way his father had said "our boys" that made his stomach twist tighter than it already was. On the dance floor petite Michelle was pulling gangly Jake onto the parquet floor next to Mel and Marc, who were dancing as if they were the newlyweds instead of new parents.

Speaking of which…

Connor scanned the surrounding tables where draped linens and colorful flower arrangements competed with guests' apparel. There. There she was. He spotted Melanie's mother Wilhemenia. She wore a navy-blue dress that reached up to her neck and down to midcalf. But despite the severe clothing, her face was softer than he'd ever seen it as she held up little Sean Jonathon McCoy, named for Sean, and Mel's late father, Jonathon. Wilhemenia's lips moved as she said something to the infant, then she pressed her mouth against his temple.

Connor's gaze moved to his nephew. Three months old. He could still remember when David was that age. And now David was married.

Where did the time go? And why did he have the unsettling feeling that it was passing him by?

Sean cleared his throat. "Certainly you didn't expect your brothers to stay single, did you?"

Connor blinked at him. It took him a moment to register what his father had said. He shrugged. "Sure, why not? What's wrong with being single?"

"Nothing. But I think the applicable question here is what's the matter with being married?"

Connor narrowed his eyes, his gaze again trailing to Wilhemenia Weber. "Are we talking about you here, Pops? Because if we are—"

"No, we're not talking about me, here. We're talking about your brothers." He drew in a deep breath then slowly let it out. "You...well, you've made it quite clear on where you stand on my being involved with a woman, so I'm not interested in revisiting that topic—especially since this is the first time you've done more than grunt at me in months."

"I don't grunt."

"Whatever you say." His father's grin caught him off guard. Connor found himself grinning back.

"Yes, well, I learned it from the best."

"That you have. And one of these days you and I are going to have a long talk about that."

"Pardon me. Connor?"

At the sound of the female voice, Connor swung around so fast, his beer nearly sloshed over the side of his glass. He found himself staring at one of the purple-clad bridesmaids. The cute one with the blond hair and the impish smile that looked all of twelve. And came to about his navel standing on the tip of her toes.

"Would you care to dance?" she asked.

Dance? Him? He'd never even set foot on a dance floor, much less danced on one. And he had no intention of starting now. "No."

The young woman darted away without so much as another peep.

Pops cringed next to him. "You were a bit abrupt, don't you think?"

Maybe he had been, but he wasn't about to admit that to his father. "Nope. I've found it's the only way to be. Try being nice and women think you're playing hard to get. Put them off, hoping they'll take the hint, and they come back." He watched the pretty young blonde hurry to rejoin the rest of the wedding party, then shrugged. "Give her five minutes. She'll get over it."

Pops stared at him in a way Connor couldn't decipher and didn't particularly like. "What?" he finally asked, inexplicably irritated.

Sean shook his head. "Oh, nothing." He gestured with his glass toward the dance floor. "You know, for David's sake, you could maybe pretend that you're having a good time."

"I've never been very good at pretending."

"No, that you haven't." He put his glass down. "You don't mind if I have a little fun for the both of us then, do you?"

Before Connor could answer, he watched his father head toward the dance floor and cut in on the bride and groom. Kelli laughed as he said something to her, then he swept her away from David like Fred Astaire on a bad dance day.

Connor turned back toward the bar. For a minute there he'd been afraid Pops meant to ask Mel's mom, Wilhemenia, to dance. He was curious at the mixture of relief and disappointment that his father hadn't.

Someone put a full wineglass on the bar next to him. "I'd like to exchange this for a glass of beer, please."

He glanced over to find Kelli's friend—*what was her name?*—standing beside him. He drew a complete and utter blank on her first name as he noticed the way the light from the chandeliers set her short, red hair on fire.

She thanked the tender for the beer then leaned against the

bar next to him. "Looks like you're having about as good a
time as I am."

Connor forced himself to take a sip from his glass. *Bronte.*
That was her name. For the life of him he couldn't figure out
why he had momentarily forgotten it. It wasn't like he hadn't
seen her enough times in the past few months, what with her
being Kelli's best friend and all.

He shifted from one booted foot to the other. Who was he
kidding? His memory of her and her name went back farther
than that cop bar where David and Kelli had first met. A lot
farther. He remembered Bronte O'Brien from George Washington University, second year.

One recollection in particular sprung forth. Although he'd
noticed her in the lecture hall before, on this day she'd taken
the seat in front of him. It had been exam time, just after
spring break. He hadn't had much time to study because
he'd spent his vacation looking after David, who had come
down with a nasty virus. The night before his brother had
been sicker than a dog. Connor had spent hours holding a
bucket up at the side of his bed and keeping a cool rag on his
head. Still, he'd fully intended to pass the exam. He'd been
twenty-five and it had taken him longer than most to make
it to college, and that had made him determined to make each
moment count. He had passed the exam—just barely. He'd
been so obsessed with the way the ends of Bronte O'Brien's
short hair curled against the back of her freckled neck that
he'd been marked wrong on questions he could have
answered in his sleep.

He took a long pull from his glass, moving past the
memory and to the present. So long as she was standing next
to him, and wasn't making a pest out of herself, he supposed
some sort of small talk was warranted, something he'd never
been particularly good at. But at least in their case they had
shared interests. More specifically, the witness she'd placed

into the witness protection program two months ago. A witness that was giving Connor his fair share of sleepless nights with her ceaseless demands for expensive items not included in the program's limited budget.

He cleared his throat. "Congratulations on convincing Melissa Robbins to testify."

Bronte appeared not to hear him at first. She twisted her lips, then glanced away. "I'm not sure if I'm deserving of congratulations yet. She's a reluctant witness at best. And her ex-boyfriend, Leonid Pryka, is a formidable target." She looked him full in the face. "Does that mean you're in charge of her protection?"

"Yeah."

Connor supposed that, on the surface, you couldn't find two people more different from each other. Where Bronte appeared at home in her sophisticated clothes and surroundings, he was counting the minutes until he could get out of there and out of his monkey suit.

But they did share something in common: their involvement in the justice system, though he found it ironic that even in that regard their roles were completely different.

As an attorney in the Transnational/Major Crimes Section of the U.S. attorney's office, Bronte O'Brien put together cases against criminals to take to trial, which sometimes required protection for key witnesses she unearthed. And as a deputy U.S. marshal in Witness Security and Protection, also known as WitSec, that's where he came in. He made sure those witnesses were kept safe and sound and delivered in time for trial.

In this particular case, Bronte had convinced Melissa Robbins to testify against her ex-boyfriend, Leonid Pryka, a once small-time importer who had become big time with noted speed, making local and federal law enforcement very interested in just how, exactly, he had come by his seemingly instant wealth. They suspected that illegal arms and possibly weapons of mass destruction might be the import of choice. And apparently the U.S. attorney's office felt that Pryka's spurned girlfriend was the witness that could help them finally prove it.

Connor's current assignment was to keep Melissa Robbins safe. Well, at least from outsiders. Protecting himself and the other marshals from her incessant, aggravating, irrational demands was something else entirely.

He squinted at Bronte, wondering if she knew exactly how…impossible her witness was. It wasn't that he doubted Bronte's capabilities. He made a point of knowing what was going on in the U.S. attorney's office. You couldn't fully protect a witness unless you knew who and what you were protecting her from. And he'd long since become aware that Bronte's conviction rate was high. If she thought Robbins could deliver the goods on Pryka, then she could. It was as simple as that.

But as far as witnesses went, high-maintenance Melissa Robbins was one of the most difficult targets he'd had to protect in all his years with WitSec—second only to a schizophrenic mob accountant who had convinced himself that the marshals protecting him had been bought. Norman Becknal had escaped their custody no fewer than four times.

Connor would count himself lucky if Melissa Robbins tried to do the same.

"I suppose I can be thankful for that," Bronte finally said. "I mean, your being in charge of Robbins's protection. At least I can be reasonably assured that she'll be…available when the case comes up for trial next month."

Connor grimaced. That was if he and his men didn't end up whacking the woman themselves.

Bronte fingered a simple silver earring on her left lobe. Connor watched the absent movement, inexplicably fascinated.

It wasn't the overt things about women that got to him. Height, hair color, breast size—none of that made one iota of difference to him. It was the small things that threatened to do him in. The way they wrinkled their noses when they talked. How they told a story, including details he'd overlook but ultimately made the tale more interesting. The way they toyed with tiny, shimmering earrings….

"What?" Bronte made a funny face. "Don't tell me. I have rice or something stuck in my eyebrow."

Connor couldn't help a smile. "No. Your…eyebrows are just fine." As was everything else about the outgoing college student turned savvy junior U.S. attorney.

He snapped upright, moving from his startlingly relaxed position.

He'd be well-served to remember what else he knew about Bronte O'Brien. Particularly that she went through men faster than a shopaholic could max out a new credit card. He narrowed his eyes. Funny, he hadn't seen her with anyone lately, though. Not at the bar when he'd first crossed paths with her again outside the district courthouse. Not during her occasional visits out to the McCoy place with Kelli.

Not that he'd been paying close attention, mind you. The last thing on his mind was women.

Bronte pushed from the bar and visibly straightened her shoulders, jolting him from his thoughts and making him realize he'd been staring. "Okay, after that thorough inspection, I know something is wrong. It's my makeup, isn't it? I forgot to put mascara on one eye. No, wait. My blush doesn't match my lipstick."

Connor looked down at his glass, fighting a half smile. "I'd be the last person to notice either thing."

She considered him warily. "Then why are you staring at me?"

He shrugged. Why *was* he staring at her? He already knew

that such steady attention only garnered unwanted interest. And while he wasn't opposed to bedding the occasional female every now and again, Bronte wasn't going to be one of them. "Just thinking."

"Uh-huh…you were just…thinking."

He put his glass on the bar. "Something wrong with that?"

"I don't know. Depends on what you were thinking."

He fastened his gaze on her face. But rather than the flirtatious look he expected, he instead found she wore a guardedly curious expression. Was that because she wasn't attracted to him? Found his company…wanting?

He frowned. What was he thinking? He didn't want her to be attracted to him any more than he wanted to be attracted to her. And he wasn't. He was merely appreciating her beauty, that's all. He wasn't any more attracted to her than he was to any of his sisters-in-law. So what if he noticed the way her breasts pressed against the thin fabric of her dress? How the slit up the side of her ankle-length skirt flashed glimpses of her long legs when she walked? How pale freckles peppered every visible inch of her skin? He'd notice the same thing about any other female within the vicinity. He was a man, after all. It didn't necessarily mean he was attracted to her.

"I was just thinking," he began, searching for an explanation that would keep him safely out of reach, yet make some sort of sense. "You went to G.W.U., didn't you?"

Her instant answering smile yanked on something inside his chest. He told himself it was relief. "I'm surprised you remember."

His brows budged upward. Her response indicated she had some memory of him being there as well. "I have to say I'm surprised you do too."

She looked down at her glass. "Yeah, well, it's hard to forget a guy who would be taller than me even when I'm in high heels. There aren't many out there."

with you?" Her smile took some of the bite out of her words, then grew genuine when he smiled back. "Okay, that's not really the reason. I didn't ask you to dance because I don't dance." She shrugged, wondering why she'd volunteered that little piece of trivia from the life and times of Bronte O'Brien. Still, no matter how many years went by, or how many men she dated, the memories from her wallflower days tagged along on her heels like a long piece of unnoticed toilet paper. Until events like these reminded her. Speaking of which… She looked down at her shoes just to make sure she wasn't trailing any t.p. The way today was going, she wouldn't be surprised to find an entire roll hanging on. "I don't know. I guess it's one of the drawbacks of having a foot on the guys in school. For some reason, they never ask girls taller than they are to dance."

His eyes darkened with something shared and elemental, throwing her for a second. "I bet they regret their actions now."

She laughed. "I doubt it."

She caught herself staring into those same eyes, now tinted with enigmatic shadows. She'd come across Connor several times in the past few months and he'd never given her the time of day, much less made an effort to talk to her. There was something different about him tonight, though. Something almost…human.

She forced herself to turn and watch the people on the dance floor, realizing she probably sounded like she was looking for a pity dance. She slanted him a covert look, relieved to find he was staring out on the dance floor much as she was. She let out a quiet, shaky breath. She should have known better. Through Kelli's dealings with the McCoy family of rebels-without-a-clue, she'd learned that while they had to be the best-looking bunch of men on the eastern seaboard, they weren't exactly the brightest when it came to women. Kelli, herself, had nearly halted her wedding plans at least three times because of some stupid stunt or other that David had pulled both on and off the job.

Her gaze was drawn to the good-looking couple, swaying to a slow, sultry song about lost loves, and her own heart gave a gentle squeeze.

This whole night had been harder on her than she would have ever imagined it would be. It was more than the loss of her heel before the ceremony that an application of Wilhemenia Weber's quick glue had fixed; the spot of brisket drippings on her dark dress she hid with the strategic placement of her gauzy wrap; the fact that, aside from Kelli and Connor, she didn't know anyone in the large room. No, what really bothered her was that she'd caught herself looking at the happy couple in a way that could be nothing but envious. Wishing it were her on that dance floor leading off the celebration with Thomas Jenkins, the man she had planned to marry. The only man who had tempted her to glimpse past her dedication to her career, made her think that maybe there was something else out there, perhaps even a white picket fence and two-point-two children. Enough to become engaged to him. At least until nine months ago, when she'd discovered he'd never had any intention of marrying her. Because he was already married.

A mixture of sadness, regret and guilt gathered in her chest, making it almost impossible to breathe as she caught herself looking at her left hand for the engagement ring that used to be there.

She tried to shake off the unwanted feelings and focus her thoughts on the man next to her, warning herself not to focus too intently. Taking on another man to get over the one before was the mode of operation the old Bronte would have employed—a mode she'd long ago chucked out the window.

"They make a cute couple, don't they?" she quietly asked Connor.

David dipped his new wife then took a whack in the arm for his efforts once Kelli had her feet back under her. "I guess."

She wondered at the tension that suddenly emanated from Connor. Did he object to Kelli's marrying his youngest brother? She found it impossible to believe that anyone would object, but she knew only too well that what she believed and what was really the truth often were two completely different things. "She loves him, you know," she felt the need to point out.

He nodded slowly. "I know."

"And he loves her."

"I know." He squinted at her, as if trying to figure out her motives.

"Then why the long face?"

He appeared suddenly uncomfortable, an emotion she would never have attributed to him. Ever. She knew her reasons for not wanting to be here, in this hall, watching two people so obviously in love with each other, but what were his?

"Would you believe me if I said I hate these things?" he asked, putting his beer bottle on the bar.

Now *that* she could understand. "Yes, I would."

"Then I hate these things."

She tilted her head to the side, considering him. "I guess that'll do. For now." She placed her beer next to his, then straightened the swath of gauzy material that had been resting in the curve of her elbows. "What's say we blow this joint for a while? Take a walk or something? I could do with some fresh air."

She slowly turned and began walking toward the doorway. She didn't know what she expected, but she was surprised when she glanced over her shoulder to find Connor following her.

CONNOR WASN'T CERTAIN WHY he'd instantly accepted Bronte's offer of a walk. Maybe it was the straightforward way she'd made the suggestion. Perhaps because she hadn't tucked her hand in his elbow in a possessive manner that some women thought brooked no argument. But the moment they stepped outside the stuffy, overdecorated hotel, he was glad he had listened to the voice that had prodded him to follow her. Almost instantly, he felt the cloud squeezing his shoulders dissipate. Immediately, his muscles relaxed. He no longer had to be the proud big brother. Pretend he was happy with events when he clearly wasn't.

Over the U.S. Treasury building across the way, the sun was setting. He realized Bronte had continued walking and followed again—this time across the street and into the park there. He hung back slightly as she leaned against a bench and slipped off first one, then the other, of her shoes. Her feet, like the rest of her, were long, slender and well-shaped, her toenails painted bright, scarlet red, contrasting against the dark navy-blue of her dress. The low-heeled pumps swinging from her fingers, she continued on, deeper into the park, away from the traffic on the street. Away from the hotel and the celebrating people inside.

She took a deep breath. He found his gaze drawn to the scooped neckline of her bridesmaid's dress. The gentle curve of flesh there expanded, revealing a few more freckles he felt the desire to explore with his fingertips. "I can't tell you how great it is to take a breath and not have your senses overwhelmed by somebody else's perfume," she said.

"Hmm?" Connor tore his gaze away from the top of her breasts. It was then he realized that he didn't detect any immediately recognizable perfume coming from her. At least not of the store-bought variety. She smelled vaguely of something soft, somewhat like a white flower he'd picked once and taken home to his mother, who had been pregnant with David at the time. Just a couple years or so before she died.

"Connor McCoy, are you staring at my breasts?"

He grinned and slowly budged his gaze up to her face, half hidden in shadow. "Yes, I guess I am." He cleared his throat and noticed the small orbs pressing against the shiny fabric. "And either you're suddenly cold, or they're staring back at me."

Her burst of laughter surprised him and when he looked up he found the same startled expression on her face. "Well, that's the first time I've heard that."

"Good. Because it's the first time I've said it."

His gaze locked with hers. A strong undercurrent of exactly what he'd been trying to ignore flowed between them like a tangling web. Attraction. Full, strong, elemental attraction. He followed the line of her cheek down to her lips, finding the top one fuller than the bottom, unpainted, the natural dusky shade unbearably appealing.

"What would you say if I told you I wanted to grab you and kiss you?" he asked.

CHAPTER TWO

WHAT WOULD SHE SAY IF HE *what?*

Bronte stared at Connor, wide-eyed, wondering where exactly she had left her good sense, and how she could snatch it back…quickly. She rested her hand against the rough bark of a cherry tree in full bloom, balancing herself before she actually fell over.

The last thing she'd had on her mind when she suggested a walk was kissing Connor McCoy. She'd simply wanted to escape the claustrophobic hotel. Gulp some fresh air. Take time to convince herself that no one noticed the envious way she eyed Kelli's dress. The way she breathed in the intoxicating scent from her tiny bouquet. The way she had clasped her hands together a little too tightly when the bride and groom had exchanged vows.

If Kelli wasn't her best friend, she would never have agreed to come to the wedding reception, much less taken on the role of her maid of honor. The whole concept of weddings made her think of things better off forgotten.

She briefly closed her eyes. She had just gotten to the point where she woke up in the morning and didn't immediately crush the empty pillow next to her to her chest and squeeze it between her aching thighs. She no longer jumped every time the phone rang. She'd even stuck his photograph into a box in her attic and had dived headfirst into a complete remodeling of her house to erase all evidence of his presence.

Then Thomas had left a message on her answering machine a couple of weeks ago. Then again last week. And yet again this morning.

It was bad enough her emotions were in disarray as a result. Now she was facing a clearly hungry Connor McCoy…and wanting him.

"What did you say?" she asked, finding her voice curiously breathless, her breasts tingling under the fine fabric of her dress.

Standing directly in the last remaining beams of the setting sun, she watched Connor's eyes darken. "The hell with the question. I'm going to kiss you."

"Kiss—"

Just that suddenly, Connor's hands were in her short hair, his mouth was slanted against hers, and the hot wetness of his tongue was begging for entrance to her mouth by way of her startled, closed lips.

Connor McCoy's kissing me. Bronte couldn't seem to wrap her mind around the possibility even as it was happening. She'd have bet anyone her life savings that he'd never even noticed her in college, much less held an interest in her. And his demeanor toward her ever since Kelli had met David at the bar could only be described as civilly chilly.

Yet here he was, coaxing her lips open and delving into her mouth like a man seeking the sweet waters of the fountain of youth.

Bronte's knees went weak and she melted against him for support. It felt so very, very good to kiss a man taller than her. To feel all her body parts nicely aligned against his without her needing to crouch skillfully lower. Thomas… She forcefully ousted the name, not wanting to think about him now. Needing to feel alive. Wanted. Desired. And desire-full.

She slowly realized Connor's erection pulsed against her

belly. She drew in a sharp breath. He groaned something, then launched a renewed attack on her mouth.

She sighed and collapsed against him again even as he backed her against the rough bark of the tree, well out of sight of any onlookers. The low-hanging branches creating a fragrant cocoon around them. The sun finally slipping over the horizon, leaving them in deep, secretive shadows.

Bronte felt a whimper gather at the back of her throat. Who knew quiet, brooding Connor McCoy could kiss so well? And who knew that she had it in her to respond so physically to another man so soon after her last relationship had failed so miserably?

She was aware of strong fingers against her rib cage, a prelude to a more intimate, probing touch. A man's way of letting a woman know what he had in mind. A warning that if she wanted to prevent the progression, now was the time to act.

And Bronte knew she should do just that. This kiss was so totally unexpected. But she didn't. Instead she found herself hungrily arching her back away from the tree trunk, telling him in her own feminine way that she wanted his touch as much as he wanted to touch her.

Then he did.

Bronte shuddered as his hand seared her flesh through her dress. His fingers expertly found and lightly plucked at her protruding nipple, causing desire to pool between her thighs and her breath to freeze in her lungs. Then he dipped his finger inside the low neckline and his hot skin made contact with hers. Amazingly, she found herself on the verge of climax, and they hadn't even done anything yet.

Yet.

The word caught and held in her mind even as she pressed her breast into his touch, straining for a more complete contact.

Yet.

No, they hadn't really done anything…yet. But if he didn't stop—

Connor widened his stance and pulled her into the cradle of his thighs with his other hand. The hard, solid feel of his erection against her belly nearly sent her reeling.

Just one touch, she told herself. She just wanted to see if he was as turned on as he seemed to be. Needed to verify that he was indeed as large as she suspected.

She thrust her hand down shamelessly between them, cupping the long, thick ridge in her palm. Oh, dear Lord. He was everything and more than she expected.

Connor dragged his mouth from hers, leaving her panting for air against his neck. Then she fell back against the tree, desperately clamping her hands behind her, finding support in the solidness of the trunk.

"Whoa," Connor murmured under his breath, pacing a short ways away, then returning. She couldn't make out his eyes in the darkness, but she didn't doubt that they held the same shock she felt from head to heel.

"This doesn't make any sense," she said, closing her eyes and shaking her head. "I mean, I'm not really sure what just happened, but…"

The sound of the grass crushing under Connor's footsteps was all she could hear over the thundering of her heart.

"But what?" he asked, startling her.

Her eyes flew open. He was standing closer than she expected. If she put her hand out, she would touch the hard wall of his chest. The same chest she'd been flush up against mere moments ago.

"But…this doesn't make any sense."

He made a sound similar to a quiet laugh. "You said that already."

"Yes, well, I'm going to say it again, so prepare yourself."

She laid her head back against the uneven bark of the tree and took a deep, calming breath. Only it didn't go very deep and it wasn't calming. "Well, since I'm momentarily incapable of describing what happened just now, maybe you'd like a go at it."

A nearby lamp flickered to life, illuminating the path some twenty feet away, and throwing Connor's features into relief. "I think I'll pass if it's all the same to you."

She smiled shakily. "Well, if it's all the same to you, it isn't all the same to me."

The way he wiped at the side of his mouth with his thumb made her knees go weak all over again. "Are you involved with anyone?"

She shook her head. "No. You?"

He grimaced. "No. And I don't want to be either."

"Good, because neither do I."

What was the matter with her? She swore after the last time that she wouldn't leap into another intimate relationship without looking first. And she certainly hadn't seen this coming.

So what did she do? Suggest they pretend their kiss hadn't happened? Dumb, dumb, dumb. She'd never been one to play coy after a good, riling bout of tongue tangling. She wasn't about to start now.

A low-frequency beep pierced her ears, followed quickly by another. She reached for her purse, then realized she'd turned her cell phone to vibrate. Nothing more irritating than someone's phone ringing in the middle of a wedding ceremony.

Connor's movements as he slipped his hand inside his tux jacket told her the ringing had come from his portable. He pulled it out and punched a button.

"McCoy here," he said, turning to walk away slightly.

She appreciated the long line of his back, the way his hair

lay neat against his head, exposing his neck as he bent forward. It took her a moment to realize that her purse had begun vibrating. She scrambled to take her cell phone out and prayed her voice sounded normal as she answered.

Connor swung to face her, his gaze snagging hers even as she understood that they were being contacted about the same thing. Her witness, Melissa Robbins, had just been found dead. And one Deputy U.S. Marshal Connor McCoy, the man she had just nearly devoured, was the prime suspect.

TWO DAYS LATER BRONTE wasn't any clearer on what had happened between her and Connor McCoy than she'd been the night of Kelli and David's wedding. Not that it mattered. She hadn't seen him since, and likely wouldn't for a while, what with David and Kelli being off on their honeymoon in the Poconos for the next two weeks.

And not with Connor being implicated in the death of Melissa Robbins.

Tightening the sash on her white silk kimono, she opened the door and scooped up the eight newspapers stacked haphazardly on the cement steps of her Georgetown town house. The spring morning was warm and clear. She hugged the papers to her chest and tilted her face toward the sun dappling the steps through the trees.

"Good morning, Miss Bronte."

She opened her eyes and smiled at the elderly woman who lived two doors up. Seven o'clock and already she was digging through the spring flowers flowing from artfully placed baskets in her front window, bright yellow cloth gloves protecting her aging hands. "Morning, Miss Adele."

The neighborhood was comprised mostly of young professionals or tenured academics and budding politicians, but Miss Adele added a little bit of the something Bronte had been looking for when she first moved to D.C.—a kind of old-world, southern charm she was coming to cherish. "Your geraniums are looking good."

Miss Adele smiled. "Nothing like a few coffee grounds mixed into the soil to perk them right up, I always say. A little trick my grandmother taught me."

Bronte waved, then headed back inside her town house. Padding into the kitchen, she slid the newspapers one after another on to the thick oak tabletop. She sighed, Miss Adele and her geraniums quickly forgotten. If the story about her witness and Connor McCoy's alleged involvement in her death wasn't on the front page, a teaser leading to it was.

When she'd first arrived on the scene at the safe house, still decked out in full maid of honor wedding regalia, she'd brushed away any possibility of Connor's involvement in Melissa Robbins's death. After all, hadn't she just spent the better part of that day salivating after him, first in the church during Kelli and David's nuptials, then later at the reception?

Then it slowly dawned on her that a good six hours had stretched between the ceremony and the reception. And it was smack dab in the middle of those six hours that Melissa's death had been approximated.

Still, she'd been unwilling even to consider that a man so obviously a steadfast believer in the law would break it so acutely. Then little circumstantial pieces of evidence began to pile up. The fact that there was a strong history of conflict between Connor and Robbins while she was in his custody; there were several minor complaints littering her file from Robbins over the past couple months claiming Marshal McCoy had been physical with her. At the time she'd written those complaints off, simply because she'd had a difficult time dealing with the demanding woman herself. And follow-ups to the complaints had proven that the physical incidents Robbins had cited were minor events brought on by her stepping outside the boundaries set for her protection, and were completely warranted. Such as the time when Connor took the phone from Robbins's hand and pulled the cord from the wall when she was going to order in from a swanky D.C. restaurant where she was well known. Or when she'd tried to ditch her protection during a visit to Bronte's D.C. office so she could squeeze in a visit to a spa that had been deemed prohibited by the marshal's office.

Separately, the occurrences could be explained away. But when combined, and coupled with no apparent outside breach of security…well, Bronte's arguments for Connor's innocence had lost a bit of punch.

Of course, it didn't help that his alibi of target practice out in an abandoned stretch of countryside during the window of opportunity couldn't be verified.

None of the circumstantial evidence was enough to issue a warrant for his arrest. But given the air around the U.S. attorney's office, the possibility was growing more likely with each passing hour.

Bronte stuck her thumbnail between her teeth and sighed. Boy, she really knew how to pick them, didn't she? Wasn't it bad enough she'd gone through what she had with Thomas? Did fate have to toss one hottie in the shape of Connor McCoy into her path so soon afterward? An alleged murderer, at that?

She snatched her hand away from her mouth, then slid into a chair. "It was just a kiss, for God's sake."

Clasping her rose-etched antique cup of Earl Grey between both hands, she took a long sip. She grimaced at the cool liquid, then glanced toward the unplugged microwave and the television tuned in to the local news next to it. She couldn't run both the microwave and the TV at the same time in the old town house, a wiring challenge she hoped to remedy with her plans to renovate the place. Plans she could put into motion just as soon as she settled on a design.

She jerkily opened the first newspaper and carefully spread it out on the table in front of her. Just a kiss. Yeah, right, and the Concorde was just a plane. First kisses didn't even remotely resemble what had passed between her and Connor in the park the other night. There had been something...explosive about the meeting of their lips. Something undeniably sexy. She'd felt the amazing urge to push her dress up and cradle him between her thighs with no thought about tomorrow. No qualms about how well she didn't know him. Absolutely no thoughts of why they shouldn't be indulging in such decadent behavior in the middle of a park in the heart of the nation's capital.

She propped her head in her hand. Who was she kidding? It wasn't so long ago that she had entertained ideas of indulging in such behavior solely because it *was* the nation's capital. While she didn't claim to be an exhibitionist, there was something decidedly erotic and intense about the idea of having sex a mere stone's throw away from the White House.

The city itself had proved an incredible aphrodisiac when she'd first started attending G.W.U. Or could it perhaps have been that D.C. wasn't the small town of Prospect, New Hampshire? She still couldn't be sure. But leaving the place where she'd grown up as the youngest of three daughters of the high-school math teacher had been wonderfully freeing. Not once had she been taunted for her height. Nor had she felt hemmed in by her lack of career choices. The sky was the limit as far as her future was concerned. And when she discovered that men were attracted to her...well, she'd taken to them like chocolate, in some odd way trying to make up for every guy who had shunned her in high school, every kid who had teased her, made her feel like a towering tree with absolutely no grace. In essence, she'd become a serial dater.

She supposed the reasons were far more complicated than

that. Still, while her personal life was littered with debris from failed relationships, she had excelled in her studies and career. Affirmative action may have made it easier for her to obtain certain positions, like clerking under an esteemed superior court judge, followed by a stint in the local prosecutor's office, then a gratifying round with a citizens' action group, but it was her unabashed ambition and single-minded purpose that had landed her in the U.S. attorney's office four years ago.

Then came Thomas.

She shook the paper vigorously, hoping the action itself would snap her from her reverie. She didn't want to think about him now. Didn't want to think about Connor either. After Thomas…well, she'd vowed to spend uninterrupted quality time with herself. And that didn't include one U.S. Marshal Connor McCoy. Especially given the cloud of suspicion now hanging over him.

The wall phone rang. Bronte slanted a look at the clock, then continued reading. Too early for her mother. Besides, she'd spoken to her the day before yesterday, so it would probably be next week before she spoke to her again, unless something important popped up. And if it was something important, she didn't think she could deal with it right now. She turned the page and continued to pretend to read the story.

Her gaze was again drawn to the phone.

The caller could be someone from work. With this Robbins witness case, everything at the U.S. attorney's office was in upheaval. While it might be good to let whoever it was think she was already on her way downtown, that call could be important, too.

She bit on her bottom lip and slowly lowered the newspaper to the table. Four rings.

She picked it up on the fifth. "Hello?"

"Bronte?"

She absently rubbed her forehead, thinking she should have let the answering machine pick it up.

"Bronte? Are you there?"

She closed her eyes and drew in a steadying breath. "Yes, Thomas, I'm here." Though she wished for all the world that she wasn't. Just five minutes later she would have been in the shower and would have missed the call. Just a half hour later, she would already have left the town house for work. But no, Thomas had to call now when he knew she would probably pick up.

"You haven't returned my calls."

She leaned against the wall. "No, I haven't."

"You mind telling me why?"

He sounded too calm, too rational, and far too familiar. "Maybe because I don't have anything to say to you?"

There was a pregnant pause, then he said quietly, "I've left Jessica, Bronte."

The words swirled in Bronte's mind. "And that affects me…how, exactly?"

"I guess that's for you to decide."

"Funny, I thought I made my decision."

"Things change, Bronte."

Her gaze caught on a grainy black-and-white photo of Connor McCoy on the front page of one of the newspapers. She rubbed her forehead. "Yeah, and the more they do, the more they stay the same." She sighed. "Look, Thomas, I'd really appreciate it if you wouldn't call me anymore."

"Okay. I can respect that."

She began to pull the receiver away from her ear, but his quiet voice stopped her, drawing her back like a dog who had either been kicked too much, or not enough. He said, "But that doesn't mean you can't call me. I'm at the Marriott Wardman Park Hotel, room 21104. And, of course, you still have my work number. Call me anytime, Bronte."

"Goodbye, Thomas."

She hung up the receiver with both hands, then stood staring it at for a long, long moment.

What was it with men? Months pass without a word, time in which you learn to pull yourself together. Then bam. One phone call and they expect you to come running. Forget that he had virtually ripped her heart out. This, after steadily dating for three months. Long after she'd fallen head over heels in love with him.

She leaned against the wall again, burying her face in her hands. Weren't women supposed to have a sixth sense about married, lying, cheating, heart-stealing creeps? Some sort of alarm that went off, saying "warning, warning, pond scum at twelve o'clock"? She'd never figured herself to be the gullible type. The exact opposite, if truth be known. On the rare occasion when she took a sick day and spent it listing around in bed knocking back Chinese chicken soup and ogling daytime television that featured shows with themes like, "She slept with my brother, emptied my bank account, killed my dog, but I still want her back," she'd harshly judged the other women as no-good home wreckers who'd known the men they were seeing were married and continued the relationship anyway.

It was shocking to have to aim her biting judgment of them at herself.

She dropped her hands to her sides. To this day, she still couldn't figure out the logistics of how Thomas had managed to keep his wife a secret from her. Or her a secret from his wife. After she'd found out, he'd explained his wife was a surgeon who chose second shift hours because she felt she worked better then. But what about the apartment he'd taken her to? The nights he'd slept over at her place?

"Stupid, stupid, stupid."

The plain truth of it was that once she'd found out, there

was no going back. She'd quickly called a halt to what-ever…strange relationship they'd had. Thrown away the clip-pings of wedding dresses she'd begun to collect. Burned the few belongings he'd left at her place. Mangled his engage-ment ring in the trash compactor. And sworn off men until an unspecified time in the future when she could think about what happened with Thomas and not feel…dirty. Could look at herself in the mirror and like herself again.

That certainly wasn't going to happen if she took up with him again, wife or no wife.

And indulging in heated thoughts of Connor McCoy wasn't going to make that happen either. Moving from a man who was too committed to women, to a man who wanted no commitment and was a suspected murderer, was *not* progress.

Gathering up the newspapers, she used her foot to open the cupboard under the sink, then stuffed them inside the waste-basket. The recycling patrol would have to forgive her this once. She kicked the door closed with her bare foot, brushed her hands together, then kicked the door again for good measure.

Of course it was only par for the course that she stubbed her big toe and had to hobble around to get ready for work. She couldn't wait to find out what else this wonderful day had in store for her.

CHAPTER THREE

THERE WERE BLASTED story-twisting, scandal-hungry reporters hiding out everywhere. When Connor went home to his D.C. apartment, they sprung from behind the bushes, camera lights blinding him, microphones hitting him in the chin. When he checked in at work, they were in the hall outside his office; he'd even found one hiding in one of the men's room stalls. He grimaced. Not that there was much reason for him to go to work nowadays. He'd been suspended with pay the instant Melissa Robbins's body had been found…and he'd been named as suspect number one.

Two days and it hadn't sunk in yet. He was good at his job. Damn good. He'd never done one single thing in his entire career to cast him in a suspicious light. He prided himself on being the one they called in for special ops, and carefully cultivated his reputation for getting the job done. He'd never lost a witness. It was only natural then that he'd fully expected his boss to stand behind him.

Not exactly the way things had gone down. Before he could get two words in, old Newton had asked for his badge and his firearm and told him he was on indefinite suspension until the outcome of the case was decided.

Politics. He knew the drill. The higher-ups in the department had to distance themselves, or at least appear like they were distancing themselves, from him in order to cover their asses. Not merely because of potential lawsuits from the victim's family. But because Washington bigwigs loved to throw their weight around when it came to high-profile cases like this one. The perfect PR opportunity to make it look like they were doing something for the constituents back home. Unfortunately, their power plays ultimately hurt the ones least responsible for the trouble. Men like his boss, Newton.

Men like him.

He hadn't been able to get a full accounting of exactly what implausible evidence linked him to Robbins's murder. But sources did tell him that an arrest was probably imminent. It was his job to make sure that arrest never took place.

Tightening his hands on the steering wheel of his silver SUV, Connor pulled up into the gravel drive of the McCoy place in Manchester, Virginia. Pops's car wasn't there. Good. And at this time of the morning, Liz and Mitch would be busy in the ranch office. Even better. His mind had been so busy whizzing through all the details of his predicament in the past two days, he hadn't gotten a wink of sleep. It wasn't until he'd accidentally poured salt into his coffee instead of sugar at a D.C. diner that morning that he realized he needed a few hours to himself to get some major shut-eye. And the old McCoy house was just the place to do that.

He distractedly eyed the pen that paralleled the parking area. Kelli's mutt, Kojak, was sitting inside with Mitch's behemoth Goliath.

Clutching the keys to the McCoy place, and to his car, he climbed out then crossed over to the pen and crouched down. Kojak ignored him, but Goliath ambled over and stuck his wet nose through the fence. He absently stroked him. "What is it, boy? Feeling a little put out?"

Could he ever relate to that feeling. For the past thirty-six hours, he'd launched an all out attack to find out why he was under suspicion for Melissa Robbins's murder. He'd come up with little more than nothing. He'd finally had to admit he needed access to inside info. Needed to find out exactly what the U.S. attorney's office had on him before he could go any further.

Goliath nudged his other hand, causing him to lose his grip on his keys. Grimacing, he bent down to pick them up, then stood up slowly as Goliath sprinted away from the fence.

Giving the quiet grounds a once-over, Connor turned from the dog, then he walked toward the house and let himself in. The door was open, which wasn't surprising. The crime rate in Manchester was basically nil. And what criminals might be lurking about certainly wouldn't think of coming all the way out here.

He stepped into the kitchen. The telltale acrid smell of something having been burned permeated the room. He was growing used to that. It was the utter silence of the place he found unsettling. In his overtired state, he found it all too easy to imagine Jake sitting in his room studying the latest in international law; Marc camped out in front of the television, soaking in whatever happened to be playing that time of the day; Mitch repairing something or other upstairs; David tossing a baseball against the side of the house, the clunk, clunk each time the ball made contact irritating yet reassuring.

David….

It was impossible to believe the kid was married. Married, for cripe's sake.

What was he talking about? He couldn't believe he was the only one of the five of them *unmarried*.

He climbed the steps two at a time, then crossed the second-floor hall to the room that had always been his, even after moving out and getting his own apartment in D.C. over a decade earlier. He started pulling off his shirt even as he opened the door. At least the reporters hadn't found out about this place yet. He could use it as home base until he figured out just how, exactly, he'd ended up in the mess he was in. And who had set him up to take a fall he hadn't earned.

He drew to an abrupt stop in the middle of his room. Only a quick, startled glance told him it was no longer his room. He backed up into the hall, looked around, then stared at the door that still held the words he'd carved when he was ten. "Private. Keep Out." He peered back inside.

It was his room, all right. Only it wasn't. A wood, spindle cradle sat in the middle, stuffed full of tiny, brightly colored toy animals. A rocking chair was angled where his twin bed used to be. And someone had painted the walls white and decorated them with…was that Winnie the Pooh?

He grimaced. Where were all his sports posters? The collection of football cards he'd kept piled up in the corner? The photograph of his mother he kept on a nightstand that was no longer there?

"Aw, hell." He realized that while he'd visited in the past three months, he'd never actually gone up to his old room. His new sisters-in-law must have turned it into a nursery for his nephew while he wasn't looking, to use whenever Marc and Mel came for visits. Which was too often for his liking.

Connor scratched his head. Shouldn't someone have asked him before doing something so drastic? And what about the other rooms? Why hadn't they chosen one of those?

He strode down the hall, throwing open doors as he went. Pops's room looked the same. So did Marc's. Jake had added a double bed to his, and his old twin now sported a pink, frilly spread, more likely than not compliments of Lili, but it was still the same. Mitch's was hardly recognizable now that his wife, Liz, had moved in, but there was no mistaking that it was still his room.

His was the only one they had screwed with.

He rubbed his hand over his numb face, feeling ridiculously like he'd woken up that morning to find he'd been evicted from his life.

He backtracked to Marc's room, stalked to the bed, then sank down on the new mattress, curious as to why Marc and Mel hadn't traded the twin for a double, or why they hadn't put the damn crib in here—but he wasn't up to dealing with the answer right now. He tossed his shirt to the corner, kicked his boots off, then stretched out, staring at the ceiling without seeing it, his feet dangling from the end of the too-short bed.

Almost immediately an image of Bronte O'Brien filled his mind.

Figured. The first free moment he had to himself and a woman intruded.

He supposed he should be used to it by now, given all the females that had taken over the McCoy place, but this was different, somehow. Bronte was different.

He closed his eyes and crossed his arms over them. Oh, he'd had his share of women in his lifetime. Mostly short-lived relationships that ended almost as quickly as they began. He'd meet someone somewhere, take her out a couple times, go to bed with her, then walk out when she started talking about something more serious.

He found it a little strange that he had never asked Bronte out. Not only now, but back in college. It wasn't as if she had a sign around her neck that read, "Interested in marriage, only." On the contrary, if she wore a sign it would probably say, "Mention of the word marriage is punishable by death."

Normally his kind of girl.

It wasn't as if he hadn't been attracted to her. She'd always commanded his attention the moment she walked into the room. And that certainly hadn't changed.

There. That was it. His epiphany of the day. He *was* attracted to Bronte. If kissing her the other night hadn't proven that, then certainly his inability to stop thinking about her now did.

He jerkily rolled over, compensating when the move nearly threw him over the side of the narrow bed. Her wanton reaction to him hinted that she was as drawn to him as he was to her. By all rights, he ought to just sleep with her and get it over with.

He remembered the way she'd pressed her breast into his touch. How she'd boldly reached down to cup his erection in her hand. Recalled her surprised gasp when she ran her fingers down and around the length and breadth of him.

Connor's stomach tightened and he turned his head the other way on the pillow. He'd never…wanted a woman the way he wanted Bronte O'Brien. He wanted to kiss her senseless. Watch her lick that full upper lip of hers right before she fastened her mouth around his erection. Grind into her like nobody's business. Tug her hair until her head fell back, giving him free access to her long neck and breasts. He wanted to possess her inside and out.

The mere thought of being between her thighs made him hard. And the feel of the mattress beneath him wasn't helping matters much.

He roughly turned back over, determined to ignore his physical reaction, though his mind kept rushing down the same path, a steam locomotive that wouldn't stop until it reached an unknown destination.

He supposed part of the reason for his different attraction to Bronte was that she'd been a secret fantasy of his for so long. For whatever reason, from the start, he'd put her aside, above other women he dated. Purposely made her unobtainable, out of bounds. He'd immediately sensed in her a…sameness. Glimpsed in her eyes a shared understanding that had nearly knocked him straight out of his shoes the instant he saw it.

Outside he heard distant sounds. Probably Mitch in the later stages of breaking one of his new fillies. He fought to concentrate on the normal sound, to stop thinking about the woman he shouldn't be thinking of, get some sleep, then get up to figure out exactly who was trying to set him up for Robbins's murder and why. His sandpapery eyelids blessedly began drifting closed.

Still, the nameless something that existed between him and Bronte tempted his attention. He'd never experienced the same thing with another woman before or since.

And that's exactly the reason he'd kept his distance—and should continue to keep his distance.

But when he finally fell into a deep, exhausted slumber, there existed absolutely no distance whatsoever between him and Bronte O'Brien.

BRONTE FIGURED SHE REALLY needed to find something more interesting to do with her down time—like defrosting the freezer.

After ten grueling hours of chaos spent juggling ongoing cases while trying to get a handle on the Pryka/Robbins development, she needed something that would take her mind off the office, allow her to take an all-important step back and look at the details with a fresh perspective.

Sitting alone at her kitchen table, Bronte finished pushing the remains of her gourmet microwave dinner around in its plastic container, then leaned back in her chair. Gourmet. Right. More like airplane food for the patently time-impaired single person. She looked around the too-quiet kitchen. The television was turned low in the corner of the counter behind her, but talking heads didn't quite do it for her tonight.

Neither did the array of interior design magazines and fabric swatches lying on the corner of the table. She reached out and leafed through the top magazine, stopping when she came to a photo of a high-tech nursery, complete with a three-camera-angle monitoring system and automatic diaper dispenser. Absently, she bent the corner of the page back and forth. There was a point when she'd believed motherhood wasn't a part of her future. A time when she'd seen herself as a lifelong career woman, being completely content, deliriously happy even, building a name for herself in the U.S. attorney's office. Then came Thomas. She not only began hearing wedding bells, she found herself slowing her step near the children's section of Saks. Began reading articles on the future cost of higher education in magazines that she usually skipped. Had idly debated cloth versus disposable and began wondering if day care was tax deductible.

Of course all those thoughts went right out the door along with Thomas.

Then why was she wondering what the nursery in the magazine would look like with a different color scheme?

She sighed and pushed the periodical aside. Maybe she should get an animal that wasn't of the human male variety. Now *that* would be a switch. Kelli's criminally ugly dog Kojak seemed to supply her with constant companionship. She twisted her lips. Then again, she'd balked so badly—obsessed with all the possible stains that could show up on her Persian rug—when Kelli had asked her to watch her prized pet, her best friend had finally taken the pooch out to the McCoy ranch in Virginia while she was on her honeymoon.

No, a dog was definitely out. And the thought of being single with a cat…well, she wasn't even going to go there.

She heard herself sigh again, then pushed her tray aside and pulled the first of the evening edition newspapers in front of her.

Today, especially, had been grueling. The buzz around the U.S. attorney's office was that there was little question as to

Connor McCoy's guilt in the Melissa Robbins case. A case that rightly should have been hers as head of the Pryka case, but notably wasn't. Word even had it that Bernie Leighton himself, the senior attorney, her superior, was working up a case against him. While running back and forth to district court juggling two other cases, one an appearance for an evidentiary hearing, the other to sit co-counsel for a rotating attorney during his first preliminary hearing, Bronte had left at least five messages for Bernie. On last check, he'd returned none of them.

Bronte fingered the grainy black-and-white photo of Connor on the front page of the *Washington Times-Herald*. He was wearing a dark bulletproof vest with U.S. Marshal printed across the chest, holding a sniper's rifle at attention. Given the handcuffed and shackled men in institution dress behind him, the picture had likely been shot while transporting federal prisoners. The expression on his face… She caught herself almost caressing that inanimate face and snatched her hand back. The expression on his face was nothing if not arrogant.

"Oh, yes? Then why did you piss off Dennis Burns today by defending McCoy? Why don't you just hand dimwit Dennis your job and be done with it?" she asked herself aloud.

She opened the paper to page four, where the meat of the story lay, and folded it back to the piece. Okay, so maybe she took a little too much pleasure in honking off a certain rotating junior attorney, aka pissant Dennis Burns, whenever the opportunity arose—which was often, given his interest in her permanent position in the Transnational/Major Crimes Section. It was an interest he'd made no secret of when he requested to assist her on the Pryka case—a request Bernie had immediately granted, putting her in nearly daily contact with the guy. Dennis had been with the section for four months and she'd caught him practically salivating outside her office no fewer than five times. And that wasn't saying anything about his overt attempts to win the senior U.S. attorney's affection by eavesdropping on her conversations and—she suspected but had yet to prove—going through her mail and beating her to the punch at status meetings whenever she got a snippet of interesting information.

If she were a man, she probably would have taken him out back and settled things with him months ago.

But she wasn't a man, and her only effective means of ammo was working her butt off to prove herself the better person for her job. The key word being "her."

She skimmed the news story. These guys really should get themselves some new sources. Most of the time they were so far off the mark—

Her eye caught on something and she traced her finger back up to the top of the section.

"This afternoon Senior U.S. Attorney Bernard Leighton has named junior attorney D.C. Dennis Burns to head up the investigation…"

Bronte leapt up so quickly, she nearly knocked over her chair.

No…it couldn't be. Pryka was her case. She'd been the one Robbins had come to wanting to testify against her Serbian-by-birth ex-boyfriend for myriad criminal activities, not limited to but including the smuggling of illegal explosives into the country, purportedly for a third-party terrorist organization. She'd been the one who had nervously made her case before the attorney general to get Robbins accepted into the witness protection program. She had even begun doing some fancy footwork on how best to shore up the hole left by Melissa Robbins's death—first and foremost, by putting a call into the FBI agents who had been working the case much longer than she had, trying to finger

Pryka as being behind the murder of his ex-girlfriend, if not directly, then indirectly.

Of course, she'd have never guessed in a million years that Connor McCoy would be the one ultimately under suspicion.

Still wearing her gray skirt suit and hose, she padded to the front of the town house and yanked open the door. On the step lay the last of the day's print news offerings. She snatched the paper up and quickly turned to the section on the case. There, in black and white, the information from the other piece was confirmed. According to two sources, Burns had succeeded in taking the case from her.

"Why that no good, scheming, conniving little son-of-a-bitch," she murmured under her breath.

The sound of a passing car caught her attention. She looked up and distantly followed its passage. For a moment, she forgot that it was after eight o'clock. The deep shadows confirmed that it, indeed, was. Policewoman-to-the-core Kelli had once warned her that she should be a little more careful when opening her front door. That her daily routines were anal and predictable and, thus, made her more of a target for crime. Bronte told her friend that the only concession she would make was she'd vary the times she picked up her much-loved newspapers by five minutes.

She shook her head then turned to go back inside.

"Wait."

Bronte nearly jumped clear out of her hose. She swiveled at the sound of the masculine voice coming from over the stoop, then continued toward her now more urgent goal to go back inside the house.

"For God's sake, Bronte, it's me."

Her heart hammering against her rib cage, she stopped herself from closing the door all the way. She craned her head through the opening. "Connor?"

The instant she said the name, she wanted to kick herself.

Admitting that she recognized his voice from the darkness and with very little to go on was far too telling in her book—both to him and to herself.

"Are you alone?"

She considered telling him no, then thought better of it. He probably already knew if she was alone or not and lying would only make her look sorrier than she already was. "Yes."

All too quickly, he stood just on the other side of the door. She had to look up to see into his face. An involuntary shiver skittered down her spine—a shiver that had nothing to do with fear and everything to do with the man eyeing her in much the same way she was him.

"So are you going to invite me in or what?"

Bronte tightened her fingers on the door. "After the scare you just gave me, I'm more in the 'or what' frame of mind."

She made out his frown in the porch light from a neighboring town house.

"Oh, all right," she said and swung the door inward.

As soon as he was inside, she peeked back out, making sure no one had seen him come in. Though why she was so concerned, she couldn't say. Maybe because this was Georgetown. And for some reason it mattered to her that her neighbors not think she was in cahoots with the person whose face was splattered all over the front page of the very newspaper she still clutched to her chest.

She closed the door and turned to face him. "An apology for scaring me out of my wits would be nice."

"Sorry."

"Gee, Connor, somehow that one just didn't hit the mark." Despite, or perhaps because of, the shiver that continued to skitter across her skin, she branded her wise-cracking for exactly what it was: her need to cover her thrill at seeing him again.

But that didn't change that she was minus one lead witness, or that the man in front of her was accused of subtracting her.

She eyed him closely. "What are you doing here, Connor?"

He stood still as stone for several heartbeats. When he finally did shrug, he looked anything but casual. "Would you believe me if I said I was in the neighborhood and decided to drop in for a visit?"

She found herself smiling at him. "Not a chance."

"Okay, then. How about I say I wanted to talk to you."

She worried her bottom lip between her teeth, trying not to notice the fresh, crisp smell of his leather jacket, or the way the snug black T-shirt she could see between the flaps hugged his abdomen to perfection. "I'd buy that."

"Good," he said, grinning. "Then I want to talk to you."

Bronte nearly took a step back. Boy, when he grinned, he was devastating. She'd have to remember not to make him grin.

"So…let's talk."

She led the way back into the kitchen, the only room downstairs that still showed significant signs that someone lived there. She plopped the paper down on top of the others, then moved to close the curtains on the back door and the window. For good measure, she switched off the television as well.

When she faced Connor once again, she found his leather jacket hanging on the back of a chair, and him standing with his arms crossed over his cotton-clad chest, his expression as dark as the one she'd seen in the picture. Only now the smart-ass description refused to spring forth. Rather words like competent, sharp and irresistibly sexy came to mind.

"What's with the clandestine stuff?" he asked, cocking a brow.

She made a face at him. "You tell me. You're the one hiding out in my bushes and scaring the bejesus out of me." *You're the one suspected of murder.*

He openly eyed the small stack of papers on her table. Right next to her half-eaten sorry excuse for dinner and the designing schemes she'd been considering. His expression darkened. She looked to find him staring at the picture of the nursery.

She rushed to clean up the place. "A little late for a casual drop-in visit, wouldn't you say?"

He didn't say.

"You could have called first. You know, given me fair warning so I could tidy up."

"I didn't have your number."

No, he wouldn't have. With Kelli away, there was no other way he could get it. Given her high-profile career, it wasn't wise for her to list her number in the book. And any unofficial channels he might have employed were no longer accessible to him. It was normal operating procedure that a government employee be indefinitely suspended when suspected of a serious crime, especially when said crime didn't reflect well on same government.

She slowly wiped her hands on a tea towel, thinking Connor had to possess a good memory to have remembered her address. It must have been at least two months ago when Kelli and David dropped her off at home after a quick dinner, Connor a silent presence in the back of the car as they did so. "I'm sorry to hear about your suspension."

Oh, but that was obtuse. *Why not just come out and ask if he did the evil deed, Bronte?*

"You got some coffee?"

She stared at him, surprised. "Um…as a matter of fact, no. I don't drink coffee. I have tea."

His grimace served as his answer.

She tossed the towel to the counter then opened the refrigerator. "Sorry, I drank the last beer last night. I have some vodka in the freezer."

"Do you have orange juice?"

She tossed another surprised glance over her shoulder. "Sure. With or without the vodka?"

"Without."

She grabbed the juice container, then retrieved a glass from one of the cupboards. She noticed the slight trembling of her hands as she poured the liquid and wondered just what he was doing there. And what, exactly, his overtly sexual presence in her last sanctuary would mean to her vow to stay away from him.

THE JUICE WAS ALMOST GONE.

Connor's fingers tensed against the cool glass. He slid a glance toward where Bronte sat at the table across from him, her gaze probing, her stance curiously standoffish.

He didn't quite know what he'd expected when he decided to show up on her doorstep to ask for help, but it certainly wasn't the blouse-buttoned-up-to-her-chin, suit-clad, tight-lipped woman across from him.

She got up for the third time in as many minutes. He watched her move to get something out from under the counter, the gray material of her skirt pulling nicely across her rounded bottom. He swallowed hard and purposely forced himself to look around the kitchen. He hadn't seen much of the rest of the shadowy town house, but this room was nice. Airy. The rough-hewn pine table was obviously the centerpiece. It was easy to picture ten people seated around it, chatting after a large meal.

"I was just about to fix myself some dinner. Have you eaten?"

Connor's gaze snapped to where she was angling a huge

pot out, then putting it on the stove. He could have sworn he spotted one of those TV type dinners on the table when he came in. He knew them all too well. "No. But I'm not hungry."

She turned and leaned against the stove, jumping when a burner switch must have goosed her. She moved over to lean against the counter instead. She crossed her arms under her breasts, bringing them into prominent relief despite the severe cut of her jacket. "Look, Connor, I don't know what you had in mind, but you'd better be out with it pretty quick. You say you came here to talk, but you're not talking. And I know you're not here for orange juice. And since you're not hungry, you didn't come all this way hoping to mooch a meal."

"I only live a few blocks away."

"Oh." She uncrossed her arms, then toyed with the spiky red bangs brushing her brows. "Then tell me, what are you doing here?"

Connor stared at the little that remained in his glass, then slowly drank it. Coming here was one of the most difficult things he'd ever had to do in his life. And now that he was here, he couldn't seem to bring himself to take the next step. He had to know what the U.S. attorney's office had on him, or else he wouldn't be going anywhere, period.

Every muscle in his body grew taut, his reaction having just as much to do with the physical tension that infused the room than his reason for being there. But he hadn't come for the physical part, no matter how enticing she looked and how much he'd like to sample that tart mouth of hers, to see if it tasted as good as he remembered.

Hell, he was the one who was supposed to help people. It was a role he had played well almost his entire life. First, when his mother died and Pops had disappeared into a whiskey bottle. Then, as a U.S. marshall in WitSec, where witnesses depended on him to see them to safety and make sure they stayed safe.

It was so foreign to now be in a position of asking for help, especially from Bronte O'Brien.

"I…um…"

"Wait a minute here." She held up her hands to halt him. He stared at her unblinkingly. "If you're here for the reason I think you are, you can just forget it, Connor. I mean, I enjoyed the other night as much as you did. But the other night was the other night. And today is today. You get my drift?"

He squinted at her. "What are you talking about?"

She gestured with her hands. "I'm talking about my just coming off a really bad relationship and not needing to get involved in another."

He got quickly to his feet. "Relationship?"

Her frown would have been amusing had the situation not been so serious. "Oh, wait. I get it. You're not interested in a relationship, are you?" She slapped her forehead then stared at the ceiling. "No. Of course, you're not. You were alone. I was alone. And you thought that maybe we could be alone together."

He widened his stance and planted his hands on his hips. "Are you done yet?"

She looked at him. "Yes. I think I pretty much got my point across."

"Good." He began to shake his head, then dragged his hand over his face instead. "Don't get me wrong. You're an attractive woman. Any man in his right mind would want to do…well, what you're implying I came here for."

Her eyes narrowed and she chewed on her bottom lip, making her upper lip look all the more plump…and kissable.

"I'm not here to sleep with you, Bronte."

Her eyes narrowed even farther. "Oh." Suddenly they

opened wide. "Oh!" She turned, fussed with the pot some more, then quickly faced him again. "Then why *are* you here?"

Say it, McCoy. Just open your damn mouth and ask her. "Because I need your help, Bronte. I need you to help me figure out how to get out of the mess I'm in."

CHAPTER FOUR

CONNOR MCCOY NEEDED HER HELP.

Incredible. Impossible. As unlikely as her waking to find the sun rising from the west. Bronte chewed on the information. Then chewed some more, not quite ready to accept it as edible. She stared at him. Stared at where the glass in his hand might shatter at any moment given his own apparent uneasiness with the admission.

Obviously, this wasn't easy for him.

Obviously, it wouldn't be easy for her, either.

What he was asking her to do was illegal—forget bad business. She'd never shared information with anyone. Not as a favor. Not even when she'd been in the middle of her rotation in the gang division and had been threatened by a Jamaican drug lord outside the district courthouse. And then she'd had a knife held to her neck.

She caught herself absently rubbing at the spot in question. "I see," she said quietly.

But did she really?

"Actually, no. I don't see. Just, um, how, exactly am I supposed to help you?"

Connor drew the tip of his index finger along the length of his brow, then sighed and dropped his hand to his side. A large hand. A nicely shaped, well-muscled, fascinating hand it was impossible to look away from. Somewhere in the back of her mind Bronte remembered the saying that a man's…intimate parts were made in proportion to his hands. She shook her head—in denial of the ridiculous notion that big, tough Connor McCoy needed her help…and to dislodge the very private images sliding through her mind. She remembered the other night in the park all too clearly. Standing under the cool shade of the cherry tree. The bark nipping at her back. Connor's heat at her front. Her hand slipping between them on a hunting expedition all its own.

She chewed on the scorched bit of flesh that was her bottom lip. "Sorry…I didn't hear you?"

"That's because I didn't answer."

She nodded. That would explain it. He hadn't said anything.

"So will you do it?"

Bronte budged her gaze back up to his face rather than his hands. "Do what?"

"You know. Help me."

Facing him wasn't helping *her.* The neck of her blouse seemed abruptly too tight, her skirt too short, the beat of her pulse far too rapid. She turned around and made herself busy. "You're talking about the Robbins murder."

"Yes."

She thrust her own hands into the sink as if the glass and fork in it were the remainders of a feast. "What exactly did you have in mind?"

"I need to see what the U.S. attorney's office has on the case. Details surrounding the murder. Evidence, both circumstantial and substantial."

Her hands stilled. "I can't do that."

"You can't or you won't?"

"I can't. But even if I could, I'm not sure that I would. Law schools are spitting out lawyers faster than you can blink. In this business, you're only as good as your word. And my word belongs to the district."

What a crock. Yes, she prided herself on her honesty and thought integrity was more than a word blithely thrown around without meaning during dinner parties. But she was known to bend the occasional rule for her own benefit, even though that rule never meant actually sharing information with anyone.

Connor cleared his throat behind her. "But you could pass whatever information you come across onto me. Or I could ask, and you could answer, without your having offered anything."

"Yes, I suppose I could do that." She'd already placed the glass and the fork in the drainer on the other side of the sink divider before she had a chance to wash them again. Now she had little choice but to face him. Slowly wiping her hands on a towel, she turned. "I have to warn you, though, I don't see myself coming across with all that much information. A co— someone else has been assigned the case."

The slight turning down of the right side of his mouth drew her gaze there. To that bit of telling flesh. "I thought Pryka was your case."

"*Was* being the operative word. As in past tense. As in I have a pesky coworker after my job and it looks like he just might get it."

"Oh."

"Yes, oh." She placed the towel on the counter, thinking that Connor looked somehow…right in her kitchen. Rather than invading it or overpowering it, he complemented it. The perfect knickknack to go with the wallpaper. She nearly laughed at the silly thought.

More than that, he appeared in no hurry to leave—which given what he'd said earlier about his not being there for…well, you know, made her curious. She glanced back at the stove. "Are you sure you don't—"

"Positive."

"Do you want some more orange juice?"

He glanced down at his hands as if just realizing that he still held the glass. He quickly held it out to her. "No. Thank you." A ghost of a smile ignited a playful gleam in his eyes. "One's my limit."

She took the glass from him, being careful not to brush his fingers with hers as she did so, though the smooth glass itself seemed excessively warm from his touch. "Good. We can't have you getting intoxicated or anything. I just might be tempted to take advantage of you."

The gleam darkened to a heated flame. "No. We can't have that."

Had she really said that? After his stinging explanation about why exactly he was there? She stomped down the urge to spend the next half hour washing his glass and instead forced herself to leave it in the sink. "I...um, can't do anything now. You know, in regards to the Pryka case." She glanced at her watch. A gift from Thomas. She had no idea why she still wore it. As a reminder of what snakes men could be? Or of what a fool she'd made of herself and never planned to do again? "It's after nine. No one's at the office."

"I didn't mean for you to do anything now."

"No, no, of course not." She turned the suddenly very heavy watch around on her wrist. Of course he hadn't meant for her to do anything this instant. He knew as well as she did what time it was. He also knew the hours of the U.S. attorney's office as well as she did.

Connor awkwardly moved first one way, then another. Bronte watched him. Was he nervous? He certainly appeared nervous. But that wasn't possible. What in the world did Connor McCoy have to be nervous about? By the same rote, what did she, Bronte O'Brien, have to be worried about?

Then it occurred to her. Connor's disposition didn't have anything to do with her personally. It didn't have anything to do with her, period. Understandably, he was upset with the events currently surrounding him and his career.

Of course.

Still, that left the reason why she was nervous around him.

And that's exactly where she intended to leave that particular train of thought. Because her nervousness went well beyond the fact that he was an attractive male—a very attractive male—and she was a female. A female who in the past few days awakened in the middle of the night clutching her pillow between her thighs.

Connor cleared his throat. Bronte cleared her mind. "Um, I think I'd better be getting going."

"Are you sure?"

He looked at her. She looked at him.

Bronte smiled. "It's just that you don't appear ready to leave."

He grimaced. Not exactly the response she was looking for. But it was the response that she got. "That's because there's a horde of reporters camped out on the doorstep to my apartment."

"Oh." Right. There would have to be given the amount of stories she'd seen in the various papers she subscribed to. And that wasn't saying anything about the television reporters sure to be hot on Connor's trail. Pryka's case was high profile. And this week was slow news-wise. No congressional scandal to sniff after. No war in lands so far away most couldn't even identify the land being fought over on a map. No extramarital affairs by people displayed in the Who's Who book. "What about your family's place in Manchester?" Bronte asked.

Connor's grimace turned somewhat comical. Not because what she said was funny, she guessed. He just appeared put out somehow—as if someone had posted signs all over his family's house banning him from entering or something equally ludicrous. "Let's just say I can't go there either." His enigmatic response ignited her interest all the more. Then his gaze suddenly locked on to hers, making her heart skid clear across her chest. "You know, you haven't asked me whether or not I did…you know, what I'm accused of."

"No. I didn't."

"And you're not going to now."

"No, I'm not."

He nodded once, as if her brief answer made all the sense in the world. In her line of work, asking a witness whether they were guilty or innocent was a dangerous practice. And one she stopped indulging in very early on in her career. It was better to consider all possibilities then make the appropriate maneuvers to protect the witness's credibility, keeping emotion well out of the equation. When she knew the person was guilty, she could never quite dislodge that fact from the back of her mind.

"Do you want to stay the night here?"

Bronte stared at Connor as though he had asked the question rather than her. But his utterly shocked expression told her what the truth was. And that was that she had just invited him to stay in her house. For an entire night. Stay. Here. Within the confines of her walls. Invade her personal space. A space she had yet to completely erase of Thomas's presence.

"Stay…here?"

She nearly choked. "Not…in that way. You know. You can camp out on my couch. The place is more than big enough for the two of us. Seeing as you're Kelli's, um, brother-in-law, I figure that makes you family, in a way. So it's not like you're a complete stranger."

The shadow of the smile he wore spread into a nerve-skating grin.

"What?" she asked.

He slightly shook his head. "I was just thinking that you don't have a couch."

Of course he was right. She *didn't* have a couch. She'd arranged to have nearly all of her furniture removed the day after she learned of Thomas's betrayal because they'd chosen it together. The dark leather hadn't done much for her anyway.

She found herself returning Connor's grin, feeling suddenly full of vinegar. "No, but I have lots of floor. And a sleeping bag."

"That probably smells of mothballs."

"Cedar chips." She shrugged her shoulders. "But if you'd rather go home and face the pack of wolves standing guard at your door…well, I completely understand."

"I think I'll take the floor and the cedar chips." The gaze that had held hers like an irresistible magnetic force suddenly dropped to the floor. "Thanks."

"Don't mention it."

He stood like that for a long moment. As did she. Then he looked at her.

"Oh! I guess I'd better go get that sleeping bag."

He caught her arm as she nearly flew for the door. "It's only nine, Bronte. Isn't it a little early for bed?"

Actually, it depended on what you had planned to do in that bed, she thought, her gaze sliding over his striking features one by one, then snagging on his all too tempting mouth. "What did you have in mind?"

"Do you have a television?"

She nodded then flicked a thumb toward the one on the counter.

"I meant in the other room."

"Actually, no, I don't." But she did have one in her bedroom. "But you can always set it up there if you'd like."

He nodded. "Okay."

She glanced down at where his long, strong fingers still encircled her wrist. He released his grasp. "Why don't you see to that sleeping bag and I'll see to this?"

"Okay."

CONNOR STOOD IN THE MIDDLE of Bronte's dark, empty living room feeling at odds with himself. Feeling more like he'd been evicted from his life now more than ever. He stretched out his fingers at his sides then crunched them into fists. A five-minute search of the room and the hall hadn't turned up a single light switch. Hell, how was he supposed to find a way out of this mess if he couldn't find a single, solitary light switch?

He drew his hand down his face, feeling the scratchiness of his stubble, then sighed. How was it that one minute all was right as rain with your life and the next it was hell on earth?

He'd never once in his thirty some odd years spent the night in a woman's house. Sure, he'd been inside his share. Saw all the little knickknacks the opposite sex had a habit of collecting. Cringed at the ultrafeminine color schemes and struggled to get up from too-soft couches and too-short chairs. But he'd never stayed more than a couple of hours. And he'd certainly never stayed the night.

He eyed the little he could make out in the darkened room. There was some sort of striped wallpaper on the walls. The mantle was bare except for a dark picture frame. Beneath him was an area rug of some sort. And a waist-high plant sat in the corner. Other than that, there was nothing in the room to reveal much about Bronte O'Brien.

He rubbed his chin. He didn't know what he'd expected. Flowers in every corner? No. Bronte wasn't a flowery type of person. Maybe some sort of animal print. Cheetah, perhaps.

No, no, maybe a tiger. Yes, that description fit much better. And made him feel even more as if he was in the middle of a lair.

A lair. He grimaced at the stupidity of the comparison. Bronte O'Brien appeared about as open to starting a relationship with him as he was with her. He wasn't exactly sure why, but aside from the fiery kiss they shared in the park the other night, she treated him with nothing more than distant politeness. He suspected she'd react the same way if she found a stray cat parked on her doorstep.

What had he expected? Given everything going on, he couldn't expect her to welcome him with open arms. Which was just as well. He recalled the picture of a baby's room he'd seen on her kitchen table and his throat threatened to squeeze tight. That being the case, and given his current situation, he was totally the wrong guy for her.

He glanced at his watch again, wondering what Mitch and Pops were doing in Manchester right now. And wondered what they'd thought of the news about his being suspected in the Robbins death. He paced across the room restlessly, then stopped at the front window, staring out at the quiet street. Of course, his father and Jake, Mitch and Marc had called him several times, leaving messages on his home answering machine, and ringing his cell phone, but he'd refused to respond. He thought about what had been covered in the newspapers and on TV and cringed. He only hoped reporters wouldn't track them down, looking for an angle for tomorrow's headline.

He'd thought about calling them back and explaining everything himself. But every time he'd picked up a pay phone, or pressed the call button on his cell phone, he'd purposely disconnected. Not because he didn't want to put their minds at ease. Or that he was ashamed of what was happening. He was innocent, after all.

No, his reluctance to return their calls had to do with the fact that he had no answers. He didn't know where he went from here. Didn't know what he could do to reverse the tide that was rushing at him.

He firmly told himself he'd call them when he had something to tell them.

But in order to get that something, he first needed some major shut-eye. His head felt like it was stuffed full of straw. His eyes were gritty as if a speeding truck had just blown by, throwing road grit into them. His muscles felt rubbery. Even now, standing still, he had to convince himself that his equilibrium was off kilter and that the floor was not moving.

He recognized the signs of fatigue from having covered more than one difficult protection case for WitSec. When he had gone days without more than a half hour of sleep.

Of course, then he'd still managed to keep alert.

Now….

Well, now, what was happening to him was personal. And personal always had a way of mucking up a man's mind.

Speaking of personal, he wondered for the fifth time whether or not it was a good idea to take Bronte up on her invitation. You couldn't get more personal than spending the night in someone's house.

He grimaced. Oh, yes, you could. You could spend the night in someone's bed.

His blood instantly heated to a simmer.

He reminded himself that it wasn't too late to change his mind. All he had to do was backtrack to the hall and let himself out the front door. Check into one of the countless hotels choking the city. His feet itched to do just that when the bare lightbulb above him flicked to life.

"It's not much," Bronte said, thrusting him a purple— *purple*—sleeping bag, then some sort of blue mat, "but it's all I have. I do have a guest bedroom, but right now it's packed full of boxes. You know, stuff I never quite got around to un-packing when I moved in last year." She motioned to the mat. "I thought that might soften the floor a bit. It's my exercise mat."

"Excuse me?"

She motioned toward the blue thingy. "The mat. It's what I use to exercise on." She shrugged. "Not that I exercise that religiously, but I do try to get in a couple of hours a week."

Connor stared stupidly at the mat, a vision of Bronte stretched out on the bit of plastic-covered foam popping into his mind. Given her taste in designer clothing and purple sleeping bags, she'd probably have a wardrobe chosen espe-cially for working out. Items that had high-cut legs, low-plunging necklines, and were made of curve-hugging material. He cleared his throat. "It'll do. Thanks."

"You didn't move the television."

"Excuse me?"

She looped a thumb toward the kitchen. "The television? You didn't move it."

"Oh, yes. No, I didn't." He moved the bag and mat to one arm and absently scratched his head. "I changed my mind. I haven't exactly gotten much sleep in the past few days and I think I'll just lie down, you know, if you don't mind?"

"Mind? Of course, I don't mind. That's why I invited you." She crossed her arms. "You wouldn't happen to want anything to help you sleep, would you?"

He stared at her, his throat going suddenly dry. "How do you mean?"

"Valium. A glass of cognac. You know."

He nearly groaned, only then realizing he had thought she was suggesting something of a more…physical variety.

Only he suspected that anything physical with Bronte O'Brien would be far from something to help him sleep. To the contrary, he was coming to believe that if he and Bronte ever had sex, he'd likely never want to sleep again. Who would want to sleep when there were all those enticing inches of flesh to explore? Her soft, sexy body to plunge into? That red hair to touch, her mouth to kiss?

"Connor McCoy, are you staring at my breasts again?"

He jerked his gaze up. Yes, indeed, he had been staring at her breasts again. He offered up a grin. Her answering smile notched up his naughty thoughts.

Oh, man, but it had been a while since he'd been with a woman. To be in the mess he was currently in, and to be thinking about leading Bronte up those stairs he'd seen in the hall and up to her bedroom where he could have at her…well, it had been a while indeed.

She glanced first one way, then the next. "There's a full bath down here. In the hall. Well, I guess I'll let you get some sleep then. I'm…I'm a little tired myself, so I think I'll just go up to my room, as well. Make a few notes on a case I brought home with me. Finish that book I've been meaning to read."

He nodded, wondering why she was telling him this. And wondering why all he could think about was her lying on a bed, any bed, in prime lovemaking mode.

Generally speaking, he'd always been drawn to women with lots of hair. Long strands that he could tug. That would fall over the pillow. Trail down over his face when their positions were reversed. But he found himself strangely turned on by Bronte's short haircut. It suited her. It was sassy. Provocative. Downright sexy. And she'd look as appealing after they had sex as before.

He forced his attention away from that same hair. "Well, good night then."

"Yeah. Good night."

She turned to walk away. His gaze immediately homed in on her backside.

"If you need anything, just, um, give me a yell."

He looked up to find her glancing over her shoulder, perfectly aware of where his gaze had been planted.

He coughed. "I will."

AN HOUR LATER, BRONTE LEANED back and stared at the case notes she had made at the small desk positioned in the corner of her bedroom. She drew her fingertips along the cool surface of the pad, wondering at the sensitivity of her skin. She hadn't been able to concentrate for more than a couple of seconds at a time. Sprinkled in along with her notes on the case were remarks like, "Make a list of who had access to Robbins"; "Check out just how secure the facility was"; "Why did Connor kiss me?"

Picking up her pen, she idly scribbled across the top of that remark until she could see nothing but a shallow, blue puddle of ink, then closed the file.

Face it, she wasn't going to be able to concentrate on much of anything right now, not with Connor McCoy literally camping out downstairs. A prime, hot male who had already proven himself capable of making her forget who she was with one simple kiss that had quickly burned out of control. Skilled at making her overlook the small fact that she didn't intend to become involved with anyone right now, much less a man with so much hanging over his head.

She slowly leaned back in her chair, her movements curiously languid, her blood seeming to meander through her veins as she gazed through the open door into the dark and quiet hall beyond. Nothing. Not even a sound to indicate someone else was in the house with her.

She glanced at her watch, then got up and silently closed the door. She opened her top dresser drawer, automatically reaching for the ratty old T-shirt and boxers she'd taken to wearing to bed at night. The side of her hand brushed against soft silk. She pushed the worn cotton aside, taking in the array of lingerie she had once collected with a passion. Something different for every night of the week. Her gaze catching on a rich blue chemise with the naughtiest of short-shorts, she glanced at the closed door, then slowly pulled out the silky set. A short while later, she emerged from the connecting bath, freshly scrubbed and scented, wearing that sexy lingerie, and feeling decidedly more wicked than was wise.

She quietly opened the door again, intently listening for any sounds. Absently picking up a perfume atomizer from her dresser, she applied the scent behind her ears and between her breasts, then sprayed the tops of her thighs for good measure.

Midspray, she realized just how ridiculous she was being. Connor was all the way downstairs. He had no reason to come upstairs. Not unless he was coming for her, but she got the impression that right now she was the last thing on his mind. Understandably so.

She started to put the perfume down, then changed her mind and shot a couple of spritzes into the hall, as though the scent would somehow waft its way down the stairs and tempt Connor to follow the path all the way back up to her room and...

And what?

Bronte's gaze trailed to her mission-style bed. It was the only piece of furniture she'd invested in so far. One couldn't sleep without a bed. Well, not for a prolonged period of time anyway.

Flicking off all the lights but for a small lamp on the bedside table, she nearly rushed the bed, feeling suddenly giddy, excited. As she fairly bounced on top of the mattress, then slid her bare legs under the crisp linen sheet, she felt vibrantly aware of every inch of her skin. Her thighs tingled.

Her breasts were slightly swollen. Her heart pounded in her chest. And she couldn't seem to stop herself from smiling.

She lay back more fully against the pillows, running her fingers over the smooth bedding. She remembered thinking when the bed was first delivered that it deserved to be broken in properly. Given a baptism of sorts. A night of wild, passionate lovemaking would do the trick.

The smile slowly vanished.

Of course, those were the thoughts of the old Bronte O'Brien. The one who would more likely than not have done exactly that.

But the new Bronte…well, she had learned her lesson in that department. But good.

For long moments she lay there, staring at where her hand still rested against the top sheet until her eyes lost focus. Her heartbeat slowed. The tingling in her thighs disappeared. And the lightness in her stomach became a leaden weight.

She didn't want Connor McCoy, or any other man for that matter, in her bed. Not right now. In fact the prospect of such a possibility made her think that it would be quite some time before she'd ever trust a man enough to let him into her bed.

She absently reached for the phone, then slowly withdrew her hand. She realized she'd been about to call Kelli. But she couldn't do that. Right now her best friend was off on her honeymoon in the Poconos with her new husband, David. Connor's brother.

She attempted to rub the gathering tension from her forehead. She'd never told Kelli what had happened between her and Thomas. She'd been so…unsure of herself then. So gullible when Thomas had requested they keep what they had together between themselves for the time being. She had thought he was being romantic and found the secrecy had lent a certain mystique to their relationship. Besides, she hadn't been so sure of what she had been feeling herself.

She'd never been in love before. Not in love, love. Not in quite that way. It had been all so new. So unshareable.

Then, of course, she had learned the truth, and she'd been too ashamed to tell Kelli. No, no, that wasn't it. She hadn't been ashamed to tell her friend what had happened. Her pain had been so powerful, so raw, that she hadn't been able to tell her. She hadn't been able to tell anyone. She'd been barely able to bear it herself.

And just as she had shared the joy of her and Thomas's relationship alone, so she endured the pain from their breakup.

Pushing herself up on her elbows, she stared down at the silky concoction she wore, hardly able to remember why she'd put it on in the first place. She threw back the sheet, peeled off the silky garments, then stuffed them back into the drawer and pulled out her old standards, which consisted of a ratty old purple T-shirt, and red-and-black plaid boxers that were nearly worn through in the bottom. She made a mental note to herself to pack away all the expensive silks and stow them in the attic. Somehow she didn't think the Salvation Army would appreciate such a gift.

Looking toward the door, she switched off the light, then moved to close the only barrier that separated her from one sexy, trouble-with-a-capital-T McCoy. Midstep, her toe slammed against the chair leg with an audible crack.

CONNOR JERKED INSTANTLY upright. He hadn't been asleep, but he had been somewhere between sleep and wakefulness. Even if he had been out cold, he was certain the muffled noise upstairs, followed by Bronte's cry, would have awakened him.

Freeing himself from the twisted sleeping bag, he leapt to his feet, then took the stairs to the second floor two at a time.

Darkness enveloped him completely. Combined with the unfamiliar environs, he had little choice but to rely on the slight shift in shadows to make his way around. There. An open door. He slid silently inside, making out the empty bed in the dim light filtering through the window behind it. Where was Bronte? A shape shifted and suddenly she was standing in front of him.

"Connor? What are you doing up here?"

He blinked at her. "Are you okay? I heard something."

"I'm…fine. I just stubbed my stupid toe, that's all."

"Can you turn on a light or something?"

The shadow before him disappeared. A moment later a small light from her bedside table flicked on.

Purple. The color of her tattered T-shirt registered before what exactly she had on did. Next came the undeniable shape of her bare breasts beneath the soft material. His breath caught and held in his chest. He held it until he no longer had a choice. The air rushed from him like a low whistle.

He caught her grimace. "You think this is something, you should have seen what I had on five minutes ago."

"Huh?"

She waved a hand, then crossed her arms. "Never mind."

The adrenaline that had rushed through Connor's system mere moments before slowly dropped. Where he hadn't felt Bronte's presence in her living room, it pressed in on him from all sides here. A soft, subtle, sexy scent filled the air. The mission-style bed was covered with rumpled, stark white, soft-looking linens. A small desk was overburdened with files and leather books slanted at haphazard angles. Framed black-and-white photos, he guessed of her family, filled the beige walls. And plants took up nearly every spare inch elsewhere.

He cleared his throat and glanced at her bare feet, noticing the way she favored one foot over the other. "Are you sure you didn't break something?"

She uncrossed her arms. "It would be no less than I deserve, but no. Everything appears to be in working order."

"Here…let me take a look."

He couldn't help noticing the way her brows rose up on her forehead, drawing his attention to her skin. Stripped of all makeup, her freckles were more prominent. And even sexier. "No, really, I'm fine."

He couldn't resist grinning at her. He'd played this game often with his brothers when they were younger. "I'm not going anywhere until you let me have a look."

Her expression shifted from surprised to puzzled. "Used to being in control, aren't you?" Even as she said the words, she backed up to sit on her bed.

"Indulge me."

He heard her swallow. "It's…the big one." She stretched her leg out and wriggled her toes.

Connor slowly moved forward, taking her lean foot in his hand, resisting the urge to run his fingertip up over her soft instep. "This one?"

She gasped and tried to pull free of his grasp.

"I'll take that as a yes." He examined her toe. Did all women take care of their feet as well as Bronte did? He couldn't say. He'd never really looked at a woman's feet. Until now.

"Will I live?" she asked.

He recognized her attempt at humor, but couldn't help noticing the breathless quality of her voice as she spoke. He released her foot, the feel of his hand against her skin suddenly unbearably personal…intimate.

"Oh, God," he heard her say. "The hell with it. I've been thinking so much my head hurts. I don't want to think anymore."

He tried to make sense of her words. "What—"

Suddenly she was standing before him, her hands on his shoulders, her mouth pressing against his.

He groaned and jerked her even closer. Mouth crushed to mouth. Hips to hips. Chest to chest.

Oh, yes. She did taste as good as he remembered. Better, even. He detected a hint of toothpaste on her tongue as she ran it the length of his, but it was more than mint he savored. Desire, passion, need…they were all there in the heat of her mouth. In the unconscious tilt of her pelvis against his. In the frantic movements of her hands as they moved from his hair, to his shoulders, then to his back, exploring, testing, grasping.

Realizing his own hands were still on her hips, he plunged his thumbs beneath the hem of her baggy T-shirt, breathing in her gasp as he touched her quivering stomach. God, she felt like heaven. Silky smooth. Hot. And so damn responsive that he ached just touching the toned stretch of her lower abdomen.

Slowly, torturously, he inched his way up, groaning when he reached the underside of her breasts. She wasn't large. She wasn't small. She fit just perfectly in his palms as he slid his hands over her straining tips.

Her own hands frenetically tugged at the waist of his jeans. This time it was he who gasped as she worked her hand inside without undoing his zipper, not stopping until her fingers caressed the hard length of him.

Suddenly she was leaning back toward the bed and he stumbled after her. The mattress gave under the weight of their bodies as she lifted her knees and cradled him tightly between her thighs.

Connor drew back, a shudder running along his spine as he pushed against her most intimate parts. Dear Lord, he'd never wanted another woman the way he wanted this one wriggling restlessly, passionately beneath him.

"Please…oh, please, don't stop…." she whimpered, rocking her hips up to meet his.

But in an instant of almost solemn insight, Connor knew that he had to do just that. He had to call a stop before things burned out of control. Before he gave himself over to something he feared would be larger than him, larger than the both of them.

He stilled her head in his hands, forcing her to meet his gaze. Even as he drew his thumbs along her hairline, reveling in the feel of the short, red strands against his fingers, he began shaking his own head. "I don't think this is a very good idea, Bronte."

She bit so hard on her bottom lip he was afraid she'd draw blood. "So don't think then. I'm tired of thinking why we shouldn't be doing this. I just want to let it happen."

He pushed from her, knowing that he had to, if for no other reason than the meaning behind her words. *Let it happen.* He'd never just let anything happen in his life. And he wasn't about to start now. No matter how much he burned for the provocative woman lying beneath him.

"I can't." He stood up, startled by the way his limbs shook from the effort it took to leave her like that. To deny his own need, her raw desire, was hands down the most difficult thing he had ever done.

He strode purposefully toward the door, his breath coming in ragged gasps, halting just this side of the entrance. He bounced a fist against the doorjamb. Behind him came the quiet sound of movement, of Bronte more than likely covering herself, recovering from what had just transpired between them. As difficult as it was, he forced himself not to look back at her. "I'm sorry."

As he continued out into the hall and down the stairs, he thought he heard her say quietly, "Me, too."

CHAPTER FIVE

"YOU WANT A ROLL OR something from downstairs?"

It took three full blinks before Bronte brought her assistant, Greg Neff, into focus. She'd been at work for exactly two-and-a-half hours and hadn't gotten more than five minutes' work done. She felt…disheveled somehow. Restless. And her demeanor had very little to do with the lack of sleep she'd gotten last night. She'd slept plenty. The only problem was her dreams had been haunted by one very sexy temporary roommate Connor McCoy, her subconscious offering up countless alternative endings to what had almost happened between them last night.

"Wow, that must have been some daydream," Greg said, leaning against the doorjamb to her office and crossing his arms.

Bronte snapped upright, not at all comfortable with his assessment. The last thing she should be doing was dreaming about anyone. Much less Connor McCoy. Either in the day or night.

Connor had been right in calling a halt to things. No matter the chemistry that existed between them, their inexplicable want of each other, had they…had sex last night, this morning would have looked most decidedly different. And she was sure regret would have factored significantly into that difference.

Better to be edgy and achy with need than to be physically satisfied and sorry.

She eyed her assistant. Greg was only a few years younger than she was, and reminded her of herself when she'd been in her first year of law school, all full of ambition and conviction. She hadn't considered it before, but she supposed that was part of the reason she'd chosen him. "I wasn't daydreaming," she objected. "This case is…well, a little more complicated than I thought."

"Uh-huh."

Bronte moved to stick her pencil into the holder and missed. Another try drove it home, causing the already overstuffed holder to bulge. There was no reason for her to believe he knew exactly what had happened last night. Or, more importantly, what hadn't happened. No. Greg had been with her back when she and Thomas were still a couple. He probably thought her distance had something to do with him.

The concept made her stomach tighten.

"Speaking of complicated cases, you wouldn't happen to know what I did with the Pryka file, would you?"

Greg grimaced. "You didn't do anything. Dennis Burns did."

Her gaze snapped to his face. "So what was reported in the papers is true. He's got the case, doesn't he?"

She sighed, then dropped her head into her hands. She'd tried getting through to the senior U.S. attorney, Bernie Leighton, no fewer than three more times this morning. Twice via the inter-office phone system, once in person. All three times she'd been told he was scheduled to begin a tedious trial that morning and his assistant had said he might be popping in from time to time, but not to expect anything.

She had decided not to leave a message. What she needed to discuss with him could only be done one-on-one.

Greg frowned. "Judging by the way Mr. Burns slipped in here before you got in this morning and lifted the file from your desk, I'd chance a yes."

She looked at him. "Did you check up on it?" She rolled her eyes. "Stupid question. So tell me, what's the word around the office? Have I officially lost the case?"

He shook his head. "Nope. Not yet anyway. Rumor has it Dennis is only a hairbreadth away from winning it though."

"Thanks for the heads up."

"Hey, just part of my job. You don't work. I don't work. If you know what I mean."

She smiled. "Yeah, I know what you mean." She briefly closed her eyes, wondering just what kind of fancy footwork it was going to take to get the Pryka case—and, by extension, the Robbins case—back on her desk. She'd spent the past four months building a case against Leonid Pryka. Had burned plenty of hours convincing Melissa Robbins that testifying against her former boyfriend was the best thing to do, the honorable thing to do after the thirty-three-year-old bombshell had discovered protective custody wasn't going to be a week at an exclusive spa complete with amenities and wanted to leave. And now with Connor's suspected involvement in the case…

She pressed her fingertips against her closed eyelids until she saw stars, then sighed. "I think I'll pass on that roll. But I could do with some hot water for more tea." She dangled her empty cup by its handle and he took it from her.

"Two cups. Boy, that must have been some night last night."

She realized Greg wasn't going to let this go unless she offered up something. Their mornings were generally categorized by playful chitchat. To divert from that routine now would be more than telling; it could prove devastating, given Greg's tenacious curiosity. She shifted in her chair. "Yes, last night was something," she said, calling up a smile.

Taking in her expression, he sat on the edge of her desk. "Care to share?"

"Nope."

"Come on, Bron, I share my dates with you."

"Unfortunately."

"Ooo, low blow."

She leaned back in her chair and gripped the arms. "I thought that was the way you liked them." Slowly, her smile vanished. "Anyway, my date last night wasn't with a person. It was with the Macmillan case."

He stood up. "You call that a date?"

"I didn't. You did."

"Things are probably pretty screwed right now, what with the lead witness in the Pryka case turning up dead."

"Probably is about the word for it." She closed the file in front of her, then slanted him a look. "Where, exactly, is Dennis right now?"

"You mean the pipsqueak weasel?"

Bronte laughed. "Yep, that would be him."

"Oh, I'd say he left his office about a half hour ago, taking off on some all-fire important meeting. This according to his assistant, of course."

"Of course. And the Pryka case file…"

Greg's grin widened. "Sitting smack dab in the middle of his desk."

Bronte couldn't help smiling back. "And what would it take to have that file back on my desk?"

"A simple please ought to do it."

"Please."

"You got it. You sure you don't want a roll along with the water for your tea? They may still have some bear claws left."

She wrinkled her nose. "No, thank you."

"Sure thing."

Pivoting her chair away from her desk, Bronte stared blindly through the window. The truth was, she couldn't have eaten a doughnut if she'd tried. She simply wasn't hungry because she had already eaten. And eaten. And eaten.

When she'd initially awakened that morning, it had taken her a full ten minutes to remember what had gone on the night before. That there had actually been a man in her town house. And it hadn't involved sex.

Well, she could say one thing for Connor McCoy. He sure knew when and how to make an exit. Her initial reaction to finding him gone in the morning had been one of abandonment, of disappointment that he hadn't stuck around to say thank you. Or at least goodbye.

But that had passed when she found the heavenly buffet he'd laid out on her kitchen table.

She didn't know how he'd done all the running around so early in the morning without waking her, but the tantalizing array of eggs, pancakes, sausage, hash browns, crab cakes, croissants, doughnuts and a special tray of a variety of teas had made her feel like she'd woken up in the wrong house. She'd never had that much food in her house at one time.

Leaning back, she slid the note he'd left for her from her pocket. "I didn't know what you liked, so I got a little bit of everything."

Bronte ran her finger over the carefully printed letters. As thank-you's went, she'd take that kind over words any day. Especially from a big, silent, sexy guy like Connor McCoy. Who knew he could be so thoughtful? Particularly with all he had going on.

"One cup of hot water…one filched file from your backstabbing co-counsel." Greg breezed back into her office, plopping the file down on top of her desk, then handing her the cup. Bronte quickly tucked the note back into her skirt pocket.

"Thanks."

"*De nada.*"

He just stood there.

"I said thank you."

"And I said no problem."

She laughed as she reached in her drawer for a tea bag. "You can leave now, Greg. I know your number if I need anything else."

"Oh."

She smiled at his crestfallen expression as the phone rang. She reached for the receiver at the same time he did. He beat her.

"Bronte O'Brien's office," he said efficiently. He held out the receiver. "It's Kelli."

"Kelli?" She took it. "She's supposed to be on her honeymoon."

Greg shrugged, apparently disappointed the caller wasn't male and couldn't shed any more light on exactly why his boss wasn't into doughnuts this morning. He closed the door behind himself.

"Hey, Mrs. McCoy, how's married life treating you?" she asked.

A discernible gulp filtered through the line. "God, it took me a moment to realize you were talking to me."

Bronte smiled. "Don't tell me. You forgot that when you get married it's customary to take the guy's name. Unless, of course, you're thinking about keeping yours. Now that would make for some interesting dinner conversation. 'Hi, I'm Hatfield and this is my husband, McCoy.'"

"Very funny."

"I thought so." She flipped open the file Dennis Burns had essentially stolen from her desk and that she'd had Greg steal right back. Instantly, she noticed it had grown fatter. She twisted her lips. Had Dennis been secretly working on the case all along? "So tell me, Mrs. McCoy, what are you doing calling me when you're supposed to be with your new husband enjoying your honeymoon?"

"David's off getting treated for poison oak…on that fabulous rear end of his."

Bronte howled with laughter. "Thank you, but that's a little more information than I was looking for."

"It's exactly what you were looking for and you know it."

The talk of rear ends and McCoys made Bronte think of Connor's nicely shaped buns. She banished the image immediately and instead leafed through the pages that had been added to the top of the case file. "So while hubby is away having some young nurse—"

"Male nurse," Kelli interrupted.

"I don't know that that's better, considering the location of the injury, but hey, he's your husband." She smiled. "Anyway, you just thought you'd give me a call because, hey, let's face it, you miss me."

"After three days? I don't think so. I'd need at least about three months or so before I even realized we hadn't spoken."

"Liar."

Bronte could practically hear Kelli smile. "You're right. I didn't call to play catch up. I just wanted to make sure you were okay."

She frowned. "Me? Why? Did something happen that I don't know about?"

"Very funny. No, it's just, at the wedding…then the reception afterward…well, you know, you just looked a little…down, I guess is the word I'm looking for."

Bronte couldn't think of a single word to say. She'd thought she'd hidden her emotions from her friend. She should have known better. She'd never been very good at hiding anything from Kelli, which was exactly why Kelli kept hounding her for the reason behind her melancholy behavior ever since her friend had returned to D.C.

"Bron? Are you still there?"

"Yeah. I'm still here." She absently flipped over another page in the file. "Is that really why you called? Because you're worried about me?"

"Yes, it is."

"Then, don't." She supposed she should be glad that Kelli didn't seem to have gotten wind of Robbins's murder and Connor's suspected involvement in it and was calling to meddle in more than her personal life. But she wasn't.

Her friend sighed. "Don't what? Call? Or worry?"

"Both. No, wait. You can call anytime you want. Only not on your honeymoon. It's the worrying thing I don't want you to do because…well, because there's no reason to worry."

"Come on, Bron, both you and I know that you're hiding something from me."

And with Connor staying the night last night, now I'm hiding two things. "Correction—you think I'm hiding something. I know I'm not. The reason behind my change in behavior is probably just something simple—you know, like impending middle age."

"You're twenty-eight."

"Okay, then, early menopause."

Kelli harrumphed.

"Well then, maybe it's because thirty is around the corner."

"You forget who you're talking to."

Bronte's gaze caught on something at the top of the page before her. Written in large capital letters was the word "COMPLAINT." She scanned down the page to find that Melissa Robbins had been the complainant and the document had been sworn the day of her death. "Actually, Kelli, the only one doing any talking on this issue is you. Me…I'm just trying to convince you that there's nothing to talk about."

"You know I'm not going to give up until you tell me what's going on, don't you?"

Bronte barely heard her friend. Her attention, instead, was riveted to the body of the complaint. *Witness contends that Marshal Connor McCoy and she were involved in an intimate relationship. That Mr. McCoy took advantage of her*

*circumstances and ingratiated himself into her life in order,
she believes, to convince her to stay and testify against Pryka.*

"My God."

"What?" Kelli asked.

Bronte shook her head. "Nothing."

She turned the complaint over, then to the front again.
Why was she just finding out about this now? And why had
Melissa gone to Dennis rather than her?

She cautiously fingered through the remaining additions
to the file, searching for any other little landmines that might
be hidden in there. A small pile of credit card receipts slid
out. She gathered them together then quickly scanned
through them. Sak's, Lauder, Cuddledown—for outrageous
amounts that rivaled her annual clothing allowance. And she
hadn't authorized a single expenditure.

She was still staring at the receipts when Greg opened her
door. She covered the mouthpiece with her palm. "What is it?"

"Guess who just returned?"

"Good," she said. "Tell him I want to talk to him. Now."

Greg gave her a little salute, then closed the door after
himself.

Bronte removed her hand from the receiver. "Look, Kell,
I appreciate your calling, but I've gotta run."

"Anything wrong?"

Bronte rolled her eyes then began rapidly leafing through
the new documents in the file, intending to copy them. "You
might consider changing the CD, Hatfield…I mean, McCoy.
That question is starting to wear on my nerves."

"Wait! Before you hang up, there is a favor I wanted to
ask of you."

She sat back in her chair. "Ah, there was another reason
you were calling."

"No, there wasn't…isn't. It just occurred to me now, while
we were talking."

She released a sigh. "Okay, what is it?"

"I forgot to take Kojak's biscuits out to the McCoy place in Manchester. Would you mind—"

"No problem," she said. "Just tell me the brand, how many, and feeding instructions and I'll take them right out."

"Thanks, Bron. I owe you one."

"You owe me more than one, but we can discuss that in detail when you get back from the Poconos, okay?"

Bronte was just about to break the connection when Kelli stopped her. "Oh, and Bron? If you need to talk—I'm not saying about what—call me, you hear? Anytime."

She squeezed the cold plastic of the receiver, wishing she could instead give her friend a squeeze. "I will," she said softly, then finally hung up.

She sat there for long moments, wondering if she should just come clean with Kelli. Lay it all out—Thomas, Connor, the case—and ask her take on everything. But she wasn't so keen on doing it over the phone.

Slowly, the items littering her desk came back into focus. Her stomach tightening, she sprang back into action.

Five minutes later, Bronte had hidden away the pages she wanted from the file, closed it in the middle of her desk, then reached out to contact Greg with the intercom. Only she didn't have a chance because her door opened. It was Greg.

"So where is he?" she asked with a raised brow.

"He left."

"Left?"

"Well, I couldn't very well stop him bodily."

She sighed. No, she supposed he couldn't. Not when Dennis had five inches on him and at least twenty lean pounds.

Greg cleared his throat. "Oh…he did want me to pass something on."

She stared at him. "Well, don't keep me in suspense."

"He told me to tell you he wants the case file back on his desk by the time he returns."

She hiked a brow. "He did, did he? A little presumptuous, isn't he?"

Greg frowned and a ball of dread settled in Bronte's stomach. "Ten minutes ago I would have said the same thing. But now…"

Bronte collapsed against her chair back. "Don't tell me. He finally managed to finagle the case away from me."

"Uh-huh. But there's more."

"More?"

"Yeah. You wouldn't happen to know where your best friend's new brother-in-law, Connor McCoy, is, would you?"

"Me?" She nearly choked on the word. "No. Why?"

"Because an official warrant has just been issued for his arrest."

CONNOR LEANED BACK IN THE diner booth, the crackle of the plastic covering temporarily drowning out the conversations from neighboring tables. He picked up his coffee cup and downed the contents. His empty stomach protested. He ignored it and motioned for the waitress to bring him a refill.

After he looked at his watch for the third time in as many minutes, he glanced back through the window and across the street at the U.S. courthouse, where the D.C. division of the U.S. Marshal's office was located. He'd called fellow marshal Oliver Platt over a half an hour ago. His friend and long time coworker had said he'd be right down, yet there was still no sign of him.

The waitress popped up and filled his cup. "Are you sure you don't want some lunch? The chicken-fried steak is really good today, I hear."

He shook his head. "No, thanks."

She frowned, making him realize she hadn't been concerned with his welfare, rather she had been looking after her tip. He made a mental note to leave her a large one as he lifted the steamy brew to his lips and took a hefty sip.

He couldn't eat anything if he tried. He was afraid his stomach would reject everything but the coffee he now plied it with. He'd barely even glanced at the breakfast he'd picked up for Bronte that morning.

He checked his watch again, only this time his interest in the time had nothing to do with Oliver and everything to do with one Bronte O'Brien and what she was doing right about now.

She'd probably be going to lunch. Or did she eat in? Judging by the scant contents of her refrigerator and cupboards, he doubted she packed anything, simply because there wasn't anything to pack.

Then again, she didn't strike him as the sort to blow money on a sit-down meal.

She probably frequented the building's vending machines, was his guess. Then probably picked at whatever she got, barely eating anything of it. At least her too slender frame indicated that's what she did.

Then again, for all he knew she ordered in and had the appetite of a cow.

He rubbed his hand over his face and sighed. Hell, what did he know about Bronte O'Brien's eating habits? She very well could have dumped every last item he'd stacked her table with into the garbage can. Why he should care one way or another bothered him.

Who was he kidding? He wasn't even remotely interested in her eating habits. He was interested in her. All of her. Preferably naked. In her bed. On her floor. Across her kitchen table. He didn't care. Last night his mind had been filled with the various ways he and Bronte could have indulged in some heavy-hitting sex. And knowing he could have seen through every single one of them when he'd gone up to her room, and that he'd turned her away, was enough to make a grown, sexually healthy man want to cry.

Connor groaned and took another long pull of coffee, grateful for the painful burning that snatched his mind from the subject at hand.

And ultimately that was the problem, wasn't it? No matter what he did, no matter how complicated his present circumstances, he couldn't seem to stop thinking about Bronte and how much he wanted to slip between the sweet, silken flesh of her thighs.

The old cowbell over the door clanged. Connor looked up to find Oliver Platt stepping inside and scanning the joint. He spotted Connor and quickly took the seat across from him.

"Jesus, Con, where have you been?"

"Here for the past half hour. Waiting for you."

"That's not what I meant."

Connor tightened his fingers around his cup, being careful not to show any of the anxiety that suddenly filled him. Oliver was nervous. "What's up?"

"Not much, except the M.P.D. was just by the office serving a warrant for your arrest, that's all."

There it was. What he had suspected. And feared.

He supposed he should count himself lucky that the warrant hadn't been served immediately after Robbins's death. Had it been, right now he'd be sitting in jail somewhere, probably denied bail—who better than a U.S. marshal assigned to WitSec knew how to make himself disappear?— and he wouldn't have stood a chance of proving himself innocent.

That the U.S. attorney's office had used the metropolitan police department over the U.S. Marshal's Service wasn't surprising either. It never boded well to have a group arrest one of its own.

"Did you get what I asked for?"

Oliver's face registered surprise. "You knew about the warrant?" he asked, ignoring Connor's question.

Connor shook his head. "No. But I figured it was coming."

Oliver looked around nervously, then reached inside his jacket. "Well, I certainly didn't. Even Newton looked like he was about to have a coronary when the guys came in."

Connor felt a brief, short shot of gratitude that his boss and coworkers hadn't believed him guilty. Well, at least not before a warrant had been sworn. Now...well, now his avenues of contact at the office had essentially dwindled down to none. Oliver, included. Not because he felt he couldn't trust him. Simply because he wouldn't place Oliver in any more jeopardy than he already had. In a case like this, aiding and abetting carried a stiff penalty. Including his job.

"Thanks for coming."

Oliver frowned. "I said I'd come, didn't I?"

"Yeah, but that was before."

"My word is my bond, Con. You know that." He slid a bulging manila envelope across the table. "Here. Just as you asked."

"A copy?"

"Yeah. Had a helluva time making it, if you want to know the truth. A messenger from the U.S. attorney's office was waiting for the master while I made the copy."

"Thanks, Ol. I owe you one."

"You owe me nothing." The waitress walked up but Oliver waved her away.

Connor sat forward. "Did you talk to Wagner?"

Oliver shook his head. Dan Wagner was the agent in charge at the time of Robbins's murder. He would have been in charge of the visitors' log. And as such, could essentially clear—or damn—Connor with one simple answer.

"No. Dan's called in sick ever since that day. No answer at

his place. And a drive by this morning proved he wasn't home."

Not good.

Oliver clasped his hands in front of him on the table. "You thinking Pryka is behind this?"

"Yeah, unless you can think of anyone else who wanted Robbins dead."

His friend shook his head. "Seems M.P.D. got a call this morning complaining of someone sitting outside Pryka's place. They contacted us to ask if we had anybody there. You?"

Oh, yeah, he'd definitely been there. Parked on the street in plain view, hoping to force Leonid into making a move. Only he hadn't. And the remote twelve-inch diameter microwave dish Connor had obtained from a local electronic store to attempt to listen in on Pryka's reaction to his being there hadn't yielded anything but white noise. Most likely produced by a top-of-the-line jamming system. It was no use planting a bug. If Pryka had a jammer, then it was safe to assume he also had his house swept for listening devices on a regular basis, as well.

Oliver was staring at him. "Look, if you need anything else, you know where I'm at, you hear? I mean anything."

Connor nodded and watched as Oliver slid from the booth and made his way toward the door. He wouldn't call Oliver again for anything. Nor would he be contacting the office again, either. From here on out, he was on his own.

He pulled out the money to pay for his coffee, then re-membered to leave the extra tip for the tired waitress. Slipping the envelope into his jacket, he strode toward the door himself. Out on the sidewalk, he caught sight of Oliver walking back toward the district courthouse.

No, he wouldn't be calling anyone at the office again until all this was over.

Still, there was something about knowing he could that made him not feel so alone.

CHAPTER SIX

BRONTE HEAVED THE HEAVY grocery bags up onto the kitchen counter, then leaned against the edge. What had she been thinking? Reaching into the nearest bag, she pulled out a fresh loaf of crusty sourdough bread and a can of coffee, neither of which she had ever bought before. Another fishing expedition yielded a five-pound bag of potatoes, three packages of different types of pasta and enough meat to choke a politician.

She wasn't sure what had possessed her to wander the aisles of the local mom-and-pop store when she'd finally called it a day at the office. A store she never spent more than five minutes in before as a rule. But an hour and five stuffed bags later—the delivery boy should be there any minute with the other three bags—here she was with more food than she could ever eat herself.

Opening a bag of corn chips, she crunched down on the rare indulgence, then followed the first with another before resuming her task.

Oh, it wasn't that she didn't know how to cook. Her mother had taught her and her two older sisters as soon as they were tall enough to reach the counter on a step stool. Lord knew she'd cooked enough while growing up in Prospect to last her a lifetime. She simply chose not to cook. Aside from it being too much of a hassle, her efforts always produced more food than any one person could ever consume. And if there was one thing she hated more than cooking, it was tossing perfectly good food away.

Fifteen minutes later, after the delivery boy had made an appearance, and she had ceased marveling at her bounty, she had every last item put away—the exception the dwindling bag of chips—then collapsed into a chair to stare at the box holding the new coffeemaker. She told herself she'd bought it because it was cute. It was one of those miniature models she'd come across in hotel rooms. And it was green.

She tried yanking open the top of the box. Failing that, she took a steak knife from the utensil drawer and poked at the tape, after much cursing and fanfare finally producing the little gem from its packing.

"Fine. Good. You're getting excited over a coffeemaker." Still, she found herself smiling. "You're losing it, O'Brien."

Truth be told, she'd lost it long before now. And while she was being honest with herself, she might as well admit that the only reason she'd bought the stupid coffee machine was in the hopes that a certain coffee lover would be stopping by.

But she wasn't up for honesty right now. No. She'd bought the damn thing because Kelli liked coffee and always groaned about having to drink tea when she came over.

Yes. That answer she could deal with.

Setting the new appliance up first next to the television, then on the other side of the counter nearer the refrigerator, she sighed with satisfaction then gathered the packing material. She opened the back door for access to the large garbage bin on the back porch and started to stuff the box inside.

"Did you buy that for me?"

Bronte nearly shrieked as she spun around to face Connor McCoy, nearly knocking the half-full bin over in the process. He easily caught it and set it upright.

Just seeing him made last night's memory of being

stretched across her bed, him lying across her, surge back with vivid, stomach-tickling clarity. She quietly cleared her throat. "Jesus, Connor, I'm beginning to think you're dead set on giving me a heart attack."

His half smile made it all too easy to forgive him. And all too difficult to dismiss the nervous energy collecting between her thighs. "You didn't answer my question."

Picking up the Styrofoam packing materials that had fallen to the porch, she lifted the lid of the bin and stuffed them inside. "Keep asking follow-up questions like that and I'm going to start wondering just who exactly is the U.S. attorney and who the marshal." She propped her hands on her hips. "And no, I didn't buy the coffee machine for you."

Somehow it wasn't as easy to lie to him as it had been to lie to herself.

"What are you doing here?" she asked a little too abruptly. He'd not only startled the daylights out of her, her mind raced with the question of just how long exactly he'd been outside her back door and just how much he'd seen. Did he watch her read the back of the pasta package for the various recipes listed there? See her demolish half the bag of corn chips? Observe her spend five full minutes rearranging the items in her refrigerator for fear that she wouldn't find them otherwise? Or, worse yet, had he seen her caressing the damn coffeemaker as though it were a priceless knickknack then take forever and a day placing it just so on her counter?

"I wasn't spying on you, Bronte," he said quietly, as though reading her mind.

"Oh?"

"I just got here. I was just about to knock on the door when you opened it."

She looked around the tiny, enclosed area. No shifting curtains from neighboring houses. No telltale lights. Everything was quiet and no one seemed to notice the appearance of a strange man on her back doorstep.

The sound of paper crinkling caught her attention. Connor held up a white take-out bag. "I brought food."

Food she had, Bronte thought wryly, suppressing a laugh at the irony of the situation. She'd stocked up so she might have something to fix if he happened by again. And he'd brought food.

She crossed her arms as though suggesting the contents would decide whether or not she'd let him in. "What is it?"

His dark brows budged upward on his forehead. "Italian."

"Italian what?"

His soft chuckle made her smile as he dropped the bag down to his side. "A little bit of everything. There's ravioli, lasagna, fettuccini, garlic breadsticks—"

"You just said the magic word." She grabbed his arm and yanked him into the kitchen, closing the door after him.

But where it had been dim and shadowy on the back porch, it was bright and revealing in the kitchen. She turned to face him, seeing him clearly for the first time since she'd opened the door, and she couldn't keep herself from gasping. "For God's sake, what happened to you?"

He slowly rubbed his long fingers against his stubbled chin. "How do you mean?"

"It's just…what I meant to say is…oh, I'm just going to come out and say it. You look awful, Connor."

His grimace was all too telling as she placed the take-out bag on the table. "Gee, thanks, O'Brien."

She waved him away. "You know what I mean." She eyed him more closely. "You haven't been home yet, have you?"

His silence said what he apparently could not.

"I see." She caught sight of the dog biscuits on the counter. The biscuits Kell had asked her to pick up for Kojak. "And have you been in contact with your family?"

He shifted from foot to foot. "Do you mind if I…go clean up a bit before we eat?"

She sucked in her lips, then shook her head. "No. Go ahead. I'll get everything set up while you're gone."

BRONTE WAS RIGHT. He did look awful. Though the words he'd have chosen would have been cruder. He looked like shit. Crap. Hell. All three rolled up into one untidy package.

Splashing cold water on his face, Connor now understood why people had begun looking at him as though they had something to fear from him. Those he passed on the streets; Pryka's neighbors; the restaurant staff where he'd picked up tonight's food. All had appeared wary of him at best, fearful at worst.

Hesitant to use one of the peach-colored towels folded on a shelf, he instead shook his hands in the sink, then used them to comb back his hair. Not that there was much there to comb, but the act of doing it made him feel somewhat more presentable. What he could really use was a long, hot shower, a straight razor, and a clean change of clothes.

And while he was at it, he'd like the real murderer of Melissa Robbins to step forward and give him back his life.

Moments later, he stood in the kitchen doorway, watching Bronte set the table. She hadn't noticed him yet and he took the opportunity to appreciate her.

She was something to look at, Bronte O'Brien. Tall, slender, almost model-like, though there was something more lively than graceful about her. Her short red bangs bounced as she moved, calling attention to her animated green eyes, her pinched nose and her mismatched lips. He had never met a woman whose upper lip was fuller than her lower and it was there his gaze was drawn to again and again.

"You're staring again, Connor McCoy."

He realized she had caught on to his quiet perusal and now stood looking at him with almost playful reproach. Today she wore red, black and white plaid trousers and a short-sleeved black turtleneck. More casual than what she'd worn the day before, though he suspected that there was a severe blazer hanging nearby somewhere. He lowered his gaze to her bare feet and fought the urge to smile. Professional to the end when at work, he guessed the shoes were the first things to go the instant she walked through the front door of her town house.

A desire to see her shuck the remainder of her professional attire ignited his groin.

He cleared his throat. "Yes, I guess I am staring. Again."

"That's bad etiquette, you know."

"I know."

She laughed. "That's one thing I like about you, McCoy. There's no lying in you. Pull up a chair."

Connor did as she asked, craning his neck to follow her movements. She liked something about him? And she'd indicated that was but one thing. What were the others?

He moved to crane his neck the other way when she reached over his shoulder and placed his silverware next to his plate. She smelled good. He nearly groaned when her breast rubbed against the back of his head. He fought the urge to lean back against her chest, burrow into the space between those small mounds of flesh, and stay until his world was set back right on its axis.

"Wine?"

He blinked. "Wine? I didn't bring any."

She smiled as she sat down adjacent to him. "I meant do you want any?"

"No. No, thanks."

She handed him a beer instead and he grinned at her. "Thanks."

"Don't mention it." He watched as she poured herself a small amount of red wine into a crystal wineglass.

They both reached for the lasagna she'd placed on a plate.

"Pardon me," she said.

"You, first," he said at the same time.

She smiled. "Tell you what, why don't I serve us both?"

Connor shifted on his chair, watching as she served first him, then herself. He wasn't used to anyone doing things for him. He was accustomed to doing for himself. In fact, while growing up often had been the time he'd served his four younger brothers only to find he'd forgotten to put something on his own plate. On one occasion, he recalled trying to hide his misjudgment, only to have Jake slide him his plate on the sly. He'd pushed it firmly back, but the action had gained him the attention of the others and they'd all chipped in, giving him portions from their plates until his was heaping full.

Well, all excerpt Marc. Marc had held out until last and, once he'd gotten a gander at how much he had on his plate, he'd pulled his own plate back.

"What are you smiling about?" Bronte asked.

Connor reached for the breadsticks and automatically put one on the side of her plate. "Nothing."

She rolled her eyes as she stuck a half a ravioli into her mouth and chewed. "Typical male response. Tell me, is it something you all are born with, or is it a learned behavior?"

He shrugged. "It just means that whatever we were thinking about isn't of the sharing variety."

"Oh." He watched pink tinge her cheeks. "Now that's a response I can live with."

His eyes widened as she reached for the fettuccini. He honestly didn't know where she was going to put all the food she was piling on top of her plate, but he was having a good time watching her try.

"So," she said, taking a sip of wine, then licking the moisture from her upper lip. "How'd it go today?"

Connor's chewing slowed, the linguine in his mouth

suddenly wet plaster. He needed the help of his beer to swallow it down. "Fine."

He found her question and his answer strange. Odd in that it seemed to indicate that everything was fine. That today had gone just like any other normal workday.

But, of course, it hadn't. Because there was nothing normal about his life right now. Even sitting here in Bronte's kitchen eating Italian wasn't normal. But in the swirling chaos that was currently his life, Bronte's kitchen was the only place he felt…calm.

"And your day?" Connor found himself asking, cringing at the continued normal sound of the conversation.

"Not so fine."

He looked at her.

"That coworker I told you about? Well, he finally got what he wanted. The Pryka/Robbins case is now officially his."

He nodded, as if what she'd said was expected.

He couldn't help noticing the way her fork began dragging across her plate and how she took tiny, distracted bites of food rather than the heaping forkfuls she had just moments before. "I, um, did come across something interesting, though."

He met her gaze, reading in it an ambiguous something he wasn't sure he liked.

She shook her head slightly. "But I don't want to talk about that right now."

Connor helped himself to more ravioli, though the last thing on his mind right now was more food.

"So," Bronte said, "tell me something about the mighty McCoys that I don't already know."

He raised his brows. "Pardon me?"

Her smile took him aback. "You know, something other than Kelli has already told me."

"No, I meant the 'mighty' part."

She shrugged. "Don't tell me you're surprised. I mean, every one of you is in law enforcement in one branch or another, right?"

At least until a couple days ago, he thought silently. "Just about," he said.

"Including your father?"

"Including my father."

"Why?"

He lifted his gaze from his plate to look at her. "Excuse me?"

"Why? Why did you choose to get into law enforcement?"

He slowly shrugged, not sure if he understood the question. What did she mean by "why"? He just had, that's all. He couldn't remember a time when he wanted to be anything other than a police officer. But during his first year in the academy, his class was visited by a recruiter for the justice department. More specifically, the U.S. Marshal's Service. He'd been impressed. And by then, the rift between him and Pops had grown so wide, he was yearning for a chance to make his own way in some other branch of law enforcement. Something that didn't have anything to do with Sean McCoy. So he'd surprised everyone by taking a job as a prison guard at night, taking college courses in the morning, and keeping after his younger, still-teenaged brothers during the rest of his day.

"You don't choose law enforcement," he said quietly. "Law enforcement chooses you."

"Have you ever come close to being burnt out?"

"No."

"It must get tiring sometimes, dealing with what amounts to the dregs of society day in, day out."

He wondered what she was getting at. "You could just as easily be talking about yourself, you know."

She appeared startled. "Yes. I guess I could." Her smile loosened the tension he'd begun to feel.

He asked, "Have you ever come close to burning out?"

She took a deep breath, then let it out, drawing his gaze to her breasts beneath the clinging fabric of her top. "No. I never have." She broke apart a piece of garlic bread. "It's funny, but I've never really noticed the similarities between what we do. But when all is said and done, we're both about putting people behind bars and keeping them there, aren't we? We just come at it from different directions."

He couldn't help smiling. "It's just that my job took a lot less schooling."

"Ha ha." His gaze glued to her lips as she chewed a healthy portion of bread. "Did you ever consider pursuing a law degree?"

His laugh was immediate and thorough.

"No, I'm serious. You were good." She waved her bread-stick at him. "Top of the class, if I remember correctly."

He realized she was serious. He fell silent.

"I also remember being incredibly pissed that you just seemed to breeze in and out of class, missing at least a third of the lectures, while I had to sit there every minute of every day, and you still beat my best score."

"It wasn't an option," he said point blank.

"What wasn't? Your getting the top score? Or pursuing a law degree?"

"Both."

"I don't understand."

"My family…well, an advanced degree wasn't in the cards for any of us, if you get my drift. There just wasn't the money."

"With your grades, you could have landed a scholarship."

"You don't understand. I had to work to help support the boys."

Her brows drew together. "The boys? You make it sound as if they were your children."

"That's because in a way they were."

Her expression grew very still. "Your dad?"

He shrugged with one shoulder, more irritated than nonchalant. "He wasn't around much."

"Sorry. I didn't know."

He wondered if she would ask about his mother and tensed at the possibility. He sincerely hoped she wouldn't. Then again, it was quite plausible that she already knew his mother had passed away from Kelli.

"How did your mom die?"

Connor's throat threatened to choke him completely. That was the one question he wasn't prepared for. Would never be prepared for.

"If it's all right with you, I'd prefer not to talk about it."

"Sure…that's fine."

For long minutes, Connor heard only the sound of forks against plates, quiet swallows, and the thud-thud of his heart in his chest.

He'd never talked about what had happened with his mother with anyone. He hadn't come close now, but he'd found himself wanting to tell her something, even if it was that he didn't want to discuss it. Which was telling in and of itself. Very telling. Usually he was silent where the topic of his mother was concerned. And the change in routine scared the hell out of him. What did it mean that he might want to share things with Bronte that he hadn't even shared with his own brothers?

Bronte cleared her throat. "My mother's paraplegic. She's wheelchair bound."

Connor stared at her. She might as well have just told him that she'd been born with two heads.

She smiled at him. "Sorry. After that awkward moment,

I felt I had to say something. And, well, you have to admit, something like that has a way of rerouting a conversation in a way nothing else can."

He considered her. "Do you have brothers and sisters?"

"Two sisters. Both older."

"How'd it happen?"

Her smile broadened. "For someone who doesn't want to talk much about his own family, you're sure asking a lot of questions about mine."

"If you don't want to talk about it—"

"No, that's okay. It's been a part of my life for so long that I don't really even see the wheelchair anymore." She chewed on some more bread, then groaned. "God, I couldn't eat another bite if I tried." She wiped her hands on her napkin. "Mom injured her back when I was nine. She wasn't doing anything especially noteworthy at the time. Gardening or something, I think. That night she felt a tingling sensation in her legs. By the next week, she was completely immobile." She shrugged. "She suffered through five surgeries before deciding to call a halt to them and accept life from a wheelchair. By then, both my sisters had already moved out, so taking care of the household duties pretty much fell into my lap."

"That must have been rough."

"I really didn't see it that way until later. It was my reality, you know? Our reality."

"Who takes care of the house now?"

"A woman comes by three times a week. Does most of the cooking and cleaning. Sees to the things Mom can't do. My sisters help with the rest. Though Mom is pretty active and can do most things nowadays, she's more busy with outside interests now."

She gave him a smile, nearly knocking his socks straight off with the jolt of electricity it sent through him.

"So, is that enough, or would you like to know more?"

Connor cleared his throat. "That's enough, I guess."

"Are you sure? Because if it's not, I can always tell you how I could never get away with anything in high school because my father was the resident math teacher. Not that I would have tried anything anyway, mind you, because, let's face it, not many kids my own age wanted to have anything to do with a girl who towered at least a head over them."

"You're exaggerating."

"You think so, huh? Hold on a minute." She pushed from the table, then disappeared into the other room. Her soft footfalls on the stairs told him she'd probably be a while. Connor started cleaning the table.

A couple minutes later she returned carrying an old, tattered photo album. "Here."

He clutched the leather bound album in his hands.

"Go ahead. Open it. Any page."

Connor did as she asked. The first picture he saw was of Bronte as an infant. All red hair, freckles and two teeth. He grinned.

"Just wait, it gets worse."

He cleared his throat and skipped about five pages. His gaze caught on a picture of a too tall, too skinny, very awkward teenager with a mouth full of braces. She was standing next to a couple of other girls, presumably of the same age, and they came to about shoulder level. Correction, she wasn't standing next to them. Rather, she was in the picture with them. They couldn't have stood farther away from her if they tried. Or her from them.

Photo after photo, Connor saw the same thing. Until he reached one taken of her outside G.W.U. Finally, she began to resemble the woman he now knew.

Bronte finished clearing the table. "So aren't you going to say anything?"

Connor slowly closed the album, unable to stop a grin. "Um, you weren't exaggerating?"

Her laughter hit him somewhere deep down in his stomach and he found himself laughing with her as they both dropped back down into their chairs.

Connor leaned back, shaking his head as he pushed the album back toward her. "Those are some really bad pictures."

She shook her finger. "No, the pictures aren't to blame. I was." She flipped the album back open. "I don't know. I suppose I wouldn't have been so bad had I learned to tame that hair and used some makeup. And my fashion sense wasn't the greatest back then." She visibly shuddered, then closed the album again. "Still, I was more interested in stretching out across the floor in the bedroom my father had converted to a library and inhaling every book in there."

"Ah, an inherited interest."

"You could say that. My oldest sister's name is Emily. My second sister Catherine. And I'm Bronte." She smiled. "Mom had a thing for *Wuthering Heights*. Dad used to joke that he was glad they never had a son because she would have stuck him with the name Heathcliff."

Connor found himself laughing again. The kind of hold-nothing-back, happy type of laughter he hadn't indulged in in a very long time—and that he probably shouldn't be giving himself over to now. It was just that when he was around Bronte, she made everything seem...well, not so bad. More than that, she was good at reaching inside him, making him forget who he was and where he came from for just a little while. Making him forget that just outside the front door, his life as he knew it had come to a crashing halt.

His laughter faded, making him realize she wasn't laughing anymore either. The tension quotient in the room shot up by at least ten degrees. He watched where she absently worried the corner of the album, her upper lip caught firmly between her teeth.

"Um…I have some photos of a kind of my own." He reached for the leather jacket he had slung on the back of the chair and took out the manila envelope Oliver had passed onto him earlier at the diner. "It's the security video taken the day of Robbins's death."

Her gaze riveted to his face. "How'd you get it?" She held up her hand. "Never mind. I don't think I want to know." She accepted the video and placed it on top of the album. "From what I know, the U.S. attorney's office doesn't even have a copy of this yet."

"They do now."

She traced the lines of the tape through the manila envelope, bringing it into stark relief. "You do know that an official warrant has been issued for your arrest."

He nodded, his throat growing suddenly tight. "I'd better be going," he said, pushing from the table.

"Wait." Bronte quickly stood up with him, color rising high in her cheeks. "There's something I've been meaning to ask you. Something that's been bothering me."

Connor considered her serious expression. This was it. She was going to ask him whether or not he had anything to do with Robbins's murder.

"You see, the case was taken from me. But my assistant managed to filch the file for a few moments so I could check on the progress. See if I could help you out…."

Her voice trailed off, and her gaze was plastered to the photo album her hand still rested against.

"And did you find anything?"

She finally looked at him. "Yes, I did. Only I don't see where this information can help you." She slipped her hand from the table and crossed her arms under her breasts. "Were you involved with Melissa Robbins, Connor? I mean, intimately?"

CHAPTER SEVEN

STRANGELY, BRONTE FELT AS if she couldn't breathe. She merely stood staring at Connor as if his answer held all the importance in the world. Why, she didn't want to explore. If he had been intimately involved with Melissa, that didn't mean he had killed her.

Though even she had to admit that things weren't looking very good for him.

Connor's eyes turned from warm, dark blue to stormy, metallic green. "What do you think?"

Bronte finally drew a breath. "Well, obviously I don't know what I think at this point or else I wouldn't have asked." She held her ground. "What I do know is that Melissa swore out a complaint against you the day of her, um, untimely passing."

He took a step closer to her. So close, she could see the specks of black in his eyes. "No, Bronte," he murmured. "I mean, what do you think? Not with your mind. With your—"

"Heart?"

Something flickered in those same eyes. "I was going to say gut." His gaze dropped to her mouth and she felt the incredible urge to lick her lips.

"I learned a long time ago that gut instincts can be very unreliable."

"I'm not asking you if you think they're reliable. I'm asking you to tell me what they are telling you."

Suddenly, Bronte was unable to breathe again. This time for entirely different reasons. Before, she had needed an answer to her question. Now, she needed to kiss him more than she'd ever needed to kiss anyone before.

"My gut's telling me that if I don't touch you right now, I'm going to die." Her laugh was more of a raspy whisper. "Just goes to show you how accurate—"

She was helpless to do more than watch as he lifted his hands to either side of her face, his gaze flicking to her mouth then her eyes and back again.

When his lips made contact with hers, the sensation was butterfly soft and overwhelmingly sweet. The feeling in her stomach was of something melting—her reserve, most likely, a small, quiet voice in her head said. But it felt so good, she didn't stop her eyes when they fluttered closed. And she was loathe to call a halt to her hands when they flattened against the solid, tantalizing wall of his chest.

He pulled away slightly. Bronte gave in to the urge to lick her lips, tasting him there. Tasting the tang of beer. The bite of garlic. The heat of passion.

"Tell me, Bronte."

She eyed his mouth. "Connor McCoy, I think you could charm a nun out of her habit in ten seconds flat."

His surprise caught her off guard. She might have expected a laugh, or a grimace, but never surprise.

She looked at him a little more closely, finding his shock genuine. Could it be true that he didn't have any idea how he affected the opposite sex? How much she burned for him after just a brief, closedmouth kiss?

"Do you really think that?" he asked quietly.

She nodded. "Oh, yes. If you put your mind to it, Hillary Clinton would be putty in your hands." She swallowed hard, afraid of what she was revealing about herself. Afraid of what *she* was seeing about herself.

Even after all she had gone through with Thomas, she realized that somewhere down the line she had opened herself up to Connor McCoy. And that by doing that, she had given him the power to hurt her.

But, right now, she could concentrate on little more than the way he grazed his thumbs over her cheekbones. The feel of his heartbeat beneath her hands. The palpable heat that drew them together as surely as a magnet. And her need for much, much more.

Drawing her palms along his solid pecs, then down his rock-hard abs, she slid them around his waist and moved closer until mere millimeters separated them. Her breathing grew noticeably more ragged as she blinked up at him. "Oh, just stop looking at me like that and kiss me again, McCoy."

And he did. He kissed her as if she were air and he was suffocating. He restlessly slanted his mouth first one way, then the other, attacking her from both sides—sliding his tongue against hers, then retreating, only to return again, making her want to whimper with need.

His hands first pushed up the back of her shirt, probing the flesh there, then dove downward, grasping her bottom then pressing her fully against his arousal.

Bronte felt as if someone had drenched her in gasoline, then flicked a match. Everywhere Connor touched, burned. Everywhere he didn't touch, ached. She tugged her mouth away from his briefly, trying to catch her breath. "Oh, God," she murmured, laying her cheek against his. "This is crazy."

"Do you want to stop?" he asked, already taking his hands from her.

"No!" she said a little too vehemently. She entangled her fingers in his hair and tugged him back toward her mouth. "That would be even crazier."

She gasped when he lifted her up, then hoisted her on top of the counter behind her. She immediately put her hands back to balance herself. He took advantage of her open position and thrust his fingers up the front hem of her shirt, seeking and finding her breasts. Bronte's elbows threatened to buckle as he tugged up the material even farther, then fastened his hot, wet mouth around her left nipple. She cried out, desire, fast and sure and all-consuming, pooling in her lower abdomen and making her thighs quiver.

Before she knew it, he was fumbling to unfasten her belt and the button to her slacks and she was helping him. Within moments, she was settled back on top of the cool ceramic tile of the counter in nothing but her panties.

He leaned back, his hands bracing her hips, and looked at her. Saliva gathered in the back of Bronte's throat, and her heart beat an erratic rhythm against her rib cage. Slowly, he moved until a finger traced the elastic edge of her panties, following it down to her crotch, then back up again. She caught her bottom lip between her teeth and bit down to quell her moan as he tunneled his index finger under the thin material then dipped it into her dripping wetness.

He leaned forward, reclaiming her mouth with his.

"Tell me, Bronte…what are your gut instincts telling you now?"

She braced herself against the counter and strained against where his hand lay between her legs.

"Tell me." He thrust first one finger deep inside her, then withdrew and followed with two.

"Please," she whimpered, grasping desperately for the front of his jeans.

He caught her hands and moved them instead to lay against the hard evidence of his arousal through thick denim. "Tell me."

Bronte shuddered, testing the width and length of him with hungry curiosity and spiraling need. "They're telling me that I want you. Badly. More than I've wanted anyone in a long, long time."

He removed his fingers from her panties, making her groan in protest, then caught and held her head as he kissed her deeply. "I want you, too, Bronte. More than you can ever know." He moved between her thighs, forcing her to remove her hands so he could rub against her. She cried out.

He dragged his mouth away from hers, his breathing sounding ragged in her ears. "But I can't...have sex with you. Not with you thinking I could have touched another woman the same way I'm touching you now. Not with that woman having been murdered four days ago. Not with you not knowing if you can trust me any farther than you can throw me."

Bronte's breath caught in her lungs. "What?"

He drew back from her, gazing at her intently. "If you think I could have been involved with Melissa Robbins, then it's possible that you think I could have killed her, as well. And that's exactly the reason why I think we should both think long and hard before we let whatever is happening between us go any farther than it already has."

He removed his hands from her face then slowly stepped backward. "Wait! Where will you go? Back to your apartment?"

He shook his head.

Bronte could do little more than stare at him as he picked up his leather jacket from the back of his chair, then shrugged into it. She opened her mouth to object, to demand that he continue what he had so skillfully started. But she was helpless to say anything as he apologized, then walked silently out the back door.

Bronte sat stock-still for long, quiet moments, then finally slid from the counter. She shook all over. Her heart beat so loudly, she wanted to put her hands to her ears to block out the sound. With trembling fingers, she pulled her sweater back down over her bared breasts. She made it to the chair and collapsed into it, drawing her knees to her chest then resting her cheek against them. A culmination of unsatisfied need, heightened frustration, and raw fear that she had gotten herself in deeper than she ever should have allowed were what made the first of many sobs squeeze from her tight throat.

DAWN'S DIM FINGERS seemed to reach through Bronte's bedroom curtains, catching her unaware where she sat on the floor at the foot of her bed, rewinding the videotape Connor had left behind, then fast-forwarding through the day in question.

By now the actions were automatic. She'd scanned through the tape dozens of times. But the images never changed. Exhaustion combined with repetitive motion made her blind to what she was seeing and numb to the emotions that only hours before had rocked her to her knees.

Connor was right. She had no business pursuing a sexual relationship with him when she hadn't faced down the question she should have demanded an answer to from the beginning.

Had he killed Melissa Robbins?

She'd skirted, avoided, and all but ignored the question… until now.

Now…well, she still didn't know what to think.

Had she grown so thick-skinned, so detached during her four years with the U.S. attorney's office that she was able to so neatly divide her professional life from her personal? Even so, what woman in her right mind would allow a man who was wanted for murder into her bed without first knowing if he was responsible for the crime?

Bronte rubbed her tired eyes. No, she didn't believe Connor McCoy had murdered Melissa Robbins. There. She'd admitted it.

The only problem was, the U.S. attorney's side had five points to her nil as far as proof went.

She squinted at the screen again, hitting the Play button when the figure of a man, purportedly Connor, appeared in the far corner, walking toward the door to Melissa's safe house.

Five minutes later, the same figure came out, head down, movements anxious.

She took note of the time and wrote it down for the third time on a small notepad she had placed near her feet.

She pushed Rewind again and sighed.

It didn't make any sense. And since Connor wasn't here to explain any of it, it wasn't likely it was going to start to make any sense any time soon.

Plucking up the remote control, she punched the power button. The screen finally went blank and it was if a cord had been cut, releasing her from some sort of trance.

Gathering everything together, she got to her feet, shaking the tingling sensation from her legs. Why had Connor given her the tape? From what she could see, it further strengthened the case against him, rather than cleared him. For whatever reason, he had gone to Melissa Robbins's house, alone, at the approximate time it was shown she was murdered.

She picked up her bedside clock as if staring closely at the time there would change it. She had forty-five minutes to get to the office. Peeling off the same clothes she'd worn since yesterday morning, she padded toward the bathroom and got into a scalding hot shower. But not even the searing heat could rid her of the knowledge that despite what she had seen on that tape, she still wanted him. Fully. Completely. She wanted him in her bed. In her life. And that, above everything, upset her the most.

She ruthlessly scrubbed her makeup off with a bar of

soap. Was she that desperate for male attention? Had she gone without sex for so long that she was willing to let a possible murderer settle between her legs?

Or was she so desperate to believe that Connor was innocent, that she was subconsciously blocking out all evidence to the contrary?

But why? It wasn't as though she knew him all that well. He was still little more than her best friend's brother-in-law.

Yet, there it was. Her immediate gut reaction to defend him, to defend herself for her belief in him.

When all was said and done, she sincerely believed that Connor didn't have it in him to break the law. Not for jaywalking. Not for embezzlement. And certainly not for murder. Even back in pre-law, he'd been as straight as they came. Even a white lie probably caused him countless sleepless nights when he was a kid. He was a man proud of who he was and where he came from. He did what he said, and said what he did.

Then why hadn't he told her he didn't murder Melissa Robbins?

He had, last night, a little voice reminded her.

She supposed he had—in a roundabout way.

Still, she needed to learn more. And she needed to know now.

She shut off the shower and rapidly toweled herself dry.

Fifteen minutes later, she called in sick at the office, leaving a message for Greg. Then she was calling the number in the Poconos that Kelli had given her.

Fifteen minutes after that, she got four phone calls, one right after the other. The first from Connor's father.

Out of all the McCoys, she'd probably spoken to Sean the least during her visits to the McCoy place with Kelli. And Connor certainly hadn't spoken of him. But their brief conversation revealed Sean cared a great deal about his eldest son and made her promise to contact him when she found out where Connor was. His parting words had surprised her. "I don't know how close you and Connor are, Bronte. But he and I have had our differences recently. In all honesty, the tension between Con and I goes back a lot further than that. But don't mistake differences for indifference. I care about my boy more than he'll probably ever know."

That particular conversation had left Bronte with far more questions than answers. But she reminded herself that now wasn't the time for them.

The next three calls came from Connor's brothers Jake, Mitch and Marc.

Now these guys she knew. While all of them were recently married, she got the impression that they saw it as part of their duty to check out any females that stepped on McCoy land, like a pack of wolves checking out the new addition. They'd given her the once-over but good. She suspected she'd gotten a passing grade from Mitch and Marc, but Jake…well, she didn't quite know where she stood with him. He was tall, dark and silent, and difficult to figure. It was only when his wife, Michelle, or adopted daughter, Lili, were around that he transformed into a man very happy with his life.

Still, her brief encounters with Connor's brothers had left her unprepared for their rapid-fire questions over the phone, a couple of them of a personal nature that left her speechless. "Just how close are you and Connor?" Jake had asked in an accusatory tone.

Funny, she'd called them with questions and instead was put on the hot seat herself.

An hour later, feeling much like she'd just spent an entire day being cross-examined by an experienced defense team, Bronte came to an eye-opening conclusion. Reporters weren't the only ones Connor McCoy was hiding from.

And after what she'd gone through, she couldn't say she was surprised.

CHAPTER EIGHT

DUSK CAST THE SOUTHWESTERN section of Washington, D.C., in contrasting shadows. Connor tossed a leather carryall into his SUV, then climbed into it and again took in the scene outside his apartment building. The six o'clock news van had come and gone, but there was still one television van parked outside, likely fishing for something to use on the eleven o'clock news. Most of the print reporters had already called it a night, however, leaving a garbage can overflowing with spent coffee cups and fast-food cartons behind.

But the reporters weren't what interested him most. No. What drew his attention was a dark sedan parked the same distance away but on the other side of the apartment building. The interior light in the car flashed on, revealing four men inside. Two in the front, two in the back. Suited men. The driver had needed the light to see his way through a white bag, likely the evening meal. The light went off again, cloaking the foursome in darkness.

Gee, did it really take four plainclothes officers to arrest little old him?

Connor shifted into reverse and backed up to the last crossroads. It wasn't until he was out of sight that he flicked on his lights and headed out of the city.

This was the first time in four days that he'd dared return to his apartment. Aside from needing to see that the place still stood, and confirm that, yes, indeed, he had a home, he had to pick up some clothes and some surveillance equipment. He'd methodically mapped out his entrance and exit, timing it for dusk, when there would be just enough light for him to see around the place, but not enough for those outside to see movement within. A simple quick in and out through the back basement window had gained him access—after, of course, riling up the dog on the corner, so that his incessant barking would draw his visitors' attention.

He pulled to a halt at a stop sign and sat staring absently at the crossroads in front of him. A part of him wanted to turn left and head on over to Bronte's house. But after what had happened between them last night…

Correction. What had almost happened between them last night. And the night before that….

He turned right.

One minute he and Bronte had been scarfing down Italian food like starved souls, the next they had been going at each other like nobody's business.

God, she had felt good. Her skin was so soft and firm and warm to the touch. He could spend forever touching her and still not get enough. Then there was the way she tasted. Spicy, hungry, and all too willing. But it had been her readiness for him that had nearly done him in. There had been a moment there, when his fingers were surrounded by her hot flesh, when he feared he wouldn't be able to turn back. Her hands had been boldly exploring his erection, then fumbling for the button on his jeans, and all he'd wanted was to be inside her. To thrust deeply into her and forget the rest of the damn world even existed.

Then she'd pleaded for release. The sound of her voice, even husky and needy, had been enough to set off a tape recorder in his head. All he could hear was her asking him whether or not he'd been intimately involved with Melissa

Robbins. And all he could think about was that if he had sex with her then, took all that she offered, and gave even more, that whatever was happening between them would take a nosedive in the wrong direction.

Within minutes, Connor found himself on the highway heading for Manchester. Oh, yeah, he thought, there was definitely something going on between him and Bronte. Always had been. But back in college he'd been too much of a coward to pursue that something.

Hell, as long as he was being honest with himself, he was still too much of a coward.

Bronte O'Brien had always made him feel…different. The instant he looked at her, background sounds seemed to fade away. When he was around her the world narrowed down to her and only her. He'd never felt that way before. And he wasn't sure he wanted to feel that way now. That's exactly the reason why he ran from her every time their paths crossed at G.W.U. And it's exactly the reason why he was running in the other direction now.

As the city slowly slipped away in his rearview mirror, so did some of his tension. D.C. was hectic and heady and demanded every bit of a person's attention. Traffic was thick. Streets many. Lights and signs and restaurants and shops all drew the eye, tempting you away from your thoughts and filling your head with others. Just being inside made Connor feel energized, pumped up, ready for anything. Only now, with his impending arrest, and his attraction for Bronte playing havoc with his mind, it was all a little too much. Overwhelming, almost. His muscles bunched, his nerves hummed, like he'd just downed two pots of full-octane coffee. He felt wired. Only this type of buzz didn't wear off with time. It only grew more acute, giving him the feeling that something was about to snap. And he was afraid that something was him.

He rubbed his face with his free hand. If he didn't shave soon, he'd end up with a full beard. He'd meant to check into a ratty hotel somewhere on the outskirts of town last night, but he'd somehow never gotten around to it. That evening he'd hoped to run into an ex-con he'd once apprehended who had recently been paroled. He'd been waiting for him to make his appearance at his usual hangout, but had ended up nodding off in his car. He'd woken up five hours later with a stiff neck, and looking even worse than he had before he'd fallen asleep.

And he never did catch up with that ex-con, a man who had a murky association with Leonid Pryka.

But there had been others. His day had been filled with them. A never-ending stream of faces and voices claiming to know nothing and no one who could help him find what he was looking for.

No, there was no word on the street of a hit being put out on Melissa Robbins.

No, Leonid Pryka, her ex-benefactor, didn't seem the slightest bit concerned about her testifying against him.

Yes, everyone believed that he was the one who had wrapped his hands around Melissa Robbins's neck and choked the life out of her.

The further he dug, the guiltier he appeared to get.

The knotting tension returned to his shoulders. It didn't make any sense. How could everything point to his having done something he never in a million years would have done? The only answer was that he was being set up. It didn't take a law grad to figure that one out. His problem was trying to figure out who and why, before he found himself sitting in a six-by-nine for what remained of his natural life.

The problem was he'd nearly exhausted every one of his human resources. His list of contacts was dwindling fast. And he was coming to the point to where he couldn't come up with another plan of action.

Hell, who was he kidding? After today even *he* was wondering if he'd done it.

Aside from the security video that seemed clearly to show him entering and exiting Robbins's room around the time of her death, there was also physical evidence linking him to the crime. No, no semen had been found. Thank God for small favors. If semen had been found, he probably would have turned himself in at the first precinct he passed, though he'd never had sex nor laid a hand on that woman in the short time he'd been assigned to protect her. In fact, he'd barely said more than the necessary words to her, such as "this way" or "stay put" or "we'll be right outside."

From the get-go, Robbins had rubbed him the wrong way. She was too blond. Too buxom. Too flirty. Too just about everything. And the unreasonable demands she'd made had set his teeth on edge. No, she hadn't wanted fast food. She'd acquired a certain taste for the good life while with Leonid and was determined to keep it. And from the start she'd complained about the accommodations. He'd decided to hole her up in the small house on the shores of the Potomac, the same house Marc had borrowed a year ago to protect Melanie. His reasons had been simple. Aside from giving Robbins privacy, the remote, coastal location demanded little outside protection after the first couple of days. Only two marshals around the clock. One close to the house, another on the perimeter.

Connor squinted against the headlights of an oncoming car. Most witnesses were thankful to be safe. At least before the reality of their situation settled in. It was only natural that restlessness and frustration would soon follow. But with Robbins, it had been more than that. She'd seemed…put out, somehow. Disappointed that the WitSec life wasn't all it was cracked up to be.

One of the interesting tidbits he had picked up on the

street was that when Leonid booted Melissa out a little over two months ago, the wealthy import/export businessman had given her little to take with her. She'd virtually been deposited outside the security gates with no more than the clothes on her back. And whatever jewelry she'd had on she'd hocked over the next few days. He deduced that she'd shown up on Bronte's office doorstep the instant her cash ran out.

He absently rubbed the back of his neck. Of course, none of that changed the fact that the U.S. attorney's office did have some sort of damning physical evidence against him. More than that damn security tape. Strands of his hair had been found in Melissa's hands.

How could she have had his hair in her hands?

He didn't have to ask how they knew it was his. The U.S. attorney's office had likely already served a warrant on his place and taken a sample from his bathroom, or even from his bed pillow. All they needed was one to compare against the evidence. And unlike DNA, hair tests were notably quicker, and nearly as irrefutable.

But that still left the question of how in the hell his hair had gotten into her hands in the first place.

Enemies. Lord knew he had plenty of them. Every con he'd ever retrieved or transported probably held a celebration bash when they heard the news of his pending arrest. But not one of them had the type of access needed to execute a plan of this nature. Protection witnesses were very well protected. He should know. He protected them.

Enemies at the department…

He couldn't come up with a single person who would want to see him fry. Sure, there might be a couple, two or three who might want to see him fired. But not fried.

The only others who had access to the witness were from the U.S. attorney's office. But even then, their access was limited. And their involvement in the murder would have come after the crime had already been committed.

Besides, the logistics didn't make any sense. Crucifying him meant letting Pryka off the hook.

In front of him, Manchester emerged from the darkening horizon. Storm clouds had begun to creep up from the west and the sun's rays bruised them, turning them ominous shades of purple and pink. Connor turned off the main road and onto an old dirt one that cut through Gerard's old tobacco field. He couldn't afford to drive through town. Lord only knew who he might run into. And the main McCoy place was also out of the question.

No, he planned to head out to his grandfather McCoy's old place that sat on some fifty acres on the other side of the new McCoy spread, the only parcel of land he'd balked at allowing Mitch to purchase when he bought Pops out last summer. Though for the life of him he still couldn't figure out why.

God, how long had it been since he'd last been out there? When he was a kid, before his mother had died, he used to ride out there on his dirt bike to escape the nonstop noise that was as much a part of the McCoy place as the paint. After she died…well, it was where he used to go to think things out. To work out a problem he couldn't get a handle on. To recover some of the peace looking after his brothers used to drain out of him.

Then, when he was fourteen, Pops had finally uncovered his safe haven. And he'd never gone back there again.

Hell, he wasn't even sure the old place was still standing. Time and the elements had a way of taking their toll on an abandoned house. Still, as he grew nearer the old southern colonial, he felt a tinge of excitement.

As immature as it was, he couldn't help thinking that this place had been his, and his alone. No one else had ever gone out there. He used to take great pride in repairing things. The front step that had rotted out. The upstairs window that had broken. The pump that had once supplied the house from the property's wells.

This was where his father had been born and raised. His mother's family had bred horses on the opposite side of the tract; his father's had farmed this part of the land. When he was younger he'd thought it romantic, his parents living on the same stretch of land, but being worlds apart. He'd once asked Pops why he hadn't continued the McCoy family tradition of farming. He'd expected to hear that he hadn't wanted to. That he'd found farm life boring and tedious. He'd been surprised when Sean had told him his decision had been based on strictly financial issues. That his own father had barely eked out a living and that he'd had to go into the city to find a job while he was still a teen. It was then, after he'd interfered and stopped a robbery at a small grocer's, that he'd formed a friendship of sorts with a beat cop. That beat cop had taken him under his wing and been a mentor to him, helping him enroll in the academy and earn a spot on the force once he was old enough.

And Pops had never looked back since.

Connor hadn't known his grandparents. His grandfather had died shortly after he was born, and his grandmother had moved to a retirement home and passed on a short time after that. But he liked to think that he would have liked them. That possibly he would have had more in common with them than he had ever had in common with his own father. Often when he was younger, he'd pretend that they were still alive. He'd ride up on his bike, lean it against one of the front columns, then rush inside to find them both waiting for him with a glass of milk and a plate full of home-baked chocolate chip cookies. Something out of a Rockwell picture he once saw.

Now, Connor grimaced. Why he should be recalling such childish memories was beyond him. It didn't make any difference now, anyway.

Slowing, he searched the dirt road for the turnoff leading to the old place. There. There it was. He turned in, grimacing when his front right tire bounced off an obstruction he couldn't see. He drove a good half a mile before the house emerged from the tangle of trees.

And spotted Pops's car sitting right out front.

He drew to a stop, staring at the new sedan. Damn. He hadn't expected his father to remember his old hangout. He glanced into the rearview mirror, considering backing out. But with his lights having swept the house and the car in front of him, he would come off looking like the coward he was.

The last person he wanted to face now was Pops. He had enough on his plate without having to pile his difficulties with his father on top of it.

He watched as Sean McCoy walked down the two front steps and came to stand in the middle of his highlights. He shaded his eyes with his hand, looking straight at him.

Connor drew up to park next to the sedan then got out of the SUV.

"Pops," he said.

"Connor."

He stood directly before his father. His father looking at him. Him looking at his father.

"We've been worried," Pops finally said.

Connor shifted from one foot to the other and crossed his arms. Of course, "they'd" been worried, not him. Not strictly his father had worried about him.

He tried to shake off the feeling. Not liking how…juvenile it came off.

"So have I," he said.

He brushed past Pops on his way to the front of the house.

He couldn't make out much in the dark, but did notice that Sean must have lighted a lamp. It shined like a warm beacon inside the otherwise deserted structure.

"Liz and Mitch came out and cleaned the place up a little this afternoon. Brought some stuff," Pops said quietly from behind him.

Connor tensed. How many people knew he'd be coming out here?

Rather than go inside the house, he instead turned, put his bag down and sat down on the steps, running his hands over his face, then gazing at his father. "What are you doing here?"

Pops strode over, stuffing his hands in the pockets of his jeans as he walked. "Kelli's friend, Bronte, called this morning. She wanted to know where you might have gone." He shrugged. "Aside from your apartment and the house, I couldn't come up with a single alternative—until I remembered how you used to come here when you were younger."

Connor considered him from under his brows, trying not to show his surprise. Bronte had called his father? Heat filled his stomach and his palms suddenly itched. He slowly rubbed his hands together. "That still doesn't explain what you're doing here."

Sean stood stock-still for a moment. Then he sighed and moved to sit next to him. Connor moved over to give him room. "You always did need me to spell things out for you, didn't you?"

"Yeah, well, maybe it's because you didn't do a whole hell of a lot of that when it was important."

"And now's not important?"

"You're avoiding the question."

"No, I'd say you are." Sean leaned back. "When were you planning on calling me? Let me know what was going on?"

He'd used the word "me" rather than "we." Not once, but twice. Connor stared out into the darkness of night. All traces of the sun were completely gone and the stars were disappearing one by one under the blanket of encroaching clouds. The wind had also begun to pick up, ruffling through his cropped hair and causing him to shudder. "Honestly...I don't know."

Sean nodded. "I know. You would have called once you thought you had things in hand."

Connor snapped to look at him.

"And since you haven't called, that means circumstances are as bad as they look."

"It can't get much worse than being wanted for murder."

"No, it can't." He felt his father's gaze on him in the darkness. "So what are you planning on doing about it?"

Connor's stomach twisted.

"Have you contacted an attorney?"

"I don't need an attorney."

"Of course, you don't. Because getting one would make you look guilty, wouldn't it?"

He hated that his father knew him so well.

"What does Bronte have to say about the situation?"

Connor straightened. What should he tell him? That Bronte thought he was guilty of having intimate relations with a witness? And that, by extension, she very well may believe him guilty of murder? But that none of that made any difference when it came to her wanting him?

He ground his back teeth together.

He felt Sean place a hand on his shoulder. He was torn between the urge to shrug him off and the need to lean into the touch from his father. "I know I'm probably the last person you want to talk to about this, Connor. And I can't tell you I'm exactly sure why that is. I know I've made mistakes in the past—"

Connor's hmmph cut him off as he caught sight of a flash of lightning in the far southwestern corner of the sky.

Pops slowly removed his hand. "But promise me some-thing—if you can't talk to me, promise me you'll talk to someone. One of your brothers. An attorney. Someone. I know you want to believe yourself invincible. But even the best need help every now and again. It doesn't make you a weaker man. It makes you human."

Connor said nothing.

How many times in his life had he wished his father would seek him out? Talk to him, one-on-one, man to man? How many times had he sought his father out, needing advice on what to do with one of his brothers? And how many times had Pops been wallowing in the contents of a whiskey bottle?

Oh, Sean no longer drank. Hadn't for years. But that didn't change the fact that he once had. Or that he had aban-doned his sons to his eldest son's care after the death of his wife.

Pops got up. "I'm here, Connor. That's not something I've always been able to say, but I'm here now. All you have to do is pick up a phone."

He stood there for a long moment, then turned toward his car.

"Pops?" Connor found himself saying.

His father stopped, but didn't turn around.

"Thanks, you know, for coming out here."

He discerned his father's nod as he continued on toward his car.

For a long while after Pops had pulled away, Connor sat staring in the direction he'd gone. How easy it should have been to get up, drive to the house and lay everything out on the table. Handle things the way he always demanded his brothers face difficult matters. But if there was one thing that the past year or so had proven, it was that each of them still felt…alone, somehow. Apart from the others. Too much had gone unsaid. Too many ghosts haunted their pasts.

No, not too many ghosts. One ghost. The ghost of their mother Kathryn Connor McCoy.

He finally hauled himself up off the steps. Gazing one last time toward his SUV and the road Pops had taken, he turned around and climbed the two stairs to the cement porch of his grandparents' old house. The light still shone in the window, but he was suddenly filled with the urge to turn around and head back into the city. To go to Bronte's. To ask her to be that someone Pops had mentioned.

He dragged his steps to a stop, the rising wind whipping around him wildly. But what could she possibly do to help? The Pryka case was no longer hers. In fact, she worked at an office that was, for all intents and purposes, his enemy. It was her coworkers currently seeking him out for arrest. It was her coworkers who believed him every bit as guilty as the charges implied. And she might very well believe the same right along with them.

Maybe it was exactly for that reason that he couldn't get her out of his head. If she did believe him responsible for Robbins's death, she would have had him arrested by now. He knew that as surely as he knew the earth would continue to turn. The fact that she hadn't…well, that said something, didn't it?

Yeah, it said that she was confused by her attraction to him.

Just as he was confused by his attraction to her.

Turning the doorknob, he stepped inside the only place he had left to go. The house he had escaped to countless times when he was younger. Had claimed as his own personal safe haven.

And stopped dead in the middle of the foyer.

One very refreshing Bronte O'Brien, dressed in baggy jeans and a snug-fitting top that accentuated her small breasts, got up from the old sofa in the living room and stood looking at him expectantly.

CHAPTER NINE

BRONTE HAD ALWAYS SCOFFED when she'd heard the description "her heart was in her throat." After all, it was a physical impossibility, wasn't it? But as she stood there, in the middle of that old, dusty house, anticipating Connor's response to finding her waiting for him…well, she felt as if something was stuck in her throat. And that something very well could have been her heart.

She watched his face intently. His surprise was plainly visible. But it was the other expression that made the object in her throat dip way low in her belly. He appeared…relieved, glad, almost pleased to see her.

She smiled tremulously. "Hi," she said, feeling utterly stupid.

"Hi, yourself."

At least fifteen feet separated them, but they could have been standing face-to-face judging by how very close she felt to him at that very moment.

She cleared her throat. "I hope you don't mind. You know that I called Kelli asking where you might be." She gave a quiet laugh. "How was I supposed to know that I'd hear from every last McCoy mere minutes later?"

"My brothers…called you?"

She nodded. "Your father first. He was very worried. Told me about this place." She glanced toward the door. "Is he still here?"

"No."

"Oh."

She turned around and picked up a thermos from the table behind her. "I, um, thought you might like this."

He eyed the metal container as though it might hold the secret to his existence. "Please don't tell me it's soup."

Her smiled widened. "Coffee. Colombian. Extra strong."

He groaned as she opened the thermos and poured out a healthy portion. He was next to her in a few strides and accepted the cup from her.

"Talk about cheap dates," she said.

His gaze met her across the cup.

"Bronte…"

She lifted her chin as she screwed the top back on the coffee. "What?"

"About last night…"

She slowly sank into the sagging couch behind her, noticing that he chose to continue standing. That was okay. She supposed she deserved to be at a physical disadvantage after what had happened between them. "Look, Connor, I don't know how else to go about this but just to come right out and say it."

"That would have been my advice."

She gave a small smile. "What I'm trying to say here is…well, I really don't know what to believe."

"You watched the tape."

She exhaled, glad he was making this somewhat easier for her when it was probably the last thing he should be doing. "Yes."

He finally sat down on the couch beside her, planting his forearms on his thighs. "Doesn't look very good, does it?"

She slowly shook her head, finding words impossible with him sitting so close.

"I don't get it." He looked at her squarely, the weighty

shadow in his eyes drawing her in deeper. "I know for a fact that I didn't go into that house that afternoon. Yet even I thought that was me going in and out of there on that tape." He clasped his hands tightly together. "There has to be some kind of rational explanation. But if there is, I certainly can't find one. I wasn't even on duty."

"Have you tried finding anyone who could verify your alibi?"

His grimace would have been endearing had it not been so fateful. "No. I only had a few hours between David's wedding ceremony and the reception." He shrugged tightly. "I was feeling wound up so I drove out to a piece of abandoned farmland a half hour inside Virginia that Marc and I used to use for target practice, and squeezed off a couple dozen rounds. The closest house is more than a mile away."

"You were alone."

"Alone."

The word held significance beyond his lack of a compelling alibi. It described how he looked right now. Alone. Lost. A man who had lost his anchor and was trying desperately to find shore.

Bronte looked down, mildly surprised to find her hand resting against his forearm. The contrast of her pale, freckled fingers against his tanned, hair-peppered skin fascinated her. The muscles beneath her fingertips bunched, then relaxed, as if she offered more than a simple touch. It was as if she'd offered him a lifeline.

His voice hummed with emotion. "Why did you seek me out, Bronte? After last night…"

She withdrew her hand, immediately noticing the loss of his warmth and suppressing a tiny shiver. She glanced out the curtainless front windows, noticing the flashes of lightning, feeling a distant rumble of thunder rock the house. The first drops of rain pinged against the pane as she swallowed.

"Last night you gave me a lot of food for thought, Connor." She rubbed her arms with her hands. "You were right. We...I had no business encouraging a sexual relationship. Not without knowing what I thought. How I felt."

She sensed his tension next to her. "And now?"

She gave him an anxious smile. "Now...well, I'm still not all that clear on how I feel beyond that I want you." She turned toward him more fully, pulling her knee up onto the couch. "Everything inside of me is screaming that you're just not capable of doing the crime you're accused of."

The uneasiness in his eyes melted into gratitude. "Despite the evidence against me."

She smiled. "Maybe because of it."

He sat back and crossed his arms over his chest. "How do you mean?"

"I don't know. Everything looks just too neat somehow. Too clear cut." She propped her elbow on the sofa back and leaned her head against her hand. "I learned early on to be suspicious of a good thing. You know that old saying if something seems too good to be true, it probably is?"

He nodded.

She quietly cleared her throat again. "Anyway, what I mean about the easy conviction is that there's no such thing. There's always something, you know? Some element that clouds the issue. A witness that steps forward and puts the defendant somewhere else. A missing weapon. Fingerprints that don't belong to the victim or the defendant. Piddly little details like that. Something that a good defense attorney can latch on to and use as a get-out-of-jail-free card." She turned one hand palm up. "But in your case, it's almost like you got caught holding the smoking gun by a hundred witnesses."

He grimaced. "That's one way of putting it."

"Sorry. I warned you that I'm not known for subtlety."

"I know. And that's one of the things I admire about you."

Bronte's throat closed around the words she was about to say. She blinked at him. Not because she was surprised he felt that way, but because he'd said the words aloud.

She'd sensed many things about Connor McCoy since first crossing paths with him in college. But she'd come to know many more details about him in the past few days.

He was a man to whom emotion of any kind didn't come easily. He felt deeply, but was loathe to acknowledge those feelings, which then, in turn, made them that much more acute. His word was his bond. If he said something, he meant it—to an astronomical, exponential degree. Truth and honesty meant more to him than freedom. It was what made him such a damn good U.S. marshal. And what made him such a fascinating, rare man.

And it was exactly the reason she was convinced he could never have killed Melissa Robbins.

She smiled at him, taken aback by the moisture in her eyes. "You better watch out, McCoy, or I might think that you're trying to change the subject."

"Maybe that's exactly what I'm trying to do."

She threaded her fingers through her hair then looked down at her jeans. Long, quiet moments passed with nothing but the sound of the rain pelting the window and an occasional rumble of thunder.

"Tell me about the guy."

She raised her eyes. "Pardon me."

He cleared his throat. "The first time I came to your house, you'd said you were coming off a bad relationship." She noticed the way he fumbled over the last word. He left out that she'd also said she wasn't looking for another relationship. "Who was he? And what made it bad?"

She moved until she was sitting straight again. What did she tell him? Considering everything else going on, she supposed the truth in this instance couldn't hurt—aside from her, that is. "Um…what can I say? The relationship itself wasn't bad. The ending was."

"They usually are."

She smiled. "Yes, I guess you're right there." She watched the thunderstorm through the window for a long moment. "He was an attorney. I was an attorney. We seemed to have a lot in common." She glanced at him. "That's why I said yes when he proposed."

Connor's brows slowly raised, then he looked pointedly at her bare ring finger.

She rubbed the area self-consciously with her thumb. She hadn't even told her best friend what had happened between her and Thomas. Still, she found she wanted to tell Connor about it. Needed to unload the weight that had been resting on her shoulders for much too long. "The only problem is, Thomas neglected to tell me something that drastically affected our future together. A fact that I feel so stupid for not having seen myself." She briefly bit on her bottom lip. "You see, he was, um, already married."

A loud thunderclap sounded overhead, startling Bronte. She laughed nervously, not daring to look at Connor. "Boy, does that ever seem like an appropriate exclamation point." She ran her palm down the length of her jeans, feeling oddly out of sorts. "I didn't even find out in a particularly interesting way. I was humiliated, yes, but who wouldn't have been? Given that we're in the same line of work, it was inevitable that his other life would eventually collide with mine." She recalled the night that had happened and wanted to wrap her arms around herself. "I'd gone to a charity event hosted at the national art gallery by a prominent D.C. attorney. And there was Thomas with his wife." She moved to tuck her hair behind her ear. Only her hair wasn't long enough to tuck. She smiled to herself without humor. "And that's the end of that story."

"You were serious about him?"

She shrugged. "I don't know. I thought I was. But now…I'm not sure if it was my heart that was broken or just my inflated pride."

What she was sure about was that she never wanted to feel that vulnerable again. That exposed. And though she trusted her instincts about Connor's innocence, she didn't dare extend that trust to her heart. To love him was an emotional risk she couldn't afford to take, though she was growing more afraid that it might already be too late.

Silence fell between them. It stretched on, drawing Bronte's nerves taut. Why didn't he say something? Tell her she'd been a fool for falling for a married man? Point out how dumb she'd been for having ended up a cliché? She shifted uncomfortably on the couch, fighting the urge to ask him what he thought.

His voice was so quiet when he spoke she nearly didn't hear him. "I was there when my mother died."

Bronte swore her heart stopped midbeat. "What did you say?"

She recalled the other night in her kitchen. When she'd asked him about his mother. How she died. He'd told her he didn't want to talk about it. And in the ensuing silence, she'd shared her own mother's unfortunate circumstances. She'd done it to break the ice. To let him know that no matter what had happened, he wasn't alone. That everyone had some incident from their childhood that changed their entire lives.

Foreboding spread under her skin.

Connor pushed from the couch and stepped to where a radio rested on the bare mantle above the fireplace. He turned it on and flipped through the stations until he came to a weather report.

Bronte stared at his back, watching him make normal, everyday movements, but knowing that there was nothing normal about what he'd just shared.

She found her voice. "How old were you?"

He didn't respond. He merely made a show of listening to the announcer report on the storm passing overhead. Distantly, Bronte heard the tinny voice telling listeners that it had blown in quickly, and had initially been expected to pass just as quickly. But the system had stalled over the area. Local residents were being instructed to be on alert for severe weather throughout the night.

Finally, Connor shrugged, the movement revealing the tension coiling his shoulder muscles. "I don't know. Nine? Ten, maybe." He rubbed the back of his neck, drawing her attention to his wide hand and long, tapered fingers.

Bronte's heart contracted in her chest. God. He had been about the same age as she was when her own mother was injured. Only she still had her mom. Connor had lost his.

She tried to imagine her life without her mother in it…and couldn't. Her head spun with all the possibilities—for both her and the man looking so alone across the room from her. What kind of man would Connor have been had his mother lived? Would he be married by now? With children of his own? Would he be in law enforcement? Or would his mother have encouraged him to take a different career path? Maybe on to law school? Or perhaps he might have followed in his grandfather's footsteps and resurrected the old McCoy farm Sean had told her about when she arrived earlier that evening.

"Nobody knows," he said, luring her away from her thoughts, "that I was there when it happened. Not even Pops."

Bronte's chest tightened unbearably. She wanted to go to him. Pull him into her arms and hold him tightly. But she was afraid that if she did, he might not continue. And he needed to. She knew without him telling her that this was something he'd kept bottled up for far too long.

But it took superhuman strength to stop herself from getting up from that sofa and crossing to him.

"We knew it was coming. Or rather, Pops knew. The rest of us suspected." His voice grew rougher, more hesitant, yet held a tender note of determination. "In the months before, she was in bed a lot. And Pops took her to the doctor at least three times a week. But they never told us anything. Never revealed she had a savage, then untreatable strain of breast cancer. And we were too afraid to ask." His chin dropped to his chest. "That morning she seemed to be feeling better. She'd gotten up to fix us breakfast, just like she always used to. And for a few sweet hours, it was almost like things had been before, you know? Almost. Pops went off to work. We went out to play...." His eyes held a faraway expression. "Then one minute she was calling me in from the old barn...the next she collapsed to the kitchen floor."

A hot, scalding tear slid down Bronte's right cheek, but she barely noticed it.

Connor rested his forearm against the mantle, his back still to her, rubbing his thumb along the length of his brow line. "Later, the coroner said it was a brain aneurysm likely brought on by the stress of her deteriorating condition. Nothing I did, nothing I could have done, could have saved her." He dropped his head. "After I realized that she was...all I could think of to do was to keep the boys from finding her. Prevent them from seeing her like that...so still...so white...in the middle of the kitchen floor." His voice caught and he cleared his throat. "I kept them outside until Pops got home. Five hours later."

Five hours later?

"Oh, God," she murmured, forgetting why she'd thought it important to stay on the couch and rushing to him. She curved her arms around his waist, crushing her front to his back. Pressing her hand to his chest and resting her head against his shoulder.

She tried to imagine that brave little boy who had watched

his mother die. That ten-year-old whose thoughts had not been of himself, or the tragedy he had witnessed, of what it would mean to him to lose his* mother. Instead his four younger brothers had been this boy's concern. A single, solitary, admirable boy who had managed to hold a family together when one catastrophic moment could have torn them irreversibly apart. She clamped her eyes tightly closed. No matter how broad and capable his shoulders now, they hadn't always been that way. Yet he had still carried the weight.

He caught her hands in his and held them tightly against his pounding heart. "I've never shared that with anyone, Bronte. Hell, I'm not even sure why I told you."

She rubbed her tear-soaked cheek against his shirt, her heart breaking for the injured adult she even now held.

"I'm glad that I'm the one you told," she murmured, catching her bottom lip between her teeth, tasting the tears there, trying to staunch them but knowing it was a hopeless battle.

She couldn't be sure how long they'd stood there like that, just the two of them, in that big old house that used to be his grandparents'. The only sounds the beating of their hearts, the drone of the radio announcer's voice and the spring storm raging outside. Her holding him. Him holding her hands. Time seemed to stand still. The courage he'd shown by sharing what he had reached out to her even more solidly than his hands. Wrapped itself around her heart. Told her that whatever may have remained of the barriers she had so carefully erected after Thomas's betrayal were now completely demolished.

Somewhere in the back of her mind, Bronte became aware that the radio announcer had signed off and a new program had begun. A lineup that included music. Old big band tunes. Recognizable pieces, with horns and strings and touching, sweeping orchestral movements. She increased the strength of her embrace, holding Connor so tightly her arms ached. As though if she held tight enough, long enough, they would become one rather than the two that they were.

Slowly, he lifted one of her hands from his chest and pressed it against his jaw line. She reveled in the feel of his stubble against her sensitive fingertips. Wondered at the generosity of this man. The kindness of his heart, his spirit.

A hauntingly familiar composition drifted from the small transistor radio. Her heart seemed to expand to the point of bursting. *Someone To Watch Over Me.*

She realized then that that's what she'd always wanted, and what Connor needed. Not in a physical sense—rather, they both needed someone to stand guard over their souls.

"Come here," Connor said quietly.

He gently caught both of her wrists and tugged her to stand in front of him. Suddenly, inexplicably Bronte felt exposed…stripped completely naked of all pretense as she hesitantly lifted her gaze to his. Until she glimpsed that same honesty, that utter vulnerability, in the depths of Connor's eyes.

She didn't realize how alone she'd felt until that very moment. Not until she felt the almost audible click of connection that bonded her with the man now tenderly grasping her shoulders, looking at her as if she was all that mattered in this life, telling her with his eyes what words could never hope to convey.

"Bronte O'Brien, will you dance with me?"

Tears gathered anew and she laughed at the absurdity of the quiet question. Had it really been just a few days ago that they had both stood in that hotel ballroom during Kelli and David's reception? When she'd revealed she'd never danced? When she'd suspected that he preferred not to dance?

Yet now here they were, just the two of them, her right

hand in his left, moving slowly to the music, their feet somehow finding the way—just as their hearts were beginning to.

Connor groaned and released her hand. She gasped when he pulled her more fully into his embrace, still somehow managing to match the rhythm of the song.

All too soon the piece ended. They stood completely still. His chin resting against her hair. Her nose tucked into the soft folds of his shirt.

Then she took a deep breath, closed her eyes and said quietly, "I think you should turn yourself in to the authorities."

She felt him stiffen in her arms. She immediately grasped his arms, hating that what she'd said had broken the magic of the moment, but needing to say it anyway. She stared up at him desperately.

He blinked once, then again, as if unable to believe she'd just said what she had.

"It's the only thing you can do, Connor. Don't you see? By evading arrest, you look even guiltier."

She watched his throat as he swallowed. "I don't think that's possible."

"Let's not argue over words. You make yourself look guilty, period."

His gaze swept from her right eye to her left. "And my turning myself in isn't going to change that."

She ignored the regret gathering in her stomach. "Maybe you're right. Maybe it won't. But then again, maybe it will. At the very least, if you turn yourself in, you'll look like a man who doesn't have anything to hide."

"I'll look like a man guiltier than hell."

She grasped his arms with both her hands, determined to get him to listen to her. "Do you trust me, Connor?"

He avoided meeting her gaze.

"I've been with the U.S. attorney's office for four years. I see cases like yours on a daily basis," she whispered, amazed she could speak past the emotion clouding her throat. "Don't you see? Running never accomplishes anything. It only makes things worse. You piss off the attorney in charge. You tick off the police trying to arrest you. And you go into the situation with two strikes already against you." She swallowed, unable to tell if she was getting through to him. "You turn yourself in, maintain your innocence, and you start everyone thinking, 'Hey, maybe this guy's telling the truth.' You make them wonder. Something that will never happen if you go the other way. When they catch up to you, and they will, they'll be so pumped up on adrenaline from the challenge, so high on having caught the big, bad criminal, they won't hear a single thing you have to say."

The muscles under her hands bunched again, although she suspected it was for an altogether different reason this time.

"Let me help you, Connor. I can do that. I have pull at the office. I'll make sure we don't contest your request for bail. You'll walk into that holding cell only to turn around and walk back out."

He appeared ready to pull away. She held tighter.

"You have my word on that, Connor."

He finally met her gaze. The intensity in his eyes nearly made her turn away, it was so difficult to look at.

Oh, how easy it was for her to tell him to turn himself in. She wasn't the one who would have to be stripped of everything that was familiar to her, including her clothes. She wasn't the one who would be locked in a tiny cell. She wasn't the one who was going to be treated like the very criminals she'd spent her life prosecuting.

She shuddered, but forced herself to hold his gaze. No matter how difficult, she felt strongly that this was the right course of action to take. There were no other options.

"Okay," he said so quietly, she nearly didn't hear him.

She blinked. "What?"

He was the one who looked away. "I said, okay. I do trust you. If you think this is the thing for me to do, then I'll do it."

Never before had Bronte felt so entrusted. Neither had she ever felt so scared.

His gaze flicked back to her face. "But I'm not going to do it tonight."

She blinked. "Why?"

"Because tonight neither one of us is going anywhere." He freed one of his arms from her grasp and curved his hand around the back of her neck. "Tonight we're going to finish what we started last night and the night before that—hell, what began years ago in college." He slanted his mouth softly against hers. "Tonight I want you to help me create something to help see me through the days to come."

He gently pulled her closer to him. Bronte all too willingly went. Her eyelids fluttered closed. Her mouth went dry. Her heart beat an erratic, anticipatory rhythm against her rib cage. When her lips finally touched his, her breath rushed from her lungs on a sigh.

She knew in that moment that she'd gone to all the trouble to find him, drove all that way to talk to him, as much for this reason as to ask him to turn himself over to officials.

He blindly maneuvered her back to the couch to sit. She immediately scooted closer to him, straining to press her chest against his. Like so many things in their blossoming relationship, this had been a long time coming. It went back further than just the kiss they'd shared in the park the night of Kelli and David's wedding reception. It went back further than when they met again in that bar over the pool table. The foundation for this moment had been laid way back in that class when she had purposely sat in front of him and felt his gaze on her as surely and potently as his touch.

She moaned, trying to get closer still. Connor deepened the kiss and grasped her hips, planting her firmly in his lap as she curved her hands under his arms and dug her fingers into the hard planes of his back. Never had she felt a man so solid. It was more than just his height or the size of his muscles. It was the entirety of the man himself. The soft reflection of herself in his eyes. What he'd had the courage to share with her. And though she had nothing to fear, she felt incredibly safe there in the cradle of his arms, felt somehow…complete. Like she'd lived her life missing half of herself, and now she had found it.

He cupped both of her breasts in the palms of his hands. She gasped, breaking contact with his mouth in order to pull in a needed breath. She absently rubbed her cheek against his stubbled one as his thumbs traced circles around her throbbing nipples. When he rolled the tips between his fingers, a bolt of lightning so much like the ones brightening the stormy skies outside struck low in her belly, leaving fire burning in its wake.

She tunneled her hands into the hair at the nape of his neck and closed her eyes. "Don't you dare pull away this time, McCoy. Don't you dare…." Even his earlobe seemed as tough as the rest of him as she pulled it between her teeth and gently bit down.

He grasped her shoulders and drew her in front of him, staring into her eyes. "I couldn't if I wanted to, B. I couldn't if I wanted to." His expression was fierce. "But I need to say something, Bronte, need to tell you something. This…our being together…making love…it won't change anything. You need to understand that I…" He dragged in a breath. "Kids are so vulnerable. Needy. It's amazing how easily you can screw up their lives. I'm a perfect example of that. My brothers, Jake, Marc, Mitch and David, are perfect examples of that. That's why I never want to have any. Never want to get married. Ever."

Bronte's heart thudded painfully against her rib cage as she smiled up at him tremulously. "Well, then…I'll just have to take what I can get, won't I?"

He stared at her for a long moment, as if gauging her honesty. Then he groaned and captured her mouth in a kiss that was as deep as the fathomless green of his eyes. Bronte liquefied against him, covering him like a second skin as he pushed her back against the cushions, simultaneously thrusting her shirt up, and her jeans down. Not even bothering with the button, he burrowed his fingers between the soft material and her flesh, not stopping until his fingertips rested at the top of her damp curls. Bronte wriggled beneath him, growing impatient, fearful that, despite his words, every moment that ticked by increased the chances of his pulling away again.

She fumbled for the front of his jeans, then switched to hers, moaning when she yanked down the zipper, giving him freer access to her throbbing parts. She spread her legs even as she tried to yank down the suddenly constraining material and he slid his fingers between her slick flesh, stroking her back and forth, back and forth until she was afraid she'd never be able to draw another breath again.

"Wait…don't…" she whispered urgently, twisting restlessly under his weight.

But the intense look in his eyes told her he wasn't about to relent. So she gathered up what remaining self-control she had left and launched an assault of her own. Desperately clutching his shirt, she yanked it up, molding her fingers against the hard silk of his abdomen, then trailing down to the waist of his jeans. But rather than undoing the button there, she sought and found his erection. She squeezed him almost roughly, relishing in his low groan and the way he instinctively stilled his own hand and ground against her. With her thumb and index finger, she traced the long, wide length of him, then came back up again, increasing the pressure of her fingers with each pass. His breathing grew more rapid, his caresses more urgent. His hips bucked and he grabbed at her hand.

She tugged her mouth from his, then slipped the tip of her tongue between his lips for one last taste. "The way, um, I see it, we have two options." She swallowed hard. "Either we continue the way we are, in which case it'll be over with before we've even started. Or—" she squeezed his rock-hard erection for good measure "—we get undressed and do this the right way."

He rolled off of her in a flash, nearly ripping off his clothes in his rush to get out of them, then helped her with hers. Her shirt flew to land dangerously near the lantern; her bra zinged over the back side of the couch; her jeans landed somewhere near the door.

Then every sweet, hot inch of him was lying against every throbbing, needy inch of her.

The only sound in the room was that of their breathing. Heavy, ragged. In and out. Connor caught and held her gaze in the warm glow from the lantern, as if asking her if she was sure this was what she wanted. Her response came by way of her hips straining up against his, driving his erection into the soft, quivering flesh of her belly.

Connor groaned then reached into the back pocket of his discarded jeans. She took the foil packet from him, swallowing when she noticed the extra-large size and the ribbing. Grasping his erection, she smoothed the lubricated latex down the length of him, wondering at his sheer size, hoping she could accommodate him.

His eyes half-lidded and full of passion, he dropped a long, lingering kiss on her lips, then guided himself to rest against her slick flesh. Bronte moaned, straining restlessly upward, seeking to extinguish the fire that seemed to have burned forever, needing to fill the aching emptiness that resonated through her and that only joining with him would satisfy.

He entered her slowly, as if aware of her need of time to adjust. She tensed, not realizing just how large he was until that very moment. She whimpered, torn between wanting him all the way inside and needing to pull away.

"Shhh," he murmured, dropping small kisses along her jaw line, then trailing a path down to her breasts. He drew circles around her right nipple with the very tip of his tongue, then generously laved the yearning nub, pulling it deep in this mouth. The instant she sighed against the cushions, he pressed inside her another couple of millimeters. Then another. Then she tilted her hips and thrust upward with needy abandon, gasping as he seemed to fill every inch of her.

He started to pull out.

"No!" she whispered fiercely. "Don't you dare go any-where. Just…stay…still…a minute." She bit on her bottom lip, feeling her unused muscles mold to him, feeling the fire in her belly rush out of control.

Then she slid back a few inches and thrust upward again, the answering pleasure almost unbearable in its intensity.

"Oh, my," he said between gritted teeth, then bent to kiss her deeply, thoroughly, as she continued her exploratory movements. "Bronte…I don't know how long…I'm going to be able to stay this way."

She kissed first one corner of his mouth, then the other. The emotional connection she'd felt so intensely a short while ago, when they'd stood in front of the fireplace, trans-formed into a potent physical connection. She slowly moved her hips up to meet his. His instinctual buck made her smile. A smile that quickly left when he made a low sound in the back of his throat, grasped her hips, then pulled nearly all the way out only to thrust all the way back in.

Bronte's back arched off the sofa and she clutched his shoulders—not in pain, but in exquisite, overwhelming pleasure. Her toes curled. Her scalp tingled. Her womb contracted. And all she could think about was how desperately she wanted this to continue.

For long minutes he stroked her both inside and out, one hand braced at the side of her hip, the other stroking her breasts, stroking her until the pressure in her belly threatened to explode.

Then his thumb sought and found the tiny, throbbing bud between her damp curls. She gasped, gripping his hips, digging her fingernails into the hard flesh of his rear, pulling him ever closer, wanting him deeper, faster, harder. Needing to follow the wispy clouds swirling through her body, up and up, around and around, twisting, turning until—

Her back came up off the sofa, her body convulsed violently, and somewhere within the whiteout that had once been her sight she heard Connor call out. He relentlessly drove into her, his muscles quaking, her body shuddering, the ultra sweet joining of their bodies culminating in soul-shaking climax.

Finally she dropped back down to the sofa, her skin drenched, her entire body quivering. She couldn't seem to take in enough air as Connor propped himself up with his forearms on either side of her and dropped his head so his forehead lay between her breasts. He virtually shook from head to toe. Bronte smiled tremulously and lightly ran her fingertips over his sweat-dampened hair.

She shifted so she could gaze down into his face. His eyes were closed, his lips parted. He looked so utterly relaxed, trustful, fulfilled. She swallowed hard, realizing how very much that meant to her, his opening to her. And something opened in her, spreading throughout her chest like warm molasses and sticking there. In that instant, she knew a brief stab of fear. What was happening right now, at that moment, was unlike anything she'd felt before. Not with Thomas. Not with anyone. And that element of the unknown, the untried, both thrilled and scared the hell out of her.

She was falling in love with him.

She closed her eyes at the thought, thinking there wasn't a cliff high enough to equal how far she'd already fallen. And, damn it, if she could just turn off her mind for a couple of hours, a few days, she could just enjoy the feeling and stop questioning it. She could delight in the lightness saturating her heart, the weightlessness of her stomach, give in to the desire to smile with no reason, and stop worrying about the rest.

She continued absently brushing back his hair with her fingers. "Now…wasn't that much better than what you had in mind?"

"Oh, yes." She watched him grin against her skin, apparently unaware that she could see him, and that sticky spot in her chest doubled in size. She laid her head back and closed her eyes, needing to savor the feeling. If just for now. If only for this one moment.

Tomorrow she could worry about exactly what all of this meant. Tomorrow she could ponder all the wonderful hows and whys and possibilities. Tomorrow they could start the long road back to getting Connor out of the mess he was in.

She bit softly on her bottom lip. And tomorrow she could find a way to get a grip on her heart.

CHAPTER TEN

SOMETHING WARM MARKED A path across Connor's abdomen. He blinked against the brightness, then raised his hand to shield his eyes against the liquid sunshine spilling in through the large, multipaned front windows.

It took him a moment to orientate himself. His grandparents' old place. On the living room floor. Bronte…

He snapped upright, staring at the sleeping bag he lay on, then searching the room for signs of the astounding, loving, inventive redhead who had turned him inside out the night before.

Nothing. Her jeans were gone. So was her shirt. And a check under the couch found her bra also missing.

Yanking off the sheet draped across his hips, he got to his feet and wound the swath of linen around his waist. A look outside found fresh tire tracks around the side of the house, marking grooves in the mud left by the rain last night. He realized Bronte must have parked at the side, which explained why he hadn't known she was there when he arrived.

He absently rubbed his face, then ran his fingers through his hair. She was gone. There was no question of that. He didn't know how, but if she was there somewhere, he knew he would have sensed it, felt it.

He padded back toward the makeshift bed they had finally made up at some point during the night. He picked up his watch and squinted at the face. Ten. He hadn't slept that long, or that well, since…before he found himself in this mess.

Even then, he never slept in past eight. His internal alarm clock never allowed it. When he was younger, there were things that needed to be done, and only himself to see to them. He'd naturally carried the routine over into adulthood, his schooling in lack of sleep serving him well on assignments that sometimes stretched to days at a time until he got a witness settled and shifts were worked out.

A flash of white caught his eye. He looked at the piece of notepaper on the sofa, then moved to pick it up. He couldn't help noticing the way his chest contracted at the mere thought of holding something in his hands that Bronte had so recently touched. He sat down on the couch and stared blindly out the front window.

If he'd been asked a month ago what love was, he would have scoffed and said something along the lines of love being some sort of imaginary, temporary state of mind that could be fixed with a little common sense and a harsh word or two.

Now…

Well, now he knew it was more than that. Much more. And he knew that what he was feeling could be nothing other than love. For one clever, sexy junior U.S. attorney, Bronte O'Brien.

He couldn't put his finger on exactly what made him so sure that what he felt was connected to the "L" word. It was everything, it was nothing. It was the way his pulse sped up when he even thought her name. It was something about her outlook on life. It was the way she had listened to him speak about his mother, and responded, as if she'd been right there with him, shared his pain.

If he felt determined to clear his name before, he was doubly single-minded now.

And the hope he had lost just the night before had come back full force.

But until he did figure out a way to clear his name, he didn't dare consider the rest.

Still, his mind ventured down that avenue on its own accord.

He recalled what he'd said to her when things between them had gotten hot and heavy, right before he had entered her hot sweetness…and felt his stomach tighten at his honesty. Before…

Well, before, he'd never told the women he'd been with prior to sex that he had no plans for them beyond tomorrow. But Bronte… He'd felt he'd owed it to her to know where things stood. Even if the design of a child's nursery hadn't been open on her kitchen table the other night, he'd sensed on a level he couldn't begin to understand that she wanted children. She had the wit, energy and drive for an entire houseful. Balancing career and motherhood would be a piece of cake for her.

For him, it wasn't even a possibility.

And she'd deserved to know that. Before things between them went any further. Before it was too late.

Unfortunately, he was afraid it already was.

He looked down to find he had crumpled the note in his fist. Swearing under his breath, he straightened it out enough to read it. "Courthouse. Noon. I'll be waiting." It was signed, "Love, Bronte."

Love, Bronte.

The bottom of his stomach gave way, making him feel larger than the house in which he sat.

And making him feel hollow, knowing it could go no further than that.

Crumpling the note back up, he stuffed the wad into his jeans pocket. Within minutes, he was dressed and ready to continue his mission to uncover who exactly had set him up.

BRONTE LEANED AGAINST THE edge of the conference table and watched the familiar scenes on the television screen in front of her. She was alone in the room, but through the narrow windows on either side of the closed door, life went on. Assistants rushed to see through tedious tasks. Fellow attorneys came in from arraignments, left for hearings. Couriers delivered court papers. And witnesses tentatively negotiated the halls, obviously feeling out of place, and looking that way.

Bronte thumbed the eject button and exchanged the security video taken at the time of Melissa Robbins's death with another. She pressed Play then leaned back against the edge of the table again.

Despite her familiar surroundings, she, too, felt out of place. Different somehow. Definitely not the same woman she'd been just the day before. Colors appeared brighter, sounds clearer, and she seemed aware of every single heartbeat.

Funny, she never remembered feeling this way about Thomas. Yes, she'd been happy. At least, she thought she'd been. But what she felt now transcended the mere urge to smile when she thought about Connor. It was as if a smile was permanently attached to her heart. As though he was a very part of her every move, with her even when he wasn't.

Leaving him that morning had been one of the most difficult things she'd ever done. She'd awakened in his arms just before dawn, and burrowed farther into his chest, wanting anything but to have to get up, to leave him lying there alone. She'd dropped off to sleep again, only to wake up again a short while later in a panic. It was bad enough she'd called in sick the day before. Being late this morning certainly wouldn't help matters. And she needed to be on her toes if she had any hope of maintaining her job, much less be able to help clear Connor.

Now, four hours later, all she could think about was Connor and how he'd react to awakening and finding her gone.

Last night completely surpassed anything she could have ever anticipated. After that kiss in the park, it had been a foregone conclusion as far as she was concerned that she and Connor would sleep together. But last night had been more than just two consenting adults having sex. Last night, she had made love for the very first time. She'd felt Connor not only with her body; she'd felt him with her heart. Every beat of her pulse, every inhale of breath, he had been a part of. She'd never shared so much with one person before. Had him share so much with her.

She glanced down at her watch. Only an hour and a half before noon.

The images flickering across the screen only a couple feet away vied for her attention. She forced herself to focus. A quick press of Rewind, then Play again, put the tape back to the beginning. It was at the point where she had stopped paying attention to anything but Connor McCoy.

Seeing what the tape held, her heart sank to her feet, making the smile on her face fade away.

She had no squabbles with her assistant, Greg. He had gotten her exactly what she asked for, which was everything Dennis Burns had compiled so far against Connor. The first tape she viewed was a carbon copy of the one Connor had left at her town house. Little help to her except to give her goose bumps.

The second video, the one she was now watching, was a compilation of clips taken from various tapes. Connor's greatest hits, she thought dryly. Each clip featured him around, talking to, or protecting Melissa Robbins. Bronte was surprised by the slight rise in her blood temperature as she watched. It was obvious to her that Connor was doing no more and no less than what his job required. But his dedication to that same job, his keen eye for detail, made him appear intense in a way that might be misinterpreted by others.

And though she knew that watching over Melissa had only been a job to him, she couldn't help feeling jealous at the thought of him giving that type of fervent attention to any other female. Ludicrous, really, seeing as she knew for a fact that they hadn't been involved intimately. More so, since the woman in question was now dead.

More than that, Bronte felt that with each millisecond of the tape that played, her chances at happiness, true lasting happiness, diminished. Because the man on whom that happiness depended might very well end up spending the rest of his life in a federal penitentiary. And she'd stepped in front of that speeding train not only with her eyes wide open, but her arms stretched wide.

She'd known before giving in to her attraction, her feelings for Connor, that the outcome of the Robbins case was anything but guaranteed. She knew firsthand that sometimes the innocent were convicted right alongside the guilty. She'd just thought it wouldn't happen to her. Believed that somehow, some way, Connor would find a way to prove his innocence, and that she would be the one to help him.

And then what? They would live happily ever after?

Her throat tightened. She'd never considered herself the rose-colored glasses type. Had preferred the Hardy Boys over Nancy Drew, and proudly scoffed at Cinderella stories in any format. Her own parents' rocky marriage stood testament to the fact that there was no such thing as smooth sailing.

Yet the first time she fell, really fell, for a guy, she found herself peering into corners for a missing glass slipper that once put on would make the real world vanish and transport her and Connor to some misty fairy-tale land where lifetime imprisonment wasn't even an option.

How was she supposed to help Connor when there was no help to be found?

Bronte rubbed her arms, then popped the second tape out as well. Her hands shaking, she gathered her things together, then made her way back to her office.

"Anything interesting?" Greg asked as she passed.

She shook her head and uttered a quiet, "No."

He frowned. "Too bad. 'Cause the man of the hour has just returned. I'm afraid our borrowing habit is about to be found out."

Bronte looked over her shoulder to where Dennis was just closing his office door. "Good. Now's as good a time as any to have a little talk with him." Still clutching the videotapes, she turned to do just that—and nearly plowed into Senior U.S. Attorney Bernard Leighton.

"Bronte. Just the woman I was looking for," he said, flashing one of his famous smiles.

It took a moment for Bronte's brain to switch tracks. To try to shake herself free of the fear clinging to her and summon up a smile. "Well, I'd chance a guess and say you've just found me." She and Bernard had always gotten along well. He was the one who had taken her off rotation and secured a permanent position for her with the Transnational/Major Crimes section.

Still, she wished this long overdue conversation could have come at a different time and a lot sooner. "What can I do for you, Bernie? I take it you're responding to my messages?"

He made a point of glancing at Greg, who, of course, appeared extremely busy with other things and completely oblivious to them, which Bronte knew couldn't be further from the truth. "You got a minute? There's something I've been meaning to talk to you about."

She motioned for him to precede her into her office. "Sure. I think I can even manage to give you two." She placed the videos on Greg's desk, giving him a loaded glance. "Hold my calls for me, Greg."

"Sure thing."

Bernard chuckled as Bronte followed him inside, then closed the door after herself. She rounded her desk, but waited for him to sit before she did. Only he didn't. For the first time since running into him, she knew a moment of concern. "Uh-oh. You're not sitting. This must be serious."

She'd meant the comment as a joke of sorts, something to break the ice, but Leighton remained serious.

She cleared her throat. "What is it, Bernie?"

"It's the Robbins case, Bronte."

Her gaze went immediately to where she could see the corner of Greg's desk through the narrow window to the right of her door. The videotapes were effectively hidden by other files, but it was enough for her to know they were there. "What about it?" she asked, looking back at Bernie.

"Word has it you've been looking in on the case on the sly."

She smiled. "I'm not sure I know what you mean by 'on the sly.' Yes, I have been following the case since Burns took it over. That I'll admit." She straightened a couple files on her desk that didn't need straightening. "Come on, Bernie, I worked on the Pryka case for four solid months—a case you assigned to me. You can't blame me for wanting to keep up on it and the Robbins case."

"Unfortunately, I can. And I do." He frowned. "Look, Bronte, you're one of my best junior attorneys. And you know I trust you implicitly. This is the first time I've heard of you doing something of this nature. And I certainly hope it's the last."

Bronte gazed at him in barely disguised shock. Then she snapped out of it, a window of opportunity opening that she was loathe to ignore. "Actually, Bernie, I'm glad you stopped by, because I've been meaning to discuss this very matter with you."

His brows raised as she rounded her desk and came to

stand directly in front of him. She had a good two inches on him at least. There was a time when her being taller than a man would have made her feel ill at ease, but no longer. "If you don't mind my asking, why did you reassign the Pryka case to Dennis?"

He crossed his arms, as if indignant at being questioned, and likely a little put off by her height, something she played to her advantage by standing a little straighter. "I understand that with the death of Robbins, there's a conflict of interest."

"Conflict of interest? How so?" She knew exactly how so, but she wasn't about to help him out.

"You're best friends with the suspect's brother-in-law, are you not?"

She smiled. "Actually, sister-in-law. And I prefer to view it as she just happens to have married a man whose brother is a suspect in the case. In fact, she's on her honeymoon now." She twisted her lips, resisting the urge to wave Greg away from where he was peering through the window. "Do you mind if I ask how you came by this possible conflict of interest?"

Bernie looked down and cleared his throat. "You know it pays to keep your ear to the ground."

"I see. So am I correct in assuming that Dennis Burns was the one vibrating the tracks on that particular point?"

A shadow of a smile appeared in his eyes as he met her gaze. "Interesting imagery."

"But accurate, I presume."

"Unfortunately, yes."

Bronte rubbed the back of her neck. "That little backstabber has been after my job since day one. And I have to admit, I'm getting a little tired of him sniffing around my skirt hem, if you'll pardon the expression." She sighed. "I really wish you would have come to me before reassigning the case, Bernie. I think you at least owed me that."

He narrowed his eyes, but appeared to be motivated by curiosity rather than wariness. "Granted. But I find it interesting that you're not asking for the case back. Shall I take that to mean that the conflict does, indeed, exist?"

She smiled. "Given the circumstances, that's really neither here nor there, now, is it?"

His chuckle reverberated throughout the room, earning her a thumbs-up from Greg.

"No, I guess it isn't." He started to turn and Greg's head disappeared from the window.

Bronte began to follow him out, just then remembering to glance at her watch. Her heart skipped a beat. She supposed she owed it to him to reveal what was supposed to happen at noon. He was, after all, the reason she was even a junior U.S. attorney. "Um, Bernie?"

"Yes?" he turned his head to glance at her as he opened the door.

"I just thought you might like to know that Connor McCoy is turning himself in to me at the courthouse at noon today."

She didn't think it was possible for his brows to shoot any higher on his forehead. She was proved wrong. "Yes. That is information I am happy to know."

Bronte gripped the edge of the door. "I also thought you might like to know that he's innocent, Bernie. And I intend to do everything in my power to help prove that point."

His brows disappeared completely. "Well, then it's a good thing you aren't in charge of the case anymore, isn't it?"

She smiled, although somewhat sadly.

"Does that mean you're not coming to the pre-season barbecue Chelsea and I are hosting this Sunday?"

"Can I get back to you on that?"

He nodded. "No problem. Though I do have to warn you that Chelsea was planning to invite a special single someone. You know how she hates having odd chairs."

"Matchmaking again. Tell her thanks, but no thanks. Right now I've got about as much as I can handle."

By now they were standing outside her office. "So…do you want me to do the honors of telling our Mr. Burns of today's news? Or shall you?"

Bronte fought to hide her frown. She would just as soon not have anything to do with the little pipsqueak. "Oh, please, allow me."

Bernie shook his head and continued walking down the hall.

Greg put the phone down from where she suspected he was only pretending to talk. "What was that all about?"

She picked up the incriminating material from the desk. "I'll fill you in later. Right now I have to pay a visit to our favorite attorney."

"Uh, Bronte," Greg called when she was halfway across the hall. "He left, like, two minutes ago. If you run, you can probably still catch him before he gets to the parking garage."

Figured. "Well, I guess I'd better run then, hadn't I?"

"Yep."

Bronte reasoned that if she didn't catch him, it would be no skin off her nose. After all, she had tried to tell him, hadn't she? And that's all that counted.

Except that she didn't want to disappoint Bernard. It didn't sit well with her that she had dented the trust that had always existed between them by filching information right out from Dennis Burns's nose.

She picked up her pace. Besides, she did want to see Dennis's face when he found out that she had arranged to have his prime suspect delivered to the proper authorities, practically signed, sealed and delivered. She didn't deem it pertinent for him to know that she also planned to spring him just as neatly.

She reached the elevator and pressed the button for the lobby. "Come on, come on," she murmured, smiling at the sole other occupant.

The doors finally slid open and she hurried to the banister overlooking the high ceiling of the tiled lobby. There he was, heading for the revolving doors.

She called out to him, but he appeared not to hear her. She stepped closer to the stairs and opened her mouth to call out again, but the words caught in her throat. She cocked her head to one side and stared at Burns's back curiously. He was dressed casually today. Actually, he was dressed casually half the time. Several of the attorneys in the office did so when they didn't have any court appearances scheduled. But Dennis tended to take things to the max. Today, he had on jeans and a leather jacket—jeans and a leather jacket very similar to the ones the man alleged to be Connor was wearing in the security video taken outside Robbins's safe house the day of her murder....

Dennis was just about to push through the revolving doors when another male attorney dressed in a navy blue suit tapped him on the shoulder and pointed to where Bronte still stood. Dennis looked up, his eyes narrowing when he spotted her. He moved toward the stairs even as she forced her feet to continue down them. They met up at the bottom of the steps, where he glanced at his watch impatiently. "I've got an appointment in ten minutes, Bronte. Can't this wait?"

Bronte's mind reeled as she silently compared Dennis's physical characteristics to those of the figure in the video. She cleared her throat, wondering how he would respond to her news. "Sure. If you want to miss one Connor McCoy turning himself over to the proper authorities."

His eyes never widened from their wary little slits. "You're kidding."

"Nope. At noon today. On the district courthouse steps." She curiously noted his deep frown and the way he rubbed the back of his neck, drawing her attention there. "You don't look pleased, Burns."

"I wish you'd have told me this earlier. This appointment is important."

Bronte drew her brows slowly together. "Considering the way you stole the Pryka case out from under my nose, I would have guessed you thought this was important."

"Yeah." He glanced toward the doors. "I've got to go. Thanks—you know, for telling me."

Bronte crossed her arms speculatively, watching as he turned around and hurried toward the door. Then the two and two floating around her brain for the past few minutes finally added up. The resulting figure was exactly the reason why she'd experienced that instant of déjà vu while watching him from upstairs. The fine hair at the back of her neck stood straight up.

Her heart beating like a thousand mallets against the wall of her chest, she pivoted and took the stairs leading back to the elevators two at a time. She had to get to a phone. She had to find a way to warn Connor away from that courthouse at noon today….

CHAPTER ELEVEN

CONNOR LOOKED AROUND THE front room of his grandparents' old place one last time. There were no visible traces that he and Bronte had been there. No telltale clothes littering the floor. No ashes in the fireplace. He'd even packed the lantern and the radio away in the pantry off the kitchen. Still, everywhere Connor looked, a fresh memory emerged and he felt the importance of what had happened there last night, making the house even more important to him than ever.

He turned toward the door, not liking that he didn't know when he would return. It was possible that time might be never. While he trusted Bronte, he knew that circumstances had a way of twisting out of one's control. Hell, if anyone should know that, he should. Look what had happened to him.

He opened the door and froze. He'd had the same reaction when he'd found Bronte last night. Only this wasn't Bronte.

He closed the door behind him as not one, not two, but four McCoys climbed the front steps to the porch. *His brothers.* His throat tightened as they spotted him at the same time he saw them. He stuffed his hands deep into the pockets of his leather jacket and squinted against the sunlight at each of them in turn.

Jake caught his attention first. As the tallest, that wasn't difficult to understand. As the second oldest, Jake had always been the one to challenge his authority, questioning when it would have been easier all around for him to just accept. Connor had a feeling he was in for some major questioning now.

Next came Marc. His military-straight posture made Connor think he was about to salute, though he was certain saluting wasn't exactly on Marc's mind. A sucker punch to the jaw was probably more his style. And boy, could the kid punch. Part of the reason was you never saw it coming.

Connor cleared his throat then glanced at Mitch. Ah, Mitch the philosopher. The shadow in his eyes told him he was hurt the most by his not coming to the family before they came to him. Still, it wouldn't stop him from trying to mediate between the two sides. Always the peacemaker, he had an uncanny ability to see a situation from all points of view, and to relate them, so that even if you didn't like where another viewpoint was coming from, you could at least understand and accept it.

Connor shifted uncomfortably as his gaze settled on David, the youngest of the McCoys.

Marc had once joked that their mother must have messed around with the mailman. Not only was David the shortest of them all, he was the only light-haired one. And he was the handsomest. But Connor knew that he was a McCoy through and through. Neither looks nor size had anything to do with the bond they all shared.

Connor's heart beat an uneven rhythm as he gave them all another once-over. His brothers. His family. God, how he'd missed them. And though he hadn't wanted to involve them in his situation, he also needed them more than he had ever needed them before.

And that was a definite turnaround. It had always been they that had needed him. They'd always had the broken bones, the scrapes, the problems with homework, the issues with others. They'd always been the ones to stumble into trouble. And he'd unfalteringly been the one to treat their ills, help them through the rough spots, fix their problems.

With their roles reversed, he wasn't quite sure what to do, what to say, how to react.

Then it occurred to him that one of them shouldn't be there at all.

He stared at David. "What are you doing here, runt? Aren't you supposed to be in the Poconos somewhere on your honeymoon?"

Emotion flashed across his face. Connor realized it was anger. "My life is a honeymoon no matter where Kelli and I are. What I want to know is why you didn't tell any of us about the nightmare you're in the middle of?"

Connor took his hands out of his pockets then crossed his arms over his chest. "Because it's my nightmare and there's no room for any of you in it."

"Uh-huh. That's what we thought you'd say," Marc muttered under his breath. He glanced at Jake. "So, do you wrestle him to the ground while I tie him up, or the other way around?"

"Touch me and you'll be sorrier than you've ever been in your life." Connor solidified his stance by widening his legs and planting his feet firmly on the cement porch.

"Well, gee, Con, looks like you're at a bit of a disadvantage here," Mitch said, the makings of a grin creasing the sides of his mouth. "From where I'm standing, it looks like there're the four of us to the one of you." He shook his head. "Not very good odds even if you're a gambling man. And all of us already know that you aren't."

"Not that that makes any difference," Marc added. "They don't come any more stubborn than Connor."

Connor grimaced. Since when had his brothers become such experts on him? "Look who's talking."

Marc's grin caught him off guard. "Yeah, well, I learned from the master, didn't I?"

Connor glanced past them. Mitch's truck and David's Mustang were parked on either side of his SUV, with Jake's four-door sedan parked directly behind it, blocking him in. Where was Pops? "Speaking of the master, where is he?"

Jake looked puzzled. "He was talking about you, Connor."

He hiked a brow. Him? Marc had been talking about him?

"Yeah, you, dunderhead," David said, shaking his own head. "Boy, you really are shooting off target, aren't you?"

Connor's neck felt suddenly hot and he found himself fighting a grin of his own. "Watch it, kid. I'm still taller than you are."

David winked. "Yeah, but I have three others on my side."

"But you can't live with them twenty-four-seven now, can you?"

"Ooo, is that a threat?" Marc asked. "That sounded like a threat to me."

"It's not a threat, it's a promise," Connor clarified.

Mitch lifted a hand. "Okay, guys, enough of the verbal sparring. If I remember correctly, the reason we're here is that one of our own is in trouble. I think it's time for us to put our heads together and devise a plan to get him out of it."

Connor's back snapped upright. "I can handle this myself, Mitch."

"I think a thank-you is more in line right now," Jake said quietly.

"Okay. Thank you all for offering, but I can handle this myself. Is that better?" Connor asked, not used to being on this side of the discussion.

"Nope."

Marc stepped forward and rubbed his hands together. "I repeat. Who wants to pin him down while I tie?"

Connor took a step back.

Mitch cleared his throat, obviously fighting a grin. "He's serious, Con. If I were you, I'd just get in the truck with me and come to the main house where we can all sit down and work this out. With or without you, we're involved."

David's expression was solemn. "But we'd all prefer it if you worked with us."

"It would work better if you did," Jake pointed out.

Connor stared at them all. As Mitch said, Marc was serious. If he didn't go with them willingly, he had the sick feeling that they would hog-tie him and throw him in the bed of the truck. And while his adrenaline level prodded him to challenge them, he knew his brothers too damn well to even attempt it. He might be able to take them one-on-one, but together they were impossible to best.

He took a deep breath. And, surprisingly, felt as though a one-ton weight had just been lifted from his shoulders. Now that he'd been forced to accept their help, he was glad they were there. Suddenly things didn't appear quite so dire. In fact, he was becoming increasingly convinced that together, they could beat this thing.

He stared at the cement beneath his boots, then cleared his throat. "Thanks."

The only sounds were those made by a dive-bombing blue jay near the cars.

"But?" David prompted.

Connor looked up at him. "But nothing." The grin he'd been fighting since he saw them all piled up on the steps looking like a posse from some old John Wayne western broke out all over his face. "I accept."

Three of his brothers grinned back at him and Jake stepped forward to drape an arm around his shoulders. But Marc...well, Marc looked disappointed that physical force wouldn't be involved.

"Damn," Marc said, trailing behind them as they headed for the vehicles. "I was hoping to get even for all those times you hammered me."

David laughed. "Sorry, bro, but it looks like you're going to have to wait until next time for that."

All of them stopped right where they were, then turned to stare silently at the youngest McCoy.

"What?" he asked, innocently.

"Bite your tongue, David. God willing, there won't be a next time."

Mitch was the first to move as he opened the truck's driver-side door. "This one's not over yet, guys. And if we keep dragging ass, it's not going to be, either. Now get your rear ends into gear and let's get going."

Without another word, all of them climbed into their respective vehicles, the air filling with the clap of closing doors, starting engines and spitting gravel.

And for the first time since Melissa Robbins was murdered, Connor began to believe that everything would be okay. It couldn't help but be. The McCoy men were together again.

BRONTE PRESSED THE disconnect button on her cell phone, then clapped it closed and slipped it into her purse, growing more anxious by the second. Almost unconsciously, she tightened her grip on that same purse, for it held more than her cell phone. It held all the evidence she hoped would clear Connor's name.

Over an hour had passed since her revelation at the courthouse. Sixty-five minutes of pure torture as she'd tried calling everywhere and everyone, searching for Connor—including each and every one of his brothers. She hadn't been able to contact a single one. And her attempts to make contact with Connor through the U.S. Marshal's office had yielded nothing but a stone wall. Normally, knowing they had tried to protect Connor from anyone asking questions from the U.S. attorney's office would have satisfied her. But now…

Well, now they were hurting him more than helping him.

She peeked at the time. Five till twelve. Twisting the plain silver watch she bought while grocery shopping the day before yesterday around and around her wrist, she scanned the spattering of people leaving the courthouse. At this time of day there were few people entering. Lunchtime. She glanced behind her to make sure Connor hadn't somehow gotten by her in the last ten minutes, then blew out a long breath, turning back toward the twenty or so cement steps below her.

As she bit down hard on her bottom lip, she couldn't ignore the irony of the situation. All her life she had hoped to find that one man who would be as good as his word. Who would make promises and keep them. Now that she was convinced she had found him, she was actually wishing he would be just like the rest of them—or at least more like Thomas Jenkins—and have lied to her. But no matter how much she wished it so, it wouldn't happen. Connor trusted her. And she trusted him. Implicitly.

Considering what she'd gone through in her former relationship, it was a major mile marker, that one—the ability to trust another man. But Connor wasn't just any other man. He was a man's man—or, more importantly, a woman's fantasy. The kind of guy most women didn't dare even dream about. Oh, he was stubborn as hell. And probably told himself in the mirror every morning that he didn't need what other men needed, probably even recited some sort of bachelor oath. But that didn't fool her, not anymore. When a man like Connor loved, he loved completely. And the mere idea that he might love her let loose a whole battalion of butterflies in her stomach.

Butterflies whose wings were instantly clipped when she remembered his quiet, but vehement words last night. He wasn't interested in marriage or having children. Two important elements that made a couple a family. Could she learn to accept those limitations? Or would she fool herself into believing she might be able to sway him to her way of thinking?

She looked around the steps and swallowed thickly, reminding herself where she was and what she was afraid was going to happen, and berating herself for her rash decision to convince Connor to turn himself in.

She bounced on her heels slightly, feeling like she could jump out of her skin at any moment.

Then she went completely still. She realized that someone was noticeably absent from the steps: Dennis Burns.

Her mind clicked. Why, after all he had gone through to finagle the Pryka case from her, and to have an arrest warrant issued in Connor's name, would he not be present for the arrest? She looked toward the boulevard, also finding it eerily quiet. Where were the news vans? The reporters? The media that would make Burns a local hero?

Her heartbeat slowed to a near stop as she counted off each of the unusual details. *Oh, God.* She closed her eyes, reciting a prayer. *Please, Connor, whatever you do, don't step a foot near this courthouse.*

A brief, piercing flash near one of the courthouse columns caught her attention. She twisted around, spotting an armed law official wearing full, black riot gear.

Her pulse leaping off the charts, she turned to her right, catching sight of another rifle as the sunlight glinted off the long oiled barrel.

Oh God, oh God, oh God.

She remembered the words on the warrant. "Armed and extremely dangerous." Secret code words for shoot first, ask questions later. A directive that worked straight into Dennis Burns's hands if what she suspected was true.

Burns wasn't there because he had no intention of Connor being taken alive.

Her feet flew into action. *What to do, what to do?* A part of her wanted to approach the armed gunmen, demand they put down their weapons. But she knew from experience that these guys never traveled alone, especially not in connection with a case like this. There was probably a whole brigade hidden behind every column and on every rooftop in sight.

Her throat refused her access to air as she climbed the remainder of the stairs leading to the courthouse doors. What had she done? She had been so wrapped up in doing the right thing she hadn't stopped to consider what could happen as a result.

She had done exactly what she promised she wouldn't do. Her actions had essentially set up a trap. And one very endearing Connor McCoy was the unwitting mouse.

She yanked open the courthouse door, stepped through the metal detector, then practically ran down the hall. If Connor was going to approach from the front, maybe his not seeing her there waiting, as she'd said she would, would stop him from coming up.

Or maybe it would just make him come inside, looking for her.

Oh, God.

Pivoting on her heels, she headed back for the door, clutching her bag tightly to her side. The bag held the evidence she needed to clear Connor's name. But what good would any of it do if Connor wasn't alive to be cleared?

She took the steps faster than she should have, her low heels clicking against the cement and echoing through the mall below. Every single last hair on her body stood on end as though she had just been zapped by static electricity. Knowing that, right now, she was in the crosshairs of at least two, probably more, high-powered rifles made her want to rush around the corner and retch.

Out of breath and with a thin sheen of sweat coating her

skin, caused both by the exertion and her fear, she looked both ways down the street. What should she do? Where should she go? Was there some way to warn Connor away, short of making a sign?

"Walk down a block the other way, then turn right."

Bronte jumped at the sound of the quiet male voice so near her ear. As the man continued walking, she noticed his dark blue officer's uniform and his dark-blond hair. David!

Her heart expanded in her chest. Connor wasn't coming! And not only wasn't he coming, obviously he had finally turned to his family for help. For the first time in long, tormenting minutes, she felt a surge of hope.

She stood on the curb for another long minute, feigning interest in the traffic rushing by, then looked at her watch. Heaving a heavy, obvious sigh for the benefit of those who were watching, she started to walk in the opposite direction David had gone, forcing herself not to look after him.

Just act like everything's normal, Bronte, she told herself, knowing that she wasn't out of the woods yet. Not by a long shot. Now that Dennis Burns knew Connor was in contact with her, she was probably under heavy surveillance and probably had been since that morning when she'd sprung the news on him. She tightened her fingers on the strap of her purse, realizing they probably already had her cell phone tapped. She cringed. That meant they knew of every single number she had called trying to get word to Connor.

Her feet automatically carried her, but she wasn't sure that doing as David had asked was such a good idea. It was her fault all this was happening. Her fault that she had placed Connor in even greater danger than he had been on his own. And by going to him now—and she was sure that's what she was doing—she'd be leading Dennis Burns, and whatever law agencies he'd enlisted for help, right to him.

Her stomach leaden, she realized she couldn't do that. She couldn't cause more trouble than she already had.

Instead of making a right at the next crossroads as David had instructed, she made a left and picked up her pace. If she couldn't help him, at least she could make sure she couldn't hurt him.

A block down, she lifted her hand to hail a taxi. Almost immediately, one pulled over. Only to have another one come up from behind and nearly rear end him, the blare of the horn deafening. Bronte frowned then noticed that the second taxi held no normal cab driver. Rather, Connor's brother Marc was behind the wheel.

Her heart giving a gentle squeeze, she told the first driver she didn't need him, then hurried to the second. She quickly crawled in the back, slightly disappointed she didn't find Connor waiting for her there.

"You made a wrong turn back there," Marc McCoy said, easily weaving back into the heavy lunch-hour traffic.

Bronte looked to where her knuckles were nearly white from where they held her bag. "I…couldn't. I was afraid I'd lead those guys back there straight to Connor."

He slanted her a glance as he put a raggedy baseball cap on his head. "Tsk, tsk. You don't give us enough credit."

Ridiculously, she felt her eyes flush with tears. "No, I'm afraid I gave myself too much." She collapsed against the seat, trying to hold her tears at bay. She couldn't give herself over to them now. She couldn't cry. She wouldn't. Remembering her cell phone, she fished through her bag for it. Eyeing the offensive instrument, she cracked the window and began to stuff it out.

"Don't!"

She jumped, startled by Marc's vehement order. She met his gaze in the rearview mirror. "Why? They're probably using it to trace me even now. Wherever I go, they'll go."

"That's what we're counting on."

She stared at him, puzzled.

He motioned toward the window in front of them. "Ahead is the Dupont Circle Metro station. You're going to get out there, with the phone, then go inside. If you're being followed, they won't have enough time to cover both exits. Go inside. At the other north exit, you'll find Mitch wearing one of Pops's police uniforms. He'll have the exit blocked off…except to you. Give him the phone, then go out that exit, walk up a block, hang a right—and this time don't go the other way. There you'll find Jake waiting in a dark blue sedan. Get in the back."

Bronte watched him, mesmerized, then nodded her head slightly.

He pulled to a stop near the south Metro entrance. "Go."

She began to, then stopped and reached out to touch Marc's shoulder. "Thanks."

He met her gaze, his own full of indecipherable emotion. "Don't mention it."

She got out, then descended the steps to the Metrorail stop. As promised, at the opposite end stood Mitch, looking formidable in an official policeman's uniform. He'd placed a black-and-yellow road block in front of the exit, and she had no doubt another was at the top of the stairs, blocking the entrance. He stood with his arms crossed, directing pedestrians to the other exit.

Bronte approached, then slid him the phone. He nodded, and she hurried up the stairs, glancing back to see him slip the cell phone into a large brown shopping bag held by a woman boarding the train.

Her heart growing lighter with hope, her mind heavier with respect for the McCoys, she emerged back into daylight. Thankful for her tendency to carry oversize purses, she slipped out of her jacket, stuffed it into the bag, then tugged her white blouse out of her slacks so that it reached down to nearly her thighs, giving her appearance a completely different, more casual look. Reaching into her bag, she took out a navy-blue, rimmed rain cap that folded down to nearly nothing, then shook it out. Within seconds, her short red hair was completely hidden under the hat. A pair of sunglasses completed the transformation. As she turned the corner, she caught sight of herself in the glass of a pharmacy. She nearly didn't recognize herself. The hat gave her an ageless type of quality. She could have been eighteen or eighty.

There. There was the blue sedan, so like hundreds of others in the city used to shuttle diplomats around. Giving a quick glance around, she quickly climbed into the backseat. She'd barely closed the door when Jake pulled away from the curb.

CONNOR IDLED MITCH'S oversize red truck, seeking out Jake's car in his rearview mirror. It didn't take him long to spot it. And it didn't take long for that weightless feeling in his stomach to reappear when he spotted Bronte.

He grimaced then ran his hand over his freshly shaven cheeks.

After his brothers had bullied him into going to the main McCoy place that morning, he'd caught a shower and a shave, and changed into the fresh clothes he'd pilfered from his own apartment last night. The routine task had made him feel somewhat human again.

He watched Bronte get out of Jake's car. He reached over and opened the passenger door for her, then pressed the automatic lock button once she was inside.

She was out of breath, but that's not what Connor noticed about her. With the floppy rain cap and sunglasses on, she looked liked somebody's mother instead of the sleek, sassy junior U.S. attorney she was.

His chest tightened even further.

"I'm sorry," she said quietly.

Connor had pulled into traffic, giving Jake a brief nod of gratitude as he passed. He looked at Bronte, wondering if she was thinking the same thing he was.

She motioned with her hand jerkily. "I didn't know that all…*that* was going to happen when I asked you to meet me at the courthouse this morning."

She was apologizing for the entire SWAT team being positioned within a one-block radius.

All it had taken was one carefully placed phone call from Pops to find out that SWAT had been alerted.

"It wasn't your fault," he said.

She quickly looked away, as if unconvinced, then said quietly, "Thank you."

This wasn't going at all as he had planned. Connor frowned, then made a fast right-hand turn without flicking on the blinker. "What are you thanking me for?"

She glanced at him, her lower lip trembling, making her look all the more vulnerable and incredibly kissable. He fought a groan and forced himself to look away.

"Thank you for keeping your word," she said quietly.

Connor made another right-hand turn a little more quickly than he'd intended, forcing Bronte almost flush up against his side. Heat instantly exploded through him at the points of contact between them, and her subtle scent teased his nose. It was all he could do not to curve his arm around her and pull her closer.

Instead, he made a left-hand turn, forcing her almost up against the door, well away from him.

"I always keep my word."

He thought he heard her say "I know" but couldn't be sure because she seemed overly interested in the objects reflected in the side-view mirror.

But he knew the instant she relaxed then turned her attention on him, for every nerve ending sizzled to life.

"You look different," she said.

He glanced at her, then wished he hadn't, because her smile was too dazzling, reminded him too much of last night and all that had passed between them. He refocused his gaze on the road. "So do you."

"Oh!" Seeming to realize she still wore her disguise, she took off the sunglasses and the ridiculous cap, then finger-combed her short red hair back into place. "I thought maybe it might help."

"It probably did."

She seemed to make a federal case out of folding the cap into a neat little square, then placing it and her glasses into her bag, while taking a suit jacket out. "Are you okay?" she asked quietly a short while later.

He gave in to the urge to look at her. "Fine. You?"

The expression on her face told him she didn't buy his answer. Not that he was surprised. Not once in the short time he'd known Bronte, had he been able to get anything over on her. Why should now be any different?

She shifted on the seat until she was almost facing him. "Okay, what is it, McCoy?" she asked, putting on her best cross-examining U.S. attorney's face. "You might as well just be out with it, because I'm going to find out what's bothering you sooner or later anyway."

"This isn't going to work, Bronte."

Even he was surprised by the abruptness of his response. But he carefully hid it behind a stone-faced expression as he negotiated the streets.

He could tell she was shuffling through possible responses. Some women would have played dumb and asked what wasn't going to work. Others might have tried to argue with him. But Bronte did neither one. Instead she sat stiffly looking out the window and softly said, "I see."

That had been easier than he thought it would be. Why,

he didn't know. And why it should disappoint him was doubly confusing.

"This has nothing to do with what just happened back there," he felt compelled to say. He cringed, realizing he should have just left things at that, let her come to her own conclusions as to why he was calling a halt to their relationship.

"Oh?" she asked. "Then tell me, Connor, what else has happened between last night and now?"

"Nothing." He glanced at her pointedly. "And that's exactly the point."

He knew by the stricken look on her face that she thought last night hadn't meant anything to him. The notion pretty near ripped his gut in half. But he stopped himself short of reassuring her.

He sighed and smoothed his hand over the back of his head. "We just weren't…meant to be, Bronte." *I can't let you put your career on the line for me. Can't let you ruin your life.*

She seemed to shrink in front of his eyes. "I see."

Damn. He had done this dozens of times before. Cut off a woman before she had gotten herself in too deep. He'd given this speech, or one very similar to it, so often he could almost recite it verbatim. But somehow blowing off Bronte made him feel like he was cutting off a limb. Perhaps revealing that he, himself, had gotten in too deep this time.

Oh, last night had meant the world to him. Despite what he'd just said, what he had experienced with Bronte…well, something had happened between them that he couldn't put a name to. Something that made him feel remarkably alive even with a death sentence hanging over his head. Something that made him want to crush her to him and never let her go—the world be damned.

But after taking a fresh look at everything this morning,

hashing things out with his brothers, he realized just how much at risk he had put Bronte merely by asking for her help—hell, even by being in her presence now. If she were caught in the truck with him, she might be charged with obstructing justice. Or worse....

He sat ramrod straight. Of course, he could never tell her any of this. If he knew Bronte, and he felt that he did, in every way a man could know a woman, she'd argue with him until she was blue in the face. She would refuse to back off. More than that, even his suggesting she do so would likely trigger a more insistent need for her to stick by his side.

And he couldn't let that happen.

Slowing, he eyed the passing town houses in Georgetown, then pulled to a stop at the curb. It seemed to take Bronte a moment to realize they had stopped. Then she blinked, glanced around, spotting her own town house a block-and-half up the street. "You brought me home."

Connor forced himself to stare through the windshield, everywhere but at her, no matter how much he wanted to erase that hurt shadow from her eyes.

"So this is it, then?"

He nodded, keeping his head straight.

"I see."

Damn. He hated when she said that. He wanted to yell that she didn't see. That she couldn't possibly see. That she couldn't understand that he was doing this for her sake.

The sound of the door opening echoed through the truck cab. Connor tightened his hands on the wheel until he was sure his knuckles would break through the whitened skin of his fingers. It took every ounce of reserve, every iota of restraint he possessed, not to grab her arm and pull her to him.

"Thanks," he managed to push out. "You know, for everything."

Peripherally, he noticed her cringe. But it was nothing

compared to the way he damned himself for the words seeming so…trivial.

"No problem," she said a little too lightly.

He reached out and pulled the door closed. Despite his vow not to do so, he looked at her one last time. And the same instant, her eyes widened and she tried to open the door. Connor pressed the automatic lock. She smacked at the window in obvious frustration.

"Connor, wait! You don't understand!"

It took everything that Connor was to force himself to pull away from that curb, watching in his rearview mirror as she stood staring at where the truck had been much like a bombing victim staring in shock at the debris.

CHAPTER TWELVE

CONNOR PULLED UP TO THE McCOY place at a virtual crawl. He wouldn't begin to link the word melancholy to his suddenly lethargic mood. That was a woman's word. Men didn't get melancholy.

Did they?

Still, he did acknowledge that leaving Bronte O'Brien standing alone on the street was the singular most difficult thing he'd ever done in his life. Nothing even came close to comparing to it. Not when Marc had been laid up at the hospital with that broken collarbone. Not when David had run away from home. Not when he'd stood up for David as best man at his wedding.

He slowly drew to a stop next to the other vehicles parked there. Sometime over the past couple of days he had come to care for Bronte in a way he hadn't thought he was capable of outside his family.

Someone knocked on the closed window. Connor whipped around, his hand on the firearm tucked under his shirt, only to find Mitch standing outside. He'd been so immersed in his thoughts, he hadn't even noticed his brother had pulled up behind him.

Mitch opened the door, making a point of looking around inside. "Where's Bronte?"

"Home." He climbed out and slammed the door. Both on the truck and the conversation. "Everybody here?"

"Fine. If you don't want to talk about it now, that's okay. There's always later."

"Not in this case." He reached out for the door handle to the house, then looked up, startled when David's new wife, Kelli, opened it for him. "What are you doing here?"

She blinked at him, frowned, then looked beyond him. "Where's Bronte?"

Connor stepped around her into the kitchen. "Home. And you didn't answer my question."

David leaned against the counter and crossed his arms over his chest. "She's here because I asked her to be here. We need all the help we can get."

Marc walked in from the living room, Melanie following in his wake. "Mel for the same reason."

Connor bristled. He didn't have to ask. He already knew Mitch's wife, Liz, would also be around somewhere, and by the sound of a little girl's laughter coming from upstairs, he guessed Michelle was there as well.

Great. Just great. It had been difficult enough having to accept his brothers' help. He'd forgotten about his new sisters-in-law. He'd seen the situation as something the McCoy men could handle.

Another aspect the women's presence emphasized was the gaping hole in his chest caused by leaving Bronte behind.

Aw, hell.

"How'd it go?" Pops asked, coming into the room.

Mitch answered him. "Like clockwork."

David unbuttoned the top of his uniform shirt. "Too bad you couldn't fit into one of my uniforms—or Kelli's, for that matter—Mitch. You were swimming in Pops's duds."

"Yeah, well, at least I didn't nearly scare Bronte into traffic. Jesus, David, what did you say to her? She looked about ready to jump out of her skin."

"Why? What happened?" Kelli asked.

Marc grimaced. "I don't know, but whatever it was, she purposely walked in the opposite direction. I didn't think I was going to be able to catch her before she got into that other taxi."

"How'd you get a hold of that ancient monstrosity, anyway?" Jake asked.

Mel sat beside her husband. "A cousin of a friend of mine let me borrow it."

"And those barricades at Dupont Circle were a work of art," Marc said. "Thanks, Kell."

"Don't mention it."

Connor listened to the conversation rolling along without him, feeling two clicks behind. The women had helped? How? When? He and his four brothers had put the plan together in this very kitchen, without any of his sisters-in-law present. And only because he insisted on making that noon meeting come hell or high water. He'd promised Bronte he'd be there and he was there.

The incongruity of the situation struck him. Yeah, he made the meeting all right. Only so he could pretend to call things off between them. Hurt her in a way that seemed to hurt him more.

Connor looked to where Pops was eyeing him from the doorway. He grimaced. Just when in the hell had the old man gotten so attentive?

"So, where do we go from here?" Mitch asked, referring to a pad full of items they had discussed earlier.

Pops pushed from the doorjamb, coming to stand next to Connor. "Can I talk to you for a minute? Outside?"

Connor wanted to tell him no. He didn't think he could handle another father-son talk with Sean right now. His nerves were too raw, his stomach too unsettled.

Still, he began to follow him out, only to be halted by his father's hand in the mudroom.

"The first thing we have to do is call you an attorney."

Connor wanted to tell him he had an attorney. Bronte. But he couldn't say that anymore.

"Why? What is it?" he asked, noticing the severe expression on his father's face.

Pops nodded toward the door. "It seems our adversaries aren't as dumb as we think. If I'm not mistaken, that's a representative from the U.S. attorney's office, along with half the state highway patrol."

Despite the conversations going on in the kitchen, everyone appeared to hear. Chair legs scraped against tile as his brothers and their wives hurried for the door.

"Plan B," Jake announced.

"Plan B?" Connor echoed.

Marc grabbed him by his collar. "Yeah. You get upstairs into the attic. Now."

Connor shrugged his younger brother off. "I've never hidden from anything in my life. I'm not about to start now."

Mitch looked at him square in the face. "There's not much you can do for yourself while sitting in jail, Connor."

He stiffened at his point. But the thought of cowering in the attic while his family dealt with officials sent to arrest him didn't sit well with him. It wasn't even an option as far as he was concerned. "What? Do you think you're just going to tell those guys I'm not here and expect them to leave? What planet are you from?" He pointed toward the door. "Those guys are not going to leave here without me."

Pops sighed. "He's right, guys."

"But we can stall them," David said. "Wait 'til dark, then devise a plan to smuggle Connor out of here."

"Not on your life." Connor straightened. "I may not know how in the hell I got into this mess, but I'm not about to run away from it either." He stared at each of them in turn. "And Pops and I certainly didn't raise any of you to be cowards either."

They all looked down at their shoes and boots like chastised children. And, right at that moment, that's exactly what they appeared to be.

Still, Connor couldn't help but feel proud of the way they all had immediately jumped to his defense, willing to risk it all in order to protect him.

The significant pounding on the door forced an unnatural silence in the room. "Connor McCoy, come out now with your hands up!"

He stood stock-still for a moment, looking at his family surrounding him, and catching sight of little Lili from where she was peeking around the doorway. Michelle followed his gaze and hurried to take the little girl away, but the image of her scared little face would remain etched in Connor's mind forever.

Exactly what he had feared would happen was happening. He was being arrested in front of everyone that mattered in his life. And, despite his innocence, he couldn't help feeling ashamed.

He started to move toward the door. Pops held his hand against his son's chest. "We'll have you out of there before you can blink, Connor."

He wanted to tell him not to bother. He'd rather rot in prison than have to see himself brought down even further in his family's eyes.

He took his father's hand from his chest, then opened the door. And the moment he did, everything came together.

"You," he said, staring into the face of the U.S. attorney who had made frequent visits to Melissa Robbins. What was his name? Dennis Burns. Yes, that was it. Could he have been the associate Bronte had referred to? The one who had wrestled control of the Pryka case out from under her nose?

He knew instantly that he was.

He also knew that he was looking into the face of the real killer.

Several state highway patrolmen stepped forward, one wielding handcuffs. The sound of a car spitting up gravel in the drive gained all their attention, as did the frantic honking of a horn.

Bronte.

Connor straightened his shoulders. With his new knowledge, he wanted to fight the men now binding him—anything but to have to bear this with Bronte also looking on.

She ground to a stop next to a patrol car, her tires kicking up a cloud of dust that made the men nearest her cough.

"Uncuff that man right now."

The patrolmen glanced warily at each other, then back at her. Bronte flashed her ID. "I'm U.S. Attorney O'Brien. Do as I say."

The guy Connor knew as Dennis Burns stepped forward. "Leave them where they are. Ignore her. She's not in charge of this case. I am."

"Not anymore you're not."

Connor eyed her, thinking he'd never seen a woman so beautiful in his life. Her green eyes sparked a warning fire. Even her red hair seemed to crackle with energy.

She pulled something out of that suitcase of a purse she carried. He realized it was a videotape. He grimaced.

"This will explain everything."

She brushed past the men, taking the keys from one of the patrolmen's belt and tossing them to Pops. "Unlock those cuffs."

Pops did as requested and they all followed Bronte into the house, through the kitchen, and into the living room like a military squadron.

She ejected Lili's video of *The Lion King* from the VCR, then popped in the one she held. Connor instantly recognized the security tape taken the day of Robbins's murder. He jerked to look at her even as he rubbed his wrists. He didn't get it. Why was she showing them something that so clearly implicated him in the murder?

"God, Connor, is that you?" David asked.

Bronte stepped in front of the screen, then slipped in another video she produced from her bag.

It appeared to be footage from another security camera. Connor squinted. It was from the lobby where the U.S. attorney's office was based. He looked at her, wanting to trust her, but afraid he had taken things too far by rejecting her so thoroughly. Was she deliberately out to hurt him? He couldn't bring himself to believe it.

She pressed the freeze button on the image. She pointed to the screen. "Looks an awful lot like Connor, doesn't it?" she asked everyone and no one in particular.

"Sure looks the same to me," Jake said, earning him stares from half the room.

Bronte smiled. "No, that's okay. That's the response I was looking for. Because you see, this—" she tapped her finger against the screen "—is not Connor. This footage was taken at the U.S. attorney's building this morning."

Connor stared at her along with his brothers. They all knew he hadn't been at the U.S. attorney's office that morning.

Dennis Burns sighed. "It doesn't matter where or when it was taken, Bronte. It's clearly McCoy." He cleared his throat. "Let me clarify that. It's clearly Connor McCoy."

Bronte's expression seemed to scream "gotcha," and Connor couldn't help the thrill that raced through his stomach. She held up a finger. "Excuse me for a minute?" She stepped a short ways away from the group, clicked open her cell phone, then spoke quietly. When she turned, she did so still holding the phone open. "Connor? Would you mind pressing Play for me?"

Unsure what to expect, he did as she asked. The man on

the screen continued to walk away, about to disappear into the revolving doors without his face being seen. Then he suddenly turned, as if summoned by an unseen someone. The image froze itself, then zoomed in on the face.

Dennis Burns.

Connor swung on the man in question. But he seemed as unmoved now as before. "So what's your point, Bronte? That Connor and I happen to have the same type of coat and haircut? That from behind we look similar?" He shook his head, a smug smile creasing his face. "You're reaching, Bronte, and you know it."

"Not when combined with this."

All of them turned to find Connor's coworker Oliver Platt entering the room. Bronte closed her phone, the smile on her face so full of pleasure Connor wanted to kiss her. Somehow he managed to suppress the desire and hear out his co-worker.

"U.S. Marshal Platt," he said, flashing his ID. "And this here is a copy of the real log from the day of Melissa Robbins's murder. On it you'll clearly see Dennis Burns's name logged in and logged out, corresponding with the times you saw on the security video."

Burns scoffed. "It's a copy. Completely inadmissible. Easily doctored."

"Yes, but when combined with the testimony of the man who logged you in and out, it's pretty convincing, wouldn't you say?" Bronte asked. "Yes, that means that we found Dan Wagner, Dennis, right where you sent him."

"This is ridiculous," Burns said, though he began backing up, making his way for the door. "You can't prove a thing."

Connor crossed his arms. Everything finally clicked into place. "I wouldn't count on it. Though you can explain the physical evidence found in Robbins's quarters away as a result of normal everyday activity, what will a forensics team pick up at your place, I wonder? Traces of Robbins's lipstick on your collar? Microscopic but conclusive proof that the two of you were intimately involved?"

Bronte's smile was telling. "I guess we'll find out soon. There's a team on its way to his place now. And a search warrant is also being served on his office as we speak." The smile disappeared. "Patrolmen...arrest this man."

The half-dozen state patrolmen looked at each other, then shrugged, stepping forward to do as ordered. But Dennis darted.

He didn't get two feet before Connor's hand grabbed the back collar of his navy-blue suit jacket. There were some advantages to having raised four bullheaded brothers. "Uh-uh," he said, yanking back the man who would have had Connor punished for his crime. "The only place you're going is to jail, Burns."

The patrolmen finished the arrest and steered Dennis Burns from the room.

Connor glanced at Bronte. Something warm and increasingly familiar spread through his chest. After what he'd said to her, what he'd done, how deeply he had hurt her—no matter his intentions—she had still come through for him. He couldn't begin to thank her for everything she'd done. So he didn't. The words got caught somewhere between his throat and his mouth.

Kelli saved him from having to say anything. She stepped to her friend and hugged her tightly. "God, I knew you were incredible, but this is awesome," she said quietly, then laughed at Bronte's startled expression. "What? Don't go getting modest on me now."

Connor looked away. Of course, Kelli had no idea what had happened between him and Bronte over the past few days. How could she? *He* still wasn't entirely sure what had happened.

There was one person who had a clue, however.

He turned to find Pops watching him from the kitchen doorway, a questioning expression on his face. Connor grimaced. Why was it that the last person he could talk to about this was the only one who had a clue about him and Bronte? Oh, his brothers might suspect something after their conversations with her yesterday, but Pops had been the one who'd seen her at his grandparents' old place last night. And it didn't take a badge to figure out that she hadn't been there strictly for the case.

Rubbing the back of his neck, he stepped away from the group. He felt Bronte's gaze on him, but was helpless to return it. What could he possibly say? *Sorry about earlier. I really didn't mean it. I was just protecting that cute little butt of yours. Forgive me?*

Still, he did have to thank her.

The only problem was…how, exactly, did you go about thanking someone for saving your life?

BRONTE FELT LIKE SHE MIGHT fall to her knees with relief.

After having gone so many days without a clue in the case, after reviewing everything in Pryka's case file and all the facts surrounding Robbins's murder, the instant she'd connected Burns with the man in the video, everything had begun to click into place. But all of it had been circumstantial until repeated phone calls to the U.S. Marshal's office that morning had finally connected her with Oliver Platt.

From the beginning, she had questioned Melissa Robbins's credibility as a witness. But she'd been so jazzed with the possibility of working on such a high-profile case she had ignored her gut instincts.

So far she had it roughly worked out that after three years as Leonid Pryka's main squeeze, Melissa Robbins had been tossed out with nothing but the clothes on her back and no way to support herself. And like many witnesses, she'd believed that WitSec not only provided people with new identities, she'd thought she'd be set for life from a financial standpoint. And in the process, she could reap a little revenge on Pryka for having dumped her.

Only Robbins had soon found that WitSec merely provided the basic necessities and that it was still undecided if she would need further aid after the trial. The information she'd supplied became a little more sketchy, her stories changed…and she'd made the fatal mistake of becoming intimately involved with Dennis Burns, thinking him her ticket to getting what she wanted.

Only Dennis Burns had had his own agenda. And a truckload of luck working in his favor. He'd wanted not only Bronte's job, but her boss's, Bernie Leighton's. But when he'd stumbled onto the fact that the woman he was using was also using him…he lost it.

Bronte had every reason to believe that Melissa's murder was a crime of passion—or a crime of ambition. Either way, when Burns was searching for a way to cover his tracks, he realized how similar he and Connor looked. From there on out, everything else was a piece of cake.

Bronte figured she should be upset that Robbins had used her that way. And even wondered if she owed Pryka an apology for having pursued him so diligently based on Robbins's testimony alone. A woman scorned was definitely a force to be reckoned with. However, all she could do was be thankful she had finally figured everything out.

Still, all that didn't change what had happened between her and Connor.

She glanced up to find him stepping toward the kitchen. Her heart contracted painfully. Even now, she was shocked that Connor had gone through all he had, arranging with his brothers the elaborate scheme to have her brought safely to him, only so he could give her the brush-off outside her town house. She'd been so upset, she'd completely forgotten about the evidence she had to clear him. She tried to fortify her legs. After all this, she refused to end up on her knees, looking like a fool in front of the room full of people milling about, slapping each other on the back. She discreetly reached behind her and braced herself against the floor-model television, unable to work everything out. They didn't make any sense, Connor's words to her earlier. She had never indicated one way or another that she expected a future with him. Why, then, his speech?

Kelli stopped midsentence, though Bronte couldn't have said what she'd been talking about to save her life. "Are you all right?"

"Hmm?" Bronte peeled her gaze away from Connor's retreating back. She gazed into her friend's concerned face and felt the ridiculous urge to cry.

"Oh, God, what's the matter, Bronte?" Her face grew stern. "And don't you dare try telling me everything's fine. I've heard the word one too many times over the past nine months."

Bronte looked down, discreetly blinking back the moisture that had begun collecting in her eyes. She was startled by the laugh that choked off her words. "Tough, because you're going to hear it again."

She shook her head. It seemed incredible that just a short time ago she'd been pining away over Thomas Jenkins. In light of what had passed between her and Connor...well, she was growing increasingly convinced that her reaction to finding out Thomas was married was more a matter of broken pride than a broken heart. What she and Thomas had shared had been convenient. This...thing with Connor couldn't have been more inconvenient. He had stumbled into her life at a time when her defenses were high, when her willingness to become involved with another man was remarkably low, and when merely associating with him threatened a job she had worked so hard to keep.

Yet, somehow, he had effortlessly moved past those phenomenal barriers and had chiseled a spot for himself inside her heart.

She visually sought him out, finding him with his back turned toward her, talking to his father. Unfortunately, he had about as much intention of marrying her as Thomas had. She was also coming to understand that he didn't trust her as much as she'd believed. Ultimately, he had decided to lock her out, just as he had turned away the rest of his family. And the thought of what his actions might have led to…

"Oh, God," Kelli said, her green eyes widening. She stepped close so that Bronte alone heard her next words. "Not you and…Connor?"

Bronte looked at her a little too quickly, was a little slow in covering her shock, and she knew it by her friend's open-mouthed reaction.

"For God's sake, Bronte, are you nuts?"

She bit hard on the inner flesh of her cheek, finding those damn tears far too close to the surface for comfort. "Yes, I guess I am."

Kelli took her arm and guided her toward the front door. Within moments, they stood on the front porch, the chaos inside the house left behind them. Kelli closed the door, apparently so she wouldn't be overheard, then crossed her arms.

"I don't know quite what to say."

Bronte stepped to the edge of the porch, looking out over the beautiful land that was Manchester, Virginia…and knowing she could never come back here. "So don't say anything." She glanced over her shoulder and smiled. "That would certainly be a refreshing first."

Instantly, Kelli was at her side, her arm over her shoulders. "When did this happen? How far has it gone? Does he feel the same?"

Bronte closed her eyes, the questions coming too quickly, her mind unable to take everything in. "It doesn't matter. Not anymore. What does is that it can never work out. Tomorrow just isn't part of the equation."

"Oh, geez, Bronte. I'm sorry."

Kelli tugged her into her arms, squeezing her tightly. Oh, how much Bronte wished she could give herself over to the emotions swirling like last night's violent thunderstorm inside her. But she didn't dare. Not when the man responsible for her pain stood just on the other side of that door.

"You know, if you had let me in on this earlier, I could have warned you that this would happen," Kelli said softly, still holding her and refusing to let go.

"I didn't have a chance to. It all happened so quickly."

Kelli pulled slightly back to look into her face. "Like you would have told me, anyway."

Bronte laughed, the emotional release giving vent to the tears gathering at the backs of her eyes. "Remind me to fill you in on everything a little later, okay? Right now…right now, I just can't."

"Everything?" Kelli asked, moving her hands to her shoulders and squeezing.

Bronte nodded. "Yes, everything."

Behind them, the door opened. Kelli finally released her. Bronte took advantage of the freedom to step away and swipe at her cheeks outside the line of vision of their new visitor.

"Is everything okay?" a French-accented female voice asked.

"Couldn't be better," Kelli said just a tad too cheerfully.

Bronte turned to greet Michelle, Jake's wife. Michelle smiled at her, then shook her head. "I know that look. It only comes when one dares to fall in love with one of the stubborn McCoy men, no?"

Bronte wondered if every single female in the house had gone through what she had. The defining difference, of course, was that they were all married to their McCoys. She… Well, she would prove the exception. The only one who hadn't fully landed her McCoy.

"Bronte?"

For the second time that day, she nearly jumped out of her skin. But this time it wasn't because she was afraid for Connor's safety. No. This time Connor had said her name and she was concerned for her own safety. Her mental and emotional safety.

She glanced at Kelli. Apparently, she wasn't the only one concerned. She touched her friend's arm, warning her not to spill the accusatory words so obviously on the tip of her tongue.

Connor cleared his throat. "Can I speak to you for a moment?" He motioned toward the large front lawn. "Out here?"

Bronte nodded, ignoring the leap of hope in her heart.

Kelli whispered into her ear, "Give me a yell if you need any help."

"Don't be ridiculous," she said, though the image of petite police officer Kelli taking down the rough and tough Connor almost made her want to smile. Almost.

Her palms overly damp, she followed the man, who had stolen her heart only to break it, toward the cars choking the driveway. The highway patrol vehicles were just backing out, but Bronte could take little joy in seeing Dennis Burns in the back of the first one, except that it meant that Connor was now rightfully cleared of any and all wrongdoing.

"What is it?" she asked, crossing her arms in the hopes of coming off more composed than she was.

Connor glanced at his boots, his grimace making her stomach bottom out. "I just wanted to say…well, I think I should…" He finally looked up, his gaze slamming into hers, the shadow in his steely green eyes making her heart skip a beat. "Aw, hell, Bronte, thank you."

Thank you? That's what he'd brought her out here for? She wanted to ask him what he was thanking her for, but she already knew. He was grateful that she had gotten him off the hook.

She forced air through her tight throat and somehow managed to conjure up a smile. "Don't mention it."

He began to walk away.

Bronte felt frustration saturate her muscles, surround them, until she was swimming in it. "Connor?"

He stopped but didn't turn to face her.

"Is that it? Is that all you wanted to say?"

For long moments he just stood there—his back impossibly straight, his shoulders drawn tight and taut—a mere instant in which Bronte's heart threatened to beat right out of her chest, not daring to hope, but hoping anyway.

She heard him clear his throat. "No. I also wanted to tell you I'm sorry."

Sorry?

Bronte ignored the squeezing of her heart and concentrated instead on all the implications of his apology.

Sorry?

Her prosecutor's mind quickly leafed through the series of events leading up to today. To this moment.

He resumed walking away. Bronte watched him for a moment as she compiled everything she'd come to know about one strikingly sexy Connor McCoy.

Then a lightbulb flicked on, shining through the pain of rejection, the cloud of confusion that made it impossible to see the truth for what it was.

Her feet sprung into action and within two strides she grasped his arm and forced him to face her. She swallowed hard at the surprised expression he wore and knew that her suspicions were true.

"Connor, do you mind telling me what you're sorry for?" She snatched her hand back from temptation and stared at him unblinkingly. "You know, just so I can be clear on what's happening here."

He looked completely stumped. And Bronte's ire rose even further. "I'm sorry for, you know…hurting you."

"Hurting me how?" She crossed her arms over her chest again, this time out of growing frustration more than the need to fortify herself.

He gestured helplessly with his right hand and she noticed the color in his neck darken. "By…breaking things off with you."

She cringed at the jab, but refused to give herself over to it the way she had earlier. There was more going on here than what was on the surface, and she wasn't going to stop until she unearthed it—no matter the price she might pay.

She bit discreetly on her bottom lip, then refocused her attention on him. "Liar," she said point-blank.

She didn't know if the risk would pay off, if she would end up looking like a desperate woman grasping at straws. But she had to know for sure if what she suspected was correct.

His slow, spreading grin made her heart bounce up into her throat. "I was afraid you were coming to know me too well."

Bronte had never hit another person in her life. But she did so now. She pulled her hand back and socked Connor right in the chest. "You moron. You said what you did to protect me, didn't you? Spouted that grandiose speech about how we weren't meant to be, pretended you didn't care about me, so you could get me out of the way."

He rubbed his chest, the amusement in his eyes shifting to growing wariness, as well it should have.

Bronte fairly shook with anger. "Boy, you really take the cake, you know that, McCoy?" She pointed a finger at him. "Have you stopped to consider exactly what that little ruse of yours could have meant? That had I had the reaction you were banking on, gone back into my town house and worked on forgetting that you even existed, you would be on your way to jail right now instead of Dennis Burns?"

His grimace was all too endearing, which made her all the madder at him.

"In fact, I bet, right now, that it really bothers you that a woman beat you to the punch, doesn't it? It eats you that you had to rely on a woman to help you out—big, bad Connor McCoy, who doesn't need anyone." She tried to calm her nerves, but the more she spoke, the more her argument gelled. "Do you know that if you had gone to your brothers before now, with their help and resources, you probably would have figured the whole thing out without my help?" She shook her head. "But no. You're big, bad Connor McCoy, who doesn't need anyone, much less a woman."

The truth of what she was saying began to sink in. No, Connor might not have meant the words he told her outside her town house. But he might as well have. From where she stood, his inability to trust anyone completely but himself…his inability to allow others to decide for them-selves…well, that made him someone *she* couldn't trust. With her life, yes. Not with her heart. Not with her soul.

"Guess what, Connor? I know you love me, even if you're too thickheaded to see that."

He began to reach out for her, but she batted him away blindly. He glanced toward the house. Bronte briefly looked to see that the entire McCoy clan stood there looking on.

"No, don't you dare touch me. I don't want you to touch

me again…ever." She swallowed past the emotion clogging her throat. "No. Wrong word. I think the word you would use would be never, right? Never will you get married. Never will you have children." She swiped at a tear that had rolled down her nose. "Well, let me add another never to your list. Never are you allowed to step within speaking distance of me again."

Giving him a long, hard look, she started to round him, her destination her car. She stopped beside him. "I can't trust a man who doesn't trust me. Who doesn't respect me as a human being capable of making my own decisions." Her voice caught. "And I can't continue to love a man who is too wounded to admit he loves me. Who understands that the word 'never' has no room in a relationship built on love."

She stepped from around his grasp and had to force herself not to run toward her car, the few tears she had been helpless to stop now a raging flood.

CHAPTER THIRTEEN

THE FOLLOWING SUNDAY, everything was just as it should be around the McCoy place. At least for appearance's sake, it was.

Many things had changed since that fateful day when the main house was swarmed by state highway patrolmen. Yet everything remained the same. Connor clutched his coffee cup and leaned against the long length of wood fence Mitch had erected to contain his growing breeding venture. While spring was still very much in evidence in the profusion of wildflowers sprinkling the pasture with vivid color, the unseasonably warm morning gave a peek at what the coming summer would bring.

He glanced toward the northeast corner of the land as though, if he looked hard enough, he'd be able to make out his grandparents' old place...now his place. But, of course, he couldn't. It was set too far away, and a large, old standing of trees blocked this tract of land from that one.

He didn't want to consider exactly why he'd decided to close up his place in the city and move out here. He knew part of the reason was his long discussion with Bronte. But to think about Bronte was to invite back a pain that startled him with its intensity.

So he merely looked forward—to the plans he had for the old house. From the way it was beginning to shape up already, he estimated it would look pretty good three months from now.

He'd yet to return to work. Oh, he'd stopped by the office, mainly to establish that there was no bad blood between him and his coworkers and superiors. But when Newton offered him an extended leave with pay as compensation for all he'd gone through, he'd surprised them and himself by taking him up on it.

What remained was what he planned to do with the leave. Initially he'd thought he'd go crazy with so much time on his hands and nothing much to do with it. But aside from those long hours between dusk and dawn, when images of a certain sexy redhead haunted him, and he'd awaken from a fitful sleep thinking she was there with him, things had gone pretty well so far.

A strident curse bridged the gap between him and where the rest of the McCoy gang was tying off the support beams of the old, hulking barn that still stood on the front corner of the land. Connor squinted against the sun, watching as Marc wildly shook his hand, as though he'd either hit it with a hammer or caught one helluva splinter. Goliath ran circles around him, barking up a storm. Connor found himself grinning at the sight.

He wasn't sure exactly what had happened last week in regards to his feelings toward his family, but he was aware of an inexplicable shift. He no longer felt…responsible, somehow, for them. He didn't jump when something happened, ready to take on the world and their problems.

Now… Well, now he simply felt a part of the family. No wiser, no more accountable, than each and every one of them.

He was pretty positive a psychologist might point to their coming to his aid, helping him when he'd never needed their help before. That rather than being the caretaker, he'd been the one in need of aid, and they had readily stepped in to fill the gap. Or it might have come as a result of Bronte's parting speech. But with that shift of power came a liberation of sorts. He didn't feel that he had to be perfect anymore. The role model to hold up to them to show them how it should be done. For the first time in his life, he felt free to make mistakes, to rush into projects—like that old house—without considering what the others might think, or what might happen if he failed.

Of course, the one person he did regret failing was Bronte.

He absently rubbed at his chest, imagining he could feel the hole in there made by her absence. How was it that in such a short amount of time one woman could worm her way into his heart so easily when others had fallen well short of the mark?

Then again, Bronte wasn't just any woman. She was a courageous, clever, sassy woman who knew her mind and held no fear of speaking it. She challenged him like no other woman before her.

And made him feel like no one else would again.

"I think you have it about right."

Connor glanced to where his newest sister-in-law, Kelli, had climbed up on the fence next to him, eyeing the others in their bid to tear down the old barn.

She nodded at them. "The safest place is right here." She smiled. "Do you think they know what they're doing?"

Connor found himself grinning back at her. She was a spitfire, this one—capable, pretty, and every bit a match for his youngest brother, David.

He caught himself up short. Since when had he stopped looking at his sisters-in-law as the enemy? He wasn't sure. What he did know was that it felt good just to sit back and enjoy them for what they were. And that was part of the new McCoys.

"Nope. I don't think they have a clue."

She tucked a strand of blond hair that had escaped from

her braid behind her ear. "I told them they should have called one of those wrecking companies. Have them come out with a ball and bulldozer. But did they listen to me? No." She drew the word out in a gently teasing tone. "They'll be lucky if they don't hurt themselves, much less kill each other."

Connor chuckled. "Welcome to the McCoy family."

She slowly turned her head to look at him, an odd expression on her face.

"What?"

She shook her head. "Oh, I don't know. I suppose I always thought you hated that your brothers got married." She caught her feet on the bottom rail. "Initially, I believed it might be because they beat you to the punch. But I quickly figured out that there are a lot of things we don't know about you, Connor McCoy. And those things are keeping you from having a healthy relationship with…a woman."

He glanced away. There was one thing he didn't think he'd ever be able to stomach about women. It wasn't just their innate ability to look straight through you and hit at the heart of the problem with a wooden mallet. It was the way those thoughts moved straight from their brains to their tongues.

She grimaced. "You know, I promised David I wouldn't hassle you about this, but…" She sighed. "Well, you and I have been family for only a short time now, and Bronte and I…we've been friends, more like sisters really, for a lot longer. Years."

Connor felt the incredible urge to move. But he couldn't budge an inch if he tried.

"Well, I don't see a hint of that stone-faced expression yet, so I guess it's okay if I continue?"

He nodded slightly, wondering what he was leaving himself open for.

"Anyway, I don't know what happened between you two. When it comes to relationships with the opposite sex, Bronte's as closemouthed as you are. But I did want to tell you that she's one hell of a woman, Bronte O'Brien. When she makes a commitment, she's in it for life. No matter what I did during our friendship, she was there, always. Without hesitation. Without judging. She was just there." She gazed past the others working on the old barn. "And I know that it's the same with you."

"She asks about me?" Connor cringed the moment the words were out.

Kelli's smile was knowing. "All the time."

He cleared his throat, trying to keep the words in, but helpless to stop them. "And what do you tell her?"

She shrugged, a decidedly wicked gleam in her eyes. "Oh, that you're just a stubborn old cuss who's even more miserable than she is."

He felt his brows shoot up to his hairline.

She laughed. "Just joshing. I don't say much, really. I did tell her about your moving into the old place on the other side of the McCoy land. She seemed pleased about that."

He nodded, knowing she would be pleased.

Another line of cussing pricked their ears and they looked to see David hopping around on one foot. Kelli leapt from the fence. "I guess that's my cue to get over there." She started walking away, brushing her hands on the seat of her jeans, then stopped and turned to look at him. "No matter what she said the other day, if you were to call Bronte, she probably wouldn't be averse to it. You know, if the thought ever entered your mind or anything." She smiled. "You'd probably get another earful, though."

Connor frowned and looked down at his T-shirt. "I wish it were that easy."

She propped her hands on her slender hips. "It is, once you get the hang of it. You pick up the receiver, punch out the number, then, voilà! There's the other person on the line." She made an astonished O with her mouth. "Imagine that."

Her grin was decidedly playful as she gave him a final wave, then continued walking toward the old barn.

Connor absently watched her go.

He wished things were that easy. He wished he could pick up the phone, punch out her number, and talk to Bronte. But he couldn't. Because Bronte was right. No matter how much had changed in his life, some fundamental things stayed the same. The fact that he never saw himself getting married. And the little issue of his never wanting to have children. He'd spent his life screwing up his brothers' lives. He couldn't handle creating brand-new lives to muck up.

Never.

The word echoed in his brain as he took a sip of his coffee then grimaced.

The question was, could he live the rest of his life never seeing Bronte O'Brien again?

An ominous creaking sounded from the direction of the barn. Connor put down his cup and pushed from the fence, ready to run.

"Heads up! She's going to go!" Jake called out.

Connor watched in gross fascination as Jake, Mitch, Marc and David all scrambled to get as far away from the swaying monstrosity as they could. Connor took a step forward, then froze as the barn chose a direction and collapsed into a pile of faded red kindling just inches away from his brothers' retreating backs.

To his surprise, rather than feeling the urge to ream them out for the stupid move that had nearly killed them all, or rushing to their sides to see if they were injured, he did something completely out of character for him. He doubled over and laughed.

It wasn't until Marc had rushed up behind him, intent on tackling him to the ground, followed by Jake, then Mitch and David, that he realized just how vocal his laughter had become. And it wasn't until they were all rolling around in the tall grass wrestling with each other, with the women cheering them on, that he really felt a part of this family, warts and all, and not just a person who was around when they needed them.

AFTER DINNER, WITH everything else in his life resolved, and feeling at peace with the family, that restlessness that seemed to have all but sunk into his bones resurfaced. Intent on shaking it off, Connor excused himself from the table and stepped into the living room, not stopping until he stood outside his old bedroom upstairs.

He stared at the words still carved into the wood of the door—Private, Keep Out—then pressed the door inward, allowing his eyes to adjust to the darkness. Miniblinds combined with curtains completely blocked out even the slightest bit of light, and most of the day's heat. Despite the sign of change, he stepped inside, only then remembering that the room was no longer his own.

The sound of something moving caught his attention. He turned toward where his bed used to stand to find the crib Marc and Melanie had put up in its place, and his three-month-old nephew Sean's wide blue eyes looking at him curiously, his tiny mouth going to town on his thumb.

For a moment, Connor forgot where he was. In that one instant, it was all too easy to forget that the infant was his nephew and instead think of him as David.

Despite the raucous man he had become, the youngest of the McCoys had been a quiet, thoughtful baby. He'd needed very little attention at all, content to lie in his crib and contemplate the world at large with the intelligent eyes of a philosopher.

But, of course, this wasn't David. David was now an adult. Not only was he an adult, he was downstairs with his new wife enjoying dessert with the rest of the family.

Connor dared step a little closer to the crib, curving his hands over the rail and peering more fully inside. Sean's gaze followed him, his bedding rasping as he moved.

God, but it was incredible to think that something so small would grow into something so large.

The baby withdrew his thumb from his mouth with a pop then extended the damp digit out as if for inspection. Connor grinned.

"No, thank you. I've already eaten," he said quietly.

The boy continued holding his thumb out, then gave a strident cry. Connor nearly jumped out of his boots.

It had been a long, long time since he'd looked after an infant. Glancing toward the still-open door, he reached out and plucked Sean up from his cutesy bedding and cuddled him close to his chest. He was surprised at the downy warmth of the child, and how well he seemed to fit against him. After a couple of moments of mutual staring, the infant tucked his head against his chest and recommenced sucking his thumb.

Connor swallowed thickly.

"No mistaking that that little guy's a McCoy, huh?"

He swiveled to find that he was no longer alone in the room with his nephew, that someone had been witness to his quiet moment with little Sean. And that someone was Pops.

Unresolved emotion twisted through Connor's stomach as he moved to put the infant back into the crib. Sean put up a protest unlike any Connor had ever heard and he quickly drew him back to his chest. The baby instantly settled against him again.

Pops laughed. "With a set of lungs like that, he's definitely a McCoy."

"I was thinking the stubbornness was more of a dead giveaway."

Sean stepped farther into the room, switching on a small Winnie the Pooh lamp on a side table. "That, too."

Connor gazed down at the infant in his arms, marveling at how light he was. "I was thinking he's a lot like David. What do you think?"

Pops was silent for a moment. "Oh, I don't know." He met Connor's gaze. "I was thinking he's you all over again."

Connor's throat threatened to close. Him? He tightened his grip on the tiny being in his arms.

Funny, while he could remember when each of his brothers had been this age, he'd never thought of himself as a baby. It was odd considering it now.

It was also odd realizing that it was nice having a baby around again. And that perhaps his decision not to have any was a poor one indeed.

Pops sighed. "Oh, yes. Definitely you. You see the way he's watching me? As if trying to figure out if I'm someone he can trust? That's an expression I saw in your eyes a lot." His voice dropped. "An expression I still see."

Connor made busy picking up a light blanket and draping it over the baby.

Pops chuckled quietly. "I remember when Kathryn and I first brought you home. It seemed that overnight the place had transformed from a house into a home." He slid his hands into his pockets. "Up 'til then, I wasn't sure how I felt about living here. This was your mother's parents' place, while I had lived nearly my entire life where you're staying now." He shook his head. "But when you were born…well, I learned that it's not a place that makes a home, but a person and family."

Connor wasn't sure why his father was saying what he was now, but he felt compelled to listen.

"Look, Connor, I know I haven't always been the father you would have liked me to be. That there was a time when I forgot that family is what's important. When your mother died, I felt as though my entire world had collapsed. You boys, the family, that was something Kathryn and I had always dreamed of doing together. With her gone…I no longer knew which way was up. More than that, I honestly didn't know what to do. I was overwhelmed by the loss."

"We needed you," Connor found himself saying, though minus the vehemence he might have used a week ago.

"I know. And I'm sorry about that." Sean looked uncomfortable. As if he wanted to reach out, but didn't dare. "I can't tell you how proud I am of you. You stepped in and took over when I couldn't. You kept this family together when I would have let it fall apart. You proved a better father than I could have ever been. I didn't realize that it was too much weight to place on your narrow shoulders until much later. When it was too late to do much about it. When it was too late to ask you to forgive me."

Connor's throat was so tight, he was afraid he was about to make a noise akin to his nephew's. "Ask me."

Pops's brow furrowed as if he didn't quite hear what Connor said. "Pardon me?"

He moved his chin from where it rested on top of his nephew's head. "I said ask me."

Sean was quiet for a long moment, then he cleared his throat. The words were so soft, Connor nearly didn't hear them. "Do you have room in your heart to forgive me, son? To understand that what happened wasn't because I didn't love you, or the others. It came about because I hated myself. I'm so very, very sorry. Especially since it appears that as a result of my inability to do what needed to be done, you're still suffering. Unable to find the love and happiness you deserve. I'm so very, very sorry."

Pops hesitantly grasped his shoulders. But when Connor stepped more solidly into his arms, they embraced, little Sean Jonathon between them. For long moments they stood there, the three of them, father, son and grandson, the three generations bound together by love.

"I forgive you," Connor said quietly, cupping the back of his father's head. "I forgive you."

They stood like that for long moments. Neither saying anything. Their actions saying a lot. Then the youngest of the McCoy's sudden inconsolable wails startled both men away from each other. Only after long minutes of rocking, cajoling, and trying everything they possibly could to console the infant did Connor look at his father, and his father look back, and they both broke out laughing.

Melanie peeked her head around the corner. "What's going on in here?"

Connor and Pops turned toward her and shrugged. "Don't know. We were just passing by and he woke up squalling like a stuck pig."

"Oh, now that's a description," his sister-in-law said, taking her young son from Connor's arms and sliding a finger in the leg of his diaper. She wrinkled her nose. "He just needs to be changed, that's all." She moved to place the still-crying baby on the changing table. "Are you sure that's all that happened in here?" she asked, looking at them both a little curiously.

Connor rested a hand on his father's shoulder and gave a grateful squeeze. "Yeah."

The sound of someone else entering the room caught Connor's attention. He turned to see Melanie's mom, Wilhemenia, standing stiffly near the door. Her gaze lifted to his, then she quickly glanced away. "Sorry. I'll come back later."

Connor caught the flash of pain on his father's face—pain he didn't want to see. Hadn't they all suffered enough? He cleared his throat, but had to go so far as to reach out and touch Wilhemenia's sleeve to halt her quick retreat. "It's all right. You don't have to go on account of me. After all, that's the reason I called you."

He was aware of a sudden hush in the room. Even little Sean's crying had choked off to a quiet hiccup.

"*You* called her?" Mel was the first to speak, although judging by the way Pops's mouth stopped moving, the words could have just as easily have come from him.

Connor grimaced. Had he really been that awful? Yes, he realized, he had. And he owed it to Wilhemenia, and to Pops, to make up for it. "Yeah. I thought…well, I think it's about time I stopped acting little Sean's age here, you know what I mean?"

Melanie looked at him and smiled. "Yeah, we know what you mean."

Connor cringed, but for the life of him, he couldn't think of a single, solitary word to say. How, exactly, did one go about talking to the woman he had shunned for so long? A woman who just might very well become his step-mother?

Mel's laugh saved him from having to say anything. "Actually, all of you might want to go outside together. The rest of them have undertaken a treasure hunt in what's left of the barn."

Connor looked at his father, then Wilhemenia, then motioned for them to lead the way out. Moments later, they were standing in the midday sunlight, watching the others ferret through the pile of wood still left in the yard. They'd already loaded a great deal of it onto the back of an old flatbed, but now, protected by sturdy leather gloves, they tossed aside some of the smaller pieces so they could gain access to the barn floor. Goliath ran back and forth along the perimeter, barking up a storm.

Pops coughed as a still uncovered portion of barn fell in on itself, kicking up a cloud of dust. "Didn't you guys check the interior out before you knocked the damn thing down?"

All five looked at him as if he was insane. "Are you nuts?" Marc asked, tossing a rusty old tool into a pile of salvageable items. "The thing could have fallen in on us."

Pops shrugged. "Just thought I'd ask. Might have been easier to find things if you had done it the other way."

"I think I found something."

Everyone turned toward where Jake was combing through another corner. He drew back, as if confounded by what he saw. "Well, I'll be damned." He picked up something and beat it against his jeans to rid it of debris. "It's my INS ID."

"What?" David looked closer, verifying that it indeed was.

"Hey! That's my wedding bouquet." Mel had come out, little Sean quietly clinging to her hip. Everyone looked at her. "Oh, sorry. It's what would have been my bouquet if Marc here hadn't convinced me to marry him instead of the other guy."

Connor tucked his chin into his chest to hide his smile. He remembered that day in the kitchen as if it were yesterday, simply because it marked the first of many changes that would come. Authorities had been at the place again, but that time because of Marc, not him. How upset Wilhemenia had been then, engaging in a battle of wills with Goliath, who'd had his slobbery jaws locked around the bouquet in question. He glanced at Mel's mother, finding her so unlike that woman, who would have had her daughter marry for security, rather than love. Now she stood smiling next to his father, every bit the image of a woman in love, herself.

"What else is in there?" Kelli asked, stepping into the sliding mess and poking around.

Connor turned his head from Wilhemenia and his father. He watched as Kelli plucked up something red and blew on it.

"I'll be damned." Mitch reached out, holding what was now noticeably a red shoe up to show Liz. "Remember this?"

The spreading of color on Liz's cheeks revealed that she did, indeed, remember. She gently took it and smiled. Mitch curved his arms around her from behind and she leaned against him, closing her eyes.

"Goliath, you little thief, you," Mitch said to the mutt panting at their feet.

Connor didn't have a clue of the significance of the find, but he could guess. He glanced at the wrought-iron archway at the end of the driveway. *Red Shoe Ranch.*

Connor turned back to find Jake bent over, frowning as he spotted something else. Using the edge of a stick, he fished around, only after two tries coming out with a scrap of neon pink material.

Kelli's gasp startled everyone. "Oh my God! David, you didn't!" She grabbed the pair of what Connor guessed were panties from the end of the stick.

David turned ten shades of red. "I wondered where those went."

"You're such a perv," Kelli said to her new husband, then whacked him in the arm when he started laughing.

"What is it?" Connor overheard Michelle asking Pops as she held Lili's hand.

Lili's face lit up. "It's a pair of underpants, Mama!" Then her face puckered up into one of consternation. "What was Uncle David doing with Aunt Kelli's underpants?"

"That's something we'd all like to know," Jake said.

The group as a whole broke into laughter.

"Well, I think that's it," Mitch said, tugging off his gloves. "I say we all call it a day. The basketball game's scheduled to start in ten."

Everyone started heading toward the house, but Connor stayed behind. It was odd how everything worked out. He glanced after the departing group, taking special interest in the way Pops and Wilhemenia walked together, yet apart, glances meant to be secretive saying a lot. Connor absently rubbed the back of his neck, trying to work out how he felt about everything, though his easy smile told him he felt good.

Sunlight glinted off something in the pile of cinder from which Jake had uncovered Goliath's stash. Connor squinted and stepped a little closer. A silver letter stood out against brown leather. C. He slowly bent over and brushed off the remaining dirt, uncovering the rest of the letters. C.A.M. Connor Alexander McCoy. His initials. In fact, as he picked up the item, he realized it was his old key chain, and dangling from the ring was a single key. His key to the house behind him. The same key he had lost the day he came out here to find his bedroom had been taken over, making him feel as though he'd been evicted from his life.

A sharp bark sounded.

He glanced up to find Goliath sitting at the edge of the debris, his tail wagging a million miles a minute. Connor stepped from the wood and motioned for the dog to come to him. He did. Connor crouched down to pet him thoughtfully. "Well, boy, either you're a scoundrel in need of punishing—" Goliath growled "—or you're much smarter than any of us give you credit for."

The dog barked and Connor chuckled. Yeah, he'd pretty much figured the latter was the case.

Strange, really, that he should recover a key he hadn't even realized was missing at a time when he'd figured out that his connection to the family in the house behind him was more tangible than any physical object.

He slipped the key chain into his pocket then stood up, leading the way back to the house, the little matchmaker in a fur suit panting at his heels.

CHAPTER FOURTEEN

"Sign here, and we're all done."

Bronte stared at the delivery man as though he was speaking a foreign language. Then his words sank in. "Oh. Okay." She took the clipboard from him and signed on the dotted line.

Within moments, she had closed the door behind him and stood in the middle of the foyer…alone.

Funny, but she'd gone so long without furniture it seemed odd, somehow, seeing her house looking again like someone lived there.

Through the archway to the living room, she distantly appreciated the neat lines of the early American design sofa and coffee table, liking the touch of Americana with the antique quilt draped over one arm. Beyond that, a heavy pine dining room table with six chairs gleamed in the early evening light, the spring flower arrangement completing the look she'd been going for.

Everything was as it should be.

Yet Bronte felt that it was all wrong.

Oh, she didn't regret the change. All the contemporary leather furniture and matching accessories had never quite fit the house. Still, she couldn't seem to bring herself to feel anything but distantly pleased by the appearance of her new furniture.

She stepped past the living room and down the hall to the

kitchen, the only room that seemed to be hers out of the whole place. The tiny television played in one corner of the counter, while the new coffeemaker she hadn't been able to put, or throw, away still gleamed on the other side. Standing in front of the table, she sifted through her stack of evening papers without much enthusiasm, then pushed aside her untouched gourmet microwave dinner.

She knew what was bothering her. It had been bothering her ever since the day Connor had effectively proven he didn't have what it took to maintain a healthy relationship. This place—no matter how nice, no matter how much in demand—wasn't home. Not like the small house in Prospect, New Hampshire, her parents had spent the past thirty-five years in. Not like the place in Manchester, Virginia, that the McCoys called home. Not even like the old place where she and Connor had finally given themselves over to the passion searing a path through their veins.

This town house was just an imitation of a home, and a poor one at that. No, it wasn't even that. Ever since her breakup with Thomas Jenkins, this place had become the equivalent of a jail for her. A pretty jail—but jail nonetheless. It's the place she had hidden out in, afraid to expose herself to the world outside, afraid of what that exposure would reveal to her. Then Connor had found her where she lived and revealed even more about her. She'd realized why it had been so easy to say goodbye to Thomas without looking back. Their type of love had been the sunny-day kind. The type that collapsed the instant rain appeared on the horizon. Had she really loved him, she would have tried to work things out when he'd separated from his wife.

She saw that now. And the reason for the fresh insight was due completely to her love for one rough and tumble U.S. Marshal.

She sank down into a chair and sighed. She didn't know

why she was even exploring this newly discovered fact. Yes, it was important to examine everything that had happened. Even learn from the experience. But every time she did, she experienced a discomfort so complete that she couldn't seem to sit still for long periods of time.

She now knew that her reaction at the McCoy place had been motivated by frustration and fear. It wasn't every day a woman found out a man had set out to protect her, especially at his own expense, and when the stakes were so very high. That's where the fear entered…quickly followed by the frustration that she should have known it was coming. Should have expected it, really. But she knew that even if she had, there would have been nothing she could do about it.

"Coward," she said to herself, jerking open the paper on top of the pile and leafing through it. Her eyes caught on a snippet that had been front page news a few days ago, but had been quickly replaced by the latest breaking scandal of a congressman with a past that included drugs.

Former U.S. Attorney Dennis Burns's Trial Date Set.

Bronte scanned the brief piece, though she already knew most of the information. It was the other information, data that the media didn't have access to, that still made her uneasy.

The more time that passed, the more she understood that Dennis's killing of Melissa Robbins had been an accident. He'd become intimately involved with Pryka's ex-mistress early on, trying to convince her to request him for her case. Only Melissa hadn't been the pushover he'd initially thought she was. She'd had an agenda of her own. First and foremost, revenge against her ex-boyfriend who had left her high and dry. Second, she wanted to be placed in a rich environment similar to which she'd grown accustomed. When it became increasingly obvious that Dennis couldn't provide her with these luxuries, she'd threatened to swear out a complaint against him. But he'd convinced her to swear one out against Connor instead, promising that the new twist would put him in charge of the case, and by extension, in a position of power to get her what she wanted.

But Melissa hadn't been able to wait. And in a fit of passion-induced rage, Dennis had strangled her.

While it helped to know those details, facts Dennis had volunteered under intense questioning with his attorney present, it was what had been uncovered next that had shown just how far he'd been willing to go to cover up the murder—and how close he had come to doing just that.

The very day he'd placed his hands around Melissa Robbins's neck, he'd paid a visit to Leonid Pryka himself, offering his services. Only it appeared accurate that Pryka wasn't the least bit concerned about what his ex-bed bunny did or did not know about his business dealings and he'd laughed Burns from his house.

Bronte closed the newspaper. For long moments, she just sat there, staring at her stone-cold dinner, and the barely touched pile of newspapers she would have inhaled every word of only a short time ago. God, her life sucked.

"Coward," she mumbled to herself again.

She glanced at her watch, wondering if Kelli was home from work yet. She could call her friend. Ask her to come over and commiserate with her over her bad luck with men.

Or she could do something to change that luck.

Her spine snapped upright.

Yes…she could do something to change it.

Or die trying.

She twisted her lips in grim determination. So Connor was a fool. Too thickheaded to see that he loved her, could trust her and believe that forever was a possibility. Okay. That didn't mean they couldn't have today. And tomorrow. And the next day.

It wasn't so long ago that she'd judged women who were determined to change men's minds as masochistic, juvenile. Now she knew her viewpoint had been nothing but a convenient cop-out. Either that, or she'd never had anything worth fighting for before.

And Connor, in all his stubborn, sexy glory, was a prize worth spending the rest of her life fighting for.

Hmm....

She already knew he was weak when it came to turning her down physically. If they were in the same room together, chances were they'd end up all over each other before either of them could say the word "boo." All she had to do was arrange to be in the same room with him.

Scorching heat spread across her skin, making her shiver in anticipation, even as her heart gave a gentle, painful squeeze.

She sat back in the chair. "Coward."

But she wasn't a coward. Despite recent proof to the contrary, she had always been a fighter. Always one to go after what she wanted and get it. Why was it any different when it came to Connor McCoy?

"Because he has the power to hurt you more than any other person you've ever met."

She fingered the pile of newspapers. Yes, that was true, but didn't it stand to reason that he could also make her happier than any other person she'd ever met? Pleasure wasn't half as sweet without the threat of pain that loomed alongside it. The fear that she might be rejected, turned away, or might never convince him to give marriage and a family a try choked off her breath. So did the thought of spending the rest of her life pondering "what if."

She slowly rose from the chair, waiting for her body to

betray her and plop back down. When her knees didn't collapse, she walked to the television and switched it off. So far so good. Okay, now all she had to do was go into the hall and put her shoes on. Good…good.

She paused in front of the closed door, stretching the building tension from her neck. So what if she had to lay everything on the line, while Connor laid nothing? It was enough to know that she loved him and that if she didn't try she'd never forgive herself.

She violently pulled open the door—then stopped dead in her tracks.

There on her front steps stood one completely delectable-looking Connor McCoy.

She blinked once, twice, then stared as if the aberration would suddenly disappear. But it didn't. In fact, it ran a hand through short-cropped hair and grimaced at her, telling her it wasn't a ghost at all, but the real thing.

Her stomach pitched to her feet.

"Hi," Connor said quietly.

She pushed the words through her tight throat. "Um, hi yourself."

He glanced behind her, as if afraid someone else might be there, then gestured toward where she held her purse. "If this is a bad time, if you're going somewhere, I can always come back another time."

Bronte dropped her purse, then clamped her right hand around his wrist and yanked him inside. "Not on your life, McCoy."

She slammed the door behind him. The expression on his face was one of a trapped rabbit. She planted her hands on either side of his head against the door, trapping him even further. "As luck would have it, I was just about to come see you."

Her gaze dropped to his throat, where he swallowed

visibly. Her own heart felt irreversibly caught in her own throat. "You were?" he asked.

"Uh-huh."

"Why?"

Only a short while ago she had wanted him here, and now here he was. A smile spread across her face. "Oh, no, Connor. Since you made it here first, it's only fair that you go first."

"Fair, huh?"

She began to nod, but was stopped when he moved his hands to either side of her face, and brought his mouth down roughly on hers.

Bronte immediately melted against him, a moan building deep in her chest. Oh, how often over the past week she had dreamed of kissing him again. Of feeling his body against the length of hers. Of having evidence of his arousal pressing against the soft, quivering flesh of her stomach. He thoroughly plundered her mouth, stealing her breath, and making it impossible to do anything but receive.

Finally, he pulled away, the searing heat in his eyes undeniable.

Bronte licked her lips. "My, you have a way with words."

His naughty grin made her toes curl in the tips of her shoes. "Your turn."

"Marry me," she blurted.

She stood staring at him as if he had said the words rather than she. But she could tell by his stunned expression that she, indeed, had just essentially proposed to him when only moments before she had convinced herself she could accept living only for today.

"Bronte, I—"

She clamped her hand over his mouth, trying to ignore how the moist heat of his lips seemed to burn her palm. "No, wait. I know why you think marriage isn't in the cards for you. At least, I think I do. After having spent so much of your life looking after others, you don't believe you have room in your heart for anything more." She smiled tremulously. Where had all her cowardice disappeared to? "But I have to ask you this. Do you love me?"

Talk about laying everything on the line…. What was she doing? Was she insane? Wasn't it enough that he was here? Admitting that he wanted her and that he'd been wrong?

No, it wasn't enough. She wanted him—now, tomorrow, and forever. She knew that as certainly as she knew her own name. And she wanted him to know that. More importantly, she needed to know he felt the same way.

"I…" he faltered, looking like he would have backed up if he'd had anywhere to go except up against the door. "For God's sake, Bronte, where did all this come from?"

She tried to still the wild beating of her heart. "Just answer me, McCoy."

His eyes shifted as he gazed into first one, then the other of hers. She was surprised by his wide grin. "Is this how you get criminals to come clean?"

"As a matter of fact, it is. Are you saying you're a criminal?"

His grin vanished, and the gravity of his expression made her stomach contract. "Yes, I guess I am. Because rather than telling you what I did the other day, I should have said what you needed to hear. What I needed to tell you but was too much of jerk to say. Words I've never uttered ever in my life." He reached out, cupping her cheek. "I love you, Bronte O'Brien…truly, deeply, madly. And I can't go on with my life without you in it."

Her throat closed with emotion and her eyes flooded with tears. "Boy, when you decide to do something—"

He interrupted her. "And my answer to your first question is an unqualified yes."

"Yes?" she asked, sucking in her lips to try to staunch the flow of tears.

"Yes." He grasped her hips, bringing her flush up against his arousal. "Oh, and another thing?"

After the heartwarming, nearly overwhelming, change in events from only a few minutes ago, she was almost afraid to ask. "What?"

He claimed her lips in a kiss that could be called nothing short of soul stirring. "I've changed my mind on the kid thing. I want to have as many as you'll let me."

Her brows shot up and she stared at him as if seeing a different man. And she realized she was. She wasn't certain what had happened to him in the past few days, but whatever it was looked very, very good on him. "As many as I let you, huh?"

One of his hands crept up under her blouse, the other slid down over her bottom, making her gasp. "Uh-huh."

Bronte tried to catch her breath, but failed. "Tell me again," she whispered huskily.

His eyes were filled with a mixture of teasing sexiness. "Bronte O'Brien…I love you and can't bear to live another day of my life without you in it."

She sighed against him. "It's even better hearing it the second time around." She bit roughly on her bottom lip. "But promise me one thing, Connor." She carefully glanced over his face. "You'll never say never again."

His kiss was all the answer she needed….

EPILOGUE

CONNOR STARED DOWN AT HIS simple platinum wedding band, then straightened his tuxedo jacket. Seemed a shame that, now that he'd gotten this best man thing down to an art, he likely wouldn't be playing the role anymore. Hell, he was even getting used to wearing these stiff monkey suits, though he doubted he'd ever actually like wearing them. But at least now he owned his own. The girl at the rental place had shaken her head when he came in again and told him to take it. Lord knew he had rented it enough times to pay for it three times over.

Connor caught sight of Bronte. As always happened when he looked at her, his throat tightened, his heartbeat accelerated and a weird, weightless feeling settled in the bottom of his stomach. She didn't even have to do anything. Just stand there and let him look at her.

Right now she was talking with the rest of the McCoy women near the front of the main McCoy place. He allowed his gaze to skim leisurely where the deep blue of her bridesmaid dress hugged her high, curvy bottom. As if sensing his gaze, his wife of four months turned and gave him a completely wicked wink.

Applause began. Tearing his gaze from Bronte, Connor turned to find the couple of the hour appearing in the front doorway to the house.

Melanie's mother, Wilhemenia, had just officially become Mrs. Sean McCoy.

Connor stood-stock still as the small gathering of friends and neighbors in Manchester, Virginia, tossed pink-colored rice and congratulated the new couple. He waited for remorse to hit him or disappointment that his father had replaced his mother. But neither emotion came. Instead, a completely different feeling rushed through his bloodstream. Pure joy. Happiness that Pops had someone he loved, and that someone loved him back. Completely. To recognize that, all one had to do was look at their faces. The way they gazed at each other and constantly touched one another. Often it was downright embarrassing just being around the affectionate couple.

"They make a cute pair, don't they?"

Connor shifted to find his wife standing next to him and the joy he felt melded into pure bliss. "Yeah. I guess they do."

He smiled warmly at her. No longer needing to hide his emotions from her. No longer caring whether or not she knew how much he loved her; hoping she did. He trusted this woman more than he trusted anyone. Including his brothers. And that was saying a lot. Bronte O'Brien McCoy had stolen his heart, his love for her indelibly etched on his soul.

"All right, everyone!" The woman Wilhemenia had hired from Maryland to take the wedding photographs clapped her hands. "Portraits over here. All McCoy and Weber family members, your presence is required. Chop chop!"

Bronte laughed, increasing that weightless feeling in Connor's stomach. "Don't look now, but the camera Nazi is bearing down on us," she said, tucking her hand in the crook of his arm.

He covered her fingers with his and squeezed. "Well, we'd better get a move on then, hadn't we?"

They followed the long line of others to stand in front of the house and take their places where the photographer indicated. Connor glanced around his familiar surroundings, only they weren't so familiar anymore. Maybe because he now saw them through different eyes, or perhaps because they truly had changed. Gone was the old barn, in its place a thriving thatch of wildflowers the McCoy women had spent an entire day planting a couple of months back. A little ways away, the new barn housing Mitch and Liz's horse-breeding operations shone warmly in the midday sun.

"No, over here," he made out Kelli's voice beside him and looked to see her tugging David to stand next to her. "And keep your hands to yourself or your expression in the picture will mirror the pain I inflict."

Connor quietly chuckled as his gaze slid to where Marc and Melanie stood farther down, little Sean animatedly chomping down on his mother's necklace even as his parents heatedly discussed something of import. Next to them, Lili was tugging on baby Sean's brand-new shoe, trying to gain his attention while Goliath had his jaws locked on her frilly blue skirt. But Jake and Michelle didn't seem to notice. Michelle was smoothing down the front of his tuxedo shirt and smiling up at him in a way that was all too provocative, and none too subtle.

"Quite a bunch, huh?" Mitch whispered, coming to stand on the other side of him.

Connor grinned and nodded, noticing where Liz was chatting with Bronte. Mitch had yet to convince Liz to have the five kids he wanted, but word had it he was wearing her down. Connor was pleased with the thought that there might be a whole brood of new McCoys running around the place soon.

"Places everyone, places!" the photographer shouted, rushing around, frantically straightening a collar here, fixing a smear of lipstick there.

Connor grasped Bronte's hips where she stood slightly in front of him. He eyed the back of her neck, recalling one of the first times he'd ever laid eyes on her, remembering how much he'd wanted to play connect the dots with her freckles.

It was hard to believe that just a short time ago he and Bronte had been at Kelli and David's wedding reception. Harder still to recognize the man he'd been then.

He bent slightly to brush his lips against the skin just below her ear. "Have I told you how wonderful you look today?"

Her answering shiver made him grin. "Thanks. You don't know how much I needed to hear that." She grasped his hands, moving them from her hips to her belly and pressing them flat. Just that morning he'd caught her standing in front of the mirror, horrified and pleased that she was beginning to show.

Yes, that's right. As incredible as it sounded, he and Bronte were four months' pregnant. Twins, the doctor had told them yesterday. The first two of what he hoped would be many. Enough to fill the six bedrooms of his grandparents' old place, where he and Bronte had moved after they married.

"I love you, Bronte," he murmured.

She increased the pressure of her hands against his, briefly closing her eyes. "Not any more than I love you."

"Smile, everybody!"

And Connor did. Because at that moment he was the happiest man in the world.

Everything you love about romance...
and more!

Please turn the page for Signature Select™
Bonus Features.

SEDUCING McCOY

How To Start a Summer Heat Wave
by Shelagh McMullan

Looking for some summer loving? You don't need to turn off the air-conditioning to heat things up: try our suggestions for starting a heat wave of a different kind in your very own bedroom!

4   Everyone has seen a summer beach movie from the '50s or '60s. Surfer girls like Gidget donned their best bikini and headed to the beach to find true love with their own personal Moondoggie.

Thankfully, women don't have to get sand stuck between their toes to turn up the heat in their relationship anymore. It just takes a bit of planning to start a summer heat wave that you and your mate won't want to see end.

Play Hooky
Greg Godek, author of *1001 Ways To Be Romantic,* says the first step is to clear time for just the two of you. No excuses, please.

Turning off the air conditioner won't heat up your relationship, but booking a morning off and leaving the kids with friends for the night will. If you have no holidays left, book a half day off without pay.

Once you're finally alone together, indulge yourselves. Turn off the alarm clock. When you do wake up, start the day with sex. "The whole thing is about breaking the routine," explains Godek.

Once you've worked up an appetite, restore yourselves with a gourmet brunch. "Part of the reason you're doing that is that it really feels like playing hooky," notes Godek.

You may just enjoy the feeling of being a bad girl and boy. As Godek points out, "Doing something naughty is fun, and that adds to the sexual excitement of it."

If you can get a whole weekday off, continue to break from your routine by catching a matinee together. Sitting in the back row and shamelessly kissing is perfectly acceptable.

Make Him Hungry for More

An evening at a restaurant with a moonlit patio overlooking the ocean can be very romantic. But if you wear a revealing outfit to dinner, that will be the only view your date needs. Godek says, "We're talking low-cut or we're talking a short skirt."

If you're not in touch with your inner exhibitionist, just wear your sexiest lingerie under your outfit. Telling your partner exactly what you're hiding under your clothes could help him work up quite an appetite, according to Godek.

Drive Him to Distraction

Hopping in the car and driving to a bed-and-breakfast is a great way to reconnect under the covers. Godek says your mate won't complain about the frilly wallpaper or lack of a TV if you say up front, "We're going to find a great environment where we can really play."

If you do decide to leave your room, you could go lingerie or even bathing-suit shopping together. Godek believes, "One of the greatest things in the world is for the guy to go into the dressing room with (you)."

All-Day Foreplay

Summer loving can be interrupted by jobs and other commitments. But you can keep the home fires burning by reaching out and touching that special someone via the phone.

Godek calls this plan "all-day foreplay."

"Call him every hour on the hour at work. And all you say, each time you call, is 'I love you.' And you hang up." If you want him home early, be more suggestive each time you call. (Dialing the right number is key to the success of this strategy.)

Start planning now to make sure this summer's forecast is hot. Your Moondoggie will be howling for more all summer long.

Roped Into Romance
by Alison Kent

8

Web designer Lauren Hollister is a thoroughly modern woman. She takes pride in her open-minded attitudes about sex. She knows what she wants when she sees it, and she's not afraid to make the first move. And right now Lauren has her eye on sexy architect Anton Neville, who is showing her and her best friend, Macy, one of the funky new lofts he's just designed.

Anton has old-fashioned ideas about dating. He likes to be the one to ask a woman out, and he expects to be the one paying for the first date. Can he handle the advances of a sensual and determined woman like Lauren, or will she turn his world upside down?

CHAPTER ONE

LAUREN HOLLISTER stood beside Macy Webb and followed her best friend's gaze up the exterior of the four-story, redbrick warehouse recently converted into four spacious lofts. The duo had been searching forever for the perfect place to live. But this didn't look promising. And Lauren said so.

"This doesn't look promising."

"Uh, hello? We're not going to be living in the chinks between the bricks." Macy reached up a hand to shade her eyes then walked down the sidewalk and cast a glance the length of the building's backside. "Besides, the facade is being repaired. The scaffoldings are set up over here."

"Hmm. He did say not to judge this particular book by its cover." Hard not to, though, since Lauren's degree was in commercial art and she had a critical eye. She glanced at the face of her wristwatch. "He also said he'd meet us here at three-thirty."

Her cursory building inspection complete, Macy walked back to Lauren's side, reached for her wrist and the watch. "It's 3:27. We were early. He's not late."

"Not yet," Lauren said just as a sleek black Jaguar purred around the corner and eased to a stop behind her SUV. She let out a long low whistle. "Okay. I'm impressed. On time and in style."

As the car door opened, Macy leaned closer. "I'm beginning to think you ain't seen nothin' yet, sister."

Lauren's *"What are you talking about?"* died on her lips as Anton Neville stepped from the car.

The architect was six foot one or two at least, and had a body to die for. For some reason—his voice? his demeanor?—Lauren had assumed from their phone call that he was older. Her father's age maybe. But he wasn't. He couldn't have been more than thirty and he was absolutely gorgeous.

His long legs ate up the distance between his car and the sidewalk, long legs displayed to advantage in a pair of tobacco-colored dress pants that were very Versace. His shirt was a lighter shade of camel and his tie a flashy brown print. He was head-to-toe delicious…the head part having snagged Lauren's attention first.

Anton Neville was not your average blonde. Both his build and his complexion declared him a swimmer. And then there was the way the sun had bleached his hair. It was long, though not unconventionally so. It was just that she'd never seen curls that were so one hundred percent male.

Windblown ringlets fell over his forehead, his collar and his ears. The look was the sexiest thing she'd ever seen, especially when she added in the barely more than stubble length of beard and mustache. But when he took off his Rays-Bans…oh, God, she was a goner.

"Anton Neville." Blue eyes flashing, he held out a hand.

Macy accepted first. "Macy Webb. Thanks for meeting us."

And then it was Lauren's turn. "Lauren Hollister," she said as his large hand swallowed her palm and long artist's fingers. She swore his touch had set her belly on fire.

"I hope I haven't kept you waiting long." He slowly pulled his hand from Lauren's.

Balling her fingers into a fist that she tucked into her pocket, she said, "No, not at all. You're right on time."

"Good." He gestured for them to go ahead, flipping through his ring of keys. "Then let's go check this puppy out."

As they made their way up the length of broken pavement to the door, Macy cast a questioning glance at Lauren and mouthed, *"You're right on time?"* Lauren simply elbowed Macy in the rib cage.

"Our contractors have done their best to utilize as many of the original fixtures as possible," Anton was saying, now leading the way down the high-ceilinged hallway that ran the length of the building. He stopped halfway. "Including the freight elevator."

Lauren and Macy looked on as he used his security key, releasing a huge red button that protruded from the cinder block wall. One smack from Anton's broad palm and the heavy steel door rolled up. When he gestured for them to enter, they did, taking the trip to the fourth floor along with the freight car's rattletrap creaks and groans.

This still didn't look promising. And so Lauren continued to think until the lift ground to a stop and Anton, again using his security key, shoved the door upward along its overhead tracks and yanked back on the loft's metal privacy grate.

12

At her first sight of the hardwood floor, Lauren changed her mind. She turned and met Macy's wide eyes, seeing the astonished reflection of her own baby blues in her best friend's whiskey-colored gaze.

"I don't believe this place." Lauren slipped off her clogs before walking on bare feet into the loft. "Talk about not judging a book by its cover. Crumbling bricks be damned. This floor is absolutely the best."

"It smells," Macy said, stepping out of her wedged sandals. "Like real wood."

"It is real wood." Anton left on his Italian loafers. "One-hundred percent maple plank. Urethane finish. Definitely shoe-proof. And the building's facade is being repaired. One brick at a time."

"I don't care," Lauren said, shaking her head. "I mean, I do care. About the bricks. Not about the floor being shoe-proof. Well, I care about that, too. But I want to experience this with my skin."

Macy had already slapped her barefooted way into the center of the loft's main room. "It's a hardwood floor, Lauren. It's not a grassy meadow. It's not Berber carpet. There's not a lot to experience with your skin."

"Maybe not with your skin." Lauren closed her eyes, held her shoes wrapped in her arms close to her chest and flexed her toes against the wood. No one, her best friend included, had ever understood how her body assimilated touch.

Her sensitivity had often been a curse. Childhood immunizations? The worst. Eyebrow tweezing? Yikes! Bikini waxes? Forget about it! But, oh, could her sensory feedback be a blessing. The right man and…

Shivering, Lauren opened her eyes—and looked straight into Anton Neville's. They gleamed with speculation. And his irises, wow. That shade of near navy was incredibly rare. She knew he wasn't wearing contacts. Just like she knew, if she had her way, he wasn't going to be wearing anything soon.

"Like I said. The best." She flexed her toes again and hoped he bought it. Then she took Macy by the hand. "We're going to take a look around."

Ankles crossed, hands shoved down in his pockets, Anton leaned back against the edge of the open elevator. "Take your time."

Once she'd dragged Macy out of the main room to the far end of the building, Lauren nearly groaned. "All night wouldn't be enough time. Give me that man and give me forever."

"You are such a slut."

Lauren grinned, unoffended. She was a sensualist, not a slut. A discriminating one, and Macy knew it. Getting a rise out of each other was tough, but they both loved to try.

Having checked a far corner and claimed it as her bedroom, Macy returned to the main room and the area prepped for a kitchen build-out. "Hey. You remember those sculptures we saw in the Sixties Store?"

Lauren's eyes widened. "They would make *perfect* room dividers. You're brilliant, Mace. Five of them at least. Right here between the kitchen and the center of the loft." Lauren's eyes widened farther as she caught sight for the first time of the balcony doors.

"C'mon. Let's check out the view." Lauren headed that way. Pulling open the sliding glass door, she slipped on her clogs and stepped outside.

"This is *so* great! Can you imagine a little candle-light, a little wine? A lotta lovin' under the stars? Listening to the traffic below and trying not to get caught?" Lauren hugged her arms around her middle, whirled back to Macy and said, "I can't wait to try it out!"

Only it wasn't Macy standing in the open doorway behind Lauren.

It was Anton Neville.

And he said, "Neither can I."

BONUS FEATURE

CHAPTER TWO

A<small>NTON</small> N<small>EVILLE</small> <small>SLUMPED</small> back in his desk chair. Feet flat on the floor, he swiveled side to side. He kept a grip on both armrests, kept his gaze on the door. It was after hours; the support staff had long since left for the night. But his partner was due any minute. And he wanted to be here to gloat.

Doug Storey, the second half of Neville and Storey, Architects, had made it his personal mission to wash the firm's hands of the loft property Anton had shown yesterday to Macy Webb and Lauren Hollister. And here, with Doug out of town, Anton had done little more than pour on the masculine charm to make the sale.

Possible sale, he reminded himself. All the women had done was inspect the property. Twice. But it was the *way* they'd done their inspection, the decorating plans they made as they walked, the looks they'd tossed back and forth, the whispers and the giggles.

Anton had been at this business long enough to know when he could sit back and let a property sell itself. But, for the loft, he'd been ready to wheel and deal his ass off. Still, this was the first time he'd ever considered offering himself as a sales incentive. And he was only half kidding. The other half seriously wondered what would've happened on that balcony had Macy Webb not walked into his tête-à-tête with Lauren Hollister.

He didn't think he'd ever hovered on the verge of anything so unprofessional in his entire career. Even if she'd made it more than clear she welcomed his attention, he knew better than to mix business with what he knew would be an unimaginable pleasure.

Lauren Hollister was a willowy thing, with pale baby blue eyes that promised all the tricks of the female trade. Her body was perfect, beautifully lush curves filling out a slender frame. Dark blond waves fell to the center of her back. And, yeah. He could see himself wrapping that silky mane around his wrist and holding on for the ride.

"Hey, Neville. You make us a million while I was gone?"

Anton looked up from his musings as his partner walked through the door. The grin that spread over his face felt like the wicked celebration it was. "Close enough. I sold the loft."

Doug stopped in his tracks, strands of blond hair falling into his face. He shook them back, tossed his satchel to the office sofa, slammed his hands to his hips. "The downtown loft. The fourth floor. The warehouse. Are you friggin' kidding me?"

Anton shrugged. "Maybe not."

"Ha!" Doug dropped down on the sofa. "You mean you *showed* it, not *sold* it. I'm not paying off any bet until that place goes to closing."

"They want it. You know the look."

"Hmm." Squaring an ankle on the opposite knee, Doug laced his hands behind his head and leaned back. "They had it outfitted before they even left, didn't they? Curtains, throw pillows, area rugs."

"Not these two." Anton couldn't get the picture of Lauren Hollister out of his mind. Her low-slung blue jeans. Her black metallic sheer lace top over a skinny black tank. "Lava lamp bubble sculptures. Hanging panels of hammered brass."

"Gay?"

"Female. Two." Anton held up two fingers.

"Gay?" Doug repeated.

"Not these two," Anton repeated, getting to his feet just as his phone rang. He glanced at the display. The number seemed vaguely familiar. He punched the speakerphone button. "Neville."

"Anton Neville? This is Lauren Hollister. From yesterday? The balcony?"

Anton jerked the receiver from the cradle, ignoring his partner's arched brow and mouthed *"The balcony?"* He flipped Doug the finger and turned his attention to the call. "Ms. Hollister. How nice to hear from you."

"I wasn't sure what time your office closed. I was hoping I might still be able to catch you. Is this a bad time?"

"No. Don't worry about it. I'm usually here this late." This time when Doug rolled his eyes and mouthed, *"Bullshit,"* Anton turned his back on the other man and leaned against the desk.

"What can I do for you?"

"It's about the loft."

He'd figured that much. And the way she said it he figured it was bad news. "Have you and Ms. Webb reached a decision?"

"Are you kidding? We love it—*ouch!*" she cried, mumbling unintelligibly from behind what Anton would guess was a hand over the mouthpiece. "What I mean is, would you have time to let me in to take a few measurements?"

"Sure." He turned back around and flipped open his Day-Timer, running a finger down his schedule. "I'm free in the morning at ten, or tomorrow afternoon around, say, two?"

"I was thinking about tonight."

Anton straightened where he stood. "Tonight?"

Doug mouthed, *"Tonight?"* before tumbling over onto the sofa and muffling his howls with a pillow pressed to his face.

"Tonight's not a problem. What time?"

"Will nine work for you?"

"Perfect. See you then." The call disconnected and Anton returned the receiver to the cradle just as Doug managed to push himself from the sofa to his feet.

He crossed the office, planted both hands on the surface of Anton's desk and leaned forward. "Let me guess. Blonde. Blue eyes. Twenty-something. Single. Not gay."

"Definitely not gay," Anton said, looking at the plain black face of the watch on his wrist.

Doug hung his head. "Does she have a friend?"

"Yeah." Anton stuffed his Day-Timer into his satchel, dug in his pocket for the keys to his Jag. "But she's not coming."

"Oh, and I suppose you will be."

Anton grinned. "You know me all too well, my man."

"I REALLY HATED calling so late, but I am *so* glad you were available." Tape measure and notebook tucked into her backpack, Lauren stepped from the elevator into the loft. The room was dark, darker than she'd expected, the only light thrown by the moon through the balcony's glass doors.

Leaving the grate open, Anton flipped a switch next to the elevator's call button. A row of track lighting above the door threw six spotlights along the hardwood floor. Nice atmosphere, Lauren thought.

Not quite as seductive as the moon but, hey. She'd take what she could get. The fact that she'd managed to get *him* here was a miracle in itself.

"Like I told you earlier. It's not a problem."

He sounded sincere enough. But Lauren wanted to be sure about that. And about…other things. "I didn't ruin your plans for the evening, did I?"

"Nope." He shook his head, the illumination catching the highlights in his hair. "No plans to ruin."

Lauren so wanted to run her fingers through those curls. She didn't think she'd ever known a guy with hair so tempting to the touch. Smiling, she reached into her backpack for her pencil and spiral pad. "I didn't want your girlfriend coming after me for making a mess of her night."

Anton walked toward her then, his eyes glittering, his mouth drawn into a seductive smile. He stopped when he'd drawn within a scant foot. Close enough that her every breath caught his subtle scent. Her heart hammered like a piston in her chest.

He took hold of the strap of her overalls, rubbed his thumb in a circle over the copper catch. "No, Lauren. I don't have a girlfriend. Is that what you were wanting to know?"

CHAPTER THREE

HE DIDN'T HAVE a girlfriend! Lauren Hollister thought she might actually jump for joy. "Yes. That's exactly what I wanted to know."

She backed a short step away and tried to pretend her skin wasn't tingling where his fingers had grazed her shoulder. "It's a girl thing. We look out for one another. Make sure not to step on toes. Or on boyfriend toes. That sort of thing."

One of Anton's blond brows arched. His mouth fought back a grin. "I see."

If he did, he would be the first. Men never did get the girlfriend thing. All the rules, and such. Still, she had to be careful. He could be one of those guys who knew a woman was lying simply by taking her pulse. Which he'd no doubt done with his hand so close to her heart. She never had been very good at deception. She was, instead, very good at the truth.

And that meant she might run into trouble convincing him she wasn't here to take his measure along with the kitchen's, or to see if her instincts were right. That, yes, her attraction to him was as much about what she saw when she looked into his eyes as when she looked at his body.

Call her foolish, but she swore she'd caught a glimpse of awareness that reached deeper than a sexual level. And that possibility, that complex attraction to both mind and matter was what she wanted to explore.

She flipped open her notebook and made her way to the space perfectly suited for the bubble sculptures on which she and Macy had their hearts set. "I knew I wasn't going to be able to sleep tonight until I found out if the sculptures are going to fit beneath the ductwork. We went by the store earlier today so I know exactly how tall they are."

While Lauren continued her decorative chatter, Anton had followed her across the main room. She'd counted each of his footsteps—she took one and a half to each of his—and now she felt his body heat behind her.

She had to talk herself out of stepping back into his solid male warmth when she so wanted to know what he felt like. Oh, but her imagination was running wild, wanting to experience more of him than she would have time to experience tonight.

"Let's see." She dug the measuring tape from her backpack, extended the strip of stiff metal far enough to reach the shiny ventilation system directly overhead. Then she let go of the casing. Gravity

BONUS FEATURE

slowly pulled it to the floor where it landed with a light *thunk*. She looked back at Anton and smiled. "And voilà! Exactly…this tall."

Anton reached over her shoulder, his large hand taking hold of the metal strip. He nodded toward the floor. "I'll do this part. You get down there and do yours."

Lauren released the measuring tape and turned beneath his outstretched arm. She had a devil of a time keeping a straight face. Anton wasn't having much better luck ignoring his own timely double entendre. "Just…go. Do. Before I get my other foot stuck in my mouth."

With a wink, she dropped to her knees at his feet. Once she noted the distance between floor and ceiling, she sat back on her heels and jotted dimensions into her notebook. "A perfect fit. You can let go now."

She made to stand. He made to reach for the tape casing. It was one of those badly timed movie moments where their faces ended up inches apart. She could so easily have kissed him. His lips were so beautifully full and she just knew that the stubble beneath his lower lip would tickle.

Imagining the feel of his mouth had kept her tossing and turning a good part of last night. But, tempting as she found his mouth and his everything else, she knew what anticipation added to the sensual equation.

She also was quite sure he would be worth the wait.

24

And so she gave him nothing more than a smile before she got back to her feet. He handed her the tape, closing his fingers around her smaller hand. "Did you get what you needed?"

"Well, that is certainly a leading question. But to answer you honestly? No. I didn't. Do you mind?" Pulling out the tape while pulling her hand from his hold, she moved away, motioning for him to step back. "Right there. Stop. How far apart are we?"

Looking at her like she was crazy before looking down at the tape in his hand, he answered, "Fifteen feet."

"Hmm." Lauren walked toward him, feeding the tape back into the case. "The base of each sculpture is three feet, so that's perfect. Now all we have to figure out is if we can afford to buy five."

"You've made up your mind then? About the loft?"

"We're getting there. Arguing over a few details still."

"And taking measurements just in case?"

"Yes. And no." Lauren took a deep breath. Here came the honesty part. "I was also hoping you'd let me buy you dinner."

She didn't know why she was nervous. Other than the obvious reason that she rarely invited a virtual stranger to eat. A stranger to whom she found herself so viscerally attracted at that. And so she held her breath.

Finally, after what seemed like eternal minutes

spent staring into her eyes, his glittering even in the room's dim light, Anton answered, "I don't think I can do that. But I would love to buy dinner for you."

Exhaling at last, Lauren grinned. She knew not to look a gift horse in the mouth. Or to trample a male ego. "Great. I'd say I'd get my things—" she shrugged and held up her backpack "—but this is it."

"Vietnamese okay?"

"Perfect. I'm famished."

They headed for the elevator. Lauren stepped inside. Anton cut off the loft's lighting, pulled the grate closed and locked it up tight, then yanked down the overhead door, leaving them with only a single bare bulb by which to see.

26

The freight car was a box of moving shadows. Lauren watched every one play with Anton's face until nerves launched from her belly on butterfly wings. She wondered what he'd do if she took that one long step toward him and—

The elevator jolted, jerked. A blood-curdling screech of metal on metal. The bare bulb swung from its wire mooring. Lauren grabbed onto the side railing to keep herself from tumbling to the floor. The car shuddered, groaned, stopped. She held her breath for a few more interminable seconds before giving a little laugh. "This is a joke, right?"

"If it is, it's on both of us." Anton spent several minutes messing with the elevator's control panel. Then he pulled out his cell phone and swore up and down at the weak signal. Lauren swore harder when she realized she'd left her phone in the car after calling Macy on the way to the loft.

He did manage to get through to his office, where he left his partner a voice mail. "Doug's a fanatic about checking messages. Unless you want me to try 911?"

She did. She didn't. "What do you think?"

Anton glanced at his watch. "Give him an hour first?"

"Okay." It made sense. This wasn't a life-threatening situation. Though her heartbeat seemed to know it could be a life-changing one. "Then, I guess, we wait?"

"We wait."

CHAPTER FOUR

ANTON NEVILLE WATCHED Lauren Hollister slide down the elevator wall until her butt hit the floor. She was wearing a pair of overalls. Micromini overalls, if there was such a thing. Which there had to be because he was looking at the evidence.

28

Damn, but her legs were long.

"You know, you'll never sell this place if you don't get this thing fixed," she said.

He moved his gaze to her face. Her eyes were resigned to the wait. Resigned, but definitely not defeated. He liked seeing that spunk. "Does that mean you're backing out of the deal?"

Lauren scrunched up her nose, stuck out her tongue and sighed. Then she sighed again and settled in for the duration, tucking her backpack up under the bed of her knees.

Damn, but her legs were long.

With nowhere to pace, Anton figured he might as well take a load off, as well. He sank to the floor, stretched out his legs and leaned back on the wall opposite the one against which Lauren had collapsed. Their feet met in the middle and she tapped his sole.

"You're going to ruin your pants."

He kept his foot pressed to the bottom of hers. "I know a good dry cleaner."

"You'd do better knowing a good tailor."

"I know one of those, too."

"At least you don't know a good girlfriend. I would be in so much trouble if you did."

"Why? This wasn't exactly a calculated move to get us alone." He knew it wasn't. She knew it wasn't. But she sure had a guilty look on her face.

"This is breaking every rule ever written. A girl does not strand herself with another girl's man." She punctuated that last statement by banging her head on the wall at her back.

And then Anton realized he didn't know for sure whether or not he was getting close to trespassing himself. "What about you? Am I going to need to be watching my back when we get out of here?"

She shook her head. "Macy's aim's not that good."

"Macy?" Uh-uh. No way he had called that one wrong!

"Never mind. No. I'm not seeing anyone right now." She dropped her head back in one last thump.

Then she smiled to herself, a private inside joke that had her shaking her head and tilting it to the side as she gave him a considering look. "And I've learned my lesson. Next time I *want* to see someone, I'll call.

BONUS FEATURE

I'll be direct. I'll do my interior decorating on my own time."

Anton wasn't sure, but he thought she'd just said she wanted to see him. His pulse began to do its own thumping. His temperature started to rise. He pointed in the general direction of the loft. "So, all that business about measuring for sculptures…"

She nodded. "I really was measuring for sculptures. But I also meant it when I said I was hoping you'd let me buy you dinner."

Anton had a sudden wish to smash Doug's voice-mail box. "No can do. My rule. No matter who does the asking, I always buy on the first date."

Lauren's pursed lips slowly parted as, in a tone both low and lightly suggestive, she asked, "Is this a date?"

"It could be." He nodded toward her backpack. "If you have anything to eat in that bag of yours that I can pay you for."

Her eyes grew both wide and bright and Anton felt a strange stirring in his gut. An unease that told him he was asking for the sort of trouble that had a good chance of turning his well-ordered life upside down.

"Hey, we're in luck. One for each of us. And my treat. None of that macho sexist crap," she added when he reached for his wallet. "We'll call this a first date warm-up if it'll make you happier."

From the front compartment, she produced two high-carb energy bars and tossed him one. Then she unzipped the main part of the pack and pulled out a bottle of water. "But the water we'll have to share."

The thought of sharing her things, of how many of his things he wouldn't mind if she shared, finally sent him across the elevator car to her side. He sat next to her, his hip at her hip.

She offered him the bottle. He pulled up on the sports cap and drank, keeping his gaze locked on hers as he handed it back, as she brought the same spout to her mouth, as she grinned before drinking, giving him a glimpse of the tip of her tongue.

He forced himself not to groan when his entire body wanted to scream.

"What was it you said yesterday? A little wine? A little candlelight?" he asked.

He cast a glance up toward the bare bulb, looked back in time to see her running the drinking spout back and forth over her lower lip. He couldn't stop the sound that seemed to roll straight out of his groin. He reached for the bottle, pulled it from her hand and set it on the floor.

She looked from the water bottle back to his face. And then she gave him a soft smile.

"That, a lotta lovin' and trying not to get caught."

His mouth descended to hers. And she was waiting. She didn't feign surprise or pretend he'd caught her off guard. She was waiting, and she responded with more than her lips and her tongue, threading her fingers into his hair and holding him close. He swore she smiled. Her lips slanted over his, even while lifting upward. Nothing had ever aroused him so quickly. Like the head of a match, he burst into flame.

And this was only a kiss. He moved his hand to the back of her neck, holding her close while he nipped at her lips, while he tasted her mouth, while he slipped his tongue the length of hers and told her with the kiss what he wanted to do to her body. To penetrate her slowly, to slide his sex into hers the way he'd taken her mouth. He wanted to feel her skin with his skin. Her mouth was soft, and the hair trapped beneath his palm slid over her nape like pure silk. His imagination already had her undressed and naked beneath him.

This time when he groaned, he knew she felt the echo in her mouth. And when she whimpered in return, the sound turned him inside out. He pulled his mouth free, his hand holding the back of her head as he stared into her eyes. So bright and so blue and so beautifully beguiled. She'd caught her lower lip between her teeth, then bathed it with her tongue, whether savoring his taste or healing the skin roughened by his whiskers he didn't know.

He didn't care.

He wanted her. He wanted her more than he'd ever wanted any other woman.

And he wanted her now.

32

CHAPTER FIVE

LAUREN HOLLISTER HADN'T known a man could kiss the way Anton Neville kissed. His hair was the texture of the softest silk, gossamer curls in her hands. His hand at her nape was insistent, his mouth on hers demanding. And she'd thought she'd known exactly what to expect from a man.

But she didn't. She'd never been looked at the way he was looking at her now. His eyes already had her undressed and she reveled in the exposure. She returned the look because she wanted to see his body, as well. To touch him. To explore and discover what spots made him shudder, which ones made him groan. Whether he liked gentle strokes of fingers or sharp nips of teeth.

She pulled his head down to hers to get her fill of his taste. He allowed her one kiss and then he shook his head, telling her with his eyes that kissing wasn't enough. He wanted more. He wanted it all. When his hand moved from her neck to the shoulder strap of her overalls, she let her head fall back against the wall, let her hands fall to her lap. Her chest lifted and fell as she struggled to breathe.

She watched his fingers work free first one loop then the second, separating the hardware from the tack button and lowering the bib so that her overalls bunched at her hips. She wore a simple skinny white T-shirt beneath and had to stop herself from pulling it off over her head. As much as she wanted to have his hands on her body, she wanted to enjoy the anticipation. And she knew without a doubt that Anton wanted to unwrap her himself.

He did, lifting her shirt hem above her bare breasts. Lauren shivered, her nipples pebbling. Anton covered her with his hands, then with his mouth, leaning down to curl his tongue around first one taut peak then the other. His hair slid over her skin like skeins of silk; his hands skated over her rib cage, the heels of his palms pressing the sides of her breasts.

She wasn't sure anything had ever so thoroughly roused her skin's sensitivity, or that any man's touch had ever felt so right, so loving. None of this made any sense. She hardly knew him, yet felt like she'd known him forever. And when his hands made their way to her thighs, she let him have his way. He looked up from beneath long blond lashes, his eyes flashing, the corners of his mouth lifted in a suggestive grin.

"Spread your legs," he said, and she did, opening to his determined search for her body's secrets. He pressed fingertips into her bare inner thighs, opening

34

her farther until he could easily slip a hand beneath the leg of her overalls. Lauren pulled in a sharp breath. His hand was hot where he skimmed her most intimate skin.

"Are you okay?" he asked, and all she could say was "Oh, yeah."

At that, he chuckled, a sexy half laugh, half moan that told of his struggle for self-control. This time it was her turn to ask of him, "Are you okay?"

"Baby, you have no idea." And then he brushed the backs of his knuckles over the crotch of her tiny bikini panties, leaning forward to murmur against her lips. "I'll stop. Just say the word."

"Don't stop." Her body was coming apart and he'd barely done more than tease her with the promise of his touch. She had never, never, never felt so close to falling from contact that was only a whisper. But she was, and this was what she wanted. She told him so with her lashes that slowly lowered, with her hungry tongue she caught with her teeth after begging, "Please. Don't stop."

But he did, pulling his hand free as he scooted to sit cross-legged in front of her and lift her legs over his. She stared into his eyes, heavy-lidded and aroused. He was as affected as she was, as taken by storm. Like her, he hadn't expected the intensity of this tryst.

And, though she'd immediately known he was special, she hadn't considered anything as crazy as love at first sight. She couldn't. For so many reasons, she couldn't. She pushed the thoughts aside and focused on this moment, this man. Concentrating on his hands sliding up her inner thighs, on his thumbs flirting with the hem of her shorts before slipping beneath to flirt with both sides of her lace-edged panties.

He used one hand to pull the wisp of fabric away from her body, giving his other hand room to slip beneath, to touch her intimately, his fingers teasing through her folds, over her tight bud of nerves, before he circled the mouth of her sex and eased a finger inside.

Lauren gasped but refused to look away from his face. Even as he began to stroke, to simulate the motion she wanted from his body, even as he moved his thumb to tease at the hard knot of sensation aching for release, she maintained the contact with his eyes. Only when he lowered his head and returned his attention to her breasts did she sag against the wall and allow passion to take over. No man had ever been so focused on her pleasure.

His tongue lapped and his thumb played and his fingers worked in and out of her sex until she couldn't stand it anymore. She cried out, she shuddered, she ground her body down into his loving hand. He continued the rhythm, seeing to her finish and easing her slowly back down. Only then did he leave her body, adjusting her panties and tugging her shirt back into place.

36

She waited for a moment, smiling, expecting him to reach for his belt and the fastenings of his pants so she could return the favor. But he only ran a caressing hand down her face to her neck and leaned forward for a too-brief kiss. Lauren frowned. This wasn't right.

"What about you?" she asked.

He shook his head. "I'm fine. I wanted to do this for you."

No. This was all wrong. She wasn't going to let him think that she didn't want to give back. And so she got to her feet, pushed her overalls down over her hips and kicked then off. Anton's eyes flared as, sitting beneath her, he took in her legs, her bare belly, the tiny slip of sheer mesh that served as her panties.

"Thank you. Now, please. Let me." She held out her hand and, when he took it, she urged him to his feet and went to work loosening his tie and the buttons of his shirt.

He stopped her hands, holding them to his chest in his much-larger fists. He captured her attention with a strange look of resignation before saying, "You don't owe me, or need to pay me back. I don't expect that from any woman."

For several long seconds, all Lauren could do was blink before she managed to wrench her hands free from his and shove them at her hips. "What? Was this some kind of test? You wanted to see how far I'd actually go? If I was all talk and no action? Is that it?"

He didn't answer. He only continued to study her

face until she wanted to pull out her hair in frustration and scream. Why did men have to have such double standards? Why couldn't they believe that good girls could love sex, too?

She asked her next question with all the calm she could muster. It wasn't much considering she was close to seething inside.

"Well, tell me then. Did I pass?"

CHAPTER SIX

ANTON GROANED. He had a gorgeous, responsive woman staring up at him like he was some kind of devil, when all he'd been trying to do was let her off the hook.

He'd known too many females who took the pleasure he gave them, then offered him the same as an afterthought, as a token payment, always out of obligation and never from the heart. He was getting older and more discriminating. He wanted a woman to want him, not to feel obliged to leave him a tip in exchange for services rendered.

But he was afraid he'd just made a big mistake with Lauren Hollister. Rather than glowing with her previous expression of replete satisfaction, she now looked ready to bite his head off. He didn't get it. He didn't get this woman at all. But, then, he didn't really know her, yet, did he?

"No, Lauren. This wasn't a test." How was he supposed to explain this from his point of view without leaving her insulted? "It was unexpected and it was amazing. You're amazing. I loved seeing you come."

She was still breathing fire. "Oh, so you'd rather watch. Is that it?"

He tried to hold back a smile. "I do like to watch. But I'd much rather do."

A faint blush crept up her neck. "You just don't want to do me. I'm too easy. You like more of a challenge. Where have I heard *that* before?"

He tossed his head back and roared. "You are not too easy, but you *are* making me crazy. I want to make love to you more than anything, and I'm about to tie my hands behind my back to keep them to myself. If that's not a challenge, I don't know what is."

"Then why—"

He backed her up, planted his hands flat against the elevator wall above her shoulders as he looked down into her upturned face. He had a number of logistical reasons, not the least of which was the lack of a single comfortable amenity, but he gave her the most obvious. "I don't have a condom."

She blinked, registering his response before her mouth broke into a self-satisfied grin. Reaching down for her backpack, she rummaged inside and produced a foil packet he wished he'd had ten minutes ago.

"Why didn't you say so?" she asked just as his cell phone started to ring.

This time it was Lauren who growled before hanging her head. Anton knew the mood would not be easily recaptured. As much as he wanted to bury himself in her warmly receptive body, he reached for the phone instead. "Neville."

"Hey, buddy. Wanna go double or nothing?" his partner, Doug Storey, asked. "You are never going to dump that dump at this rate."

"I wouldn't be so sure," Anton answered, keeping an eye on Lauren as she slipped back into her overalls and swiped the elevator dirt off her backside. "Where the hell are you, anyway?"

"Downstairs with the elevator crew and your Ms. Hollister's roommate." Doug lowered his voice. "You two might want to get your story straight. Looks like you'll be outta there in a few."

"Thanks, bud." Anton ended the call, returned the phone to his pocket and took great pleasure in watching Lauren run a brush through her hair. Then she straightened her clothing, smoothing down her T-shirt as well as the legs of her shorts. Once she'd finished, he held out his hand.

"You want my hairbrush?" she asked.

He shook his head. The elevator jerked to a start and he knew he didn't have much time. "I want the condom."

She swung the backpack strap up onto one shoulder.

One brow lifted as she gave him a haughty look. "What, you don't have a supply of your own at home?"

"I do." He wanted to make it clear that her assumptions had been wrong. That he didn't think her too easy. Her expression told him she wasn't convinced. But the problem was more complicated than he could get into with only two floors left to descend.

The rest of what he wanted to say would have to wait. The elevator groaned and creaked and finally hit the ground floor. Anton continued to hold out his hand. Lauren continued to consider him with her worldly eyes. Finally, just as the overhead door began rolling up along its tracks, she slapped the condom into his palm.

He closed his fingers around hers and around the foil packet, only letting her go when she insisted. The condom he tucked into his pocket, holding it tight in his fist.

"I'm going to hold on to this. And I'm going to call you and invite you to dinner. A real dinner. A real date. Next time, and there will be a next time, I don't want to be caught with my pants…up."

"WHY DO I EVER BELIEVE a man when he tells me he's going to call?" Three days had passed since Lauren and Anton's elevator adventure and she was not a happy camper as she paced back and forth in her best friend's gIRL-gEAR office.

Macy Webb sat cross-legged behind her desk in a chair that seemed to swallow her diminutive form. She'd been working on copy for the gIRL gUIDE column when Lauren took over the office with her ranting and raving about men.

"C'mon, Lauren. It's been three days, not three weeks. And not the three months you're acting like. If he calls, he calls. If you can't wait, call him. It's not a crime, you know."

Lauren stopped pacing and collapsed in one of Macy's visitor's chairs. She rubbed her fingers to the headache building in her temples. "I can't call him. I can't explain. But I think he's sorta old-fashioned about wanting to be the one to do the calling and the paying. Stuff like that."

Macy leaned across her desk. "Yoo-hoo. Lauren? Since when do you do old-fashioned? Waiting for *the man* to call? Letting *the man* pay? Don't you think you're borrowing trouble here when there are about a bazillion men out there who wouldn't think twice about you calling or paying? Especially the paying part."

Lauren sighed, dropped her head back against the headrest and stared up at the ceiling. Macy was probably right. Lauren knew she wouldn't be able to deal with having a man call all the relationship shots.

Anton Neville seemed the type who got off on being in charge. He'd certainly been in charge of their elevator date, hadn't he? What kind of guy said no to sex, anyway?

And why was she even thinking about seeing a guy who did, again?

44

CHAPTER SEVEN

"I'M SORRY it took so long to get back to you. All hell's broken loose at the office. Doug and I have hit a streak of bad contractor luck lately. Not to mention clients who can't make up their minds."

Sitting across from Anton Neville in the restaurant known to serve Houston's best Vietnamese cuisine, Lauren Hollister listened to his architectural woes. The last part about clients being unable to make up their minds, had her rolling her eyes.

"Is that what this is? A business dinner to talk about the loft? You're wanting to know what Macy and I have decided?" She didn't know why she'd gotten her hopes up otherwise. But she had. She liked him a lot and hated that they might actually be facing a problem as out-of-date as equality of the sexes.

Anton laid his chopsticks on his plate, propped his elbows on the edge of the table and laced his fingers, looking at her over his joined hands. His blue eyes were brighter than she remembered from the dim elevator and lit with an intensity that would've stolen her appetite if she'd thought it was intended for her. But she didn't.

"If this was a business dinner, this conversation would be business specific," he said. "As in, what build-outs you've decided on. If you want us to arrange them, if you plan to hire your own contractors. Or, if you've even decided whether you want the loft at all."

"So, that wasn't a dig? That comment about clients making up their minds? Because we have. We do want the loft." Why, oh why, did he have to look even yummier than her spring rolls? All dressed up in the dark browns and greens that did such amazing things to his coloring?

"Good." He picked up his chopsticks and dug into his steamed rice. "Now, can we get back to the date? I promised you a good time and I intend to see that it happens."

Yeah, *his* idea of a good time, Lauren silently groused. He wanted to call, he wanted to pay. He wanted to coordinate the when, where and how of any sexual encounter. And now he wanted to be in charge of what they talked about. Typical overbearing man. She had a feeling that she was going to miss out on experiencing his good qualities because his bad ones *so* got on her nerves.

True, some women did like sitting high atop a pedestal, safe from problems, decisions and sin. He couldn't know that she hated looking down at the action. That she thought duking it out eye-to-eye was a much more honorable way to live.

Not to mention a helluva lot more fun. "Did you bring our condom?"

"As a matter of fact, I did." His lips drew taut, almost into a grimace as he dug his wallet from the back pocket of his chocolate-colored pants. "Did you want it back?"

Still holding her chopsticks, Lauren slumped back hard in her chair, her hand on the napkin draped over her crossed legs. "Oh. Now you've changed your mind."

Anton leaned into the forearm he'd braced on the table and reached for his beer. He took a drink from the longneck, keeping his gaze locked with Lauren's as he did. "Can I ask you something, Lauren? Do you want to be here with me? Or did you feel indebted to go out with me because of what went on in the elevator?"

Indebted was the last thing she felt. But she could understand where he was coming from, considering the way she was acting. Time to stop dancing around the ring and take it on the chin. Returning her chopsticks to the table, she smoothed down her simple salmon-colored skirt.

She tried to smile but, since the feeling failed to reach her heart, was afraid she wasn't very convincing. "I'm sorry. I just don't think this is going to work."

Anton blew out a huff, as if he'd been anticipating her decision. "You're calling this off before we've even gotten to know each other?"

She was calling it off before she was in over her head and ended up being hurt. "I think I make you uncomfortable. And that makes me uncomfortable."

He frowned. "Why would you make me uncomfortable?"

"Because I am who I am. I say what I think. I go after what I want. I play by my rules and I'm afraid that might cause me to inadvertently step on your more traditional toes." There. She didn't think she could be more honest without telling him he needed to loosen up.

48

"My toes are traditional?" he asked, a small quirk to the corner of his mouth.

This time her response was genuine. She felt her own smile work the muscles of her face. His smile she felt other places and she held the feeling close. She wanted to feel so much more, but they seemed to be coming from two disparate places. "Since I haven't seen them yet, I can't say for sure. But I'm leaning in that direction."

"What do you want me to do with this?" He held the condom he'd pulled from his wallet between two fingers.

Lauren felt a flush heat her cheeks. She might be the more free-spirited of the two, but even she didn't want an entire restaurant wondering if they were in for a show. She took the foil packet from his hand and tucked it down in the low-draped cowl bodice of her sleeveless white blouse. "I'll hang on to it. Just in case."

One blond brow went up. "Just in case you change your mind?"

She shook her head. "In case you come to your senses and realize that you don't have to be the one on top to have a good time."

LAUREN AND MACY finalized the deal on the loft not long after. Doug Storey represented the firm of Neville and Storey, Architects at the closing. He explained that neither he nor Anton usually handled the financial end of any property they sold. But the loft space had been an anomaly since they'd acquired it and they'd sworn to see its sale through to the end.

Lauren couldn't have cared less who showed up. She and Macy had found the perfect place to live and nothing else mattered. And Lauren told her best friend that very thing.

"Oh, that's a bunch of crap, Lauren," Macy said, her head next to Lauren's as they lay side by side on the hardwood floor of the loft's main room. Feet pointing opposite directions, they stared up at the exposed piping Lauren had decided to paint red, purple and green. "You wanted Anton there and you

BONUS FEATURE

know it. You may not have said so, but you wore a business suit to the closing, for chrissakes."

"It was an important occasion and I dressed accordingly."

"You dressed like you thought Mr. Uptight would want you to dress."

"That's not true. He is not uptight. He's just… traditional."

Macy snorted. "Traditional, my ass. He's a stick-in-the-mud. Face it."

Anton Neville was anything but a stick-in-the-mud. He was a veritable god. Seeing to her pleasure? Without expecting anything in return? Had she ever known a man so unselfish? So considerate? So incredibly kind and thoughtful? And did she mention *hot?*

Lauren groaned. She'd been so worried about her precious equality that she'd told him it wasn't going to work before they'd gotten to know each other.

Now she was afraid she'd thrown away the best thing to ever happen in her life.

CHAPTER EIGHT

"So, YOU'RE GOING TO GO? After all that bitching about your date with the man, after the way he dumped on you at the closing, you're still going to go?"

Macy Webb stood in Lauren Hollister's bedroom doorway, watching as Lauren settled on a periwinkle suede fringed skirt and a silver silk corset that left the biggest part of her assets bare. She left her legs bare, as well, and slipped her feet into a pair of easily slipped-out-of periwinkle blue mules.

"And that's what you're going to wear?" Macy's brows both went up. "What happened to conventional and old-fashioned?"

They'd closed on the loft yesterday. And they needed to get busy packing. But Anton Neville had called and asked Lauren to meet him at the loft. Alone. Tonight. At nine.

Lauren turned side to side and examined her reflection in the full-length mirror. With this outfit and her hair in a wispy knot on top of her head, she looked hot, if she did say so herself.

"Yes, this is what I'm going to wear. Anton Neville can take conventional and old-fashioned and shove it. He wants to see me? He's going to see me."

"A whole lot of you, in that outfit," Macy added.

"What's wrong with that? I'm a fun, fearless female. Screw him if he doesn't like it." Lauren only hoped she could keep up the charade. Her insides were melting like butter and she was afraid if he came too close she'd pour herself all over him.

Equality be damned. He was sexy as hell, both his mind and his body. The combination was an incredible turn-on. More than that, however, the combination had captured her heart. She only hoped she hadn't messed things up forever the day she'd walked away.

Macy gave a quick nod. "Looking like that? I'd say screwing is a definite possibility."

ANTON STOOD on the loft's balcony, leaning against the railing as he watched the taillights of the traffic four stories below. He was waiting for Lauren and he wasn't sure he wouldn't still be waiting come morning. She'd vaguely agreed to meet him, as long as nothing else came up, or so she'd said.

He still had a key and he'd let himself in. He didn't think Lauren would mind, *if* she showed up and *if* she hadn't already written him off. He wanted to give this a go. If he had to rein in his insistence on having things his way, he'd give it his best shot. Lauren Hollister was too special not to work out a compromise.

He heard the newly installed elevator motor engage and his heart flipped on his chest. He glanced quickly around the balcony where he'd set up a chaise lounge with a coverlet and pillows. On the table beside, candles still burned. The wine was chilled.

He wondered if Lauren had brought the condom. He had others, of course, but there was something about that particular one....

"Anton?" she called.

Even the way she said his name was enough to make him weak in the knees. "Out here. On the balcony."

He'd left the sliding glass doors open and now he leaned his backside against the railing and turned to face the darkened loft. He heard her footsteps as she made her way across the floor. He couldn't see her, but he knew she could see him. He wasn't sure he'd ever had so much trouble drawing a breath.

His heart thumped furiously in his chest. And when she finally reached the doorway, a vision of glittering silvers and blues, he knew he was in more trouble than he'd ever imagined possible.

"Hi," she said, and stepped outside into his world.

She glanced around and, even with nothing more than the light from the moon, he knew she could see the romantic stage he'd set. She grinned and Anton held his breath, hoping she wasn't about to laugh at his plans for seduction.

She did laugh, but it was the purest sound of joy, a filling of her soul with the moment and happiness spilling like bubbling champagne and, God, but he needed to be committed, writing poetry in his mind instead of talking to the flesh-and-blood woman holding his heart in her hand.

"I can't believe you. I can't believe this." She pressed her fingers to her lips as she circled the chaise lounge, plumping the pillows and running her palm over the coverlet.

54   He remained standing with his arms crossed and his ankles crossed because he still wasn't sure if her disbelief was a good thing or bad. But then she made her way back to where he stood.

She took him by the hand, guided him to the chaise and, with a palm planted in the center of his chest, forced him to sit. "You did good. The candles and the wine. There's even traffic down below. And there's always the possibility of getting caught. We're only missing one thing."

"The condom," he stated, his palms growing damp.

Nodding, she planted her hands at her waist. "Find it and you get that whole lotta lovin'."

Hands shaking, he started with the tiny silver

hooks holding the corset together. The front separated and fell to the ground, revealing nothing but bare skin from her tiny waist to her beautifully long neck.

Pressing his lips between her breasts and breathing deep of her softly scented skin, he skimmed his hands around her hips, finding the skirt's rear zipper and easing it down. One smooth tug and it fell to her feet, leaving her standing in a wisp of sheer silver mesh.

The condom was caught between the elastic and her skin.

He stripped her free of both, leaving her standing bare before him. He took a deep breath, struggling for control, even as Lauren urged him to his feet.

"My turn." She tugged his shirt from his pants, releasing the buttons from bottom to top as he got busy with his cuffs. By the time he was out of his shirt and his shoes, he was so hard he thought he might burst. And then Lauren went to work on his belt and his pants.

"Careful," he whispered, as she eased his zipper over his erection. At the bold touch of her fingertips, he released a gut-deep groan, groaning again as she shoved his pants and his briefs to his ankles. He kicked them aside and she dropped to sit on the lounger, patting the seat for the condom and smiling when she found her prize.

Taking his penis into her mouth, playing the ridge of his head with her tongue, she used nimble fingers

BONUS FEATURE

to rip into the foil packet. Anton grit his teeth and threaded his fingers into her hair. When she sheathed him, he was more than ready.

He lowered them both down to the cushion, covering her with his body. She opened her legs, taking his weight and accepting him deep inside. He shuddered. She shuddered. Her warmth enveloped him; her wetness welcomed him and he knew he'd found a place to call home.

"I want to ask you something," he said, knowing they had so much to talk about, so much to settle. Knowing, too, that time would come but, for now, this was what mattered.

56   "Anything."

"Do you believe in love at first sight?"

She lifted her hand and cupped his face. "Yes, I do. And, yes, I did."

Her words slowly brought their sensuous dance to a stop. He turned his lips toward her palm for a kiss, his eyes maintaining contact with hers that shimmered by the light of the moon and the softly glowing candles. Reaching for the coverlet, he pulled it up until they lay enveloped in a cocoon of warmth and romance.

He didn't think making love had ever felt so right. Had ever resonated with so much emotion. Her heart snared his, as did her eyes. And her body held him tightly in her intimate embrace.

He began to move again, trying to take his time.

But holding back quickly became impossible. His body ached with the need for release. Lauren's eyes gave him permission to come, promising she'd stay with him every second of the ride.

He picked up the pace, harder, faster, meeting each upward thrust of her hips with a powerful downward stroke. Seconds later, she cried out, a soft gasp, a sweetly unexpected catch of breath as she shuddered beneath him.

Her completion sent him over the edge. His body clenched and he groaned, his climax exploding through him in one final driving burst. He buried his face in her hair, holding his weight on his elbows braced above her head, feeling for the first time in his life like he'd never recover. And loving the feeling of being in love.

Finally he raised his head and looked down into her smiling eyes. "So, about that love-at-first-sight thing? Are you sure?"

Lauren gave a quick little nod. "I wouldn't be down here naked beneath your godlike body otherwise." When he raised a brow, she added a small shrug and said, "Hey, it sounded good anyway."

"Uh-huh. I thought so." He brushed hair back from her forehead, loving her sense of humor yet knowing this one thing, at least for him, couldn't wait. "I can be as cynical as anyone, Lauren, and

I've always believed in love. I just never expected to be hit—"

"Shh." She placed her fingers to his lips. "I promise. Next time I won't hit you."

"That's what I wanted to know. About next time. That there will be one." He knew she had to feel his heart racing, his chest pressed to hers as it was.

"Maybe one or two." And then she smiled. A smile that touched him where a woman had never touched him before. Where he knew no woman would touch him again.

"One or two? Is that all?"

"Or however many times we can squeeze into the next forty years," she added, pulling his head down for the sweetest imaginable kiss.

Here's a sneak peek...

Just One Taste
by
Wendy Etherington

Another Harlequin Temptation author making her debut in Harlequin Blaze...

CHAPTER ONE

FROM BEHIND HER post at the chocolate fountain, Vanessa Douglas watched the posh crowd of Atlanta society schmooze with each other.

Prominent doctors and lawyers, chairmen and women of the board and business moguls turned out in jewels and designer clothes, decorated by elegantly dressed first spouses or young, hard-bodied second ones. Vanessa fought the urge to yawn.

But when a girl made penis-shaped cakes for a living, a lot of things seemed staid by comparison.

"Have you seen *any* cute guys?" her best friend and business partner, Mia Medini, asked.

"Nope. And hardly anybody under forty."

"What we expected. Your mother never listens." She planted her hands on her trim hips. "People our age go to *night*clubs for fun, not the *country* club."

"Except my sister." Angelica stood across the room with a group of elderly women. Nearby, their parents socialized in an intimate circle of longtime friends.

60

Even though her mother had sent catering business Vanessa's way instead of steering it in the other direction, hell, apparently, hadn't actually frozen over.

"But your sister is a fifty-year-old in a twenty-five-year-old body," Mia said.

"She hooked the best cardiac surgeon in the South."

Mia elbowed her. "Like he's a damn herring. And, personally, he's too staid for me."

"Wearing a bow tie is *not* a good sign."

"Though I once knew this stripper who wore his bow tie on his—"

"Mia, please," Vanessa said, glancing around furtively to see if they'd been overheard. "Not here."

Mia looked wounded. "You turn into such a stuff-bucket around them."

She knew. But she was tired of the estrangement from her family. She'd had her rebellion, and she was ready for compromise. "I'm just trying for peace. For once."

"I wish you luck on your journey, Don Quixote."

Ignoring her roommate's negativity, Vanessa rearranged the stack of napkins on the table, which were highlighted by elegant shrimp canapés and delicate chocolate puff pastries. No anatomically correct—or incorrect—body parts in sight.

Damn it.

BONUS FEATURE

"Though everybody *has* been complimentary," Mia went on. "You think we'll actually get more business from doing this shindig?"

Vanessa shrugged like she hadn't given the idea much thought. "Maybe. We could use it."

Of course she'd given the idea *a lot* of thought. Her family was a cornerstone of the swanky society laid out before them. Her father was a senior partner in one of the oldest, most prestigious law firms in the city. Her mother was a premier society queen. Vanessa and her sister had been raised as pristine, pure debutantes.

And she'd chucked it all to slave in the kitchen making chocolate sauce and leaven bread for a living.

Crazy? Her mother thought so. As well as most of the people she'd grown up with. But Vanessa had never felt more normal, free and alive the day she'd packed her jeans, T-shirts—and the scandalous red bra she'd worn under a white shirt once and nearly sent her mother into a dead faint—as she moved out on her own.

After being cut off from the family money at the urging of her mother—she was the power behind the throne, no matter what her father claimed—she'd put herself through culinary school and started her own business. After years of having to *sneak* into the kitchen to help their housekeeper make cookies—since debs didn't cook, they nibbled elegantly—she'd found a profession where getting messy was just part of the process.

For years, she wondered if sneaking was her only attraction to cooking, but after moving out and working in a restaurant, she realized that being a chef appealed to her need for excitement and variety. From a practical aspect, she could eat and get paid. Emotionally, it gave her instant gratification—she fed people, and they were happy. She didn't disappoint them, and they didn't try to change her.

Rejection of her efforts was rare.

Which brought her thoughts back to her family. Her sister, believing that a woman wasn't complete until she married, constantly tried to fix her up with men who were completely wrong for her. While Vanessa fought to keep her fledgling catering business afloat, her mother discouraged everyone she knew from using her services. And her father seemed too busy to notice there was a rift in the family at all.

Still, seven years after her big rebellion, she could say she didn't regret the choices she'd made. She had great friends who supported her, she threw her energy and hopes into her business and she planned for the future.

And yet…she wanted nothing quite as much as a reconciliation with her family. Just not at the expense of her pride.

How's that for a contradiction?

BONUS FEATURE

"Do you think her usual caterer really canceled on her at the last minute?" Mia asked, her tone as suspicious as Vanessa's had been when her mother called her less than a week ago to ask them to cater this party.

"It's possible."

She'd like to think her mother was softening, or at least getting used to the idea of a daughter in the—shudder—"service industry." Or maybe actually—*big gasp*—accepting Vanessa's chosen career and life rather than doing everything possible to turn her into a society princess and carbon copy of both her and her younger sister. But she wasn't holding her breath.

64

"I guess I'm a sap for bailing her out," Vanessa continued.

"Since she's done so much to help us."

"She thinks she's doing what's best for me."

"Yeah, well, you're twenty-seven. I'm pretty sure you've figured out what's best for you on your own."

"Here, here."

"And we did a classy job here. I bet fifty bucks your mother didn't sleep a wink last night, wondering if we'd show up with boob-shaped suckers and a cock-shaped champagne fountain."

Vanessa's eyes widened, and she temporarily shoved aside her vow for peace. She exchanged a knowing look with Mia. "That's not a bad idea."

"For that bachelorette party this weekend."

"We could have champagne spurting out the top."

"Crude, but fun."

"My mother really would faint."

Mia flicked her hand in dismissal. "Well, she's not going to be there, is she? And let's quit talking about her. It's too frustrating." She craned her neck to try to see around and over the crowd. "This place is a crush. Somehow the staid and boring really have found their own place in the world. Imagine that. Still, there's got to be a least one scrumptious, eligible man— *Oh, my God.* What's *he* doing here? Hide me."

Vanessa looked around and quickly spotted the problem—Colin Leavy was heading their way. He'd been in love with Mia ever since he'd come into their bakery and catering shop to order a cake for his mother's birthday two years ago. Unfortunately, he was an accountant and the epitome of "staid," so Mia wouldn't have anything to do with him.

Vanessa thought he was cute, and his devotion to Mia adorable. She might even reveal her chocolate-chunk cheesecake recipe to have a man look at her with the devotion Colin showed Mia.

Somehow, in her relationships, Vanessa always managed to be the pursuer, not the pursuee. Because she knew what she wanted? Because she knew how to get what she wanted? Or because she impulsively jumped in with both feet without bothering to ask too many questions?

She highly suspected it was the latter, especially after the last guy she went out with turned out to have a fiancée.

"Good grief," she said to her partner. "There are worse things in life than having a bright, successful man grovel at your feet."

"Depends on the man."

As Colin approached, and Mia realized she didn't have anywhere to hide, she simply crossed her arms over her chest.

"Hi, Mia. Would you like to dance?"

"I'm working—"

Vanessa pushed her friend forward. "She'd love to."

Mia glared at her over her shoulder. "But, I—"

"Come on, Mia," Colin said. "Please."

Who could resist those sweet, puppy-dog-brown eyes?

Apparently not even Mia, who sighed, but held out her hand to take Colin's. Vanessa hoped she let him lead.

While her partner was dancing, Vanessa roamed the perimeter of the room, making sure the platters of appetizers and pastries were filled, and the wait-staff kept the drinks flowing. The party doubled as a fund-raiser for a local children's hospital, so once her mother presented the check to the chairperson at ten, the crowd would probably disperse and Vanessa and

Mia would be free to clean up and go. Still, it would be midnight before they got home, as they had to pack everything, then run it all through the industrial-quality dishwasher at the shop.

Dessert First was started on a whim, quickly became a challenge, but it fulfilled Vanessa as nothing else ever had before.

She'd met Mia in culinary school, where her friend had excelled at organizing and managing much more than she had at cookies and pastries. They'd become close buds, then business partners and room-mates. Vanessa knew she could count on Mia like no one else in the world, and that safety net allowed her to handle the tension between her and her family with much more confidence and panache.

Maybe, with Mia's business savvy and her sugary concoctions, they wouldn't have to struggle so much someday. Maybe this party could be the beginning of healing and understanding with her family.

Oh, yeah, and maybe the man of her dreams was going to pop out from behind the fruit bowl and whisk her to his castle in the sky.

EXCEPT FOR HER, the party was a dead bore.

Lucas Broussard prowled the edges of the room, knowing he'd have to endure many more of these things if he was going to be accepted in this city. Net-working in his profession was a necessity. A sacrifice, like so many others, he'd just have to buckle down and endure.

Were they all genetically programmed for this stuff? Small talk, gossip, bragging. Trophy wives and pedigreed family trees.

At least, though his mistakes and faux pas were many, he'd never been accused of boring his audience to death.

As expected, and like everyone else, he'd flashed his Rolex. He wore a custom-made designer suit. He'd made plenty of money as a respected attorney, even if the money was a little too new to be decent and his tactics sneered at by some. He held his champagne glass by the stem. He could even tell the brand was that ole reliable Dom Perignon and not the now-hipper Cristal.

And still the boy from Cypress Bayou Trailer Park of Lafayette, Louisiana, lurked inside him. Inescapable. Maybe even necessary.

All in all, he'd much rather snag that hot blonde in the red dress, a bottle of whiskey and head home.

Even as he managed not to choke over yet another story about hunting lodges and the advantages of buying a personal Learjet, he watched her. He smiled internally as she accepted a breath mint from her dark-haired friend. His body tightened as she snitched a chocolate truffle from a tray of sweets and slid it into her mouth with a sigh of pleasure, her tongue peeking out to skim the last drop of chocolate from her bottom lip. He noticed as she slipped into the kitchen, then return moments later with a large silver platter of strawberries.

At first glance, he'd pegged her as a guest. With her sparkling dress, tall, trim body and sleek curtain of blond hair falling just past her shoulders, she had class written all over her. But when he'd maneuvered himself closer, he saw her nails were painted bloodred, and she had a small butterfly tattoo on the back of her left shoulder.

And he'd smiled genuinely for the first time all night.

Now, while a local cardiologist—whom his company was panting over as a client to represent in nuisance malpractice suits—explained the advantages of jetting to Brussels in the spring, he watched the chocolate-loving blonde rearrange strawberries on the fruit platters and considered how she'd feel about comparing body decorations.

Even as the arousing picture of that played through his mind, he strangled his libido and remembered his career. His life. His future. And the future of those who depended on him.

He'd come to Atlanta to change direction. To amend for the past. To remind himself why he'd started down the road of law in the first place.

Beautiful, butterfly-tattooed blondes would just have to wait.

He tuned into the European vacation discussion. He smiled at appropriate times. He didn't talk too much. Or too little. And when the esteemed doctor excused himself to dance with his wife, Lucas's card was in his jacket pocket.

With a smile, he turned to find the next conquest. But as he continued to schmooze, she was there. He felt her. Her smile and her grace. Her glowing skin. The heat her body would undoubtedly radiate.

Why couldn't he forget her? Or at least set her aside until the business of the night was done?

Nothing came before business. At least nothing ever had.

Tonight, though, he knew where she was every moment. He knew she hovered nearby. Lovely. Tempting. *Forbidden.*

His muscles grew tired of holding back. His fingers tingled in anticipation. He even got a crick in his neck from craning in an effort to constantly keep her in sight. For a man who'd fought for and gained control over his life and his emotions, the night was becoming both a torture and a curiosity.

Oddly enough, the moment he buckled was when he saw her holding out a tray of strawberries to an elderly couple.

After they moved away, he approached her. "I'd rather have them dipped in chocolate."

Her head jerked up, and she met his gaze with a surprised jolt, as if she'd been lost in her own thoughts.

Smart move, cher, *with this crowd.*

"They're better with a bit more sweetness," he added, somehow knowing he wasn't through giving in to temptation.

...NOT THE END...

Look for JUST ONE TASTE *by Wendy Etherington in bookstores July 2006 from Harlequin Blaze.*

BONUS FEATURE

Silhouette
BOMBSHELL

THE GIFTED.
MAGIC IS THEIR DESTINY.

DAUGHTER
OF THE FLAMES
by Nancy Holder

June 2006

When a mysterious stranger helped her
discover her family's legacy of fighting evil,
things began to make sense in Isabella
DeMarco's life. But could she marshal her
newfound supernatural powers to fend
off the formidable vampire hell-bent on
bringing Izzy down in flames?

More dark secrets will be revealed as
The Gifted continues in

Daughter of the Blood
December 2006

HOTEL
MARCHAND

Four sisters.
A family legacy.
And someone is out to destroy it.

A captivating new limited continuity, launching June 2006

The most beautiful hotel in New Orleans,
and someone is out to destroy it. But mystery,
danger and some surprising family revelations
and discoveries won't stop the Marchand sisters
from protecting their birthright…
and finding love along the way.

Page-turning drama...

Exotic, glamorous locations...

Intense emotion and passionate seduction...

Sheikhs, princes and billionaire tycoons...

This summer, may we suggest:

THE SHEIKH'S DISOBEDIENT BRIDE
by Jane Porter

On sale June.

AT THE GREEK TYCOON'S BIDDING
by Cathy Williams

On sale July.

THE ITALIAN MILLIONAIRE'S VIRGIN WIFE

On sale August.

With new titles to choose from every month,
discover a world of romance in our books written
by internationally bestselling authors.

Paying the Playboy's Price

(Silhouette Desire #1732)

by

EMILIE ROSE

Juliana Alden is determined to have her last—
her only—fling before settling down. And she's
found the perfect candidate: bachelor Rex Tanner.
He's pure playboy charm…but can she afford
his price?

Trust Fund Affairs: They've just spent a fortune—
the bachelors had better be worth it.

Don't miss the other titles in this series:

EXPOSING THE EXECUTIVE'S SECRETS (July)
BENDING TO THE BACHELOR'S WILL (August)

On sale this June from Silhouette Desire.

*Available wherever books are sold, including most
bookstores, supermarkets, discount stores and drugstores.*

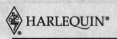